IN THE HOT ZONE

She felt herself go cold with fear. She was breathless, all right, but not with anger. The airpack was giving out.

She stood up, looking around wildly. She had two choices, neither one good. Run straight back through to the locker room, breaking decon procedures and spreading lethal pathogen all over the room and beyond. Or find a way through to Level Four and the air hoses. The first choice might not be as bad as it sounded, she thought; the peruvia virus was transmittable only through blood and bodily fluids. But who knew what refinements had been added? Removing her spacesuit without deconning was risking death.

So she was not breathing. . . .

Nancy Fisher

CODE RED

A SIGNET BOOK

SIGNET
Published by the Penguin Group
Penguin Putnam Inc., 375 Hudson Street,
New York, New York 10014, U.S.A.
Penguin Books Ltd, 27 Wrights Lane,
London W8 5TZ, England
Penguin Books Australia Ltd, Ringwood,
Victoria, Australia
Penguin Books Canada Ltd, 10 Alcorn Avenue,
Toronto, Ontario, Canada M4V 3B2
Penguin Books (N.Z.) Ltd, 182–190 Wairau Road,
Auckland 10, New Zealand

Penguin Books Ltd, Registered Offices:
Harmondsworth, Middlesex, England

First published by Signet, an imprint of Dutton Signet,
a member of Penguin Putnam Inc.

First Printing, February, 1998
10 9 8 7 6 5 4 3 2 1

PUBLISHER'S NOTE
This is a work of fiction. Names, characters, places, and incidents either
are the product of the author's imagination or are used fictitiously,
and any resemblance to actual persons, living or dead, events, or locales
is entirely coincidental.

For Sarah,
with love

ACKNOWLEDGMENTS

Many thanks as always to my brother, Dr. Robert Fisher of Minneapolis, for sharing his impressive medical expertise with me. I'm also grateful to the eminent cardiothoracic surgeon Dr. Barry Gold for the opportunity to soak up operating room atmosphere while watching him do the impossible, and to Dr. Barry Hartman, noted infectious disease specialist, who was so generous with his time and expertise. Cecelia Wennerstrom and Chester Huie welcomed me into their virology laboratories and patiently answered my many questions. And Linda Urmacher, a generous friend and efficient volunteer researcher, supplied me with much interesting data. Any errors are mine, not theirs.

As always, the contributions of my agent, Robert Diforio, and my editor, Hilary Ross, are highly valued and much appreciated. And my daughter, Sarah, and my mother, Tema, lavished upon me their usual love and encouragement.

CODE RED: A call to action to deal with an urgent, life-threatening emergency.

THE FOLLOWING ADVISORY HAS BEEN
POSTED ON THE INTERNET SINCE MARCH 1996

THE CENTERS FOR DISEASE CONTROL HAS
REQUESTED THAT THE FOLLOWING ADVI-
SORY BE ISSUED TO ALL MEMBERS OF ASV
IN LIGHT OF RECENT DISTURBING EVENTS
INVOLVING REQUESTS FOR SHIPMENT OF
DANGEROUS BIOLOGICAL AGENTS TO
QUESTIONABLE RECIPIENTS:

11 March 1996
Centers for Disease Control and Prevention (CDC)

In recent years, the threat of terrorist activity involving the use of biological agents has raised increasing
concern from the perspective of both public health
and national security. Accordingly the Centers for Disease Control and Prevention (CDC) has serious con-
cerns about the illicit use and the interstate
transportation of certain human pathogens that could
have adverse consequences for human health and
safety.

To immediately address this issue, CDC requests that
all those who authorize the acquistion and transfer
of dangerous human infectious agents increase their
vigilance to minimize the risk of illicit access to infectious agents by:

1. reviewing all requests prior to transferring pathogens and toxins, particularly any request regarding the
agents causing anthrax, botulism, brucellosis, plague,
Q-fever, tularemia, and any agents classified for work
at Biosafety Level 4;

2. determining whether agents will be used for legitimate medical or scientific purposes; and

3. immediately reporting any suspicious inquiries or transactions to CDC's Office of Health and Safety, at (404) 639-3235 (nights and weekends, call the CDC Duty Officer at 404 639-2888).

These voluntary safeguards are a first step toward strengthening regulatory and statutory protections. CDC co-chairs a Federal interdepartmental working group that is developing a framework for controlling the acquisition and transfer of infectious agents. This framework will include safeguards to control access to microbial agents of particular concern while ensuring that researchers and others who have a legitimate scientific need for these agents have appropriate access to them. This approach will require close collaboration among researchers, their institutional biosafety officials and committees, and providers of these agents.

The CDC will soon be proposing new regulations regarding the acquisition and transfer of certain biological agents. The regulations will be developed with input from professional associations, the research community, law enforcement authorities, and concerned members of the public. A Notice of Proposed Rule Making will be published in the Federal Register for public review and comment in approximately 120 days. In addition, the Department of Justice is working to strengthen relevant criminal statutes to enable prosecution of those who attempt to gain illicit access to these agents.

Sincerely,
David Satcher, M.D., Ph.D.
Director
Centers for Disease Control and Prevention

Chapter One

She was still half asleep when her feet hit the floor, her hand reaching for the bedside clock while her mind puzzled over its strident ringing. She sat for a moment on the edge of the metal cot, blinking in the darkness. She felt dull and edgy. She shivered in the early morning coolness, knowing it wasn't just the temperature. The blood was starting to get to her. Not the blood itself—she was used to blood—but the horror that was in it.

She turned to the figure beside her and shook him gently. "Time to get up, Jean."

He groaned and rolled over, then sat up. "*Merde*. What's the time?"

"Five-thirty. The pilot wants to leave by seven."

"Are you sure you want to come? It's over an hour to the airstrip. And you'll be driving back alone."

"I've done it before. I picked you up when you flew in, remember?"

"How could I forget? You drive like a marine." His smile warmed her. He ran his fingers through her short dark curls, then swiveled around and began the daily ritual of shaking out his boots; who knew what might have crawled through the chinks in the rough wood floor during the night? "But tiredness can cause mistakes, sometimes fatal ones." The words floated back over his shoulder. "And you've been going flat out for days."

"So have you," she answered.

"Yes, but tonight I'll be sleeping in a soft bed in Lima. You'll still be at risk in this godforsaken jungle. You should sleep while you can."

"I'll get plenty of sleep," she told him with a smile, "with you off to France for two weeks." She knelt on the bed and wrapped her arms around him from behind. "Anyway, I'll be going home, too, in a few days. Back to New York."

He dropped the boot and turned to embrace her. "I'll call you from Marseilles the night you get back. Three days from now, yes? And before you know it, my aunt will be feeling better, and I will jump on a plane and come flying home to you."

They kissed deeply and long. How quickly it had happened, this *affaire de coeur*. Two doctors, sent on a mission of mercy by the prestigious International Medical Aid organization, clinging together in the midst of death. Finally he released her and they began to dress.

They loaded his suitcase and small carryall and the equipment bag with its distinctive blue-and-white IMA logo into the muddy Jeep, and went rattling across the still-sleeping compound. Beyond the wide, bleach-filled ditch that separated and protected the staff's living quarters from the "hot zone" of makeshift lab and hospital buildings, Lucy could see a faint flashlight beam bobbing along a rutted path—a nursing sister going to check on her patients. Brave woman, she thought. Dr. Lucy Nash had trained in a hospital fellowship for infectious diseases, then done a rigorous two-year stint in epidemiology and virology at the Centers for Disease Control in Atlanta, where she'd achieved a coveted Level Four clearance. She'd seen a myriad of viral illnesses, but nothing as horrific as this.

The overcast sky lightened a little as they bounced along the rough jungle track toward the small airport

some twenty miles away, where a plane waited to take
Dr. Jean-Pierre Didier across the mountains to Lima.
Lucy studied his strong hands on the wheel. Healing
hands. "No new cases for over ten days," she said.
"I'm pretty sure we've contained it. Thank God it's
not airborne."

"Jesus, yes," he agreed with real feeling. Airborne,
this thing would be impossible to control. "You think
we'll ever identify the host?"

Lucy shrugged. "I've been concentrating on the
most likely carriers: birds, insects, rodents, and monkeys, but the microscope studies haven't turned up a
damn thing so far. Still, it took Mackenzie four years
to identify the host of the Machupo arenavirus in Bo-
livia, back in the sixties. . . ."

"A mouse, wasn't it?"

"Yes," she said. Around them, the rain forest
chirped and grunted and whistled and buzzed. So
much life; so many possibilities. "Of course the virus
could have been imported by someone from outside
the region, someone who ate infected monkey meat
miles from here. Or came in contact with mouse or
bird droppings. . . ." She paused, thinking. "Trouble
is, aside from the anthropologist who came through
here, the one who told the IMA what was going on,
no one's visited the village for months, they say.
They're pretty isolated here. And even if it *was*
brought into the area from any distance, the carrier
would have had to run here—literally *run*—after being
infected. Sangre negra kills so incredibly fast."

"The official name's peruvia," he corrected her.

"Sangre negra's better." Sangre negra was the name
the local people had given the disease. *Sangre negra.*
Black blood.

"What's the count now? Forty-six dead?" His voice
sounded tight, nervous. He glanced up at the lowering sky.

"Forty-eight. More than half the village."

"Well, at least it's not as lethal as Ebola."

"Lethal enough." Lucy hesitated. "Remember that old man, the one with the crescent scars on his neck? He said sangre negra is an evil spirit that's come back."

Jean-Pierre shrugged. "He was raving, half crazed with fever. He cursed the nurses, me, everyone who tried to help him. He was so nuts, he and his wife left the isolation tent and ran off into the bush. . . ."

"Yes, but he had the blister scars. So did his wife. If it really *is* something that's come back—"

"Then he'd have been immune, or at least resistant."

"But he had the scars."

"He also had peruvia," Jean-Pierre reminded her.

"Well, he had a bad fever. He disappeared before the classic sangre negra symptoms set in, so I can't be certain—"

"Come on, Lucy. The peruvia virus was in his blood sample, yes?" She nodded. "Then he had peruvia. So did his wife. And they both died of it, somewhere out there." He waved a hand at the sea of green through which they were driving.

Lucy nodded again; Jean was right, of course. One of the earth's oldest life-forms, filoviruses were only just emerging from the rain forests of the world. Who knew how many variations lurked there, undiscovered? "I'm still surprised that it turned out to be a filovirus rather than a hanta or an arena." She paused. "It's the first filovirus ever found outside Africa."

"Marburg was found in Germany," Jean-Pierre reminded her. Identified among laboratory workers handling vervet monkeys in 1967, Marburg was a lethal form of hemorrhagic fever caused by a filovirus resembling that of Ebola, another newly emergent killer.

"Yes, but Marburg was directly traceable to an African source," Lucy replied. "Sangre negra—excuse me, peruvia—has no such connection." She thought of the dark hemorrhages that filled the lungs and poured from every orifice of the body during the final stages of the disease, of the black blood blisters that formed on neck and chest and thighs, leaving crescent-shaped marks on the skin of the survivors. Coming face-to-face with such terrible human suffering every day was far more emotionally wrenching than studying lethal viruses in a lab environment, as she had at the CDC. "Sangre negra . . . black blood." She thought of her heavy, sealed bodysuit and boots, the surgical gown, the thick latex gloves, of the pits in which their gear was burned and then buried at the end of every day. Had the flames been hot enough? Were the ashes buried sufficiently deep?

Jean-Pierre glanced over at her, sensing her mood. "Your first IMA mission has been especially difficult."

"Are they ever easy?" she replied. "You've made, what? Ten, twelve trips for the IMA over the past three years. Are they ever easy?"

"No, of course not."

Lucy smiled at him. "You really are . . . admirable, Jean."

Jean-Pierre looked over at her, surprised. "Me?"

"You give so much of your time, take such risks. And yet it would be very easy for you to not to care about any of this." Jean-Pierre cocked an eyebrow at her. "You're rich, you're very successful. . . . You paint, you collect antiques, you play the piano. You're not quite what I'd imagined an IMA volunteer would be like."

He laughed. "You thought we all had beards and backpacks and sandals, like the Peace Corps?"

Lucy laughed, too. "Maybe. Anyway, I think it's all pretty terrific. I think *you're* pretty terrific."

Jean-Pierre ducked his head in embarrassment. "I like to help others," he said softly. "It's a way of giving something back. I know you feel the same." He glanced up at the sound of distant thunder. "I hope the plane can take off. Jorge—" He broke off as the Jeep hit a root and bounced hard.

"Jorge?"

"The friend I'm meeting in Lima. He has only this evening to spend with me, and I must leave for New York tomorrow. . ." He fell quiet at the sound of thunder, closer now, and turned onto the approach road for the airport.

Despite the early hour, people were already gathering inside the small terminal as Lucy and Jean-Pierre maneuvered his bags toward the counter. A thickset man in his mid-thirties, sporting a toothbrush mustache and an official-looking identification badge, hurried across the room to intercept them. "Jack McNulty, IMA rep, South America," he said energetically. "Believe we met in New York last year, Dr. Didier." Jean-Pierre nodded and smiled as McNulty pumped his hand. "And you must be Dr. Nash," he added, turning to Lucy. "Heard a lot about you. Good to have you on the team. Now why don't you two get some coffee? I'll take care of these." Lucy handed over the heavy equipment bag with relief, but Jean-Pierre hesitated, one hand grasping the leather handle of his suitcase, the other clutching the small carryall. "Go on," McNulty urged. "They're still refueling, so you've got twenty minutes or so. I'll see this stuff gets aboard."

"Thanks," Jean-Pierre said. "Good idea." But still he hesitated, glancing around as though looking for someone.

"Gate Three," McNulty told him. "Something wrong?"

Jean-Pierre shook his head, frowning. Slowly he relinquished the suitcase, but held on to the carryall.

"Better give me your ticket," McNulty told him.

"For the luggage." Jean-Pierre handed over his ticket folder and McNulty leafed through it. "Lima . . . New York . . . Marseilles . . . back home to New York again. No rest for the weary, eh?"

Jean-Pierre shrugged. "My aunt is quite ill. I promised my mother I would go to see her."

"You prefer living in New York to living in France?" McNulty asked. "Can't say I would."

"Professionally, there are many advantages," Jean-Pierre said. "And I manage to return to Paris now and again to see my family."

"But you're ticketed to Marseilles."

"My aunt lives in Marseilles," Jean-Pierre told him somewhat testily. "I think we'll have those coffees now."

"Sure, you go ahead. I'll see you at the gate." McNulty hefted the luggage and moved off, and the two doctors started toward the makeshift coffee bar. Suddenly Jean-Pierre stopped. "I need a pit stop," he told Lucy. "Would you get the coffees? I'll be right back."

"Okay." Lucy watched him head toward the restrooms. His body language was anxious and strained. Can't blame him, she thought. It's rotten weather for flying. She bought the coffees, took them to a bench and sat sipping. What was taking him so long? She'd nearly finished when she heard him call her name. She turned; the door to Gate Three stood open and he stood just inside it, gesturing to her. Beyond, the rain was pelting the runway.

"They want to get off right away," he said as she hurried over. He took a gulp of the coffee she handed him and glanced outside, his expression anxious.

"Dr. Didier?" A member of the flight crew appeared at his elbow, a ticket folder in his hand. "Follow me, please," he said, handing it to Jean-Pierre. "Hurry."

"Uh, are my bags aboard?"

"Yes. Mr. McNulty said to tell you the claim checks are in that folder. Please board the plane, doctor."

Jean-Pierre glanced quickly around the terminal. "Where is McNulty?"

"He's already boarded."

"Boarded? He's on this flight?" The crewman nodded. Outside, the rain increased. Turning back to Lucy, Jean-Pierre took her in his arms. His lips brushed her ear. "Be careful."

"What?" Startled, Lucy jerked back, but he pulled her close again. "Be careful," he repeated softly.

"I'm always careful," she told him, puzzled. "Double gloves, bodysuit—"

"That's not what I mean."

"Dr. Didier, please. You must board now," the crewman urged.

But still Jean-Pierre held her. "There is something for you in my suitcase," he whispered.

"A present? I love presents." She had no idea what was going on, but every instinct told her to act naturally. "You can give it to me when I see you in New York," she said lightly, and smiled up at him.

But he didn't return her smile. "I hope so," he said. His eyes signaled a message she couldn't read. Then he turned abruptly and followed the waiting crewman out into the rain.

He retrieved his passport from the immigration officer and entered the baggage-claim area. Luggage from the Lima–New York flight was already revolving on the metal carousels. The last few days had been busy and somewhat tense, but he was on the home stretch now, and glad of it. A brief stop at his apartment in New York, then on to Marseilles in the morning. He was loading the last of his bags onto a luggage cart when the two men appeared, one at each side.

"Dr. Didier? Would you come with us, please?"

"What? Why?" Jean-Pierre eyed the two U.S. Customs agents with surprise and dismay. IMA personnel were treated with great respect by every government in the world. Their progress through airports was expedited, their bags never inspected. "Do you know who I am?" he asked, then felt stupid. Of course they knew who he was; they'd addressed him by name. "Is there a problem, officer?"

"Just come this way, please, sir." One of the customs agents grasped his elbow while the other took control of the luggage cart. "Just in here, sir."

"I don't understand," he protested as they whisked him through an unmarked door into a small room.

His suitcase and the IMA equipment bag were removed from the cart and laid on a scarred wooden table. "Would you open these for us, doctor?"

He tossed over the keys. "This is ridiculous. I'm a physician, an IMA volunteer." He was still protesting when they found the first bag of heroin.

The aircraft was parked well away from the terminal building, and a portable staircase had been rolled up to allow Lucy and the crew to disembark. Now she stood on the tarmac in the failing light, watching the sealed biohazard containers of live peruvia virus being carried out of the cargo hold and checking off their numbers on her list. Called "hatboxes" because of their distinctive shape, the containers had been locked into explosion-proof plastic carriers for the flight from Peru to New York. A windowless IMA van stood nearby, ready to transport the hatboxes from Kennedy Airport to their ultimate destination, the Centers for Disease Control.

The last container was being locked into the van when the black Range Rover appeared. It braked to a stop and a slim, sandy-haired man in an Armani blazer, jeans, and sneakers leaped out and hurried toward the small group around the van. "Congratulations," he called to Lucy. "Well done."

She turned, surprised but pleased. "Dr. Miller? Bill?"

The new arrival embraced her warmly, then pulled back and looked at her. "You're exhausted. And I'm afraid I'm not going to make your day any easier."

"What do you mean?"

But he didn't answer, turning instead to the van driver. "All set? Papers in order? Better get going then." As the van moved off, he took Lucy's arm and led her toward the Range Rover. "I'll drive you home. We can talk in the car."

"What is it? What's happened?" It had to be something pretty bad, she thought, to bring Bill Miller, IMA's charismatic chairman and a renowned physician in his own right, out to the airport this evening.

"Let's get out of here." They swung onto the Van Wyck Expressway. What he had to tell her was so terribly difficult. But it would have been cruel to let her find out any other way. "Dr. Didier . . . Jean-Pierre . . ."

"Is he all right?" Lucy felt her pulse quicken. Bill glanced over at her. Was there something between them? he wondered. That would make what he had to tell her so much harder, so much worse.

"He was arrested two nights ago, when he arrived here from Lima."

"Arrested? What for?"

"Customs got a tip of some kind, they said. They searched his bags." Lucy was staring at him fearfully. "They found drugs. Heroin."

"That's not possible!"

"Six kilos."

"I don't believe it," Lucy said numbly.

"Neither did I," Bill said gently. "But after what happened—"

"There's got to be some explanation," she interrupted. "He's innocent, I'm sure he is. Where are they keeping him? I need to talk—"

But Bill shook his head. "I'm afraid that's impossible." He hesitated. "They arrested him, as I said, and locked him up. He kept saying he was innocent, that he had no knowledge of the heroin."

"Of course he didn't. He couldn't!"

"But during the night, he . . . God, Lucy, it's terrible. During the night, he committed suicide in his cell."

Lucy gasped. "No."

He leaned over and touched her arm, his kind face creased with sympathy and concern. "I'm so very sorry," he said. "I don't know what to say."

Her body felt cold, her mind numb. Jean-Pierre, a heroin dealer. Jean-Pierre, dead. "Jean and I . . ." she began. "We were . . ."

Bill glanced over at her. So there *had* been something between them. Poor woman. "You shouldn't be alone tonight," he told her. He reached for his cellular phone. "Is there anyone I can call for you?"

Lucy shook her head. "I'll be okay." Impossible; the whole thing was impossible. Or was it? She recalled Jean's furtiveness at the small airport, his reluctance to let McNulty take his bags, his anxiety about possibly missing Jorge in Lima. Then with a chill of fear, she remembered his warning to her to be careful, and the mention of a gift for her in his luggage. What had he gotten her involved in? She began to shiver, gazing out of the window with unseeing eyes as the car rushed through the night.

Several times during the thirty-minute drive into the city Bill started to speak, but each time thought better of it. What could he say? Better to let her assimilate

the news in silence. But as he pulled off the FDR and
headed down York Avenue, he looked over at Lucy.
Her arms were wrapped tight around her body, the
knuckles white, her face very pale.

"Are you all right?" Bill asked.

Lucy nodded, her stomach churning. At the first red
light, she opened the door and vomited into the street.

Chapter Two

Perhaps it was because her father, an Army surgeon, had uprooted his family so many times; perhaps it was because she herself, once she was on her own, had never stayed anywhere long enough to put down roots: college in Colorado, medical school in Michigan, residency and fellowship in New York, then two years in Atlanta with the Centers for Disease Control before returning to New York eight months ago. Whatever the reasons, Lucy tended to make friends quickly but not deeply. Now, at the age of thirty-two, she found herself with many far-flung acquaintances but few close friends. Which had made her romance with Jean-Pierre all the more precious.

She lay tangled in the sheets, her face stained with tears. Bill Miller had asked if he could call anyone for her, but who could she call? Kathy in Hong Kong? They hadn't spoken in months. Lynn in Seattle? Monica in Atlanta? She knew how the conversations would go. They'd be horrified, of course, and then comforting and supportive. But sooner or later, the old familiar questions would start, gently at first, then more insistent. Did she really believe she could have been in love with Jean-Pierre, truly in love with him, after only three weeks together? Hadn't it been just another of her fast and furious relationships, with great intensity but no staying power? And she'd begin to wonder whether they were right. And that would make her pain so much worse. Because only time would have proven them right or wrong. And time had run out.

She fell into a troubled sleep just before dawn, mind and body exhausted. She awoke around noon, blinking in the weak November sun that streamed through the blinds she hadn't bothered to close the night before. She felt rotten. She showered, washing away the grime of her trip but not the bone-deep sadness, then collapsed on the bed again, the tears starting. Forcing herself to her feet, she wiped her eyes and went and packed a gym bag. Keeping fit had always been a passion with her, and she'd found over the years that rote repetition of physical exercise helped her heal mentally. The end of love affairs often found her in the gym, banging away on the light bag or doing push-ups at a furious pace.

She hurried past the doorman and into the street, her short dark hair curling around her face. As she turned the corner onto Second Avenue, a stocky, unkempt man shambled up the street toward her, waving his arms and muttering to himself. He was clad in multiple layers of shirts and sweaters topped by an old quilted jacket, and his shaggy, graying hair was partly covered by a worn blue baseball cap that proclaimed FBI in dirty yellow letters. As his pale blue eyes focused on Lucy, he smiled broadly, revealing several missing teeth.

"I know you," he said, looming over her five-foot-three-inch frame. He held out a paper cup containing several coins and shook it at her. "You're the doc, right?" He beamed at her with the childlike candor of the mentally challenged.

"That's right. I'm the doc." Lucy had never been able to decide whether the man was truly deficient, or if his medication was responsible for his mental state. Either way, she had come to consider Ray her special charge. "How're you doing, Ray?"

"Good. I'm real good." He frowned. "You went away, huh?"

"I was working in Peru. Now I'm back."

Ray nodded emphatically. "I been workin' too," he proclaimed.

"Really? That's terrific." Lucy's face lit up. For months she'd been trying to convince Ray to seek help from one of the many organizations and missions that catered to the city's homeless population. The best she'd been able to do had been to get him to accept the address and phone number of a group the hospital had recommended. "So where are you working?"

"Yeah, gonna start next week, prob'ly," Ray told her. "Gonna get me a real good job."

Lucy's smile faded. "Did you talk to the people I told you about?" she asked. "Did you call that phone number?"

Ray looked blank. "Phone number?"

"I wrote it out for you before I went away. . . . Never mind, I'll write it again."

"Oh, *that* phone number. Gonna call them tomorrow, I surely am. Meanwhile, I could use a little help, doc, get me something to eat. . . ." He extended the paper cup and shook it at her.

Lucy sighed. "Sure, Ray." She dug in her jeans pockets and came up with a quarter. "That's all I have with me," she apologized as she dropped it in. Ray scowled at her. "My wallet's at home. I'll catch you later, I promise."

Ray stared at the quarter with deep disgust. Then, with an angry gesture, he shuffled off down the street, muttering and cursing. Lucy watched him go. She'd been told it was wrong to give money to homeless people, that it just prevented them from seeking long-term help at centers that could offer rehabilitation and work. But Crazy Ray, as he was known in the neighborhood, obviously refused to consider himself a candidate for such places. Besides, she'd seen him in line at the McDonald's up the street, and knowing that at least some of the money he collected actually went for food made her feel better about giving him a dollar or two whenever he approached her. Over the past eight months, these relatively munificent contributions had produced a doglike devotion at such times when Ray actually recognized her, and even the occasional semi-lucid conversation.

There were other homeless people who haunted Lucy's neighborhood: a ragged young woman with a large, dirty bandage on her neck, a man in dreadlocks who seemed permanently attached to a supermarket cart in which he collected empty deposit bottles from the trash. Lucy dropped coins into their outstretched hands from time to time, but she took a special interest in Crazy Ray. Several people had complained to the local police about the panhandlers, especially when Ray forgot to take his medicine and became agitated. There had even been talk of forcibly removing him from the streets. But as long as he was still around, Lucy would keep putting money in his cup. The truth was, there wasn't anything else he would allow people to do for him.

She continued down the street, thoughts of Crazy Ray overshadowed by images of Jean-Pierre. His talent as a lover. His skill as a doctor. His love of beautiful things. Jean-Pierre a drug runner? It simply didn't make sense. Despite what Monica and Kathy and Lynn would say, Lucy believed she'd come to know Jean well enough, even after only three weeks, to be certain of that much. So what should she do? What *could* she do? she wondered as she pushed through the gym door and headed for the locker room. I can try and prove it, she decided grimly. Changing direction, she hurried toward the pay phones.

*   *   *

Bill Miller, known to his staff as Doctor Bill, leaned around the open door to his office. "Alicia? Lucy Nash is on her way," he told his secretary. "I want to see her as soon as she gets here."

"But you've got Dr. Wolff—"

"Yes, I know. See if you can catch him and ask if he'd mind postponing our meeting until tomorrow."

"I'll try," Alicia said doubtfully, "but he's probably already left."

"Well, let's give it a shot. Unless you want the job of entertaining him out here for twenty minutes." His grin, wide and infectious, made him seem younger than his fifty-one years. He tended to grin a lot.

"Not me," Alicia told him firmly. Though a major supporter of the IMA, the bad-tempered Dr. Wolff was not popular with the staff.

"Then dial," Bill said, laughing. "Dial! Dial!"

Alicia laughed too, and reached for the phone, and Bill returned to his desk, his smile fading. What the hell had Didier been involved in? he asked himself for the hundredth time. He sat down, put his hands behind his head and leaned back in his chair. His expensive dark blue blazer was slung casually over the back, and as usual he was tie-less, although he kept a small, expensive selection in his bottom drawer for meetings with people to whom such things were important. Despite his wealth, he liked to present himself as a man of the people. He glanced around the paneled office high above Park Avenue, his gray eyes taking in the framed articles heralding the IMA's many heroic missions, then moving on to the coffee table where a selection of newspapers, not all of them tabloids, were having a field day with the drug arrest and suicide of an IMA volunteer. He sighed deeply. What a frigging mess.

The IMA was Bill Miller's baby. He'd given up the hands-on practice of medicine some six years earlier

to found the organization, and now devoted himself
to its management and support, spending much of his
time in fund-raising and medical recruitment activities.
He kept in contact with the medical community
through consulting work, and had been delighted, on
meeting Lucy Nash at a medical conference, to find
her interested in volunteering with the IMA. She was
just the sort of person he was looking for: smart, professional, and idealistic. Her youth and physical fitness
were also plusses; conditions in the field were usually
very difficult. Her training had made her the perfect
person to deal with the viral outbreak in Peru and, by
all accounts, she'd done the job with skill and sensitivity. He'd been looking forward to sending her on other
missions, perhaps eventually offering her a staff position. And then this had to happen.

He stood and paced the polished parquet floor,
stopping at a narrow side table to pour himself some
coffee. The news had hit everyone hard, but Lucy so
much harder because of her personal relationship with
Jean-Pierre. He was glad Lucy had called and asked
to talk with him; if she hadn't, he would have waited
a day and called her. He was anxious to learn how
she felt about the IMA and its mission now. It was
bad enough losing Jean-Pierre; he hoped they
wouldn't have to lose Lucy, too.

"I caught Dr. Wolff just as he was leaving." Alicia
appeared in the open doorway, interrupting his musings. "He wasn't very happy."

"He's never very happy." Bill gave her a small
smile. "But he's always very generous."

"And Dr. Nash is here."

"Good." He rose quickly and stepped around his
desk as Lucy came through the door. She wore tai-
lored tweed slacks and an aqua sweater, and carried
a leather bomber jacket. She looked pale but determined. "What can I say?" he murmured as he led her

to the leather sofa and seated himself in an upholstered wing chair across from her. "Such a terrible
thing to happen. A real shock to us all."

"I still can't quite believe it," Lucy replied, slinging
her jacket onto the sofa beside her.

"We all feel the same. Can I get you some coffee?
Something stronger?"

"No, thanks. The thing is . . . Bill, it's not just that
I can't believe it. I *don't* believe it."

"I'm afraid it's true all the same," he said gently.
"The heroin was there."

"That's not what I mean. I can't believe Jean *knew*
it was there."

"I'd like to think that, too," Bill told her sadly. "But
if he really had no knowledge of the drugs, why would
he commit suicide? If he were innocent, surely he'd
want to clear his name."

Lucy was silent. Bill was right: Jean's suicide did
seem like an admission of guilt. And yet . . . "I'm not
going to let it rest," she told him firmly.

"How do you mean?" He frowned.

"I mean I want to get to the bottom of this, try and
clear his name. Will you help me?"

"Of course, of course. But . . . what are you planning to do?"

"I don't know yet. Talk to someone at the Drug
Enforcement Agency, and maybe some of his friends,
colleagues. . . ." She paused. "How long has Jack
McNulty worked for the IMA?"

"McNulty?" Bill frowned. "Why do you ask?"

"He met us at the Mayaruna Airport. He put Jean's
bags on the flight to Lima."

"And you think he may have slipped the heroin into
the bag?" The idea seemed to amuse Bill. "Highly
unlikely," he told her firmly. "Jack's worked for us
for years."

"So did Jean."

Bill shook his head. "No, I know Jack McNulty. I knew his father, too, when he worked at Langley. There's no way he'd be involved in anything like that. Besides, the DEA people think the drugs were put on board at Lima."

"How can they know that?" Lucy asked.

"The difference in the weight of the bags. All baggage was weighed in at Mayaruna because of the size of the plane and the weather conditions. The DEA weighed them again in New York, once they found the drugs."

"He could have put something else in his bag in Lima."

"Something weighing exactly six kilos?" He smiled sadly. "Unlikely."

Lucy thought of Jean's anxiety over possibly missing his meeting with Jorge in Lima. It all fit so neatly, but it still didn't ring true to her. "Has anyone told his family?" she asked at last.

Bill nodded. "I called his mother as soon as I heard. The IMA will arrange to have his body flown to France for burial—I'm sorry," he added as he saw her expression. "And someone will have to sort out his belongings."

"Will you give me Mrs. Didier's phone number? I'd like to call her."

"She doesn't speak English."

"That's okay, I have a little French, enough to say what I want to say."

"I understand. Alicia will get you the number." He leaned toward her earnestly. "Clearing Jean-Pierre's name would be wonderful, of course. This whole business is causing terrible problems for us in the press, and with our fund-raising efforts. But what can we really do? The only person who knew the truth is dead. And if he really was involved in drugs—I don't want to believe it either, but it does seem likely—

wouldn't it be kinder to let the truth die with him? Wouldn't it be better to move on?"

But Lucy shook her head. "I can't. I have to know."

Bill sighed. "Well, I'll support you, of course. But . . ." He paused, his brow furrowing. "Have you thought about the risk you're taking?"

"Risk?"

"Think about it. If Jean-Pierre was involved in drug running, even peripherally, and you start asking questions . . ."

Lucy smiled. "Aren't you being a little melodramatic?"

"We're talking heroin, Lucy. Organized crime, Cali cartels . . ." He watched her smile fade. "Better to let it rest." But she shook her head. "Well, it's your decision. But keep me in the loop, okay? Sure you won't have some coffee?" He rose and refilled his cup. "When are you due back at the hospital?"

"A week from next Monday. I took a six-week leave. But I'm thinking of going back sooner. Better to keep myself busy just now."

"Good idea. You did strong work in Peru," he told her, returning to his chair.

"Thanks. There's a lot more to be done, of course."

"And your friends at the CDC will do it." He paused. "I hope this terrible business hasn't soured you on the IMA. We really value your contributions. We need you."

Lucy smiled. "Now that I've seen it all first-hand, I'm even more committed. What you do is so important."

"I'm glad to hear it."

She reached for her jacket, then hesitated. "Bill . . . you don't really believe he did it, do you?"

Bill leaned over and touched her hand. "I don't know what to think," he said gently. "But then, I wasn't in love with him." He removed his hand and stood up. "Let me get you that phone number."

The managing agent was waiting for her in the elegant lobby. Yes, he'd received the authorization from Madame Didier to admit her to Mr. Didier's apartment. Some suitcases had just been delivered. Did she want them brought up? The porter would see to it. Here was the key to 34G; would she kindly return it to the doorman when she left?

An exhausting day and a half had passed since Lucy's conversation with Bill Miller. She'd had two emotionally and linguistically difficult phone conversations with Jean-Pierre's mother in Paris, offering her sympathy, explaining her relationship with her son, reiterating her determination to clear his name, and suggesting she go through his things and arrange for an international moving company to pack up and ship to France anything of value. Lucy was an expert at moving.

Talking to the Drug Enforcement Agency had been worse. Despite a call from Doctor Bill, they had not been anxious to speak with her, telling her mostly what she already knew. As to how, despite a strip search, Jean-Pierre had managed to conceal a "death pill" with which he'd committed suicide, they refused to comment, and they obviously thought the "why" was self-explanatory. The one victory she'd wrung from them was a promise to return his luggage when they'd finished with it. Apparently, they'd done so.

Now, feeling a little spooked, she turned the key and stepped into Jean-Pierre's apartment. A grand piano dominated the living room. Beyond, a wall of windows looked out at a sea of rooftops and a cloudy sky. The walls were painted the lightest of creams, and a Chinese carpet in blues, whites, and pinks covered much of the pale wood floor. The artwork was eclectic, a mix of the best of many periods and hands, including several African masks and a small stone figure that, to her unschooled eye, looked pre-Columbian. She wandered through the apartment, orienting herself, trying to decide where to start. The bedroom faced out over town house gardens, its walls painted a dove gray. Gray-and-blue-striped bed linen covered the king-size bed, and matching drapes were tied back with gray velvet ropes. An old-fashioned rolltop desk stood along one wall, its top closed.

The entire apartment was almost obsessively tidy. Not a glass sat in the sink of the bright small kitchen waiting to be washed; every towel in the spotless bathroom was carefully folded and hung at the same length. She thought of her own rather haphazard housekeeping and decided she and Jean would have driven each other crazy.

She went back into the living room and sank into a chair. She'd offered to pack up his things because it would give her an opportunity to snoop. But what, exactly, was she hoping to find? His innocence would be proved not by the presence of evidence, but by the absence of it.

The arrival of the suitcases interrupted her musings. As the door closed behind the porter, she began emptying their contents onto the floor. Clothes . . . medical equipment . . . books . . . toiletries . . . Everything was jumbled and creased, and in some cases, ripped apart, and the bottoms and sides of the cases had been slashed open. Jean had told her there was something for her in his luggage, but she didn't really expect to find it. The DEA would have removed and retained anything that seemed the least bit significant. So it was with some surprise that, at the bottom of the second case, she came upon two ugly wooden figures, sawn in half by the DEA in their search for drugs. She was

certain they hadn't been used to secrete drugs. If they
had, the DEA would have kept them.

Remembering her conversation with Bill Miller, she
hefted the hollow pieces of wood hopefully. No, there
was no way they weighed six kilos. She set them on
the coffee table, balancing the upper sections on the
lower ones, and studied them. Could these tacky-look-
ing figures be what Jean-Pierre had been referring to
when they'd parted? One was of a man, the other of a
woman, both with exaggerated sex characteristics. They
certainly didn't look as though they had any value, she
thought. Or was that simply because this sort of thing
had never been to her taste? No, she decided, they definitely looked like cheap, mass-produced imitations of
the sort of thing she'd seen in the windows of galleries
specializing in primitive art. The carving was crude,
the figures charmless. Why would a man with Jean's
exquisite taste, with his keen appreciation of genuine
artifacts, have such things in his possession?

She turned back to the suitcases and emptied the
last of the clothes onto the floor, then stuffed everything back in the cases again. Any undamaged clothing
could be donated to the thrift shop, the rest thrown
away. She and Madame Didier had agreed that only
the good furnishings and art should be shipped to
Paris. The rest could be sold or given to charity. She
set the statues on top of the cases; the thrift shop
could have them, too, if they cared to glue them
back together.

Now what? The rolltop desk, she decided. She went
into the bedroom. Outside, the clouds were thick-
ening. She switched on the track lighting and went to
the desk. The slatted wooden cover seemed jammed,
and she worked it back and forth trying to free it.
Suddenly it released and rattled open, and she gasped.
The space beneath was crammed with paper, all in a
hodgepodge of disarray. Pages had been torn from a

diary, letters and papers pulled from cubbyholes, the
desk blotter slit into ribbons. The desk drawers revealed the same sort of mess, including a bankbook
and two Merrill Lynch CMA statements, all with impressive balances. Obviously this chaos was not Jean's
doing. Could it be the work of the DEA searchers?
But they'd been so neat elsewhere in the apartment.

She went to the intercom and buzzed down to the
lobby.

"This is Carlos," the doorman answered.

"This is Dr. Nash in 34G. Who's been in Dr. Didier's apartment?"

"No one except yourself, miss."

"Are you sure?"

Yes. No one has been in the apartment except for
the two times the government men came."

"Two times? When?"

"You want to know exactly? I have to check the
book." Lucy could hear the rustling of pages. "A man
came from the drug agency on Tuesday night, just as
I was going off duty." The night Jean-Pierre died.
"And then two men came back the next afternoon."

"Did they show you any papers?" Lucy asked. "A
search warrant?"

"Not the first time, no. The man just said he was
with the Drug Enforcement Agency. He showed me
his ID, so I gave him the key."

"How about the men who came back on Wednesday?" Lucy asked. "Did they show you a search
warrant?"

"Yes, miss."

"And you didn't think it was strange that one of
their people had been here the night before?"

"He said he was from the government," Carlos replied defensively. "He showed me his ID."

"And was he one of the men who came back the
next day?"

"No, those were different men. They were black. The first drug agent was white."

Drug agent, my ass, Lucy thought. The DEA had told her they'd searched Jean-Pierre's apartment the day after his suicide and found nothing incriminating; there'd been no mention of an earlier visit. Besides, the real DEA searchers had obviously taken pains to leave the apartment as they found it, so the desk must have been trashed before they arrived with their warrant on Wednesday afternoon. She wondered if the impostor's search had been successful. "Never mind," she told the doorman. "It's all right."

She went back into the bedroom and surveyed the chaos on the desk, then angrily pulled the cover into place again. If anything of significance had been there, it was obviously gone now. She found a Yellow Pages in a bedside table and began calling thrift shops.

Half an hour later, all arrangements made, she emerged from the apartment and rang for the elevator. It arrived and she stepped inside, but as the door began to close, she suddenly shoved it open again and stepped back out. Returning to the apartment, she found a white plastic trash bag in one of the kitchen cabinets. She retrieved the wooden statues from the suitcase, jammed them inside, and tied the bag closed. Ugly they certainly were, but if Jean-Pierre had really intended them as a gift for her, they might not be as valueless as they seemed. Only an expert could tell her. Besides, they were all she had left of him.

She left the apartment again, locking the door carefully behind her, and took the elevator to the lobby.

"He showed his identification," Carlos insisted earnestly as she handed him the key. "I hope there is no problem."

"No problem," she assured him. Sure.

The doorman looked relieved. "And you are all finished up there?"

"No. I'll be back next week," Lucy told him, "to meet the thrift shop people and the movers." She paused. "What did he look like?"

"The men from the government?"

"Just the first one, the one that came on Tuesday night."

Carlos frowned, trying to remember. "He was in a suit," he said at last.

"Was he young?" Lucy asked. "Old? Tall? Short? What color was his hair?"

"Brown, I think. Brown or black. And not too tall."

"How tall?"

"Taller than you, shorter than me." The doorman was about six feet tall.

"How old was he?"

Carlos shrugged. "Probably younger than me. I'm forty-one."

"You've got a good memory," Lucy told him.

He smiled. "Comes with the job," he said. "I have to recognize all the tenants and call them by their names if I want good tips at Christmas."

The clouds were spewing forth a hard, cold rain as Lucy exited the building. "Damn," she said aloud. She considered going back upstairs and borrowing an umbrella from Jean-Pierre's apartment. Never mind, she told herself; a little rain won't hurt you. There was a bus shelter on the corner and she ran for it, clutching the plastic trash bag to her chest. A dark-haired man of medium height leaned out from a recessed doorway and watched her.

Chapter Three

It felt strange to be back at work after her four weeks in the jungle. New York General seemed more imposing, the halls more crowded than she remembered. She showed her ID to the guard, then entered the staff elevator and hit the button for the seventh floor, home of the epidemiological research lab.

Several staff members greeted her as she went along the hallway to her office, raincoat and umbrella dripping. The showers that had begun on Friday evening had continued right through the weekend, and the clearing skies promised for the beginning of the work week had so far not materialized.

She hung her wet things on a hook behind the door, then drew from her large handbag the two crude wooden statues she'd retrieved from Jean-Pierre's luggage. She'd managed a fairly neat job of glueing, and they now stood whole and triumphant in their ugliness. She set them on the windowsill—the rain coursing down the glass made a fitting backdrop, she decided—and turned her attention to her cluttered desk. She hadn't been at it for more than ten minutes when a voice interrupted.

"I heard you were back. How'd it go?"

Lucy looked up from the pile of pink message slips that had accumulated during her absence. Jake Weiss, chief of the epidemiology department, stood in the

doorway. In his arms were a stack of patient charts.
"Tell me those aren't for me," she begged.

"Only one. I need a consult. So how was it?"

"Tough. And scary. And fascinating. We found the
first filovirus outside Africa."

"A *filo*? No shit." He settled himself on a corner
of her desk. "Any ideas about the host?"

"Nothing conclusive, but I have a gut feeling it's
some kind of bird. Someone will need to go back, do
a lot more studies."

"You?"

Lucy shrugged. "I've got plenty to do right here at
the moment."

"You've got that right." He smiled at her. "So you
did your usual superb job, you finished early, and you
came straight back here to me," he teased.

"I couldn't stay away." Lucy smiled back.

"I have that effect on people." A burly bear of a
man some twenty years her senior, Jake Weiss had a
reputation for brilliance that terrified the residents
who rotated onto his service. But Lucy had found him
both generous and amusing, and the two had quickly
developed an easy, collegial relationship.

"I see you brought me a present." He gestured at
the two crude statues on the windowsill. "You
shouldn't have. And I do mean that."

She grinned. "Awful, aren't they? They were given
to me by . . . a friend." Her smile faded. "Jake, you
know anything about art?"

"Art who?"

"Seriously, do you think these things are
authentic?"

Weiss dumped the charts on her desk, then reached
over and picked up the female figure. "Authentic
kitsch, maybe. Hell, I don't know anything about this
stuff. Why not ask the friend who gave them to you?"

"I wish I could."

Weiss studied her. "That Didier guy, right? The doctor who was arrested for drug running?" Lucy nodded. "I saw it on the news." He hesitated. "You want to talk about it?"

"Not really, Jake. Not right now."

"Okay," Weiss said easily. He turned the statue around in his hands. "Look like this thing's been broken apart and glued back together. You do that?"

"The second part, not the first." He raised an eyebrow, but Lucy was silent.

He reached for the male figure and held them together. "Cute couple. You planning on breeding them?"

Lucy gave him a small smile. "Actually, I thought maybe Joe Carr in Radiology might be able to tell me about them. Isn't his wife involved in some gallery in SoHo?"

Weiss looked doubtful. "I think they do modern stuff, but you could ask." He replaced the statues on the windowsill. "You look tired," he told her.

"Nice of you to mention it."

"Maybe you should take a couple more days. . . ."

"I need to work, Jake. Work and working out are the best therapies I know. Now, which one of these cases is for me?"

He'd been sitting in the parked car for several hours, scanning the street, when he saw the nannies returning with their strollers. The rain had stopped around midday, though the afternoon remained cloudy, and the two women had essayed a quick trip to the park. As they approached the large, multistory apartment building, a grocery delivery man arrived and began unpacking bags from his wheeled cart and carrying them into the lobby. Deciding the setup was as good as he was likely to get, he got out and headed up the street, intercepting the two women just as they got to the canopy. "You work for the Boyds in 12B, don't you?" he asked the younger of the two as he opened the heavy outer door for them. "I'm in 12G." He gave a reassuring wave to the doorman, who was attempting to make the delivery man understand that the groceries had to be taken around to the service entrance.

"No." The woman frowned. "I work for the Leesons."

"Sorry. I guess you look like her." The charming young man in the suit and tie smiled down at the stroller's occupant. "He's cute." He leaned down and waggled the fingers of his right hand at the baby as they entered the lobby. "How ya doin', fella?" The baby gurgled. "My wife and I are expecting in the spring," he announced, straightening up and keeping his left hand out of sight. His longish brown hair had fallen over his forehead, and he flicked it back with a boyish gesture. "We're looking for someone to help out. Either of you know someone who could work for us?" Both women smiled at him, the older one started to reply, and the harried doorman, now busy with the intercom, barely glanced at the friendly little group as it moved past him toward the elevators.

The man got off at twelve and walked down to seven, found he was in the wrong wing, rode down to the lobby, and took another elevator up again. The seventh floor corridor was empty, and his keys made short work of the two guaranteed-unpickable locks.

He stepped inside, closed the door behind him, and looked around. He was standing in a typical high-rise layout: a short, narrow hallway with closets on one side and a kitchen on the other, beyond it a rectangular living room with dining area, then another short hallway to bedroom and bath. He decided to start in the living room.

The room was comfortable but not lavish: a sofa

and matching loveseat upholstered in yellow paisley, a glass dining table, and several pieces of old pine. The built-in bookcase along one wall contained a broad assortment of reading matter: novels, biographies, medical texts, cookbooks. An old pine table with a center drawer that served as a desk revealed nothing untoward. He was neater with its contents than he'd been at Didier's, knowing its owner would be back. He then turned his attention to a low pine chest along one wall. Carefully placing various objets d'art on the floor, he opened the chest, but found only blankets. He pulled books from the shelves and looked behind them, ruffled through pages to make sure they *were* books and not hollowed-out containers, then placed them back. He lifted the area rug, peered behind pictures and mirrors, felt under tables.

The bedroom was done in shades of peach and green, with peach balloon curtains. The bed was rumpled, its green print duvet pulled roughly up over the matching sheet and pillows. He checked under the mattress and inside each pillow case, then pulled the duvet up again in a close approximation of its original position. The closets contained nothing of interest to him either, though he went through each one carefully, removing and inspecting every shoe, every sweater box.

Back in the front hallway, he explored the linen and coat closets, then turned his attention to the kitchen. Working quickly, he checked the interior of each cabinet in turn, feeling inside the pots and bowls, looking behind the china and inside the freezer. He shook rice and spaghetti boxes to make sure their contents were as described, hefted cans, peered inside the trash bin.

The bathroom was easier but no more rewarding. Damn, he thought, as he lifted the top from the toilet tank and stared glumly inside. What the hell had she

carried away from Didier's apartment last Friday in
that plastic bag, and what had she done with it?

Dusk was falling as they pulled away from the Salva
Regina Mission on Eighth Avenue. As Doctor Bill
was always quick to explain to IMA contributors, his
car and driver weren't the luxury they seemed. If he
had to depend on public transportation, or take his
personal car in and out of parking garages all day,
he'd never get through his rounds.

When Bill Miller had given up his lucrative medical
practice, he hadn't given up practicing medicine. Charity work, he liked to say, was as rewarding as a Park
Avenue office. It was just that the rewards were emotional rather than financial.

Of course he could afford the luxury of being paid
in gratitude rather than dollars. A wealthy man in his
own right, he'd amassed a tidy fortune during his years
of private practice and invested it wisely. Now he was
as familiar a figure at missions and shelters around
town as he was at charity balls, advising and diagnos-
ing, doctoring wounds and illnesses that weren't serious enough to bother the local hospitals about, and
providing free inoculations during flu and measles
epidemics.

He checked his watch: nearly five. Not too bad. A
quick stop at the Homeless Coalition to drop off the
samples of antibiotic cream he'd promised, then downtown. There was plenty of time; his reservation at
Bouley wasn't until eight. But traffic around the Lincoln Tunnel area was unusually slow, and they didn't
pull up outside the five-story brick mission building
until six-thirty. It was dark now, and the light mounted
high above the doorway painted the deserted pave-
ment below. This seedy, light-industrial section near
the docks had not been gentrified, and streetlights as
well as passersby were few and far between.

Sister Margareta, and the smells of franks and beans and disinfectant, greeted him as he entered. "Busy tonight," he offered as she led him past the line of homeless people waiting to be fed.

"We're always busy when it is cold and wet," the nursing sister replied with a heavy Dutch accent. A severe, columnar woman of sixty-four, Sister Margareta had recently emigrated to New York to take over the running of the mission, which she did with great firmness and greater compassion. Bill had taken to her the first time he'd met her, and her medical training, combined with her independent, no-nonsense attitude, had caused him to make this mission one of his regular stops.

"What have you got for me?" he asked as they continued along the green linoleum'd hallway toward the infirmary.

"The usual. Coughs. Colds. One case of flu. A few scrapes and scratches. And that poor woman with the neck sore has pulled off the bandage again. It looks badly infected."

Bill dealt with the neck sore first, cleaning, medicating, and rebandaging it, then giving the woman some antibiotic pills. "Now you take them. Don't throw them away," he told the woman firmly, but he knew the chances of his instructions being followed were no better than fifty-fifty. The scratches and scrapes were minor and quickly doctored, but the coughs and winter colds were less treatable. He dispensed the cough drops and vitamin C pills with a sense of futility. The mission had only limited overnight space—twenty-two beds—and a three-night limit. And it was no good telling people who lived in cardboard boxes on heating ducts to keep warm and drink lots of fluids. Victims of flu, measles, and other more serious sicknesses were kept in the mission infirmary that lay just beyond the examination room, but colds and coughs would quickly overrun the tiny five-bed unit, and had to be turned away.

The patients shuffled out into the hallway, and Bill and the nursing sister turned their attention to the patient suffering from what Margareta had diagnosed as flu. A thin black man in his mid-twenties, he had been wrapped in several blankets in an effort to control his chills, and settled in a threadbare reclining chair behind a screen.

"Bill, isn't it?" the doctor asked kindly. "An easy name for me to remember." He put a gentle hand on the man's shoulder. "How long have you been feeling sick?"

"Since yesterday," the man said softly. His eyes were jumpy and afraid.

Bill examined him carefully, frowning as he put his stethoscope to the man's chest, then turned to Margareta. "Have any other of your regulars shown up with these symptoms?"

"No."

"Any of your staff sick?" The nurse shook her head. "I'd like him to have a chest X ray."

"I could have someone take him to Bellevue—" Margareta suggested.

"Not Bellevue." The young man levered himself out of the chair, blankets falling around him. "Not going to Bellevue. They lock you up in Bellevue. You never come out."

"No, no," Bill tried to reassure him. "That's not what she means."

"I'm gettin' out of here," the man announced, tottering toward the infirmary door. Bill reached out a hand to stop him, but he shrugged free. He got as far as the doorway before he stopped and stood swaying, eyes hot.

"I suppose we might take him to Dr. Jensen's office on West Seventieth," Bill mused. "He's one of our volunteers and I'm sure he'd do us the favor. It would be easier for this guy."

"Not going to Bellevue . . ." The man hesitated, weaving.

Margareta went and draped a blanket around him, but when she tried to lead him back to the recliner, he resisted. "Not Bellevue," she assured him. "You have my word."

"I could have someone pick him up, bring him back here," Bill said. "Let me make a call."

"What do you think he has?" Margareta asked softly, drawing the doctor aside.

"I'm not sure. But it could be TB."

"That would be bad. Especially in a place like this."

"Yes, very bad."

"What're you two whispering about?" the young man asked suspiciously. "You gonna take me somewhere, lock me up?"

"No one's going to lock you up," Bill told him firmly. Turning back to Margareta, he asked, "Do you think you could keep him here? At least until I'm sure of the diagnosis?"

She nodded. "We'll isolate him in the infirmary. Only three of the beds are occupied at the moment, and we can move those patients in here after we disinfect." She glanced back at the young man. "I know the hospitals do what they can," she continued, "but they are so impersonal. And being sick can be a frightening experience for anyone."

"It'll mean extra work for you and your staff."

Margareta drew herself up. "We are used to work," she told him sternly. "Besides, who will care for them if we don't?" She smiled at the young black man. "You can stay here. The doctor will take you somewhere for X rays and bring you back. But you must do exactly what I tell you."

The young man smiled sweetly. "Yes, ma'am," he

said. His eyes rolled back and he collapsed slowly onto
the scuffed green floor.

Lucy tossed her jacket and oversize handbag onto
a chair. Carr's wife's gallery did indeed specialize in
modern art, and neither Joe nor his wife, whom he
was kind enough to call, could offer a valuation of the
statues, although she noticed the radiologist wince
when he saw them. She stood the figures on the pine
chest, then continued on to the kitchen where she
poured herself some wine from an open bottle in the
fridge and thought about food. Vietnamese, she decided. She wasn't in the mood to cook, but there was
a good local place that delivered.

Back in the living room, she ordered red curry
chicken in lemon grass and coconut milk, then
checked her answering machine. Monica's voice
boomed out, reminding her that she and Howard were
expecting her next Wednesday evening, along with her
famous duck recipe, and asking how the hell she was,
anyway? Lucy smiled. Monica was a research scientist
at the CDC and the two women had become friends
during Lucy's stint there. The second message was from
the international shippers she'd contacted, confirming
the dates of the New York pickup—next Tuesday, at
his apartment—and the Paris delivery of Jean-
Pierre's things.

She went to the bookshelves and scanned her cookbook section. An enthusiastic cook when the mood hit
her, she'd collected many recipes over the years. The
duck recipe was in a flimsy pamphlet, and tended to
work its way back between the more substantial volumes. She'd located it and was pulling it out when
she stopped, frowning. What was *The Salterton Trilogy*
doing between *365 Ways to Cook Pasta* and *The Food
of Greece*? She glanced at the shelf above; *Hungarian
Cooking* beside Somerset Maugham? Strange; she

hadn't read Maugham for months, nor had she used the Hungarian cookbook. With a mental shrug, she reshelved the offending volumes in their proper sections and carried *Game Bird Cooking* across to the desk, where she copied out the duck recipe for transport to Atlanta, then put the pamphlet back on the shelf. She was glad Monica had agreed to ducks for Thanksgiving; turkey was so boring.

She returned to the desk to call Madame Didier in Paris. It took her a moment to find the number; apparently she'd left it under her appointment book on the top of the desk, and not in the drawer as she'd remembered. The phone rang for some time before it was answered, and Lucy realized belatedly that it was eleven in the evening in France.

"Madame Didier? Here is Lucy Nash again." In her phone conversations with Jean's mother, Lucy was finding her command of French not nearly as commanding as she'd remembered it.

"Ah, Lucy," the older woman said warmly. "How are you?"

"I'm fine, Madame, thank you. I hope I am not calling too late. I wish to tell you about the shipping persons."

Jean-Pierre's mother rattled away in rapid French, and Lucy sighed. While her college French allowed her to communicate, sort of, she didn't always understand the responses she got back. "Please speak more slowly," she begged.

"I wish to thank you for your help," Madame Didier said, speaking at a snail's pace. "What of the shipping?"

"I hear today from the shipper with confirmation. . . ." Somewhat laboriously, Lucy managed to explain what was being sent and when it would arrive, and to supply the name and phone number of the local French ship-

ping agent. "I give everything else to the charity people as we agreed," she added. "Yes?"

"Yes. I would not want his clothes," Madame Didier replied, picking up speed. "It would be too sad.
Again, I must thank you, my dear. Jean's family
thanks you for all you have done."

Don't want clothes, Lucy managed to translate. Too
sad. Thank you. Jean's family.

"We will have a memorial service here in Paris,"
his mother continued. "All the family will come.
There are cousins I have not seen for many years. It
is a sad reason to see loved ones."

Memorial service. Paris. All the family. Sad
grape . . . Grape? No, that couldn't be right. . . ."And
will your sister be well enough to travel from Marseilles for the memorial?" Lucy asked. "I understand
she is very ill."

A silence greeted this question, and Lucy was beginning to wonder if she'd really said what she thought
she'd said when Madame Didier spoke at last. "My
sister lives in Paris," she said.

"I'm talking," Lucy persevered, "about your sister
in Marseilles. The one who is very ill. Jean was going
to visit her this week."

"But . . . I have no sister in Marseilles." Madame
Didier sounded perplexed. "You said this before, and
I told you. Perhaps you did not understand. My sister
lives in Paris." She paused. "You say Jean was coming
to France this week?"

"My French is not good," Lucy apologized. "I must
have misunderstood."

"I think you did. Jean was coming to visit me for
Christmas."

He was? "Yes, that must be it. Well, Madame Didier, I mustn't take up any more of your time. Let me
know if there is any problem with the shipping."

"Yes. And thank you again."

Lucy replaced the receiver and leaned back in her chair. So Jean-Pierre had lied about having a sick aunt in Marseilles. But why? The answer, terribly obvious, was not one she wanted to think about. Marseilles was a major port of entry for drugs.

She rose and went to the window. A half-moon peeked from behind the departing clouds. The Vietnamese food she'd ordered would arrive any minute but she was no longer hungry. She went to the kitchen and refilled her wineglass. Sipping, she returned to the living room and sank onto the sofa. She'd convinced herself that Jean was innocent, that someone had planted the heroin in his suitcase. But if that was true, what was the real reason for his trip to Marseilles? And why did it require a cover story about a fictitious aunt?

Chapter Four

"Nothing? Not at his place or hers? Nothing at all?" The older man sipped his beer and scowled.

"We've been all through this," his companion replied tiredly. Although their booth, with its patched mock-leather seats and scarred table, was set well toward the back of the noisy bar, they spoke softly.

"But she did take something from Didier's apartment when she was there last week."

"Well, I saw her leave with a bag she didn't bring in with her, yeah. As for what was in the bag . . ." He shrugged.

"Drugs? Cash?"

"I didn't find any. I didn't find a goddamn thing."

"Maybe you didn't look hard enough."

The dark-haired man rose angrily. "Dammit. You don't believe me, search the place yourself." Faces turned toward them in anticipation. This small Irish pub down by the docks did not cater to the most genteel crowd in town.

"Sit down, Rossetti." Rossetti sat. "So what's her story? Didn't you learn anything at her place?"

"Yeah, well, she's pretty, she's a lousy housekeeper, and she likes to cook."

"Oh, that's useful. Look, I want to know what she took from Didier's place, and I want to know why."

"Hey, maybe she took back a bunch of love letters

she wrote him. Maybe she was reclaiming a couple of books he borrowed."

"And maybe *she's* the one dealing drugs now. In which case—"

"She's a doctor. Cut her some slack."

"Didier was a doctor, too."

Rossetti sighed. "Yeah, I know." He stood up. "Look, I gotta go. I'm already late."

"Keep in touch," the older man said.

Rossetti gave him a wry smile. "Like I have a choice."

". . . and in here," Lucy continued, leading the three packers from Cartright's International Expediters into Jean-Pierre's bedroom, "there's just the desk."

"It's a beauty," one of the men commented, inspecting it. The name stitched on his coveralls identified him as Chad. "It's the real thing; old. Don't see many of them around." He turned to Lucy. "Any chance you want to sell it instead of ship it?"

"I'm afraid not," Lucy told him. "It doesn't belong to me."

"Pity," Chad said. "Kind of a hobby with me, Victorian furniture." He bent and studied the drawer fittings. "See this? Real brass." He pulled open a drawer. "You empty it all out?"

"Yes, of course," Lucy replied, puzzled. Surely the man could see that the drawer was empty.

Catching her tone, he looked up at her and winked. "I mean the other drawers. The secret ones."

"What?"

"All these Victorian rolltops have secret compartments. Didn't you know that?" Lucy shook her head. "People hid love letters in them, jewelry . . . here, I'll show you." He pulled the open drawer completely out of its frame and set it on the floor, then felt around inside. "There's usually a sort of spring release . . .

got it." He drew out a small, rectangular wooden compartment, open at the top. "Empty. Let's try another one." He slid it back in and replaced the drawer.

"How many are there?" Lucy asked, her eyes wide.

"Oh, a couple. There's usually one behind the small drawers on top." He rolled the desktop back. "May I?"

"Please," Lucy said. "By all means."

"Come on, man," one of Chad's partners interjected. "We've got a schedule, you know?'

"Just take a second," Chad replied calmly. He pulled out the small drawers and felt behind each in turn, stopping at the third from the left. He manipulated an unseen mechanism and Lucy heard a tiny thunk as the catch released. "Drawer's sticking." Chad frowned. "I think something's stuck back there." He looked over at Lucy. "If I pull hard, I can probably get it out. But I might rip it. Or damage the drawer."

"Go for it," Lucy said. "You have my permission."

Chad's large fingers fumbled and twisted inside the narrow cavity. "I've got hold of it," he reported at last. "Feels like leather . . ." With a final twist and pull, he brought forth a small leather-bound diary amid splinters of wood. "Afraid I broke the drawer," he apologized, handing the book to Lucy.

"No problem," Lucy assured him. Her pulse quickened as she leafed through the maroon diary. The first page was blank; the second, covered in cryptic symbols and abbreviations, was in Jean-Pierre's handwriting. "I can't thank you enough," she began.

"Sorry it wasn't, like, jewels," Chad told her, but Lucy shook her head.

"Don't be. This is better."

While the three men padded and crated Jean-Pierre's belongings, Lucy sat on the floor in the emptying living room and puzzled over the contents of the diary. There were letters and dates, and symbols she couldn't interpret, and names—*Vieillesse, Sun God, Stanislas, Noone*—with sums of money next to them, some rather large. She was pretty sure that *Vieillesse* was French for old age, which made no sense to her. But *Sun God* sounded like it could be the street name of a drug of some sort. And *Stanislas* and *Noone* could be buyers. One name that appeared several times was *Jorge M.*, and as she recalled Jean's anxiety about missing Jorge in Lima, she wondered whether he might have been Jean's South American drug connection. Suddenly aware of where her thoughts were taking her, she snapped the book closed. Jean couldn't be a drug dealer. There had to be another explanation for the words and phrases. And the large sums of money? Yes, she told herself fiercely, there could.

"All done." Chad stood before her. "If you'd just sign here, please."

Lucy rose, slipping the diary into her jeans pocket. "Thanks again for showing me those secret drawers," she said as she signed the shipping release. "Uh, wait a sec." She retrieved her handbag and pulled a twenty from her wallet. "Please take this," she told Chad. "I'm really grateful."

"My pleasure," he assured her, pocketing the money. "Like I said, I love those old desks."

When the shipping people had left, Lucy took a last look around. The apartment felt cold and sad and empty. Jean was truly gone. With an air of finality, she went out and locked the door behind her.

But as she walked home through the darkening streets, she felt no closure. Nor would she, she knew, until she had cleared Jean's name of the drug charges. Or confirmed them, an inner voice whispered.

As she turned onto Second Avenue, she reached into her purse for a few dollars to give Crazy Ray, but surprisingly he wasn't at his usual evening spot in front of the video store, nor was he stationed outside

McDonald's, opening the door for customers and waving his cup in their faces. Well, she'd catch up with him in the morning.

The phone was ringing as she unlocked her door, and she ran for it, grabbing it just before the answering machine cut in.

"Lucy? Monica. Just wanted to double-check when your flight gets in tomorrow. Howard says three twenty-five, but I thought you were coming in earlier. . . ."

"Howard's right. I tried to switch to the ten o'clock, but it was sold out."

"Then three twenty-five it is. We'll meet you at the baggage claim. Sure you'll recognize us after lo these many months?"

"Now don't try and make me feel guilty. It hasn't been that long."

"Only since last May."

Lucy smiled. "Well, you can't have changed all that much."

"I keep getting blonder. Howard just gets balder. Women age so much differently than men." Lucy laughed. "Oh, and I've got your ducks. I bought them from a local game farm, and they're real beauties. And five oranges, like you said. And wild rice. Sure that's all you need?"

"I'm bringing the spice mix with me, and a bottle of Hennessey. Whatever I don't pour on the ducks we can drink."

"Good plan." Monica hesitated. "Hey, Luce, you remember Ted Wiley? Well, he's been working with those peruvia samples you sent. And he's come up with something kind of interesting."

"Yes?" Lucy lowered herself into her desk chair. "What?"

"There seems to be a second strain of the virus. It's real, real close to the original."

"Curious," Lucy said. "We saw only one version of the disease. . . ." She recalled the man with the scars and the fever, the one who'd cursed them all and disappeared into the jungle. "Although there was a man who claimed peruvia—he called it sangre negra—was an old disease that had come back."

"Well, we're just discovering filoviruses. It'll probably turn out there are thousands of the little buggers. Anyhow, if you can stay until Monday, Matt might let you have a look at it."

"You think so?" Matt Kravitz was in charge of the CDC's Level Four section, and Lucy's old boss.

"If not, you can watch the video feed from the electron microscope. Can you stay?"

"Five days? Sure you won't get sick of me?"

"Of course not. We never see you anymore. It'll be fun."

Lucy thought for a moment. "Okay, as long as the hospital can spare me, I'll pack an extra pair of undies and change my flight home."

"Terrific. Oh, and bring some good, sturdy boots. Howard's plans for Saturday involve mud."

"Uh-oh." They both laughed at Lucy's tone. Howard, a high school chemistry teacher, was a notorious outdoorsman, and the more uncomfortable the experience, the better he liked it. "Oh, and Monica?" Her voice became more serious. "I have something curious to show you. It's a diary that—well, it's a long story. I'll tell you about it when I see you."

"Can't wait."

"Me neither."

Atlanta was a popular destination on Thanksgiving eve, and her flight circled for half an hour before landing. Lucy hurried through the brightly lit terminal, pushing from her mind the memory of a small airfield in Peru, and concentrating on ducks and mud and old friends.

Monica and Howard had stationed themselves by the baggage carousels and they waved enthusiastically as she appeared, Monica a lot blonder and Howard only slightly balder. Despite her protests, Howard grabbed her large green bag as it came around, and talking nonstop, they headed out into the parking lot to retrieve the couple's Cherokee. In the front seat, a rather silly looking Corgi barked fiercely at their arrival.

"Don't mind Max," Monica said. "He's all mouth and no trousers."

"New acquisition?"

"New*ish*," Howard replied. "He got us around Halloween." He opened the door. "Max," he said firmly, "stay!" The small, low-slung animal immediately leaped out of the car, raced over to snuffle at Lucy's outstretched hand, marked the left rear tire as his personal property, galloped around to supervise the loading of her bag, and jumped into the backseat, claws scrabbling on the upholstery and stubby tail going a mile a minute.

"You train him yourself?" Lucy asked, all innocence.

"Very funny." Howard slid behind the wheel, then turned and patted the Corgi's brown head. "Good boy."

"Ah, the Reverse Reinforcement Method," Lucy said, laughing.

"Joke all you want," Howard replied defensively. "The fact is, Corgis are very smart dogs. And they're great sheepherders."

"Such an important skill out here in the suburbs," Monica added, smiling. "Now let me tell you who-all's coming to dinner tomorrow. . . ."

*   *   *

The four Rhesus monkeys howled and rattled their cages at the arrival of their Thanksgiving dinner, carried by the man in the yellow jumpsuit. He put the food on the steel examining table and went over to the cages. No change. Well, he hadn't expected any. When he'd examined them thoroughly several hours before, they'd seemed completely healthy. It had been over a week, after all. If they were going to succumb, they would have done so by now.

He went from cage to cage, carefully unlatching the small sections that allowed access to the interior and retrieving the empty food dishes, then latching them firmly in place again. Although he was anxious to finish here and go home to his own holiday meal, he worked carefully and slowly. At the steel table he refilled the dishes, then went back to the cages and began to feed the animals. Usually the monkeys withdrew when he put his gloved hand into the cages, repelled by the nearness of the bright yellow color and the smell of disinfectant. He was placing the last dish when it happened. Without warning, the Rhesus swung down from the far side, grabbed the glove, and bit down hard on his thumb.

He dropped the food dish and jumped back, cursing. His heart was beating wildly, but he had the presence of mind to slam the cage section back into place and set the latch before examining his ripped glove. Had the teeth gone all the way through?

Normally he would exit the lab and decontaminate in the airlocked disinfectant shower before removing gloves or suit. No time for that now. To one side of the small animal lab was a decon sink. Using the foot pedal, he started the flow of disinfectant as he stripped off the heavy glove. Both pairs of the surgical gloves he wore underneath were punctured. Shit. He ripped them off, thanking God when he saw no blood, and thrust his bare hand under the flow. He felt no sting, and the skin of his thumb appeared unbroken.

Slowly his breathing became normal. Hell, he told himself, there's nothing to worry about. The monkeys aren't infected. But he knew that wasn't completely accurate. The fact that they weren't sick didn't mean they weren't infected. Simian hemorrhagic fever was fatal to chimps, but harmless to humans. The reverse could be true, too.

"So what do you think of him?"

Lucy scraped the remains of a bounteous Thanksgiving dinner from the last of Monica's pretty Mikasa dishes, then set it in the sink with the others. The ducks had been a huge success, and only the bones remained. "What do I think of whom?"

"Charlie. Charlie Moss."

Lucy looked over at her friend. "Oh, no," she said. "You didn't invite him for me."

"Of course I did. He's perfect for you. And Howard says he's a great woodsman."

"One of my first requirements in a mate." Lucy turned on the tap and began rinsing the dishes. "You know how I hate that matchmaker stuff."

"Just give him a chance," Monica begged. She took a rinsed dish and stood it in the dishwasher. "He's smart and he's cute. And I know he's looking."

Lucy stopped rinsing and turned to her friend. "I know you mean well, sweetie, but this isn't a good time for me."

"What do you mean? What's wrong?" Monica's brown eyes filled with concern.

"I . . . got involved with somebody in Peru," Lucy began. "And then a whole bunch of shit happened. . . ." Haltingly, she told Monica about her romance with Jean-Pierre, about his arrest and death, and about her determination to learn the truth. Sounds of laughter and barking drifted in from the dining room as she spoke, making her words seem overly dramatic and unreal.

Monica listened silently. When Lucy was finished, she put an arm around her shoulder. "I'm so sorry," she said softly. "I had no idea. Why didn't you tell me before?"

"I was planning to, this weekend," Lucy replied. "That diary I mentioned on the phone? It was his. It's the only clue I have, and it seems to say exactly what I don't want to believe."

"I read about it in the papers," Monica said, "but I had no idea. . . . You really think he's innocent?"

"I did, in the beginning," Lucy replied. "I still want to, but . . ."

"Pumpkin pie and apple strudel, coming up!" Howard called back over his shoulder as he entered the kitchen. "Lucy, Monica, leave the dishes. Charlie and I will do them later."

"A veritable prince among men," Monica announced, shutting the dishwasher firmly. She turned to Lucy. "We'll have a long chat when everyone's gone home."

"Ah, girl talk." Howard gave Lucy a broad wink. "That Charlie's really something, isn't he? And a helluva trekker. You know, one time—"

Lucy rolled her eyes and Monica gave her husband a long-suffering look. "Howard? Go find out if anyone wants ice cream on their pie."

The day after Thanksgiving brought an early snow to New York City, big wet flakes that sank heavily through the cold air and flattened themselves in sodden layers on sidewalks and awnings and roofs. Bill Miller traditionally spent Thanksgiving in Vermont. He had several close friends in the Manchester area with whom he ate his turkey, and his Stratton Mountain condo was right on the liftline. Bill loved to ski, and he could usually count on a few good runs being open by the end of November, even if most of the snow was man-made. But this year, he was too busy to spare more than a few days, and Thanksgiving Saturday found him back in the city. It had been years since he'd spent this particular weekend in town, and as he made his rounds, he marveled at the exodus that had left the streets pleasantly empty and still.

Sister Margareta hurried to greet him as he entered the mission. "There is not much improvement," she said without preamble.

"Give it time." He followed her white-coated figure toward the rear of the building. "Quiet around here," he commented.

"We've eliminated all overnight infirmary stays as you suggested," she explained. "And the soup kitchen now stops serving at three. We will resume our regular schedule once this is over, of course." They stopped at a steel door, obviously new, that proclaimed in large red letters: QUARANTINE. NO ADMITTANCE.

"I'm glad you got us permission to keep them here," she said.

"It wasn't as difficult as I'd feared," Bill replied. "My buddy at the Board of Health was very anxious to avoid a panic. The quieter we can keep it, the happier we'll make him." He turned and looked at her severely. "But it's absolutely essential that you and your staff be religious in following the safety procedures."

"Absolutely. We understand."

"And none of the staff or volunteers is sick?"

"No, thank God." She turned aside and opened the door to a small changing room. "I have laid out your things. Thelma and Pat are already inside. They'll help you." Margareta paused. "We are all so grateful to you, Dr. Miller."

He gave her a warm smile. "I'm glad to do what I can. I'm afraid it's not the last we'll see of antibiotic-resistant TB," he added, his smile fading. "And I'm still not totally convinced that hiding them away here is the right thing to do, even though the commissioner seems to like the idea. . . ."

"The hospitals are overcrowded," Margareta said firmly. "Besides, if word get out that a few homeless people are carrying antibiotic-resistant TB, there will be a panic. You said so yourself." Bill shrugged his agreement. "The shelters and the missions will all be shut down, and those poor people will be out in the snow."

He nodded slowly. Sister Margareta had made her feelings and intentions perfectly clear, ever since that young man had collapsed in the examining room last week. All Bill had done was follow her lead. "Well, let's just make sure we don't add to the problem," he told her. "I agree we're probably doing a service by containing the illness here. And perhaps what we learn will help others. But we must be scrupulous in our sterilization procedures. And our security."

Inside the changing room, he stripped off his street clothes and hung them in a locker, then donned the clean green scrubs and fabric booties Margareta had set out on the bench. Hanging from a padded hook on one wall was an orange RACAL bodysuit with a self-contained, battery-powered air supply. A communications microphone and headset were built into its hood. He struggled into the suit, hating the confined feeling it gave him. He'd always been slightly claustrophobic. He took a few experimental breaths; the mechanism seemed to be working okay. He pulled on the two pairs of surgical gloves Margareta had left for him and Velcro'd the suit's sleeves tight around the join. Feeling like an orange version of the Michelin

Man, he waddled out into the hall, took a deep breath, and pushed through the steel door.

He went quickly through the tiny airlocked decontamination chamber that Carl Anders, head of the IMA lab, had recently installed. Its chemical shower, with the powerful disinfectant known as Envirochem, would only be needed on the way out of the ward.

Thelma looked up from the rolling tray stand on which she was laying out the blood-collection implements—butterfly needles, Vacutainer tubes, alcohol swabs—and smiled at Bill through the clear faceplate of her RACAL suit. Thelma was an excellent nurse, and the mission could afford her services only because of a special contribution made by the IMA. Pat, a nurse's aide, turned from the patient she was tending and waved. She, too, was gowned, gloved, and RACAL-suited.

Four beds had been added to the shelter's usual twenty-two, and two rows of thirteen beds, set at right angles to the walls, now marched the length of the long narrow room. Men were placed on one side, women on the other. Thelma rolled the tray to the first bed on the right, and she and Bill got started. He examined each patient in turn, Thelma making notes and drawing blood samples. Occasionally Bill asked for certain Vacutainers to be used; the colored tops indicated the specific tests to be done on the blood inside.

"They're still pretty lethargic," Thelma told him as they worked, her voice thin and muffled in his headset.

"That's normal," he assured her. "Actually, they're in better shape than I expected. Are the coughs still productive?"

"Some yes, some no. The fever and sweats were pretty bad in the beginning, but they seem to be over the worst." She hesitated. "I've noticed a sort of rash, though. A number of them have it."

Bill frowned. "Show me." Thelma led him to the bed of a plump-faced, middle-aged woman with graying hair.

"Doctor wants to look at that rash," Thelma told the dozing patient as she gently pulled back the hospital gown. The woman opened her red-rimmed eyes in sudden alarm, but Bill smiled at her reassuringly and patted her hand as he bent to examine the small dark welts. "Yes, I've seen these lesions before," he told Thelma. "A form of subacute hematogenous TB. It's a not uncommon complication with these antibiotic-resistant strains, especially in the reactivation of old TB cases." The nurse nodded and they moved on to the next patient.

It was nearly eight when they finished and Thelma began packing up the vials of blood for decontamination and collection.

"The improvement's small but it's steady," Bill told the two women. "I think we're going to beat this thing. You both doing okay with the RACALs?"

Across the room, Pat gave him a thumbs up, but Thelma shrugged. "They get in the way," she said. "Are you sure we need them? Wouldn't a jumpsuit and mask and gloves—"

"The RACALs may be a little overkill," Bill replied, "but we're talking about an airborne, blood-borne tubercular pathogen with no known cure. I'm still surprised that it didn't spread all through the mission before we realized what we had and isolated it. Hell, Margareta and I both examined the first victim, leaned over him, touched him. Wear the suit." The nurse nodded.

He frowned as he entered the decon chamber for his seven-minute disinfectant shower. He was pleased with the progress of his patients, but very concerned about the risks. He stood in the center of the small cubicle and let the spray play over him. Well, there was no turning back; they were into it now. He turned and raised his arms so the disinfectant could reach the undersides of the sleeves. As long as the proper precautions were taken, the mission could handle this. As long as everybody decon'd. As long as nobody screwed up.

"Oh, God. Please help me. Please . . ." The man moaned softly, and bloody tears ran from his eyes. His pillow was smeared with the blood that seeped from his nose, his mouth, his ears. The nurse stood beside the bed, her eyes large and terrified. Around her, sixteen other patients lay moaning and thrashing, dying in their own dark, bloody discharges. What was this strange and terrible disease?

She shivered as she filled the hypodermic needle. Nothing she or the other two nurses did seemed to help, but they did it anyway, because they couldn't just stand by and not try. She wore a blue hospital shirt and pants, and over them, a full-length, long-sleeved gown. Surgical gloves covered her hands and wrists, and a surgical mask was tied tightly behind her head. They'd told her the disease could only be spread by contact with bodily fluids, but why take chances?

She held the hypodermic up and squirted a drop from the tip, then glanced over at the clock on the far wall. Half an hour more, and her eight-hour shift would be finished. She couldn't wait to strip off her bloody clothes and get some sleep in the staff's tiny living quarters. More and more, lately, she regretted having signed on for this duty. But who could have imagined it would be like this? The first day, the patients had seemed like any others. . . .

The wages she'd been offered were three times her hospital pay; of course, that should have warned her. And she hadn't really understood she'd be living in complete seclusion. At least she had the other nurses and the orderlies for company. And that man who called himself a doctor, although she had her doubts about that.

"Help me . . ." The man's body shook with spasms.

"I'm here." She bent toward the patient and put her free hand on his shoulder. "I have something that will help you."

The man turned his bloody face toward her, his tremors slowing. "Help me . . ."

She reached behind her for an alcohol swab and rubbed his twitching arm, knowing such procedures didn't really matter anymore. The man was dying. They all were. She dropped the swab, took a firm hold on his arm, and plunged the hypodermic into the bruised and mottled tissue. The man moaned. She emptied the contents into his arm, knowing it was hopeless. His eyes were fixed on her face, searching for some reassurance, some spark of hope, and finding none.

She was withdrawing the needle when the man's body spasmed again. His arm jerked from her grip, hitting the hypodermic and sending its bloody tip through the sterile glove on her left hand and deep into the flesh between thumb and forefinger.

With a guttural cry, she dropped the needle and stood staring at her hand.

"What is it? What have you done?"

She looked up fearfully. One of the orderlies stood beside her.

"I need to decon," she said, brushing past him. She ran toward the locked door that led out of the ward, but he was faster.

"Let me see your hands," he demanded, barring her way.

"Leave me be." Her heart beat fast as she tried to pass him. If she could just get to decon, maybe it would be all right.

He grabbed her wrists and looked down at the gloves. "You broke the skin."

"No, it's nothing," she said, pulling away. "Just let me decon."

"Like hell. Ali!"

In an instant, she was surrounded. The two orderlies, big men both, held her firmly while Nurse Raphaela, the one she didn't like, stripped off the punctured left glove. The streak of blood was bright against her cocoa skin. She struggled fiercely, screaming, knowing what would happen, but the orderlies were strong. Raphaela injected the soporific and they tied her into a bed. The drug worked fast, and her screams diminished, then ceased. They stood looking down at her, gripped by a white-hot dread. An accident like that could happen to any of them. She had been a good nurse.

In the early hours of the Monday after Thanksgiving, a white decontamination truck bearing no identification drew up to the curb and waited, its motor turning over softly. Three men in black spacesuits emerged from the shadows. They dragged eleven plastic body bags to the rear of the truck. From inside the cab, the driver unlocked the sealed compartment, and the men shoved the body bags inside. The compartment locked again with a click, and the ghostly truck slid away into the night.

Chapter Five

It was all so different from the way she remembered it, Lucy thought, as she and Monica pushed through the airlocked door and entered Biosafety Level Four. She plugged her suit into one of the thick black air hoses dangling from the ceiling, and looked around. An eerie blue light pervaded the empty lab. Where was everyone? Monica took her elbow and guided her to a workstation where a rack of stoppered test tubes stood, their contents glowing redly.

Lucy leaned closer to read the label: PERUVIA. Why were they glowing like that? Monica reached over and unstoppered one of the tubes, releasing a pinkish vapor. It swirled up out of the tube, expanding, filling the air around the two scientists and covering the face-plates of their RACAL suits. Lucy gasped and stepped back, knocking Monica's hand and sending the tube stand crashing to the floor. The tubes exploded, sending shards of glass flying. She felt a sharp sting and looked down. Her suit was slashed open, her leg exposed and bleeding. She stared at the gash in horror, feeling the cold vapor seep into the wound, then fell to the floor, screaming silently into her suit. Monica grabbed her shoulder and began pulling her toward the airlock, but they both knew it was too late. Her leg, freezing cold, dangled out of her suit as Monica dragged her along the tile floor. . . .

"Come on, Lucy. Get up!"

Lucy opened her eyes, her heart beating fiercely. Monica was standing over her, kneading her shoulder. "It's nearly seven. Time to get your butt in gear."

Slowly Lucy took in the patterned wallpaper, the blue curtains, the portable TV on the dresser. Her pulse began to slow. She looked down. The pink blanket had slipped off during the night, exposing her right leg to the unseasonably cold air that had arrived the day before. "You ever rip your RACAL?" she asked softly.

"Sleeping Beauty wakes at last," Monica said, then noticed the strain in Lucy's face. "Bad dream? I used to have those a lot when I first started at the CDC. You okay?"

"Couldn't be better," Lucy said firmly. She sat up and swung her legs over the side of the bed. "A dream's just a dream."

"Then let's shift. Traffic can be murder after eight-thirty."

They arrived at the cluster of buildings that made up the CDC's Special Pathogens Branch just before nine, ran the strict security gamut, and grabbed some coffee in the cafeteria. Nothing could be done without Matt Kravitz's approval, and Monica's eagerness to beat the traffic had gotten them there ahead of him.

As she munched a cinnamon roll, Lucy thought again about her nightmare. Unlike Monica, she'd never experienced bad dreams while working at the CDC. Lucy took pride in her toughness, and the idea that peruvia might be getting to her was very annoying.

"Sorry I wasn't much help with that diary last night," Monica said, interrupting her thoughts. "But there's not a whole lot to go on, is there?"

"Frankly, there's too much to go on, and it all says drugs," Lucy replied bitterly. Her blind faith in Jean-

Pierre's innocence had been rocked by the diary's contents. "I wish I'd never found the damn thing."

"Every piece of evidence is valuable, even if you don't know where it fits," Monica replied. "You're a scientist; you know that." She stirred the remains of her coffee idly. "So what's your next move, Sherlock?"

Lucy shrugged. Bill Miller was right. If Jean-Pierre had been dealing drugs, pursuing the truth could put her in real danger. "I'm not sure I have a next move," she said.

"Then just let it percolate for a while," Monica advised. "Who knows? Maybe one day you'll be sitting in your office and suddenly the names and initials will take on a whole new meaning."

"Oh, right. And maybe one day Howard will say, 'Max! Stay!' and Max will stay."

Monica laughed. "Hey, it could happen."

"But not in our lifetime. Now, if you've finished toying with that stuff they're attempting to pass off as coffee, why don't we go see if Matt's decided to come to work today."

Matt Kravitz was just coming down the hall when the two women arrived outside his office. He was surprised but obviously pleased to see Lucy, and eager to hear about her experience in Peru. "But I'm afraid our insurance coverage won't allow you inside the Hot Suite," he told her, using the slang term for the Level Four labs. "Current employees only. If you want to see the electron microscope feed, I'll call Ted and set it up."

Which is how she and Ted Wiley came to be sitting in front of a computer monitor, studying the images she'd come to know so well in person: a riot of viral filaments that resembled shepherds' crooks. Color enhanced for clarity, the tangled strands of virus showed red against a pale yellow background.

"This is peruvia," Ted told her. A short, blond researcher in his mid-thirties, Wiley specialized in filoviruses, and had extensive lab experience with Ebola. "Now here's the other strain," he continued as he typed in a command. "I've called it peruvia two." The image changed, but the filaments looked the same. "Can you see the difference?"

Lucy studied the images carefully as Ted switched back and forth between them. "I give up," she said at last. "I can't see it."

"Neither can I," he told her. "That's the point. It's like the Ebola strains, Reston and Zaire. You can't tell the difference just by looking."

"Thank goodness for that," Lucy said, smiling. "I thought I was losing my touch. So how did you find it?"

"I was working with the genetic code of one of the three proteins we can actually identify"—Lucy nodded; four of the seven proteins that constituted all filoviruses were completely unknown—"and I found a very slight difference in the code. Tiny, really. Of course, I can't say exactly how that genetic difference changes the protein, or what such a change might mean in terms of the action or transmission of the virus. That'll take time and testing."

"Including the kind of testing you're not mandated to do," Lucy reminded him. The testing of deadly pathogens by government agencies was tightly constrained in order to avoid any charges of attempting to create biochemical weapons.

Ted nodded. "Anyway, all I can tell you at this point is that we appear to have two strains of peruvia."

"How much of what I sent you is the original peruvia, and how much is this new one?"

"It's pretty much all the original strain. I found peruvia two in only one sample." He frowned. "Kind of weird when you think about it."

"Maybe not," Lucy replied. "A man and his wife who were brought to the compound with fever both had old peruvia scars. They're probably the source of this second strain you found."

Ted nodded. "Sounds right. But . . . a man and his wife, you say? I only found it in one of the samples you sent back. It should have been in two at least. You did take multiple samples?"

"Yes," Lucy said, "but not from those two. They left the compound almost as soon as they got there." Ted raised an eyebrow. "The man was raving about sangre negra—that's what they call it down there— being a white man's disease. He was cursing at us, shouting, even tried to hit an orderly."

"We certainly brought them measles and TB," Ted said, "but these filoviruses walked straight out of the rain forest." He paused. "So there should be two samples?"

"Yes. Could you have missed one?"

"I don't think so. When I found the second strain, I got excited and checked all forty-five samples thoroughly. Nada."

"Forty-five?" Lucy shook her head. "That can't be right. I packed fifteen samples in each hatbox. Fifteen times five hatboxes makes *seventy*-five—"

"Three hatboxes."

"What?"

"We got three hatboxes, not five."

Lucy stared at him in horror. "I brought back five, Ted. I watched them being offloaded at Kennedy. I saw them go into an IMA van."

"Well, two of them never got to us."

Lucy stared at the deadly images on the screen. Thirty test tubes—shatterproof, unlike the ones in her dream, but their contents just as lethal—were out there somewhere, unaccounted for. "Where's the nearest phone?"

Ted led her to a small office across the hall and stood by as she dialed. "Bill Miller's office, please . . . Alicia? It's Lucy Nash. I need to talk to him urgently." She listened for a moment, frowning. "What time tonight? Damn. No, it can't wait. Can you reach him anywhere? Well, do you think he'll call in? Give me his home number so I can call him as soon as he gets back. Dammit, Alicia, this is very important." Calm down, she told herself. Cursing Miller's secretary wouldn't help. "Okay, put me on his calendar for first thing tomorrow." She slammed down the phone and turned to Ted. "Miller flew to Chicago this morning, didn't leave a contact number. His secretary won't give me his home phone number, which, she was kind enough to inform me, is unlisted, but she said she'd leave a message on his home answering machine."

"And Miller is—?

"The head of the IMA. He was with me at the airport when the hatboxes were unloaded. He saw them go into the van, too."

"Call me after you talk to him," Ted requested. "If the samples really *were* delivered here and we screwed up—"

"A CDC screw-up?" Lucy said doubtfully. "It's not very probable." The security of the CDC's pathogen-handling procedures was legend. "But of course I'll let you know what I find out. Meanwhile, let's not—"

"—start a panic."

"Right."

They went back across the hall. On the monitor, the peruvia filaments glowed blood-red in the darkened room. "Nasty little buggers, filoviruses," Ted said softly.

"The nastiest."

They stared at the screen for a long moment. Then Ted typed in a command, hit a button on the keyboard, and the screen turned black.

                        *   *   *

Lucy had booked herself on an afternoon flight from Atlanta to New York, planning on an early lunch with Monica after her morning at the CDC. But now she was too anxious to sit still, let alone eat, and Monica, overloaded with work after the long holiday weekend, didn't protest too much when Lucy begged off. She called a car and headed for the airport, thinking she might be able to switch to an earlier flight. But she wasn't the only person who'd extended the weekend by a day, and everything was booked solid. She consoled herself with the thought that there was nothing she could do until Bill got back.

It was nearly six when the taxi dropped her in front of her building. She dumped her suitcase with the doorman and went around the corner to the Korean greengrocer for a carton of milk. The slushy snow that had fallen while she was in Atlanta had turned black and crunchy in the cold, and she found herself shivering despite the lining in her trenchcoat. As she left the small grocery, she remembered to shove two dollar bills into her jacket pocket for Ray, but she didn't see him. Perhaps he was huddled in some doorway, sheltering from the wind. It was a sad thought.

She unpacked her suitcase, then made a sandwich and ate it in front of the TV. An old Bogart movie was on, one of her favorites, but her mind kept wandering as she repeatedly checked her watch and willed the phone to ring. Finally, at eleven-fifteen, it did.

"Lucy? Bill Miller. Sorry to call so late, but Alicia left me a message saying it was urgent."

"That's right, Bill, it is. We've got big trouble."

A brief silence. "What kind of trouble?"

"The worst. Remember how you met me at Kennedy when we were offloading the peruvia? Remember how we watched them load all five hatboxes into the van?"

"Yes . . ."

"Well, only three of them arrived. The other two are missing."

"Missing?"

"Well, unaccounted for. We're talking about peruvia, Bill—a hot agent. What the hell are we going to do?"

"We're going to stop worrying," Bill told her firmly, "and get some sleep. The hatboxes aren't missing."

"But the CDC didn't get them."

"They weren't meant to."

"But—"

"Calm down, Lucy. They're perfectly safe."

"I don't understand."

"Of course you don't. You're not involved in that part of our work." He paused. "Look, I'll explain it all in the morning. I understand we have an appointment first thing."

"But—"

"I'm exhausted, Lucy. I've had a long, full day. Tomorrow, okay?"

"You're telling me it's safe, though. The peruvia is safe."

"Yes, perfectly safe. We'll talk in the morning."

Lucy lowered the phone, reassured but puzzled. Just what part of the IMA's work had Bill been referring to? Well, the peruvia was safe; that was the important thing. With a mental shrug, she switched off the TV and headed for the bedroom.

She slept well and dreamlessly, rising refreshed at seven for a half-hour workout before her appointment at the IMA. The weather was still cold, and clouds were moving in as she headed for the gym, pulling on her gloves. She scanned the streets, but Ray was still among the missing. Had her neighbors made good their threat to remove him from the neighborhood? Or had he finally taken her advice and sought help from one of the city's homeless organizations? Maybe, with the weather turning so much colder, he'd taken refuge in a shelter. Having arrived in the neighborhood the previous April, Lucy had no idea of Ray's normal winter routine.

Alicia apologized profusely when Lucy arrived at Bill's office. "I was wrong not to give you his unlisted number last night," she told Lucy. "Dr. Miller was quite angry."

Lucy shrugged. "You were just doing your job."

Alicia nodded eagerly. "Thank you for understanding. You can go right in. He's waiting for you."

Doctor Bill rose from his breakfast of croissant and coffee as she entered. "Help yourself," he told her, gesturing toward the sideboard. Lucy went and poured herself some coffee, hesitated, then took a croissant, too. "Sorry to scare you like that," he added as she seated herself across from him at the small round conference table. "But as I told you last night, there's nothing to be concerned about."

"Good. So where are they?"

He smiled. "You're always so direct, Lucy. I like that about you." He took a sip of coffee. "Three hatboxes were delivered to the CDC as planned. The other two went to the IMA lab here in New York." He set his cup down.

"Your lab isn't set up to handle a hot agent," Lucy exclaimed.

"We are now."

"But that kind of research is tightly controlled. You need special licenses—"

"I know that," he said gently. Lucy flushed with embarrassment; of course he did. "We've recently been given a special, limited license to do specific viral pathogen research. Millions of dollars have gone into readying the IMA lab to meet the challenge."

"I'm impressed," Lucy said. She was. "But why

spend your money that way? The CDC is already working on it."

"Along with a hundred other things. Another croissant?" Lucy shook her head. "Lucy, I feel a personal commitment to the forgotten people of the world. The rain forest is being destroyed, primitive cultures erased . . . I have the greatest respect for the CDC, of course. But let's face it: peruvia, and viruses like it, are viewed by most of the scientific community merely as interesting scientific challenges. The world's major commitments of time and money are put against sicknesses that affect large numbers of people. Mostly mainstream people."

"That's not—"

"Fortunately, not everyone agrees with that philosophy," he continued, overriding her interruption. "*I* certainly don't, and many of my supporters don't, either. Thanks to their generosity, the IMA has the funding to redress that."

"I had no idea."

"Of course you didn't. Our expanded capability is a well-kept secret. But it's all perfectly legal, I assure you." Lucy sipped her coffee. The concept was intriguing, but a hot lab in the heart of New York City? "We've been inspected by OSHA, the EPA, the Department of Health. . . . Would you like to see the papers?" he added with a smile, as though reading her thoughts.

"I'd like to see the lab."

Bill looked surprised. "I suppose that could be arranged. Although entrance into the restricted areas is limited to a few employees."

"I understand. But I *am* a member of the IMA."

"Volunteer. Not staff."

"That can be changed."

Bill frowned. "You want to give up your hospital job?"

"No, I wouldn't do that. But maybe I could give you a couple of afternoons a week. I could probably adjust my schedule for that," she added, her enthusiasm building. "I'd really like to be involved in the peruvia research."

"Oh, peruvia isn't the only thing we're working on. We're also running several bacteriophage projects. I believe genetic engineering holds the key to the viral scourges of the Third World."

And elsewhere, Lucy thought. "And you're completely self-funded? That's pretty amazing." The sort of research Bill was talking about would cost many millions of dollars.

"Well, if there's one thing I'm good at, it's fundraising." Bill smiled self-deprecatingly. "And as I say, many of our supporters feel as I do." He rose and went to the sideboard. "More coffee?"

"No, thanks."

"So, are you serious about coming to work for us?" he asked as he refilled his cup.

"I'd certainly like to consider it, after I've had a look around." She sipped the remains of her coffee. If the lab was run properly, if all the safeguards were in place . . .

"I'll see what I can arrange," Bill promised, returning to the table. "Of course, the decision won't be mine. Carl Anders runs the lab. He's a brilliant scientist, and very dedicated." He studied Lucy across the table. "He can be a little . . . stiff. Brusque. But you're a tough cookie." He grinned at her. "I think you can handle him."

Hmm. "I'll look forward to meeting him," Lucy replied evenly. "I'm curious to know what he makes of that second strain of peruvia."

"What? What second strain?"

"Ted Wiley found it. In Atlanta." So much for Bill's claim that the IMA was more fully committed to helping the world's unfortunates than the CDC, she thought. "I believe the strain came from the two people who left the compound—I wrote about them in my report. I was only able to get one sample from each of them. The CDC has one, so I assume Carl . . .?"

"Anders."

"Anders, yes. He must have the other one."

"I haven't heard about a second strain. Do you think it's significant?"

"In research like this, everything's significant until proven otherwise," she assured him. "But ask Anders what he thinks. If he knows about it."

"You think he might not?"

"Well, you can't see the difference between the two strains under the microscope. Ted happened on it while he was playing around with the genetic code of one of the proteins."

"I'll talk to Carl," Bill said, looking thoughtful. "Sure you won't have some more coffee?"

"No, I'm due at General in twenty minutes." Lucy rose. "Let me know when it would be convenient for me to visit the lab. Thursday would be good for me."

Bill stood, too. "I'll see what I can do. Oh, and Lucy? Have you made any progress with the other thing?"

"Other thing?"

"Jean-Pierre. All that."

"Oh." She thought of the diary that now lay hidden in her underwear drawer. "Uh, no. No progress."

"Well, maybe it's for the best. Let sleeping dogs lie."

"Jake, you ever hear of a hot pathogens lab being run privately?" The two doctors had retreated to the staff lounge to discuss the two new cases Lucy had been handed that morning.

"Privately?" Jake set his clipboard on the coffee table. "Sure. Cornell has the only existing license to grow and study live AIDS viruses. If that isn't hot, I don't know what is."

"That's not exactly what I mean." Lucy stood and walked to the small window. Outside, Central Park looked gray and cold. "Bill Miller tells me the IMA has a special license to study peruvia."

"Wow."

"Yeah, that was my reaction, too."

Jake thought for moment. "Well, if he says they have a license, they have one. I mean, it would be impossible to do something like that without it, and he'd be nuts to try. Besides, he told you about it, so it's obviously not a secret."

"He called it a well-kept secret, actually."

"Christ, I would think so, a hot lab here in the city. Where is it?"

"Downtown somewhere. I'm getting the grand tour next week. They're also doing some DNA work with bacteriophages. Jake, why would the government approve an IMA lethal pathogens lab when we already have the CDC, USAMRIID, other established labs . . . ?"

"He said the government was providing the funding?"

Lucy hesitated. "Actually, he said his fund-raising is what really supports the place."

"Well, that could be your answer. Miller's a highly respected doctor, with supporters who are willing to pay for the pleasure of saving the world. He gets a limited license, with the proper controls, and the taxpayers save a bundle."

"But he's never done this kind of work before," Lucy said, settling herself in one of the blue fake-leather chairs.

"So he hires someone who has," Jake said. Lucy

thought of Carl Anders and nodded. "Look, the man's a heavy hitter," he continued. "He moves in the right circles, knows important people. . . . And that IMA of his does an awful lot of good in the world."

"It does, yes."

"And so do you, and all the other doctors who give their time."

Lucy smiled. "Thanks. I'm thinking of giving a little more of mine."

"Oh? Where are you off to now?"

"Nowhere very exotic. I'm considering joining the IMA lab staff on a part-time basis."

Jake looked crestfallen. "I was hoping we could get you to expand your time with us," he said.

But Lucy shook her head. "I brought peruvia back from the jungle, and this is a great opportunity to follow it through."

"Well, I guess we can't compete with a gen-u-wine filovirus."

"Nope." Lucy grinned. "It's hot stuff."

It was after nine when Lucy finally left the hospital that evening. By the time she'd dealt with two new cases—an AIDS patient with pneumocystis carnipneumonia who was allergic to Septra, the drug of choice, and a young woman with a recurrent kidney infection—three more cases had arrived on her desk. She'd managed to grab a minute to call Ted Wiley and reassure him that the viruses were safe, but hadn't eaten much of anything since Bill Miller's croissant breakfast. Now, tired and hungry, she shivered in the light snow that had been falling since late afternoon, and searched for a taxi.

The light on her answering machine was blinking as she came into the apartment. Slinging her coat over a chair, she pressed the play button and listened as Alicia's voice informed her that Carl Anders couldn't ac-

commodate a visit from her until the following
Thursday. Well, that was fine with her. Those five hospital cases would need all her attention just now.

She changed into jeans and a sweater, and flipped
on the TV. They'd finally identified the homeless man
who had frozen to death in Central Park the night
before. Although his description hadn't matched
Ray's, she'd found herself worrying about him. She'd
scanned the streets on her way home, but he was nowhere to be seen. She hoped he was somewhere warm.

Next morning the sky had cleared and the cold had
moderated a little. On her way to the hospital for
an early epidemiology departmental conference, she
checked out the neighborhood, but Ray was still a
no-show. The evening told the same story. Her mind
crowded with the details of her new cases, it wasn't
until Friday evening that it occurred to her that not
only was Ray gone, but she hadn't seen the young
woman with the neck bandage for some time, either.
And the man with the dreadlocks was no longer rifling
through trash bins in search of bottles. In fact, she
realized with a start, all the homeless people in her
neighborhood had disappeared.

Chapter Six

"I'm still not convinced we need her," Carl Anders growled.

Bill sighed. "We've been over it and over it," he said, shifting the phone from one ear to the other. "She's got an excellent reputation in the field, she's familiar with peruvia, and she's already one of us."

"One mission," Carl scoffed.

"But an important one." He massaged his ear and repositioned the phone again. In his mind's eye, he could see people in white coats—not a female among them—moving to and fro beyond the glass that separated the lab director's small office from the laboratory proper. Carl's antipathy to women was well-known. Well, he'd just have to get over it. "You've got her for one, maybe two afternoons a week," he continued. "You can deal with that, surely." Carl was silent. "Once you get to know her—"

"I'll love her? Doubtful." Anders looked at his watch. "She's twenty minutes late," he said triumphantly. "Not a great beginning."

"Relax, Carl."

"Well, I have work to do. Where the hell is she?"

Where the hell am I? Lucy asked herself. What with her residency and fellowship in the city several years ago, and the eight months she'd spent here this time, she'd come to consider herself a real New Yorker. But at the moment, she felt as if she'd just stepped off the bus from Kansas City. The subway line she'd taken downtown had deposited her some distance to the east of her destination. No problem, she'd thought; I'll catch a cab. But the only taxis she'd seen were off duty and moving fast. Okay, she'd walk. She headed west and south, asking directions as she went of the few passersby she saw, several of whom seemed as confused as she. Down here where the island of Manhattan narrowed tightly, many streets were only a few blocks long, and unlike the numbered streets farther north, names like Laight and Renwick gave no hint of any orderly geographic progression.

She passed auto body shops, warehouses, loading docks, and, finally, a cab company. A driver, waiting for his car to be gassed up, pulled out a well-thumbed street map and together they worked out a route that took her, four minutes and six blocks later, to the front of a run-down factory building some five floors in height. Large old-fashioned windows, metallic threads set into their frosted panes, looked blindly toward the river. Could this be right? She checked the address she'd been given against the numbers stenciled above the plain, wide steel door. Yes, this was it. She tried the door, but it was locked. To one side was a security keypad; next to it was a push button and an intercom speaker. A small video camera was bolted to the wall above. She pressed the button and announced herself.

"Welcome, Dr. Nash," a masculine voice told her. "Please come to the second floor." The door lock clicked open and she went inside.

She found herself in a high, square entrance hall, its brick walls freshly painted a glossy white, its floor covered with black and white ceramic tiles. The only furniture were a wooden desk and chair, now deserted. An elevator was set in the wall ahead of her, its door just sliding back. She got in and rode it up to two, stepping out into a hallway similar to the one below. Steel double doors were swung back against the far wall, revealing a plate-glass door and beyond it, a tiny reception area. A man in a lab coat hurried toward her, opening the door to admit her.

"Doctor Livingstone, I presume?" His grin was infectious.

"It *is* rather an adventure getting down here." Lucy smiled. "In fact, I'm not quite sure where 'here' is."

"I came here from Stanford in September, and I still feel like I'm charting new territory just getting to work in the morning. Oh, I'm Richard Hollander." He extended a hand and Lucy took it. His grasp was firm and cool. "Molecular biologist, senior researcher. I hope we'll get to work together."

"That would be nice, Richard," Lucy said neutrally as she studied the friendly young man. Well, not that young, she decided, noticing the tiny creases at the corners of the smiling gray eyes that looked at her from behind thin wire spectacles. Late thirties, probably. His face was interesting rather than conventionally handsome, his brown hair neatly cut and combed, his manner easy and open.

"Richard's so formal," he said with a smile. "Call me Rick. It'll be nice having a woman around," he continued as he led her into the lab. "You're the one and only."

"You're kidding."

"I think our Dr. Anders has a wee problem in that area," he said sotto voce. "He gives new meaning to the term 'conservative.' But you'll charm him."

"I have no intention of charming him," Lucy said firmly.

"Even better." He grinned at her, then turned to hail a tall, slender man in his late fifties who was just emerging from a glass-sided office to one side of the wide, high room. "Ah, Carl. This is Dr. Nash. We were just coming to find you."

Anders turned, hesitated, approached. He was ascetically thin, with fair hair cut so short it was difficult to define its color. His pale cheeks bore the faint scars of an ancient acne, and his nose was sharp enough to cut a steak. At six-foot-three, he towered over both Lucy and Rick. He bared his teeth in an imitation of a smile. "Dr. Nash. Delighted to have you with us."

"Delighted to be here," Lucy responded evenly.

"Come into my office and let's chat for a few minutes," he said. "Then Hollander here will show you around."

Rick gave her a mock salute and moved off as Lucy followed Carl into the small office. "I understand Rick joined you several months ago," she said conversationally, seating herself in one of the two guest chairs. "Is a lot of your staff new?"

"Yes, it is. We've expanded recently, as Dr. Miller must have told you."

"Yes, that's what Bill said." She noted with amusement Carl's reaction to her use of Miller's first name. Don't play silly buggers with me, Anders, she thought. I'm not one of your new hires. "I understand that's quite a facility you have out there."

"Isn't it? We have a small animal lab, too, not that I expect you'll be involved with our *in vivo* veterinary studies. Let me tell you a little about our work. . . ."

Lucy listened attentively as Carl described the methodologies, techniques, and equipment currently being used, all of them up-to-date and horribly expensive. Miller's claim that he was good at fund-raising was obviously an understatement. But as Carl droned on, Lucy found herself a little surprised at the emphasis on attempting to alter the genetic structure of the filovirus and then testing how the changed structure affected virulence and transmission. At the CDC, the emphasis had been on gaining an understanding of the underlying genetic structure, and searching for an agent that could alleviate or cure. She recalled the Ebola research Wiley had been involved in, and the computer-assisted modeling he'd done, working with the fusion area of the AIDS virus in an attempt, so far unsuccessful, to design a drug with which to treat Ebola.

". . . don't you agree?"

Oops. Her thoughts drifting, she hadn't caught Carl's last few sentences. "Um, perhaps," she muttered, hoping he wasn't proposing Newt Gingrich for president or an end to Medicare. "And what do you think about that second peruvia strain?"

Carl scowled. "Dr. Mi—Bill mentioned that, too. There is no second strain."

"But there is. I saw it myself at the Centers for Disease Control."

"You saw what, exactly?"

Lucy paused. "Perhaps I phrased that incorrectly. You can't actually see the difference between the two strains. But the researcher I spoke with found that the genetic code—"

Carl shook his head. "An aberration. Or contamination of some kind, a common problem in any virus lab."

"I'm certain that's not the case. There were these two Peruvians—"

"Yes, I read your report. But here we have found no second strain. Not that it matters for our purposes," he added. "Now"—he rose, ignoring the surprised look on Lucy's face—"I believe Hollander is waiting. Afterward you can tell me what part of the work you'd like to get involved in."

So much, thought Lucy as she followed Carl out into the lab, for Bill's claim that the IMA was more committed to this research than the CDC. Well, Carl's attitude didn't matter in the least. Ted Wiley would do a proper job on the second strain.

But her reflections on Carl's attitude quickly faded as Rick took her through the lab complex. Impressive was hardly the word. The ceilings of the open lab area were double-height, combining the second and third floors, and lit from above by a cool fluorescence. There was no evidence of the windows she'd seen from the outside of the building. A double skin had been built inside the original factory walls, Rick explained, to seal off the lab space and allow for the EPA-required air filtration system. Beyond the open-bench work area, the floors resumed their original two levels. The third floor was divided into several sections. One area was set aside for computer and other imaging procedures, including micrograph duplication, and the demanding technique of computer viral image reconstruction. Another section contained a series of labs specially designed for "cold" work such as column chromatography. The temperature was kept roughly akin to the inside of a refrigerator so as not to inactivate the enzymes with which the researchers worked. "The animal lab's through there," Rick explained as they passed a steel door festooned with biohazard signs. "It's kept locked, of course."

"Do you do much *in vivo* work?" Lucy asked.

"Very little. I think Carl has a couple of programs running at the moment, that's all."

The second floor had more labs, as well as a large freezer storage area, an electron microscope, and an ion shield room.

"The lab has an arrangement with BioScan," Rick explained, "that allows us to use some of their fancy technology on a temporary basis." Lucy nodded. Private industry often made such arrangements with government biomedical research groups, allowing them access to special technology and personnel the groups wouldn't need on a regular basis. BioScan was a major player, and such an arrangement with the IMA would explain the presence of the high-ticket toys she saw around her.

"What's on the two floors above us?" Lucy asked.

"Nothing at the moment," Rick answered. "Room for expansion, I guess. The rest of the building's empty."

"And below?"

"The sterilization vats, and the filtration and pressurization systems for the hot lab." Lucy nodded. All liquid from the hot lab was thoroughly boiled to decontaminate it before it was discarded, and the air was treated as well. He led her down a short corridor toward a set of steel doors covered with red biohazard symbols. "The lethal pathogen lab is through there. I'm not cleared for it, but I understand you are. Carl said you'd probably want to suit up and have a look. . . ."

"Yes, I do."

"You'll find a 'blue suit' with your name on it in the staging area. And they've set up a lab area for you. It's at the end, on the right."

"Very efficient." She smiled at him.

He didn't smile back. "I don't know how you guys do it," he said. "There's not enough money in the world to make me go in there." He shuddered. Lucy nodded understandingly. Although she herself was thankfully free of any tendency toward claustrophobia or panic, these were not uncommon reactions to sealing oneself into a pressurized space suit and entering a Level Four containment area. Which was why very few people were cleared to do so. As the changing room door closed behind her, she looked back. Rick was still standing there, looking after her.

She stripped off all her clothes including her underwear and put them into a locker. Then she took a sterile green scrub suit from a shelf and put it on.

Next came the surgical gloves and white socks, which she taped to the cuffs and sleeves of the scrub suit, making a tight seal. A door labeled STAGING AREA led to an inner room where bright blue Chemturion space suits hung on a rack. She found the one with her name stenciled across the chest, laid it on the floor, and stepped into it, pulling it up around her body and fitting her hands into the built-in gloves. She put on the plastic helmet and Velcro-sealed the suit, and her face mask began to fog up. Grabbing a black air hose that dangled from the ceiling, she plugged it into her suit. With a *whoosh,* the suit pressurized and her mask cleared. The flow roared in her ears as she breathed in the cool, dry air and looked around.

To one side was a steel door covered with more biohazard warnings and the words LEVEL FOUR CON-TAINMENT. She unhooked the air hose and pushed through the door into a stainless-steel air-locked room, feeling the pressure change. The entire hot lab was positively pressured so that air flowed into it, but not out; yet another safeguard against the escape of a lethal pathogen. She'd spend seven minutes here in the steel room on the way out, allowing the nozzles that lined the walls to shower her with disinfectant. But now she continued across the room and through a second steel door. She was in a small concrete cubicle. A closed cabinet ran along one side, and air hoses were suspended from the low ceiling. She plugged in, took a pair of yellow boots from the cabinet and put them on. A few feet away, yet another steel door led to the lethal pathogens lab space. She took a deep breath, centered herself, unplugged the air hose, and went through it.

The hot lab was smaller than the one she'd worked in at the CDC, but what it lacked in space, it made up for in equipment. Black air hoses hung from the ceiling, and she grabbed one and plugged in, then looked around her. The space, tiled in white from top to bottom and bathed in cold light, was divided into a series of well-equipped work areas. She moved along the central walkway, glancing this way and that at the blue-suited workers, few in number, who labored there. Several looked up; no one smiled. This was intensely serious business.

As she neared the end of the walkway, something caught her eye. At a workstation to her right stood a rack of test tubes. The setup seemed familiar. She moved closer; the contents of the tubes glowed a faint red in the ambient light. She leaned in and read the label: PERUVIA. She reached for one, then stopped dead, her heart pounding, the flow of air roaring in her ears.

She was living her dream.

"She's inside now." Rick leaned against the door frame of Carl's office. "Looking around, as you suggested."

"She's been in there a long time," Carl said, frowning. "I hope she knows what she's doing."

"Oh, I should think so. Didn't you say she spent two years at the CDC, with Level Four clearance?"

Carl nodded. "But I can't get used to the idea of women doing this kind of work. They're such emotional creatures."

I can't believe what a dinosaur this guy is, Rick thought. Aloud he said, "I think it's more a matter of temperament than gender. I myself would react very emotionally to being sealed in a space suit and handed a vial of peruvia." He paused. "I think that Lucy Nash of yours is terrific."

Carl scowled. "She's not mine, I assure you." No kidding, Rick thought. "I prefer my women softer, less aggressive," the director continued. "More . . . womanly."

" '*Kinder, kuchen, und kirche,*' eh? Not a very progressive attitude."

"Not all progress is good," Carl replied stiffly. "There are certain old-fashioned values, including children, cooking, and church, as you put it, that are worth keeping—" He broke off, looking faintly embarrassed. "You'd better go and wait for Dr. Nash outside the changing room. We don't want her blundering all over the place, getting herself lost."

"My goodness, no, we wouldn't want that," Rick said innocently, unattaching himself from the door frame.

Carl watched him go. Cocky bastard, he thought. Still, Hollander was a conscientious worker, always willing to put in long hours. And he'd been very highly recommended by Hugh Bechner at Stanford.

A dream is just a dream, Lucy told herself fiercely. All hot labs have a similar look. And the rosy glow of the tubes? Pure coincidence, and so what? But she could feel her pulse racing, her breath coming in short gasps. If she touched the tube of peruvia, would it shatter as it had in her dream? Would it cut her suit and her leg? Would they have to drag her from the lab, seal her into a bubble stretcher, and lock her into an isolation facility somewhere? Suddenly Lucy couldn't wait to get out of Level Four.

Rick looked at his watch. She'd been in there for nearly an hour, rather a long time for a simple lookround. Was she all right? Of course she was, he chided himself. She was experienced, she had clearance. He leaned against the wall. She was also quite pretty, he reflected. Smart, too. It was after five. He wondered if she'd agree to have a drink with him after she'd finished up with Anders. . . .

*   *   *

Lucy stumbled into the dim, gray decon room and hit the button that would start the chemical flow. It was a stupid dream, and it was a stupid reason to panic, she told herself angrily. How long had she stood in front of the workstation, frozen with a mindless fear, before turning and fleeing, back through the hot lab, back through the boot room, back into the air lock in which she now stood? She closed her eyes to the EnviroChem mist that swirled around her. How much longer until the timer would turn the nozzles off and she could leave? Five minutes? Two?

It wasn't in her nature to panic, and she didn't like the feeling one bit. You've got to work in there, she told herself angrily, so get a grip. This cannot happen again.

"Anders was starting to worry," Rick teased as she came through the door, "you being the weaker sex and all. . . ." He broke off as he saw her face. "Are you okay? You look kind of pale."

"I'm fine," Lucy said.

"So do we pass muster? You'll work with us?"

How can I say no? Lucy wondered. And why should I? A dream is just a— "Of course," she replied. "I'm looking forward to it."

Rick studied her for a moment. Something had happened in there; he wondered what it was. He led her back to Carl's office, introducing her to several people along the way, and making his pitch to buy her a drink. She looked like she could use one, and he was only faintly surprised when she agreed.

"Rather a luxury, keeping a car in New York," Lucy said lightly. The ride uptown had restored her equilibrium.

"We Californians are attached to our cars," Rick replied, smiling. "At the hip."

They were sitting at a window table in the Plaza's Oak Bar, Lucy sipping a white wine, Rick, an imported lager. There were no decent watering holes within walking distance of the lab, he'd explained, so they'd retrieved his ten-year-old Volvo, still bearing its California plates, from a nearby garage, and driven north to civilization.

As they left the lab, he'd removed his glasses, saying he only wore them for close work, and traded his white coat for a rather smart tweed blazer, revealing for a brief moment an impressive musculature moving beneath his crisp cream shirt. The transformation, Lucy reflected with amusement, was a little like Superman stepping out of a phone booth.

"Ever live in New York before?" she asked now, reaching for a cashew.

"First time. I've visited a lot, though."

"Still, Stanford to the IMA . . . that's quite a jump."

Rick nodded. "I wanted a change, and I sure got one." He smiled. "I really like it. There's more independence, and fewer administrative levels." He sipped his drink. When he looked back at her, his eyes were warm. "I hope you're going to join us."

Lucy nodded. "An afternoon a week is all I can spare. But I'm eager to work with peruvia."

"You brought it back from South America, right? Probably used up all your vacation time doing it."

Lucy felt a pang at the thought of Peru and Jean-Pierre, but brushed it away. "When you love your work," she said, "ordinary vacations are so boring."

"Ah, a fellow workaholic." Rick laughed and drained his glass. "More wine?"

Lucy hesitated. She had nothing planned for the evening, and she was finding Rick attractive and interesting. "Sure, why not?" The waiter was called and new drinks ordered. "So you're working on the bacteriophage studies? Is that what you did at Stanford?"

"More or less. My group was working on inserting a DNA sequence that slows aging into a tomato bacterium."

"You ever do any clinical work?"

Rick shook his head. "Pure research is what I like. My folks wanted me to go to med school, but I knew I didn't want to work with patients. I understand you do both clinical and lab research."

"That's right. I did pure research at the CDC. It was fascinating and I learned a lot, but I found I missed the clinical side, the people side. And I like the variety of challenges I get, working at General— why are you smiling at me like that?"

"I'm smiling because I'm having a such nice time," Rick said. "I'm smiling at *you* because you're the *reason* I'm having such a nice time." He paused. "Have dinner with me? I know a great little French place about six blocks from here."

"Well . . ."

"Come on, Lucy. Here I am, a stranger in the big city—"

"A stranger who seems to know his way around rather well," Lucy replied, laughing.

Flurries drifted by the high window, glowing with the reflected light of the streetlamps. "They have a real fireplace," Rick said. "And a wonderful coq au vin."

Lucy swirled the remains of her wine around in the glass. I do not need a romantic relationship right now, she thought. I'm barely over the last one. But Jean-Pierre was gone; nothing could bring him back. And her feelings for him, feelings that had arisen so suddenly, had been ebbing just as quickly, as evidence of his involvement with illegal drugs had surfaced. If Jean really had been running drugs, she owed his memory nothing.

She swallowed the last of her wine. What the hell, she thought; it's just dinner. She set down the glass and smiled across the table at Rick's open, eager face. "I'd love to," she said.

Chapter Seven

"The good doctor does himself very well," Rick observed as the taxi drew up in front of Bill Miller's double-width brick town house. A golden glow spilled from the high arched windows, and white fairy lights festooned both the miniature trees in the front patio and the oversize wreath suspended from the wrought-iron balcony a floor above the heavy oak door.

"I guess he can afford to," Lucy said, smiling. "I'm told this Christmas party of his is legendary."

Rick squeezed her hand as he helped her from the car. "That dress is a knockout," he told her.

"That's because you only ever see me in whites or jeans," she teased. But in fact, she'd chosen the expensive black cocktail dress with care.

That first dinner together two weeks ago had been followed by another. Then a drink and a burger after Lucy's first afternoon at the IMA lab. A movie several days later. And last Sunday, they'd driven to a small inn in Connecticut for lunch, then explored the snow-covered countryside. So it seemed natural for Rick to suggest they go to Doctor Bill's famous Christmas party together.

But although Lucy was finding Rick more and more attractive—intelligent, funny, attentive and, she had to admit, sexy—she was determined to break her pattern of high-intensity, short-lived relationships. She vowed to take it slowly this time and, fortunately, Rick seemed to want the same thing.

The sounds of laughter and live music greeted them as they entered the high marble foyer. A servant took their coats and directed them past a wide staircase, its banister rail twined with ropes of fresh balsam, and toward the center of the house.

The town house's two large reception rooms had been combined into one large, comfortably furnished space. Fires blazed in the two marble fireplaces. Bars and buffet tables were set up at both ends, and in one corner a five-piece combo played show tunes. People danced and chatted, ate and drank, and admired the artwork mounted on the walls and carefully displayed inside shallow glass-fronted display cabinets. Waiters circulated with trays of champagne, and Lucy and Rick each took a glass as they searched the crowd for their host. Lucy waved to Alicia, Bill's secretary, as they worked their way through the room.

"You know all these people?" Rick asked.

Lucy shook her head. A number of faces were familiar to her from the IMA offices and labs, but many others were strangers to her. "I think he's mixing business with pleasure," she said.

"Or business with business." Lucy gave him a puzzled look. "His medical associates and contributors to his charities are probably here, too," Rick explained. "Not just friends and the IMA crowd. Hey, Enrique." He stopped to greet the research assistant, and Lucy's smile froze on her face. Beyond Enrique, the cadaverous Dr. Anders had turned and was staring balefully at her. Ah, well, she thought; can't be liked by everyone. She gave Anders a luminous smile, then turned and pretended to examine a large, colorful painting hanging nearby.

"You like that sort of thing?" Rick asked, his brief conversation with Enrique finished.

"Not really my cup of cappuccino," Lucy replied. "I can see the beauty in it, but it's a little too . . ."

"Crude? Strong?" Bill Miller stood behind them. "Primitive art is like that, sometimes. It taps into our primal instincts, our primal joys and fears."

"Guess that's why it's called primitive," Rick offered.

"Actually, that's not the reason," Bill replied pleasantly. "The 'primitive' in primitive art means unschooled in technique. Lucy . . ." Bill reached for her hand. "So glad you could come." He regarded Rick with a vague yet friendly expression.

"Richard Hollander." Rick extended his hand. "IMA lab."

"Yes, of course. Please forgive me." Bill turned to a towering, strikingly beautiful woman in a daringly cut backless dress, standing nearby. "My dear, this is Dr. Lucy Nash, an IMA volunteer. And Richard Hollander, one of our researchers." He put a possessive arm around the woman's bare waist. "May I present Renée, Contessa dePalma."

"Contessa." Rick reached for her hand with its talonlike nails and kissed it, and it seemed to Lucy that he held it just a beat too long.

"Please call me Renée, Mr. . . . ?" Her accent was soft and liquid.

"Hollander. Richard. Rick."

"Rick." The contessa gave him a lazy, rather suggestive smile, then leaned toward Lucy, her long tawny hair swinging against her shoulders, her expensive perfume filling the air between them. "And Lucy Nash. A pleasure." Her eyes flicked over Lucy's dress, then she smiled the same long, lazy smile. Lucy felt vaguely uncomfortable.

"Are you here on a visit, Contessa?" Rick asked.

"You must call me Renée." The contessa's smile widened, revealing small, sharp, white teeth. "No, I live here," she said. "Well, as much as I live anywhere."

"Here in New York," Bill hurried to explain. "The contessa has an apartment on Sutton Place. And a villa at Amalfi, south of Naples."

"And a flat in Mayfair," Renée added, "although I rarely go to London, these days. So grim."

"The contessa is a major contributor to the IMA," Bill told them proudly. "A big supporter of our work."

"I like to help the less fortunate," the contessa said.

"Very commendable." There was something in Rick's tone that made Lucy shoot a glance at him, but his expression was pure admiration. "Your family is from Naples?"

"No, my family is from Villarosa, in the south," Renée replied. "It is my husband, the Conte dePalma, who lives in Naples."

"An awful man, the Conte dePalma," Bill confided grimly, giving the name its Italian pronunciation. "It was common knowledge, even then. I can't believe you married him."

"I was very young." Renée smiled her seductive smile. "And he was very rich." At least she's honest, Lucy thought. "We have lived apart for many years, now," the contessa continued. "He is nothing to me." She waved a deprecating hand and the large rings on her fingers sparkled. "Ah, you have finished your champagne," she exclaimed. "You must have more, mustn't they, Bill? And something to eat."

"Indeed they must."

"And you must dance," Renée added. Her eyes lingered on Rick. "It is a party. We must all dance." Behind them, figures swirled and dipped on the parquet dance floor.

"And so we shall," Bill said, taking Renée's hand. "Please excuse us."

Lucy stood looking after Renée, then turned to Rick. "An interesting character, isn't she?"

"I suppose." The band segued into a popular disco tune and the decibel level rose appreciably. "How about some food? I'm starved."

Progress through the crowd was slow, but at last they arrived at the buffet tables set up in front of the French windows at the far end of the room. The garden beyond was illuminated by strategically placed lights. "Must be a helluva place in the summer," Rick commented before turning to the feast laid out before them.

"The smoked salmon is supposed to be absolutely amazing," Lucy told him, reaching for a serving fork. "Flown in from Scotland. Can I give you some?"

"Pile it on." He extended his plate. Lucy served him, then herself. When she looked up from the table, Rick was staring at the dance floor. Following his gaze, Lucy saw Renée turn in their direction, and a look passed between her and Rick. Or did it? A microsecond later, Renée turned away and Rick took his dish from Lucy, chatting animatedly as he garnished both their plates with brown bread and capers and led her to a recently vacated sofa.

As they ate, Lucy found herself sneaking looks toward the dance floor. Aside from the contessa's obvious interest in Rick, there was something unsettling about the woman.

Rick, misunderstanding her glance, set his plate on a side table. "Would you like to dance."

Renée and Bill were just leaving the small dance floor as Lucy moved into Rick's arms. He was a good dancer, and their bodies fit together well. He held her close, and she could feel the strength in his arms and shoulders, the flat muscles of his stomach as he pressed her to him. When the song was finished, they stood entwined for a moment, reluctant to let go, but at last they drew apart, their eyes fixed on one another. Lucy could feel the intensity of his stare shoot through her body. Whatever she'd thought she'd seen pass between him and the contessa had obviously been a figment of her imagination.

"May I?" Bill Miller stood smiling at Lucy, his hand outstretched.

Shit, Lucy thought. But there was no polite way to refuse. She looked over at Rick, pleased to see that he looked as disappointed as she felt, then turned to Bill and smiled. "Of course."

"And I will give you a tour of the house," Renée told Rick, smiling her lazy smile as she took firm hold of his hand.

"Why don't we dance?" Rick said quickly. Renée looked disappointed, but followed Rick onto the dance floor. She towered over him, and Lucy was pleased to see him holding the contessa far more formally than he had held her.

"It's a fabulous party," she told Bill as they performed a sedate fox-trot. "And I had no idea you were an art collector."

"Oh yes, a hobby of mine for many years. That Haitian painting you were admiring was one of the first to be shown in this country. It actually started the Haitian primitive craze, years ago. And you must see my temple paintings from Ceylon—Sri Lanka now. They're in the study."

"You have catholic tastes," Lucy said. "Most collectors choose a period or a country and stick with it."

"True. But my 'period' is a state of mind rather than a particular time or place. I admire the unschooled eye, the instinctive reaction of the primitive artist to his or her surroundings, beliefs, culture. I find myself moved by their artistic purity, uninfluenced by Western thought."

"It's hard to find any culture that hasn't been

touched by Western civilization, these days," Lucy said. "Certainly not Haiti."

"Unfortunately, you're right. Which is why my most treasured pieces are quite old. Those two cases over there"—he gestured with his chin—"contain some interesting examples of pre-Columbian art. And I have several Assyrian amulets. . . ."

"Isn't it a little risky, keeping such things here?" Lucy asked.

Bill smiled. "My security measures are quite thorough, I assure you. And the rarest items have been lent to museums. Let them worry about protecting them." He chuckled. "Not my favorite dance," he added as the fox-trot became a samba, "although Renée and Hollander seem to like it. Let me show you some of my pieces, instead."

Ignoring what appeared to be an attempt by Renée to consume Rick's left ear, Lucy followed Bill through the crowd to one of the illuminated cases. "I don't know much about art," she began diffidently.

"You don't need to," he assured her. "Just let the pieces speak to you." Together they peered at a collection of small statues, some of stone, some of wood, behind the glass. "Fertility figures are found in nearly every primitive culture—"

"Uh, Dr. Miller? Sorry to interrupt," the waiter apologized, "but there's a phone call for you. Long distance. The caterer took it in the kitchen. They said it was important."

"Please excuse me," Bill told Lucy, then turned to the waiter. "Bring the lady some champagne, will you?"

Lucy watched him hurry away through the crowd, then turned back to the figures. Let the pieces speak to you, he'd said; how mannered could you get? But she leaned in for a closer look. Well, they were certainly beautiful, if a trifle overblown; not to her taste, but she could appreciate their artistry. As in a museum, a printed label identified the origin of each piece. She glanced at them, working her way down the case. Colombia . . . Brazil . . . Peru . . . Was it her imagination, or was there actually a faint similarity between these Peruvian pieces and the two figures currently residing in her apartment? These were far more subtle in their modeling, more finely finished. And yet . . .

What these pieces are saying to me, Lucy thought, is that I could be wrong about the value of the statues in Jean-Pierre's suitcase. . . .

"A little too obvious for my taste," Rick said, coming up behind her.

"Me, too," she agreed, straightening up. "Give me the Impressionists any time."

"I meant our Italian friend."

"She's very beautiful, isn't she?" Lucy said.

"If you like the type." Rick put an arm around her. "Personally, I prefer this type."

Lucy smiled. "Who would have thought Bill would have such exotic taste in women?"

"Who would have thought he'd have such exotic taste in art?"

"Who would have thought he'd have such excellent taste in champagne?" Lucy said as the waiter arrived with a tray of filled glasses. "To Bill Miller."

"Long may he wave."

After the champagne, they danced again, and then went back to the buffet table. The crowd, already thick, thickened.

"Hollander. Dr. Nash." Carl Anders pushed his way toward Rick and Lucy, a glass of amber-colored liquid in hand.

"Evening, Carl," Rick said. "Heck of a party."

"Isn't it?" Carl stumbled slightly as he came up to them. "I wonder, Dr. Nash, if you would excuse us for just a moment? I realize it's bad form to discuss business at such a gathering, but something most urgent has just come up—"

"I don't think—" Rick began.

"Just take a minute," Carl insisted, the words slurring slightly.

"Of course, Carl," Lucy said quickly, moving away. Behind Carl's back she turned and rolled her eyes at Rick, who gave a small shrug. Carl put an arm around Rick's shoulder and began talking; she could see Rick wince at the liquor fumes. She moved through the crowd, stopping here and there for a word with the few people she knew and several she didn't, and ended up at the bar, where she traded her empty wineglass for a full one. What the hell, she thought; it's a party.

"And where is that terribly attractive man of yours?" said a soft Italian-accented voice. "A Perrier with lime, please, bartender."

"I'm afraid he's talking business," Lucy told Renée. "With Carl Anders. Do you know Carl?"

"I have met him, yes." Renee's eyes raked the room. "There he is. But he is alone." Lucy turned; Anders, indeed alone, was making his way through the crowd toward them.

Lucy shrugged. "They must have finished," she said lightly. She sipped her wine and wondered where Rick had gone.

"You like champagne?" Renée asked, leaning back against the bar. "I hate it," she continued, not waiting for a reply. "All those bubbles. Too cute. Scotch is what I like."

"And Perrier," Lucy pointed out.

"Yes. But not together." She smiled. "Some things go together well, others not. You agree?" Huh? Lucy thought, but she nodded. "You have such a lovely skin," Renée said, drawing her fingertips lightly along

Lucy's arm. "And such a beautiful cameo necklace."
She touched the amber ornament gently.

"Thank you," Lucy said, stepping back. "Please excuse me. I must—" She looked around quickly. Whom could she pretend to know, to need to speak with?

"There are people you must talk with," the contessa said, amused. "I understand. We will see each other again." Lucy hurried away to lose herself in the crowd, and Renée watched her go, a faint smile on her porcelain face.

Halfway across the room, Lucy's progress was arrested by a hand on her shoulder. "Dr. Nash. Dr. Nash." She turned and found herself face-to-face with a somewhat flushed Carl Anders. "A word with you, please." His alcohol-laden breath was unpleasantly hot against her face as he moved closer. I've had about enough of this party, she decided. "I feel I must apologize," Carl continued, "for being so negative about your, ah, your coming to work at IMA. I'm afraid I'm a little, um, conservative about women in science." Welcome to the nineteenth century, Lucy thought. "But over the past few weeks, I've come to know and, er, respect you. I want you to know that you are truly welcomed." He gestured widely with his glass, spattering nearby partygoers.

"Thank you, Carl." But will you still love me when you're sober?

"Richard has told me of your skill, your dedication. . . ."

So Rick's responsible for this change of heart, she thought. She wasn't sure whether that pleased or annoyed her. "Thank you so much," she repeated. "And now I really must have a word with . . . uh, Alicia."

"Of course. I just—"

"Yes. So kind. See you next week." Lucy moved off quickly, depositing her half-empty glass on a coffee table as she went. The wine she'd drunk had begun to make its presence felt, and she headed back toward the entrance hall in search of a powder room.

The bathroom off the foyer was occupied, and a caterer's assistant directed her down a short hallway to the den which, he told her, had its own bathroom. But she could hear voices behind the den's firmly closed door. Back in the foyer, the powder room still in use and her bladder protesting the wait, she ascended the wide, carpeted staircase in search of another option. The darkened second floor of the town house was as magnificent as the first, but Lucy barely paused to take in Bill's shadowy bedroom as she hurried through it in search of a bathroom.

Feeling like a trespasser, she closed the door and flicked on the light. Green marble everywhere: walls, floor, Jacuzzi bath. The commode was a low-slung, quiet-flush custom model in avocado porcelain. Even the toothbrush hanging in the built-in holder was green, she noticed with amusement. But that and the hairbrush lying beside the sink reminded her that she was invading Bill's personal space. Get in and get out, she told herself.

Her business done, she switched off the light and began to open the door, then stopped. Someone was in the bedroom.

A rustle of fabric. Whispers.

She peered around the edge of the nearly closed door, her eyes adjusting slowly to the darkness. She could just make out a figure, no, two figures intertwined.

"Ah, so big," said a voice Lucy recognized. "You say no, but this says yes."

"Not here," came a harsh, masculine whisper. One of the shadowy figures pulled away from the other. "Not now." His voice, pitched low, was impossible to identify.

"No one will come," Renée assured her partner, rubbing against him. "God, I want you."

The man groaned, then pulled back. "Don't," he whispered.

"Don't stop, you mean." A rustle of clothing. "Here. Touch them. They are aching for you—" But the man was moving backward toward the door, his hands at his crotch. Lucy heard the sound of a zipper being closed.

"Why did you follow me up here, if you didn't want to?" Renée demanded of the shadow-man. Bill Miller? Lucy wondered. It must be; the height and build seemed right. And if Bill hadn't followed Renée up here, if she'd found Lucy in here instead, would the contessa be attempting a similar scene with her? Lucy felt sick.

"Go, then," Renée said angrily, adjusting her clothing. "It is not so big, after all. I have known men—"

In an instant, the man was back in the room, taking hold of Renée, his mouth hard against hers, his hands moving over her body. The contessa cried out. "You're hurting me. Not so rough."

"You like it rough," the man whispered fiercely. He pulled back and grabbed her by the shoulders, holding her immobile for a moment before throwing her across the bed. In three strides he was at the door, then through it.

Go after Bill, Lucy pleaded silently. Get out of here.

The contessa slowly raised herself from the bed. Expecting curses, Lucy was surprised to hear a low, guttural laugh. Surely she'll leave now, Lucy thought, watching the contessa smooth her dress. Then the woman's hands went to her head and Lucy realized she wasn't leaving, not yet. She was going to comb her hair and fix her makeup first. In the bathroom.

Feeling slightly foolish, Lucy dropped to the marble floor, then swung the door open just enough for her to crawl through onto the bedroom carpet. Hugging the wall, she headed toward the bed, keeping an eye on Renée's progress, and rolled underneath just as the bathroom light stabbed through the darkened room. She worked her way beneath the king-sized box spring, emerging at the other side. The door to the corridor was some ten feet away, easy if Renée was concentrating on her face. She peeked over the top of the bed. She couldn't see into the bathroom from this angle, but that was okay; it meant Renée couldn't see her, either. She stood up and walked quickly into the hall, where she brushed herself off and ran her fingers quickly through her curls. Well, that was fun, she thought dryly. Time to go home. Definitely.

As she rounded the bottom of the stairs, Bill Miller hailed her. "Have you seen Renée? There's a new arrival I want her to meet." Behind him, a white-haired man in a dinner jacket stood waiting.

Lucy froze. "Uh, no. I haven't."

"Well, if you do, tell her I'm looking for her, will you?" Lucy nodded. "Enjoy yourself." He and the white-haired man moved off in the direction of the bar, and Lucy went slowly into the foyer. Not that it was any of her business, but if it wasn't Bill Miller up there, then who—

"Hey, watch it." Lucy looked around. "Sorry, but you walked right into it," a woman said.

Lucy looked down at the long smear of crab salad on the skirt of her dress, the broken plate on the marble floor. Just what I needed to round off the evening, she thought. "I'm terribly sorry," she apologized.

"You're the one with the stain," the woman replied. "I suggest club soda. The kitchen's through there. And you might tell them to send someone out to clean this up."

The caterer's assistant supplied a small bottle of Schweppes and a towel and directed her to the powder room. Which was, of course, occupied. She was about to head back to the kitchen when the door opened and Rick emerged, his hair freshly combed. "Lucy. There you are."

"Yup, here I am, crab salad and all."

His eyes went to the stain on her dress. "Can't take you anywhere," he teased as he took the towel and bottle from her. He drew her inside and closed the door. "Let me do it." He knelt and began to sponge away the stain.

"Thanks." Lucy looked down at him fondly. A cellular phone peeped from his breast pocket. She didn't remember it being there before.

"So where'd you get to?" he asked as he worked. "I looked all over."

"Powder room," she said. No reason to go into the details.

"*I* was in the powder room."

"You think a house like this has only one?" Her eyes were laughing. "So do you usually call people from the john?"

"Hmm?" Rick said, concentrating on the stain. "Oh, the cellular." He glanced at the phone, then up at Lucy. "Anders wanted me to call a firm we work with; check something out for him."

"At ten o'clock at night?"

"It's already tomorrow in Japan. And no," he added with a laugh, "I did not call them from the john."

"I didn't think so." She smiled. "Still, making Anders's calls isn't your job. Why do you let him use you like that?"

"It's no biggie," Rick said. "It gives Carl a feeling of power, I guess. And I don't mind. There. All done." He set the towel and bottle on the sink, opened the door, and flicked off the light. For a brief moment his body was silhouetted against the bright foyer and an impossible thought came to Lucy, but she immediately brushed it away. Of course not. Anyway, there must be thirty men out there in the living room, of a similar height and build, Bill Miller included.

"Speaking of our friend Anders," Lucy said as they stepped into the foyer, "I understand you're responsible for a rather rambling speech he made me this evening. He respects me, he likes me, he thinks women are the salt of the earth. . . ."

"Well, he can be a real jerk, sometimes. I just set him straight. Nicely, of course. I hope you don't mind."

"I guess not. But I'm kind of surprised he would listen."

Rick shrugged. "For some reason, he's taken a liking to me." He grinned at Lucy. "I think he enjoys my boyish irreverence."

"The son he never had?"

"The *life* he never had is more like it." Rick looked around. "How about getting out of here, maybe have a drink somewhere? Or do you want to stay?"

"Not me. Let's find our host and say good night."

They moved through the crush of people to where Bill and Renée held court, and said their good-byes. Bill kissed Lucy lightly on the cheek and clapped Rick on the shoulder, but Renée barely looked at them. They retrieved their coats and went out into the street. The night was cold but refreshing.

"Where to?"

"Let's walk a little."

"You're quiet," Rick said after several blocks. "Tired?"

"A little."

"Cold?"

"Not really."

Rick put an arm around her waist and held her close. "Warmer?"

"Mmm."

Their footsteps slowed, then stopped. He put his other arm around her and turned her to him. Again she felt the intensity of his gaze. Slowly he drew her to him and kissed her, a long, deep kiss that took her breath away. "How about coming back to my place for a drink?" he said at last, holding her close. "Or coffee."

"Coffee sounds good," she said slowly. "But . . ."

"What?"

"Don't take this the wrong way, Rick. But I think I should go home." She hesitated. "I just think it would be better."

"You mean because we work together?"

"No, I don't care about that. I . . . I just want to take things slowly. And that's hard to do, with you."

"I'll take that as a compliment." He smiled at her. "Okay, you set the pace. Whatever you want."

"I think I want to go home now."

"Home it is." He kissed her nose and released her, then went to the curb and flagged a taxi.

Outside her apartment building, he kissed her again, gently. "Sleep tight."

She smiled. "You, too."

He watched her as she went past the doorman and disappeared into the lobby. Then he turned away, reaching under his coat for the cellular phone, talking softly into it as he headed down the empty street.

Chapter Eight

The next day was Saturday and Lucy slept late, waking at ten to a cold, bright day. A quick shower, a boiled egg on toast, and a cup of coffee, and she was ready to tackle the last of her Christmas shopping.

With the holiday just over a week away, she still hadn't decided where to spend it. Monica was agitating for another visit, and her mother had been touting the joys of Christmas in Santa Fe for months. But New Mexico would be difficult, even if Lucy had planned ahead and booked a ticket, since she couldn't expect to wangle more than a couple of days off from the hospital. And Christmas in New York was a lot more appealing now that Richard Hollander had appeared in her life.

Not surprisingly, the festively decorated stores were crowded, but Lucy managed to find a lot of what she wanted, including a rather elegant blue chenille sweater for Monica and, in the unfortunately named Pet Empawium, a set of brown plush antlers, held on by an elastic neck strap, that were guaranteed to put both Max and Howard "in the ho-ho-holiday spirit." She still hadn't decided what to get for Rick.

She stopped for a moment to watch the skaters whizzing around the Rockefeller rink, tempted to join them. Another time, she decided; when the tourists go home. She checked out the Christmas windows at

Saks, and treated herself to a hot chocolate at Godiva. She bought herself a new cookbook at Doubleday, thinking Merry Christmas to Me. She put loose change in several Salvation Army baskets, wishing for live caroling instead of the canned music coming from their boom boxes.

And as she dropped the last of her dimes and quarters into the outstretched hands of the homeless people who approached her as she headed up Second Avenue toward her building, she silently wished Crazy Ray a good Christmas, wherever he was. And the rest of her "regulars," too, all of whom were still missing.

Inside the apartment, still carrying her shopping bags, she went over and checked the answering machine. Nothing. Well, she'd told Rick she wanted to take it slowly; he probably didn't want to crowd her. She looked around, seeing the apartment through his eyes. Not bad, she thought. Maybe a little messy.

She tossed the packages on the sofa and her coat over a chair, then surprised herself by retrieving the coat and hanging it up. She unpacked her purchases on the coffee table and started balling up the paper bags the way she usually did, then stopped, folded each one carefully, carried them into the kitchen, and tucked them away under the sink. Last Sunday's papers were spread out all over the floor behind the sofa, and she scooped them up and piled them neatly by the front door for disposal. She went and retrieved her breakfast dishes from the dining table along with a long-forgotten coffee mug, took them into the kitchen, and began to wash them. The coffee in the bottom of the mug was solid, and the remains of her morning egg had dried hard. She scrubbed at the egg with a tired sponge, but it wouldn't come off. Hell with this, she decided suddenly, and shoved everything into the full-to-overflowing dishwasher. I yam what I yam.

She poured herself a club soda and went back to the living room to wrap the presents.

As she crossed to the desk for scissors and tape, her eye fell on the statues standing on the pine chest. She dropped the tape and went over and studied them. God, they were ugly. But she did think she saw a faint resemblance to several of the pieces she'd seen the night before. Of course, she was no expert. Perhaps she should take them to Bill Miller; he'd know. But somehow she didn't think he'd take kindly to anything to do with Jean-Pierre. No, an impersonal expert was what she needed, and here in New York that should be easy to find.

She went back to the desk and pulled out a Yellow Pages, thumbing through it to the Art Galleries section. There were three pages of them: where to start? She ran her finger down the list from the top, looking for names that might indicate the types of art they dealt in. She'd gotten as far as the *L*'s when the phone interrupted her.

"Lucy? Monica. So what's the story? Are we going to see you at Christmas?"

Lucy sighed. "Don't hate me, sweetie, but I don't think so. There's my work at the hospital, and the IMA lab—"

"And a man named Rick," Monica teased. Lucy had mentioned to Monica that she'd had dinner with Rick a few times, and Monica, being Monica, had turned it into a big romance. Well, maybe it was. Or would be.

"Frankly, I'm not sure of Rick's plans," Lucy said. "He might have to go back to California for Christmas. Some family business to attend to, he said. Anyway, I really do have a lot of work—"

"As long as you won't be alone," Monica said. "By the way, did you hear? Ted Wiley's gone."

"Gone? Gone where?"

"They cut the funding for his program, and he decamped. Said he'd had enough of government work. Took a job in Texas somewhere."

"What about the peruvia project?"

"His replacement'll pick up the pieces, I guess. Although it's not exactly high priority: one small, isolated outbreak, fully contained, miles from anywhere. And you know what the budget situation is down here. We're being cut to ribbons; USAMRIID, too. So I wouldn't expect much. Guess it's up to you guys."

"Poor Ted. He'd been there for years."

"Yeah, but he was getting itchy. I think he was due for a change. And his wife's from Texas, so it's kind of nice for her."

Lucy had continued glancing idly through the gallery listings as they'd talked. Now something caught her eye. "Monica? Hang on a second." The Noone Gallery. Noone. Why did that name seem familiar?

"You okay?" Monica asked.

"Sorry. I was looking up art galleries when you called. I thought I'd take those statues of Jean's to be appraised."

"I thought you said they were worthless."

"I did, but what do I know?" Noone, she thought. Noone . . . "There's a name here I seem to recognize, but I don't know—Jesus. The notebook."

"What?"

"Jean-Pierre's notebook. The one he hid in that old desk. Hold on." She dropped the receiver and ran to unearth the small leather-bound book from her underwear drawer. Back at the desk, she tucked the receiver under her chin and leafed through the book. "Here it is," she told Monica excitedly. "Noone."

"Noon?"

"With an *e*. It's one of the names Jean wrote in his notebook. It's also the name of an art gallery here in New York."

"Could be a coincidence," Monica said cautiously. "Any other matches?"

"Let's see . . . Stanislas, Stanislas . . . yes, there's a Stanislas Arts," she announced triumphantly. "And Sun God Gallery . . . and Gallery Vieillesse." She paused, thinking. "Monica, you know what this means? Jean-Pierre must have been distributing the heroin through a network of art galleries. It's the last piece of the puzzle." Suddenly she felt very depressed. "I was wrong and Bill Miller was right. Jean *was* smuggling drugs."

Monica was silent for a moment. "I thought you were smarter than that," she said at last.

"What do you mean?"

"They found heroin in his suitcase, sure. But that doesn't mean he put it there." She paused. "Jean-Pierre wasn't smuggling drugs."

"He wasn't?"

"Of course not, Lucy. Think about it. He was smuggling art."

Chapter Nine

The young man eyed the statues she placed on his desk with distaste. "Typical tourist tripe, I'm afraid," he said. "I hope you didn't pay a lot for them."

"Actually, they were a gift."

He looked up at Lucy, his left eyebrow lifting. The Benton-Busch Gallery's clientele were, apparently, not the sort of people to whom such tawdry objects were given as gifts.

During the intervening week since Monica had made her surprising statement, Lucy had thought of little else. But gallery hours and her own work schedule had not allowed her to do anything about it until today, Christmas Eve. Meanwhile, she'd made a plan. She'd decided to start by getting a benchmark valuation of the statues from legitimate galleries, ones not listed in Jean-Pierre's notebook. Then she'd move on to the suspect ones, mentioning Jean's name and looking for a reaction. If she got one, she'd probe further, eventually offering to continue where he'd left off, and see if anyone took the bait.

Although the streets were thronged with last-minute shoppers this cold Saturday morning, art work wasn't nearly as popular as sweaters, books, and ties, and Benton-Busch's owner had been eager to attend to her. Until he'd looked at what she pulled from her shopping bag. It was the third place she'd stopped at, and so far the experts agreed: the statues were junk. Thanking the man, she repacked the wooden figures and left. Time to hit the hot spots, she thought. The Noone Gallery was just around the corner.

But if she'd thought the sight of the statues and her description of their origin would cause a suspicious flurry among the staff there, she was disappointed. Even the mention of Jean-Pierre's name didn't produce so much as a blink from the gallery's owner, a brittle, middle-aged woman in a designer suit, who immediately dismissed the statues as valueless, realized Lucy wasn't about to purchase any of her overpriced artifacts, and turned away to help a wealthier-looking customer.

The story was the same at Gallery Vieillesse. Although she thought she saw a flash of recognition at her mention of Jean-Pierre's name, Lucy's broad hints that she had more and better artifacts to sell were met with polite coldness, and she soon found herself back on the street again.

She sighed, hailed a taxi, and headed uptown to Stanislas Arts. Obviously, her approach was flawed. Traffic was sluggish, and she had plenty of time to think. By the time she got out in front of an antique store on Columbus Avenue, she had a new plan.

But where was the Stanislas gallery? She checked the number against her list; yes, this was the right place. Then she spied it: a tiny sign beside a grimy door next to the store. This outer door was unlocked; inside was an intercom plate with a labeled push button for each of the seven tenants of the small, dingy-looking row house beneath which the antique store was set. She pressed the bell marked STANISLAS ARTS.

"Who is?" The man's heavily accented voice came tinnily through the speaker.

"Lucy Nash. I'm a . . . a collector. A friend told me about you. He said you had very special things."

"Who has told you this?"

There was only one art collector Lucy knew, but he was a man of such eminence that Stanislas could well have heard of him. If so, it might give her the leverage she needed to get inside. "Dr. Bill Miller," she said.

For a long moment, nothing happened, and Lucy began to wonder whether she'd miscalculated. Perhaps Bill wasn't as well-known in the art world as she'd assumed. Then, "Come to the third floor," the voice said. "I will meet you at the landing." The inner door buzzed open, and Lucy went in.

She mounted the chipped stone stairs in semidarkness. It was quite a contrast to the other galleries she'd visited, and that made her feel strangely hopeful.

A dapper, birdlike man in his seventies, wearing a well-cut dark suit and patterned silk tie, stood on the third-floor landing. He leaned heavily on an ebony cane, studying her carefully as she climbed up toward him. "So," he said when she stood beside him. "Lucy Nash."

"Yes."

"I am Beno Stanislas." He extended his hand and Lucy shook it. "What do you collect, Lucy Nash?"

"I collect South American art," she said. "Old pieces."

"I see. Pre-Columbian?"

"Yes."

"And this Bill Miller you mentioned, he told you to come and see me?"

Lucy nodded. "He said you had some very unusual things."

"And so I do." His eyes hardened. "But I do not know any Bill Miller."

"Uh, Mr. Stanislas, could we talk inside?"

"Inside?"

"In your gallery." Lucy looked around. It seemed an unlikely location for such an establishment.

Stanislas frowned. "You have made a mistake. I have no gallery."

"But it says—"

"I am a dealer, Miss Nash. I buy from private sellers, and I sell to private buyers. I am not open to the public." He turned away.

"Wait. Please. I'm a friend of Jean-Pierre Didier."

The man stopped. "I know no one of that name, either," he replied without turning. "Good day."

"I have his notebook."

That brought him around. "And why should that interest me?"

"Because you're in it."

The old man lifted his cane, and for a moment Lucy thought he would strike her with it, so enraged had his face become.

"It's all right," she said quickly, stepping back. "I'm his . . . friend. His business partner. He said," she continued, improvising, "that I should come and see you if anything happened to him."

Slowly Stanislas lowered the cane, breathing deeply in an attempt to bring his emotions under control and muttering to himself. Another pause. "I don't know what you're talking about," he said, but his tone was uncertain and his expression furtive.

"We both know you do." He stood staring warily at her. He thinks I'm the police, Lucy realized. Or a customs agent. She was uncertain what agency would be involved in an investigation into art smuggling, but undoubtedly there was one and Stanislas thought she was part of it. She pulled her hospital identification badge from her purse and thrust it toward him. "Here, look. I'm a doctor, just like Jean-Pierre. Dr. Didier. I work at New York General. We were together in Peru, when he— I'm a doctor. See?"

Grudgingly, he examined the badge, turning it over in his arthritic fingers, then shoved it back to her. "Inside," he said briefly. Lucy followed him down the short, dark corridor and into a tiny, overheated room.

"Sit," he told her. "Over there, on the sofa."

Lucy sat and looked around. She was in a small sitting room. The furniture was an eclectic mix, old but good. A faded oriental rug hid most of the polished wood floor, and the walls were covered with an old-fashioned red-flocked paper. A faint smell of cooking lingered in the air, and Lucy realized that this was no gallery. It was Stanislas's home.

"So, *doctor,*" he said, seating himself in a chair opposite her. "Why did this person whom I do not know tell you to come and see me? And why should he think something would happen to him?"

Lucy sighed. "Come on, Mr. Stanislas. I know all about your, uh, business with Jean-Pierre. He told me himself. Jean was one of those private sellers you mentioned, the source of those unusual, those special things you sold." Stanislas gave a noncommittal shrug, but his eyes never left her face. "As for why he was afraid something would happen to him," she continued, still improvising, "maybe he thought someone knew about his art smuggling and what he was doing with you. And he was right, wasn't he? Something did happen to him."

"Heroin, that is what happened to him," Stanislas responded angrily. "The art wasn't enough for him; he had to involve himself in narcotics."

"Perhaps you bought that from him, too," Lucy said. "And sold it to those private customers of yours. Was art enough for *you,* Mr. Stanislas?"

The old man rose, shaking with rage. "I do not deal in drugs, Dr. Nash," he said. "It was only when Jean was arrested that I learned—" He leaned heavily on his cane, breathing hard. "You will please leave now."

But Lucy didn't move. Instead, she studied the old man carefully and found that, for some reason, she

believed him. "Sit down, Mr. Stanislas," she said at
last. "I can see you're telling me the truth." But still
he stood glowering down at her. "Please. I'm sorry. I
didn't know myself, until he was arrested. I was
shocked; it just didn't seem possible that he'd be involved in drug running. I couldn't believe it was true.
I still don't want to believe it. . . ." Tears flooded
her eyes as she recalled that terrible night, Bill
meeting her at the airport, telling her what had happened. But through her rekindled grief, she remembered to maintain the fiction she'd built for
Stanislas, saying, "I thought maybe you and he— I
had to be certain."

Slowly the old man lowered himself back into his
worn leather chair, studying her, deciding. "He was
your lover?" he asked at last.

Lucy colored at the man's bluntness. "Yes. Yes,
he was."

For some reason, that seemed to reassure the
dealer. "Yes, I see," he said, his expression softening.
"Lovers tell each other many secrets. But why did he
send you to me?"

"Well, he had told me what he was doing," Lucy
said carefully. She reached into her bag for a tissue
and dabbed at her eyes. "In fact, I even helped him
a few times. I think he meant for me to continue the,
er, business relationship he had with you."

"And is that what you mean to do, Lucy Nash?"

"Yes."

"Frankly, I'm glad to hear it. I had recently begun
to feel that Jean might have been—I hardly like to
say cheating me. Let's just say I felt he might be attempting to sell his purchases directly to my clients."
His eyes went to the shopping bag in which the
wrapped statues lay. "So what have you brought me?"

"What?" Lucy followed his glance. "Oh, nothing

yet. This is just some Christmas shopping. I thought we should meet first, talk . . ."

"Of course. Would you like some tea?"

"Yes, thanks," Lucy said, surprised. "Can I help?"

"Please do not trouble yourself. It is easily made." He shuffled into the kitchen and eventually Lucy heard the whistle of a teakettle. "Perhaps if you would just help me with the tray," he called out, and she rose and went to the tiny kitchen. Two mugs of fragrant tea and a plate of frosted biscuits sat on a Chinese lacquer tray. "A mug I can manage," he told her, "but all this . . ."

"What a beautiful tray, Mr. Stanislas," Lucy said as she carried it into the sitting room and set it down on the low table between them.

"Beno," he told her, seating himself. "If we're going to be business partners, you must call me Beno. The biscuits are excellent. Imported."

Lucy smiled and took one. "So how shall we work this, Beno?"

He blew on his tea, then sipped thoughtfully. "Jean had many contacts in many countries, built up over the years. You have his notebook, so you must have the names."

Lucy nodded. "There's Jorge in Lima," she offered.

"Jorge Melendez, yes. Of him I have heard." He reached for a biscuit and broke it in two. "You met with him when you were in Peru?"

"Jean did."

"Ah, that is most interesting. You see, Jean had hinted to me that Jorge had located something very special. An ancient artifact of some kind of course, but what it was, he wouldn't say, although it was obvious from the way he spoke that it was quite old and extremely valuable. And yet you say you have nothing for me?" He looked at her searchingly.

"No. Jean had, er, hinted the same thing to me, but

unfortunately I had already returned to the States when he met with Jorge. Then he was arrested, and I never found out—"

"But they gave you his things? You checked them carefully?"

"Yes, very carefully. There was nothing."

"And you are sure you would recognize it if you saw it? You have that knowledge?"

"I've never studied art," Lucy admitted. "But I'd certainly know a pre-Columbian artifact if I saw one, even if I didn't know its value. There was nothing."

"And why do you suppose it must be pre-Columbian?"

"Peru, Jorge Melendez . . . I naturally assumed—"

"Never assume," Beno cautioned her. "Jean's work took him to many countries, as does yours, apparently." Lucy nodded. "The same is true of Jorge Melendez." He smiled and took another biscuit. "How much do you know about the world of ancient artifacts, Lucy?"

"Very little. Nothing, really."

"Then you must study, or you will be badly cheated. Even by so reputable a man as Jorge Melendez," he added dryly. "The buying and selling of primitive artifacts is cloaked in secrecy, my dear. Secrecy is practically written into the contract of sale, and unlike Bloomingdale's"—he smiled at the shopping bag by her feet—"there is a 'no-returns' policy." His eyes grew solemn. "You must be sure of what you are buying, and very careful to whom you sell it. It can be very difficult."

"But isn't it equally difficult for you? Don't your buyers ask where you get the things you sell them? Don't they suspect the pieces are smuggled, and aren't they afraid of getting caught with them?"

Beno chuckled. "Oh, no," he assured her. "My buyers are far more concerned with the authenticity and

value of an object than they are with whether it was
looted or stolen. Don't look so shocked," he added,
seeing her expression. "They realize there is little
chance that such artifacts were legally obtained, not
with the current laws against international trafficking
in ancient artifacts. Although frankly, it wasn't so very
different before 1970. It's the nature of the business,
you see. And the nature of collectors."

"What happened in 1970?" Lucy asked.

"The UNESCO Convention is what happened. An
international agreement that was designed to stop, or
at least limit, trading in objects of national heritage.
Africa, India, South America . . . so many valuable
pieces had already gone, sold to the highest bidder.
And sometimes not sold at all, merely taken by con-
querors. Oh, it has been going on for ages. The Elgin
Marbles, for example . . ."

"So the UNESCO Convention made it harder to
buy and sell ancient artifacts?"

"Harder, perhaps, but by no means impossible. It
all depends on geography, you see."

"Geography?"

"Yes. Many countries, France, for example, are not
as . . . fastidious, shall we say, as the government
of the United States, in detecting and seizing ancient
artifacts and returning them to their countries of origin, as the Convention requires."

Jean-Pierre had been planning to fly to France, Lucy
recalled, just two days after his meeting with Melendez. And Beno had said he'd suspected Jean had been
planning to sell his wares to others. If France was
more likely to turn a blind eye to art smuggling, it
would make sense for Jean to take his business there,
especially if he had something really special to sell.
But if it *was* stolen art that Jean was bringing to Marseilles, where did the heroin fit in?

"Another biscuit?"

"No, thank you. I really should go." Lucy stood, and Beno levered himself erect, leaning on his cane. He went to a small rosewood desk.

"Here is my card with my private number. Call before you come next time. We must be careful. That notebook of Jean's," he added as he walked her to the door, "I hope you are not so foolish as to leave it where a friend . . . or a lover . . . can find it."

"Of course not," she answered, thinking what a stupid hiding place her underwear drawer was.

At the door he stopped her, putting a hand on her arm. "Recently I have noticed certain people in the street below," he told her softly. "They walk about, they look into store windows, but they are not real, you understand me? And two people have telephoned, claiming to be collectors and asking strange questions."

"And yet you let me in."

"I thought you might be one of them. Don't look so surprised, my dear. Better the devil you know than the devil you don't. I decided it was time I had a talk with one of them, face-to-face. I thought I might learn what things they actually knew, and what they only suspected."

"But what about Bill Miller?" Lucy asked as she stepped out into the dingy hallway. "Didn't my mentioning his name play a part in your seeing me?"

Beno shook his head. "I have already told you: I do not know this Bill Miller." His birdlike eyes peered sharply at her. "Why should you think I would?"

"Bill's the head of the organization that sent Jean and me to Peru," Lucy replied. "He's quite the collector, and I thought you might have done some business with him."

"Unfortunately, no," Beno said, his face clouding. A beat, and then he smiled, all affability now, as he offered his hand and Lucy took it. "I am going away for a while," he said. "For a month; perhaps a little longer. You will excuse me if I do not send you a postcard." He smiled bleakly.

"But you're coming back?"

"Oh, yes. My business is here. I simply want to allow the heat, as you Americans so colorfully say, to die down. Well, Merry Christmas, my dear. I will look for you in the new year."

"Merry Christmas," Lucy replied. *Don't hold your breath.*

So what have I learned? she asked herself, out in the street and heading south.

One: Monica was right. Jean-Pierre was smuggling art. But I don't know for sure that he wasn't smuggling drugs as well. Although that would be stupid, and Jean wasn't stupid. Greedy, immoral, and unethical, apparently, but never stupid.

Two: The United States is tough on art smugglers. Had the customs agents at Kennedy Airport actually been looking for smuggled art when they found heroin? Had they been tipped off that artifacts were coming in? Perhaps, but that still left the problem of the heroin. If Jean hadn't put it there, who had?

Three: Beno had suspected that Jean-Pierre was cheating him. He'd seemed upset when I said that Jean and I both knew Bill Miller. He must have thought Bill was a private customer Jean was keeping to himself. Not that Bill's the sort of man who would buy smuggled art, but Beno couldn't know that.

A chill wind had come up, and she pulled her coat more closely around her. What if Beno's suspicions had been correct? There were several sets of initials in Jean's notebook that didn't correspond to any galleries listed in the Yellow Pages. What if those initials represented a few of Beno's buyers, people Jean had sold to directly, thus doing the dealer out of his cut?

Now that was an interesting thought. Might Beno have tipped off the customs agents out of a desire for revenge? But no, that would put Beno himself at risk. Unless Jean died before he could implicate Stanislas Arts. Which he did. With what the newspapers had called a "death pill."

Why would an art smuggler be carrying a death pill?

And she still couldn't fathom why Jean would have brought back those ugly, worthless carvings. Hell, even the customs agents hadn't been able to figure that one out, and they'd sawn the damn things in half.

A scattering of flakes began to fall; perhaps it would be a white Christmas after all. Not that it mattered much to her. With Rick in California for the holiday, and all planes out of New York booked solid, she had been at loose ends for Christmas Day. So when a colleague at the hospital had asked her to trade days off so that he could be with his family, Lucy had decided to go for it. It seemed reasonable to exchange a lonely Christmas Day for an Easter Sunday of possibilities.

She passed a movie theater showing a comedy she'd been wanting to see, and thought, why not?, enjoying the freedom of having no plans. The film started in twenty minutes, so she bought her ticket and went across the street to a nearby coffee shop to check her answering machine. A message from Rick wished her a happy Christmas Eve from rainy California and promised to call again soon. Another, from Jake Weiss, reminded her that she was expected for dinner after work on Christmas Day, which was also the first day of Hanukkah, and that his wife made the best latkes in town, and that all Lucy needed to bring was her appetite. Lucy smiled and wondered what latkes were.

In the theater, she treated herself to popcorn and a

soda, then settled back for a little escapism. She could use some, she decided. Although the day had certainly been illuminating, she was still left with more questions than answers.

Chapter Ten

For many businesses, the period between Christmas Eve and New Year's Day is a slow one. Vacation days are taken, clients are out of town, everything winds down. But in the arena of hospital medicine, it is a time as busy as any other, often busier. Lucy's days were full, and an outbreak of what turned out to be a virulent form of *E. coli* bacteria at the local restaurants of a well-known fast-food franchise stretched her to the limit.

Which was why she was already fast asleep when Rick called from California at nine-fifteen on Wednesday evening.

"Merry three-days-after-Christmas," he announced cheerily. "And how's the *E. coli* Kid?"

"Tired," Lucy said.

"I can imagine. I've been reading about it in the papers out here. Even the local Santa Barbara newscast picked it up. Sounds like you guys have your hands full."

"That's putting it mildly." Lucy yawned mightily.

"Did I wake you?" Rick asked with concern. "I'm really sorry. Maybe I should call back in the morning."

"No, it's okay. I can't think of anyone I'd rather be woken up by."

There was a brief silence as they both considered the ramifications of this. Then, "Let's work on that," Rick said, and they both laughed. Lucy reached for the bedside light, then stopped. It was kind of cozy talking to Rick in the sleepy darkness. "My flight gets in pretty late on Friday," he said, "but Saturday is New Year's Eve, and I was hoping we could spend it together. If you don't have any other plans."

"I'd like that."

"Great. So what would you like to do? I guess I should make a dinner reservation somewhere before things get too booked up. Any place special you'd like to go?"

"You choose," Lucy told him. "You have great taste in restaurants."

"And in women. Hey, I got you a present."

And I still haven't chosen one for him, Lucy thought. Get busy, girl. "What is it?"

"Oh, no." Rick laughed. "It's a surprise. Now go back to sleep. I'll call you Saturday morning. Not too early," he added, and she could hear the smile in his voice.

"That would be wise." She felt herself smiling, too. "Good night, Rick."

"Good night, Lucy. Sleep tight."

She put the phone down and snuggled into her pillows. New Year's Eve with Rick, she thought sleepily; what a nice way to start the year. She remembered his body pressed against hers at Bill's party, the intensity with which he'd kissed her afterward. Taking things slowly was all well and good, but she wasn't sure how long she'd be able to keep it up.

Rick palmed the cellular phone, flushed the toilet, and came out of the bathroom into the darkened bedroom. His jacket was thrown over the back of a chair, and he slipped the phone back into a side pocket as he passed.

She was spread out on the bed, eyes closed. He stopped and looked down at her. Her eyelids flickered open, and she reached for him greedily. "Come back to bed."

"You're insatiable."

"Mmm." She kneeled and came toward him. "And you're delicious."

She took him in her mouth and he groaned with pleasure. She was very skilled, and he soon toppled onto the bed, flushed and spent. She gazed at him with her green cat eyes, tawny hair falling around her face. "Merry Christmas."

"Christmas is over."

"Happy New Year, then." She smiled her lazy smile. "Now we will have a shower, and then you will take me to dinner."

"Not a chance." He sat up, frowning. "You know we can't be seen together. We agreed."

"Well, now I *dis*agree."

"No."

"You are scared?" she taunted. "A man like you?"

"Damn right I'm scared. Bill Miller pays my salary."

"Oh, he won't care what we do."

"Like hell he won't. Look, I won't keep having this argument."

"You're being silly," Renée told him. "This is not Italy. And he is not my husband."

"A good thing, too. Back in that village you were born in, your husband would shoot us both. Or your father." But he was smiling now.

"Yes, and then we would spend eternity fucking each other." She moved across the bed and settled herself in the curve of his arm. "Do you think they fuck in heaven, *caro*?"

"I doubt they could stop you."

She laughed, then reached over and began to stroke the inside of his thigh.

"You're going to put me in the hospital." Rick grabbed her hand and bit it lightly, then rolled quickly off the bed and stood up. "I need a drink. You want something?"

"You know what I want."

"You'll have to settle for scotch and water," he told her, evading her reaching hand.

"For now."

He went through her small, ultra-modern apartment to the kitchen and soon returned with two cold glasses. "So what was it like, growing up in a tiny town in southern Italy?" he asked, handing her one. "And how did you learn to speak English so well?" He perched on the arm of a nearby chair, just out of reach.

"I came to America when I was fourteen," she told him, sipping her drink. "My father died, and my mother and I came to live with her sister."

"In New York?"

"No, Miami. But when I was nineteen, I got married and went back to Italy."

"To Amalfi, with the count?"

"Yes. Why are you so interested in these things?"

Rick smiled. "I'm trying to picture you as a little girl. You must have been very sweet."

"I was a hell-raiser."

"That would have been my second guess." He paused. "I can understand your wanting to go back. Italy's a very beautiful country."

"Do you know it? You have been there?"

"Only once. To Rome. And to Latino, to visit my grandfather's grave."

Her eyes widened. "Your grandfather was Italian?"

"No, but he died there." Rick took a pull at his drink. "He was in the army during the Second World War. He was killed in the fighting around Monte Casino."

"How sad. He was young?"

"Thirty-two."

"And your father? He too was in the army?"

"Navy. But he wasn't a career man. He did his time and got out."

Renée regarded him over the top of her glass. "So you come from a family of patriots. Very noble."

"You don't approve?"

"Fighting the politicians' wars? It is stupid."

"Rather cynical sentiments from a woman who donates megabucks to the IMA."

"Ah, but that is not politics. That is charity." She finished her scotch and set the glass on a low table beside the bed. "Take me out to dinner, Rick. I promise no one will shoot you."

"No, Renée."

"Well, I will take my shower, and then we will see." She got up and walked to the bathroom, her hips swaying provocatively. "Join me?"

"Soon," Rick said. "Let me surprise you."

He waited until the shower was running, then put down his glass. She'd left the bathroom door half open, and he went behind it and quietly pushed it shut. Then quickly and methodically, he began to search the apartment.

Despite the extra load the *E. coli* outbreak placed on her work schedule, Lucy was determined to get down to the IMA lab for her regular Thursday afternoon session. But somehow the day got away from her, and it was after four when she closed the last patient file and turned off her computer. She always ran her eye over the next day's schedule before leaving the office every evening, and she did so now. The yellow Post-it, her reminder to herself to call Alicia, had been there since Monday, but she hadn't had a minute to make the call. She glanced at her watch. She was already three hours late getting down to the lab; a few minutes more wouldn't matter.

"Alicia? Lucy Nash. I have a quick question for you about Bill's schedule. No, I don't need an appointment. It's about that business with Jean-Pierre. I'm, uh, just trying to reconstruct Jean's movements around that time, and he'd mentioned something about a meeting with Bill. Do you think you could you tell me when that was? Probably around the time Jean and I went to Peru. Well, could you check the month before? Thanks. Yes, I'll hold on."

Jake Weiss waved a file at her from the doorway, but she shook her head. "I'm out of here in two minutes," she told him, putting a hand over the receiver. "Rosemary's still here, if it's urgent."

"Not urgent. Can we talk first thing in the morning?"

"You've got it. And you better have that latke recipe with you. Yes, Alicia, I'm still here . . . when?" Lucy frowned as she wrote down the date. "You sure that's the only one? Did Jean happen to say why he wanted—no, of course not. Well, thanks a lot, Alicia. And a happy New Year to you, too."

Lucy hung up, then flipped back through her desk diary. The date Alicia had given her was the day after Jean had died. And the day before he was supposed to fly to France.

Carl Anders was pulling on his overcoat as she came through the glass doors. "It's after five," he said without preamble. "Surely you're not planning to work this evening."

"Merry Christmas to you, too, Carl," she said, shucking her coat. "Was Santa good to you this year?"

Carl gave one of his imitation smiles. "Yes, very good. I apologize for my abruptness. I'm late for an appointment." He paused. "Ben and Corrin will be leaving soon, and everyone else is already gone. How long were you planning to stay?"

"Not long," she responded. "I've got a bunch of tabulations to enter, and this seemed to be a good time to get them out of the way."

"You're not going into the hot lab?"

"Not today, no."

He nodded. "Good. It's a bad place to be when you're tired. Well, see you next year."

Lucy gave this limp witticism a broader smile than it deserved, and headed inside.

As she passed Carl's office, she noticed that his computer was still on, the bouncing-ball screen-saver moving in slow motion. Should she shut it down? No, better not touch it. One wrong keystroke and she could wipe out a month's work. She went through the nearly deserted benchwork area to the small lab she occupied when not inside the hot lab, put down her coat, and activated her own computer terminal.

"Like the filovirus Ebola, the peruvia virion contains seven polypeptides," she typed. "The function of protein VP402, found in the viral membrane, is unknown. In this, as well as in its molecular weight, it resembles VP40, found in the Ebola virion membrane."

In her early attempts to separate and identify the seven proteins of the peruvia virus, she'd been surprised by their uncanny resemblance to the virion proteins of Ebola and Marburg, two filoviruses which had their origins in Africa. But on reflection, she'd decided that perhaps it wasn't so surprising after all. Eons ago, Africa and South America had been one continent. Considering the fact that filoviruses were some of the planet's oldest life-forms, they would have had plenty of time to migrate across that huge land mass before it split apart.

She finished transcribing her notes, then closed the PROTEINS file and opened the MORPHOLOGY file. That, too, needed bringing up to date.

"Virion density is 1.34 g/ml as determined by centrifugation in a potassium tartrate gradient," she typed. "The single molecule of linear, negative-sense, single-stranded RNA it contains is approximately 12.9 kb in size and constitutes 1.3 percent of the virion mass."

"So long, Lucy." Ben, one of the lab researchers, stood at the door. "Happy New Year."

"You leaving?"

"We both are," Corrin said, appearing behind Ben. "Don't work too late. It's kind of a creepy neighborhood at night."

"I won't," Lucy promised.

They disappeared toward the elevator, and Lucy yawned and stretched. It had been a long day. "Peruvia appears as either a long filament, sometimes branched, or in a shorter U or 6 shape. While filamentous forms vary in length, up to 12,000nm as observed in our samples, the length for peak infectivity appears to be approximately 1050nm. . . ."

How curious, Lucy reflected, that the length of each separate viral strand affected its virulence. Curious, too, that virulence increased with length up until 1050nm, and then dropped off as virions got longer. A viral strand of 10,500nm was far less lethal than one of 1050nm. The same was true of Ebola, although the actual measurements were slightly different. And nobody knew why.

"The mode of entry of the peruvia virus into cells remains unknown," she typed. "Messenger RNA is abundant in infected cells, but virion RNA is not detectable, suggesting rapid packaging of genomic RNA."

In a recent discussion of her research with the closed-mouth Carl, she'd managed to winkle out of him the fact that he was attempting to clone peruvia's genomic RNA in order to produce an RNA diagnostic probe specific for the virus. Using such a probe, she knew, one could then develop a polymerase chain-reaction diagnostic assay. She wondered how he was getting along.

The lab was deserted, and his computer was on—dare she have a look?

All the lab computers were networked together, since researchers frequently traded data. She could access Carl's files through her own terminal. She typed in his name and a file request, followed by the word PERUVIA, scanning idly through the list of documents that appeared on the screen. RNA CLONE; yes, there it was. She'd highlighted it and was about to call it up when her eye drifted lower. SANGRE NEGRA.

Now that was odd.

Sangre negra was the local term for peruvia; it wasn't actually a separate virus. Was it?

She recalled the old Peruvian, angry and fevered, insisting that sangre negra was an evil spirit that had returned. Returned as peruvia, obviously. So why would Anders have a separate file marked SANGRE NEGRA? Why should he even know that purely local name for the disease? She tried to think whether her report had mentioned sangre negra; presumably it had. Still, why should Anders have created a separate file for it?

One way to find out, she thought. She tried to call it up, but the screen turned red, and the word RE-STRICTED appeared.

Odder and odder.

She closed the program's windows and started again, asking the computer to search for all references to the words *sangre negra*. It provided her with a list of two, the first reading SANGRE NEGRA, the second, SANGRE NEGRA followed by a date. The date was two years old.

She closed the window and typed in the second ref-

erence. Again, the screen turned red and the RE-
STRICTED warning appeared.

"Why are you attempting to access my private
files?" Lucy gasped and swung around to face a furious Carl Anders. "Shut down that terminal now."

"Jesus, Carl," Lucy stuttered. "You scared the hell
out of me."

Anders didn't reply. He simply reached around her
and hit a few keys. Instantly, the screen turned black.
"My private files," he told her with barely controlled
anger, "are none of your business."

"You're right. I'm sorry. I just wanted to see your
progress on the RNA clone—"

"Then you ask me to show it to you." Carl's normally pale face was flushed, his fists clenched. "I told
Miller we didn't need you here, I told him you'd be
nothing but trouble."

"Trouble? I'm the most experienced researcher
you've got, Carl. I'm sorry if you have a problem with
women—"

"I have a problem with *you*, Dr. Nash. Those files
are restricted. How dare you—"

For a moment Lucy thought he might hit her. She
forced her chair back against his legs, stood and faced
him, keenly aware of the dark, empty lab in which
they stood. "It was an accident," she said as calmly
as she could manage. "I was looking for the genome
file." She tried to think if there was anything on the
desk behind her with which she could defend herself.
Maybe the lamp . . . "I told you I was sorry—"

"Shut up." A pause. "Is that why you came here
so late today, when you knew everyone would be
gone? To try and read the sangre negra file?" He fixed
her in a cold, unwavering glare and she saw anger in
his eyes, and something else. Fear.

"Of course not," she said hotly. "I was looking for
the RNA clone file, and I happened to notice the san-

gre negra listing, that's all. It's the local name for peruvia, and I wondered . . ."

"You wondered . . . what?"

I wondered why you had a restricted file that's dated two years before the disease that its name describes was actually discovered. Aloud she said, "I . . . I was just curious."

"Curiosity killed the cat." He stared balefully at her.

"Are you threatening me, Carl?" Her hand inched across the desk toward the lamp. She wished fervently that Corrin and Ben were still here.

He held her gaze for a moment longer, then stepped away from her. "No, of course not." He ran a hand across his forehead. "I've had several unfortunate experiences in the past, with people stealing my research." He scowled at her. "Now I guard my work carefully."

"But sangre negre . . . That's peruvia. It's my work, too."

Carl shook his head. "No, the file you saw has nothing to do with peruvia."

"But the local Peruvians—"

"The term is a generic descriptive," he said impatiently. "Black blood, dark blood. It could fit any number of tropical illnesses—dengue fever, for instance." He paced the length of the small lab, his anger dissipating. "The file refers to some old research I did privately in Mexico. It has nothing to do with the IMA. The name is a coincidence." He turned to her, his expression daring her to disagree.

Old research? The file was dated only two years earlier. But she just nodded.

"And now I think we've both done enough work for this evening," he said firmly. "I'll walk you out and get you a taxi. This is a rough neighborhood."

And getting rougher, Lucy thought, reaching for her coat.

Her alarm woke her at six the next morning, and she was on her way downtown by six-thirty. She'd heard that Carl rarely got in before nine. She had plenty of time to have another go at those restricted files and be at New York General for eight o'clock rounds.

She gazed out of the taxi window at the Hudson River, silver-gray in the early light, the near shore patched with ice. After that first, confusing visit, she'd always taken taxis to the lab. It was expensive, but far more direct: a straight shot west, and then down along the river.

She rode the elevator to the second floor, fumbling in her purse for the keycard she'd been issued. As with many businesses in the city, the heavy glass doors were kept locked, even during the day. She stepped out into the dark hallway and peered through the glass. A faint glow illuminated the short hallway that led from the reception area into the lab. Carl must have left a light on last night, in his rush to evict her.

Or was someone else already here?

Cautiously, she inched her way along the hallway, then stopped. The high, open work area was in shadow, the only light source a half-open door. Beyond the door was a lab. A lab that should have been empty.

She tiptoed across the floor. He was seated at the computer terminal at the far end of the room, studying something on the screen with great concentration.

"You're supposed to be in California," she said to his back.

He started violently, then swung around and stared at her. "Jesus. Lucy. What are you doing here?"

"I could ask the same of you."

"Christ, you practically gave me a heart attack."

They looked at each other for a moment, then Rick laughed. "Anders changed a timetable on me. Suddenly decided he needed this stuff pronto." He hit a key as he rose, and the screen went blank. "I grabbed a 'red-eye' flight, got in around four this morning." He enfolded her in his arms. "God, you smell great. I was going to call you at the hospital this morning," he continued, releasing her. "I never imagined you'd turn up here." He eyed her questioningly.

"I just came by to print out some data. I was so exhausted last night, I forgot." For a fleeting moment she considered telling Rick about the restricted files, then remembered how tight he was with Anders and thought, better not. It wasn't that she didn't trust Rick, but she doubted he would react positively to the idea of her snooping through Carl's private files. "I guess I'd better get busy," she said.

"Want some coffee?" he asked, putting an arm around her and walking her through the open-bench work area toward her lab. "There's a fresh pot in the kitchenette."

"No, I can't stay long. I have an early consult." She eyed him critically. "You look exhausted."

"I am. Those night flights are murder." He stood in the doorway and watched her as she slid into the chair in front of her computer terminal. "You, on the other hand, look wonderful. I really missed you, Luce."

"I missed you, too." She smiled up at him. He did look awfully tired.

"Tomorrow night'll be great," he said. "A corny, old-fashioned New Year's Eve at the Rainbow Room. Champagne, funny hats, a dance band, the whole nine yards."

"Sounds like fun."

"Well, I better let you get to work. I'll call you later. Maybe we can meet for a drink or something."

"Maybe. Although my days at the hospital have

been turning into nights this week. And you look like you could use some sleep."

"I could. Well, let's see how today goes." He came up behind her and kissed the top of her head. "It's good to be back." He went to the door, then stopped. "Sure you don't want any coffee?"

"No, thanks."

"Okay, then."

Lucy watched him head toward the kitchenette, then turned her attention to the computer screen. She brought the screen alive, then typed in the same series of commands she used the previous evening. Nothing. No SANGRE NEGRA, no red screen, no restricted warning. Hmm . . . She tried again, and managed to bring up Carl's file list. She scrolled down it to the bottom, then back up again, carefully scrutinizing every entry. The sangre negra files were gone.

"Shit," she said aloud. "Goddammit."

"Something wrong?" Rick stood at the door, a steaming cup in his hand.

"No. It's nothing," she said, shutting down the terminal. "All done." She stood and came toward him.

"Don't forget your printout again," he said, smiling.

"Right." She went back to the workstation, grabbed some papers at random, and stuffed them in the pocket of her coat. "Thanks. Wow, I didn't know it was so late."

"Talk to you later," he called to her retreating figure.

He watched her disappear into the hallway, listening for the soft thunk of the heavy glass doors closing behind her. Then he went to her desktop printer, raised its lid, and put his hand inside. Stone cold.

He sank down in front of her computer terminal and contemplated the dark monitor screen, sipping his coffee and wondering.

Chapter Eleven

The blue silk suit or the black dress with the matching jacket?

This dinner invitation from Bill Miller had surprised and unsettled her. Had Anders complained to him about her snooping? She hadn't seen Carl since their run-in two weeks ago; he'd been out of the lab on business this past Thursday. Could this be Bill's way of sugarcoating a request that she no longer donate her time to the IMA? No, that was silly. He might take her to lunch for such a purpose, but hardly to dinner at Le Regence.

The black, she decided. And the gold-twist earrings.

New Year's Eve had come and gone, and with it, Lucy's will power; she and Rick had become lovers in his surprisingly impersonal one-bedroom apartment. They'd spent the following day curled up together, eating Chinese takeout, watching the rain drip down the windowpanes, and exploring each other's bodies.

But despite the bliss of that first night and day, Lucy felt a certain reserve, whether in him or in herself, she couldn't say. Yet she'd felt no reticence in telling him about her brief affair with Jean-Pierre, and her determination to clear his name. He seemed untroubled by the former and approving of the latter, but he didn't push when she turned down his offer of dinner and a movie the following evening. He seemed content to let her set the pace. In the ten days since then, they'd seen each other a total of four times, their evenings together always ending with lovemaking at his apartment. Rick was a gentle and attentive lover, and an amusing and pleasant companion. But for some reason she couldn't define, Lucy was not yet ready to invite him into her own space, or to spend another entire night in his. So far, Rick had accepted this.

She pulled out a pair of black sling-back heels and stepped into them, then surveyed herself in the full-length mirror. Not bad, she thought. Not bad at all for a woman who's spent the past nine hours at work in one of the city's busiest medical centers.

He rose to greet her as the maître d' led her to the corner banquette he'd commandeered. "I'm so glad you could join me," he told her. "How very beautiful you look. No one would guess you'd been up to your elbows in gore all day."

Several nearby patrons turned to stare. "Infectious diseases isn't a particularly bloody specialty," she replied, smiling.

"Of course not. Now, what would you like to drink? Champagne?"

"A glass of the house white would be—oh, why not? Champagne."

Bill nodded his approval. "Another Perrier Jouet," he told the waiting maître d', then turned back to Lucy. "Have you been here before?"

"No."

"It's one of my favorite places. And the lamb is excellent."

It was obvious that Bill was a favored patron. The wine arrived immediately, as did a small dish containing four delicate hors d'oeuvres. An obsequious waiter hovered with menus, but Bill waved him away. "To you, doctor," he told Lucy. "I think you'll enjoy this."

Lucy sipped. "It's delicious," she told him. It was, very.

"I'm not much of a drinker," he said, "but what I do drink, I like to enjoy." He swirled the pale liquid around in his glass. "What's that old saying? 'Life's too short to drink bad wine.'"

"A good philosophy if you can afford it."

"Sorry," he said, his smile fading. "I didn't mean to be insensitive."

"And I didn't mean to get heavy," Lucy said. "God knows, you do more than your share for people who can't."

"Yes. Well." Bill looked modestly down at his glass, then raised his eyes to her. "As do you, Lucy. Which is what I wanted to talk to you about." Uh-oh, Lucy thought. "But let's deal with the menus first, shall we?"

They decided on the lamb, and a good Bordeaux to go with it, Bill transmitting their order to the waiter and consulting with the wine steward in perfect, colloquial French. "It's my mother tongue," he explained to Lucy. "Literally. My mother was French."

"It's a beautiful language."

"Isn't it?"

"Were you born in France?"

Bill laughed. "Good lord, no. My father was career navy; ended up at the Pentagon."

"My father was in the military, too. An army surgeon."

Bill looked surprised but pleased. "I didn't know that." He took a small sip of wine. "Anyway, I did two years at the Sorbonne, mostly to please my mother." He paused, remembering. "At the time I was considering a career in the diplomatic corps."

"Mostly to please your father?" Lucy teased.

"Afraid so." He fell silent as the waiter refilled her glass. "When my mother died," he resumed, "I went back home—well, I went to Harvard, actually. And I had an epiphany of sorts: I realized medicine was what I really wanted to do."

He leaned back against the cushioned seat and looked out over the well-heeled crowd that filled the expensive restaurant. "I lead a double life, Lucy. It's true," he insisted, smiling at her startled expression. "I live in the world of missions and homeless shelters, of third-world people struggling against the legacy of colonial powers, of illness and poverty. . . . But this is my world, too." He gestured at the scene before them. "Money and power and success. These are the people who pay the bills. I get my funding from this world. I draw power and support from it. And frankly," he concluded, turning to smile boyishly at Lucy, "I enjoy it."

"Who wouldn't?" Lucy replied automatically. Where was he going with this?

"What I mean is, it's important to be pragmatic." He tasted the red wine and nodded to the sommelier. "I've always been something of a left-wing revolutionary, Lucy. I've always supported the underdog. I'm probably the only person in this room who ever sent money to the Black Panthers." He chuckled. "But people are so very black-and-white in their thinking. In many people's eyes, enjoying myself with a beautiful woman in an expensive restaurant makes me a traitor to the cause, no matter how much I support it with money and personal commitment. Yet this is where the money and power for social change comes from, not the back alleys of the poor and victimized."

"I didn't realize you were a political activist, along with everything else," Lucy said, somewhat at a loss as to how to react to this sudden dialectic.

"But what else would you call what we do, if not political activism? Caring for the underdog is a political statement."

"I think it's more a social responsibility," Lucy replied lightly. "Surely you can work at a homeless shelter or vaccinate children in the slums of India and still vote Republican."

Miller shrugged. "The point I was trying to make is that the achievement of the goal is what's important. Attitude without action is worthless." He tore off a piece of warm bread and ate it. "I like you, Lucy. You're action-oriented, you're courageous, you're smart. I know about your work in Peru, of course. I've been hearing excellent things about you from colleagues in the medical community."

"You've been checking up on me?" Lucy found she was more amused than annoyed.

"Oh, that phrase has such an unfortunate connotation." Their Caesar salads arrived, and Lucy ate a forkful and realized she was hungry. "Of course, we checked your references fully before the IMA accepted you as a volunteer. But now it's even more important."

Lucy frowned. "I don't care for mysteries, Bill," she said. "Why don't you tell me what's going on?"

"Your directness is one of the things I like best about you. But I'm not going to tell you until dessert. It's good news, I promise." He smiled conspiratorially and attacked his salad. "Meanwhile," he said between forkfuls, "why don't you tell me how things are going at the lab?"

Lucy hesitated—either Carl hadn't told Bill about the incident, or Miller considered it unimportant. In either case, Lucy decided, he ought to hear about it from her. "How well do you know Carl Anders?" she asked him.

"Carl? Been with me for years. Tops in his field, absolutely dedicated. Not the easiest person to get along with, but completely reliable." He looked sideways at her. "You guys had a run-in of some kind, I understand."

"Yes. As Carl probably told you, I was scanning through his data lists." Bill nodded. "I was looking for his work on an RNA clone. I probably should have asked him for the file, but the rest of us trade information through the network all the time. . . . Anyway, he went ballistic, but that's not the point." She reached for her wineglass, then changed her mind and drank some water. "I found some files marked 'sangre negra.' One had a date of two years ago. Carl acted really funny about it, and the next day, the files had disappeared."

"And?" Bill leaned back, an expression of casual interest on his face.

"Sangre negra is peruvia. How could Carl have information about peruvia that's two years old?"

Bill smiled and shook his head. "That's not peruvia." The salad plates were cleared and the lamb arrived. "Carl has permission to pursue his personal research projects at the lab—that's always been part of my deal with him—and he keeps his private data in the computer."

"But sangre negra—"

"Let me finish, Lucy. I had a long talk with Carl, when he came to complain that you'd been trying to access what he termed 'classified information.' His term, not mine."

"But why should important research information be kept secret? I'm working on peruvia, too."

"I just told you," Bill said impatiently. "The sangre negra files you found have nothing to do with peruvia. How's your lamb?"

"Delicious."

"You haven't even tasted it. Go on. You eat, I'll explain." He waited until she picked up her cutlery, then continued. "When Carl came to me, ballistic, as you put it, I went into the whole matter thoroughly. It seems that some years ago, Carl did a study of a small localized illness in rural Mexico. The people there called it sangre negra."

"And now sangre negra has spread to Peru? My God, that's—"

"No, Lucy. The Mexican 'sangre negra' turned out to be a hantavirus, a very close relative of the Sin Nombre hantivirus that broke out in Four Corners back in 1993. Remember?"

"Yes. The vector was a deer mouse." Lucy ate a piece of roast potato. "Still, doesn't it seem a little odd that the name the local Mexicans gave the Sin Nombre lookalike would be the same as the one the local Peruvians gave peruvia?"

Bill shrugged. "Not really," he said, turning his attention to his plate. "Both the Mexicans and the Peruvians were merely describing a symptom. Hantaviruses produce symptoms similar to filoviruses. Hell, you know that; it's your field."

"But why would those sangre negra files be in Carl's peruvia folder?"

"Who knows? Maybe he was doing some cross-referencing, comparing genome sequences or something."

"Then why did they suddenly disappear?"

"Hell, they were his private files, Lucy," Bill replied testily. "He could move them wherever he wanted to." He looked around for the wine waiter to refill their glasses. "Look, he's assured me the files have nothing to do with peruvia, and that's good enough for me." He gave Lucy a hard look that said "and it should be good enough for you, too."

"Has he shown them to you?"

"I haven't asked him to." Bill frowned.

"Maybe you should."

He sighed. "Don't go looking for mysteries where none exist, Lucy. We all have better things to do." He put down his fork and reached over to touch her hand.

"I know these past few months have been a terrible strain on you. Jean-Pierre's death hit you hard—his suicide, his involvement in narcotics. It's natural for you to be a little . . . emotional in your interpretation of events—"

"Emotional? I'm a physician, a professional scientist." Lucy's eyes flashed. "Don't treat me like some lovesick teenager, Bill. I saw what I saw, and I drew a perfectly reasonable conclusion."

"Yes, of course," he said soothingly.

"And don't patronize me."

A beat. "I'm sorry. It's just . . . I hurt for you, Lucy."

"Well, don't."

"I'd like to help you put it all behind you."

Lucy froze; was he making a pass at her? His eyes locked on hers, and she thought, oh, shit, and looked away, reaching for her wineglass. "I can see why you love this restaurant," she said. "The food is excellent."

Bill smiled a sad little smile of understanding. "I saw you with Rick Hollander at the Christmas party, but I wasn't sure . . . You've been seeing each other?" Lucy nodded. "I'm happy for you. Uh, Lucy? About Jean-Pierre. Alicia tells me you called her about a meeting we had scheduled." He paused. "I thought you'd dropped that whole business."

"I have, more or less. It's just that I remembered Jean mentioning a meeting with you, and I thought I'd follow it up. One last lead."

"Well, as Alicia told you, the meeting never happened. He died the day before."

"Yes. Did he tell you what he wanted to talk about?"

Bill frowned, thinking. "He didn't arrange the meeting with me directly. He called Alicia and asked to be put on my calendar."

"And she didn't ask him why?"

"No. People come and talk to me all the time." His tone was amused. "Do you think he wanted to sell me some drugs? Sorry," he added quickly, seeing her face. "That was uncalled for."

He wanted to sell you something all right, Lucy thought grimly, but it wasn't drugs. "Never mind. It's not important." Telling Bill about Jean's art smuggling would only add weight to his conviction that Jean was smuggling drugs, too.

The waiter approached with dessert menus. "You must try the apple flan," Bill said as Lucy took the card. "Or the hazelnut vacherin." A beat. "So you're still trying to clear his name?"

"No," she said, studying the list of sweets. "I've decided to take your advice. I'm still not convinced he put the heroin in his suitcase, but whoever did— well, it's just too dangerous to pursue."

"Good decision."

They ordered dessert and coffee, and Lucy, attempting to lighten the conversation, told him again how much she'd enjoyed the Christmas party. "And your art collection," she added. "So many beautiful things."

"Ah, my great indulgence." Bill beamed at her. "I could tell you that it's my way of preserving the culture of indigenous people, many of whom have been colonized out of existence. And that would be the truth. But"—he smiled conspiratorially—"not the whole truth. The fact is, I'm a fanatic about the stuff. That's what real collecting is about, you know: the fanatical desire to possess something of beauty."

"You don't look like a fanatic." Lucy smiled.

"It's my only failing." He smiled disarmingly and signaled the waiter to refill her wineglass, but Lucy shook her head.

"I have early rounds tomorrow."

"Yes, and speaking of work . . ." Bill stirred sugar

into his coffee, sipped it, set it down. "I'm thinking of offering you a job."

"I *have* a job." Lucy turned to look at him.

"I can offer you a better one, starting in June when your contract with the hospital is up for renewal. How does President of IMA Medical Services sound?"

"Chuck Bennington's job?" Lucy frowned.

"He's being moved abroad." Bill paused. "Think about it. Travel, hands-on medicine, a job with full-time social importance. And a fifty-percent pay raise over what you're making now. How about it?"

"I don't know, Bill," she said slowly. "I'm pretty happy doing what I'm doing."

He looked nonplussed. "It's a great opportunity."

"I'm sure it is."

"Most people with your social conscience would jump at it."

"Let's not make this into a sociopolitical issue," she said lightly. "There's a lot to consider."

"Well, frankly, it *is* a sociopolitical issue," Bill replied. "That's the whole point. I thought you understood." He sipped his coffee. "I thought you agreed with my theory of political activism."

"I believe in taking positive action to combat social ills," Lucy said slowly, "but I'm not real big on political theory. And I certainly don't want to make career decisions that way."

Bill was silent for a moment. "Then think about it in terms of a career move. I promise you, it's a good one."

"I'll think about it, Bill. That's all I can say right now."

"Fair enough. And whatever you decide, I know you'll never stop working for social justice. You're as committed to the underdogs of this world as I am." He beamed at her. Lucy frowned. All this talk of political activism was making her feel distinctly uncomfortable. "I can see that such praise embarrasses you," he continued. "Your modesty is part of your charm."

Jesus, she thought; he's laying it on a bit thick. "You give me far too much credit," she told him firmly. "I'm a doctor, not a social reformer."

"And an excellent one, so I'm told. I really want you on our team, Lucy."

"I'll think about it," she repeated. No way would she trade her current position, with its balance of hands-on medicine and lab research, for an administrative sinecure. Still, she should at least acknowledge his generosity in making the offer. "Thank you for your, er, confidence in me."

"I have every confidence in you, Lucy," he said heartily. "Despite what Carl Anders says."

Chapter Twelve

The sleek black car drove slowly along the quay, heat waves shimmering off its hood. The scents of tropical foliage and saltwater floated on the air, but the passenger, insulated behind tinted windows and air conditioning, was oblivious to them. The car rolled past an assortment of million dollar vessels, all sporting satellite dishes, and one with a helicopter perched on its upper deck. A playful breeze tousled the heads of the royal palms lining the marina and sent a chorus of wavelets dancing along the surface of the aquamarine sea.

"There it is, sir," the driver announced through the intercom. "That's the *Cristobel.*"

The car slowed, then stopped in front of a broad teak walkway leading up to a large white wedding cake of a ship, no helicopter garnishing its upper deck but with plenty of room for one. A uniformed steward rushed forward to open the passenger door. "Welcome, Dr. Miller," he said deferentially, his English softly accented. Greek, Bill thought. Or Cypriot. "Mr. Kiamos awaits you in the salon."

Bill followed the young man up the walkway and onto the ship. It was not the first time he'd been invited onto the vessels of the rich and occasionally famous, but the *Cristobel* was beyond his experience. As was her owner's pocketbook.

Alexander Kiamos rose with difficulty from the gold

brocade sofa. Short, bald, and impressively fat, with a
handsome, rather trivial face, he bore a faint resemblance to the late Aga Khan. But despite his fondness
for florid decor and ornamental women, one of whom
was currently curled beside him, there was nothing
trivial about Kiamos's mind or his fortune. He embraced Bill warmly, then waved his hand at a servant
who immediately dispensed preprandial drinks.

The salon was icy with air conditioning, and Bill
wondered why the older man spent half the year in
the tropics. But of course it was where the action was,
if the action you craved was high-stakes gambling and
screwing around with the dim descendants of deposed
royalty. Kiamos himself was the full stop at the end
of a deposed royal line, and had spent serious amounts
of money over the years on misguided schemes to res-
urrect and seat himself on one throne or another.

But it would be wrong to write him off as simply
another royal wannabe, Bill knew. Kiamos had his
blind spot, but he was a brilliant financier. From this
floating control center, he managed a pool of funds
with more than a billion dollars in assets, built via a
strategy of risky, highly leveraged speculations. He
was also, surprisingly, a philanthropist, contributing
many millions to such noble causes as educational programs in Central Europe and the promotion of democ-
racy in Africa.

Financial genius that he was, Kiamos made sure he
got exactly the sort of return on his investments that
he desired. Supported by his enormous, carefully
placed gifts, he'd begun to make a reputation for himself as a minister without portfolio, befriending, sup-
porting, and advising powerful heads of state with
keen political savvy.

The two men had been introduced by a mutual acquaintance and had taken to each other, each recog-
nizing in the other a pragmatism and an unemotional

appraisal of the world's realities that were as unique as they were refreshing.

"People think of me as selfless," Kiamos had told Bill during their first meeting. "But I'm really quite self-centered."

Bill, understanding precisely what the man was saying, had nodded, smiled, and filed away the illuminating remark for future contemplation.

Now he was ready to put it to use.

The conversation was desultory as the threesome moved from cocktails through a superb dinner, served in the walnut-paneled dining room. Afterwards, Kiamos's nubile companion was sent below, and the two men retired to the overly decorated salon. There they sat over cigars and brandy, discussing the proposal that had brought Bill to Curaçao.

". . . not just a humanitarian gesture," Bill was saying, "but a self-serving one, as well. For the good of all, and for the good of oneself. An unbeatable combination for realists like ourselves."

Kiamos was smiling and nodding, his small eyes glittering in the soft light of the lamps that had been turned on as the sun dropped into the sea. "I am intrigued," he said, drawing on his Macanudo. He exhaled luxuriously and reached for his brandy. "But such a large donation . . . I must be sure I am getting value for my money. Political value, if you understand me."

"Of course. That's why I came to you, sir. It's good for you, and it's good for the work of the IMA."

Kiamos studied the doctor over the rim of his crystal snifter. "I like you, Dr. Miller. But you puzzle me. I ask myself, does he really believe all those fine words he speaks about working for the common good, for the good of his fellow man?"

"Of course I do," Bill said stoutly. "Don't you?"

Kiamos stared at Bill for a moment, then laughed

heartily. "Oh, yes, assuredly I do. Oh, yes. I love the poor, the sick, the downtrodden. Just keep them far away from me." Still chuckling, he levered himself erect. "No, stay and finish your brandy, doctor." He waved Bill back into his seat. "I have arranged some after-dinner entertainment. You will pardon me if I do not join you; the Japanese exchange opens in twenty minutes." He traversed the room, moving lightly for such a large man, then turned back. "You will have your answer before you leave," he promised. Music began to pulse from hidden speakers. "Ah, the entertainment has arrived. I am certain you will enjoy it." He slipped from the salon.

Moments later, a scantily clothed woman appeared. She came toward him, smiling suggestively as she gently pressed him back against the cushions. Bill frowned as he watched the stripper undulate above him. Money, not sex, was what he'd come here for, he thought impatiently. All he wanted was a quick answer from Kiamos and a night flight back to New York. The woman leaned down and placed his hands on her pendulous breasts, then squatted lower, brushing his face with the filmy scarf that barely covered her crotch. She was plump and swarthy, not a type he usually found attractive, but he felt himself coming erect in spite of himself. The woman whipped the scarf away, and performed some gyrations of a particularly lewd nature that left her spread out in front of him like a plate of hors d'oeuvres. She held out her arms to him, but despite his physical reaction to her nudity, Bill felt no desire to participate.

The woman hesitated, then rose, swiftly collected her garments, and left the salon. The music died. Bill drank off the last of his brandy. Maybe now Kiamos would get on with it. He set the glass on a side table and gazed out of the window toward the ocean, its dark surface alive with green phosphorescence.

A faint sound turned him back around. A different woman stood before him—a girl, really, and one much more to his taste. She was completely naked, her pale skin untouched by the sun. He'd never seen a woman of such total whiteness; even her small patch of pubic hair was a silvery-white, matching the mane that hung nearly to the rosy tips of her breasts. She held out her hand, smiling faintly, her eyes the color of seaglass.

So what if Carl Anders dislikes me? Lucy thought as she stowed her clothes in the staging room locker. I'm not crazy about him, either, but that doesn't mean we can't have a reasonable working relationship. It's not as though we actually work on the same project. Besides, Bill Miller had thought so little of Carl's criticism of her, he'd gone ahead and offered her a plum of a job. Not that she would seriously consider taking such a job, but it certainly was a vote of confidence from the man who would actually be paying her salary.

Still, Carl's attitude didn't make for a healthy working environment. Perhaps she should talk to him, clear the air.

She checked her spacesuit carefully for tears in the fabric, then suited up as usual and went through the various airlocks leading into Biosafety Level Four, plugging and unplugging and replugging her air hose. It still amazed her that the IMA had been able to construct such an expensive and intricate containment center with private money.

Quiet today, she thought as she entered the empty lab. There were usually two or three other scientists seated at the biosafety cabinets, large work areas closed on five of their six sides in order to contain any aerosols created in the experimentation process. Today she saw no one.

From a storage cabinet she selected a twenty-four-well panel: a shallow lucite square about twelve inches on a side, with twenty-four small, circular depressions built into it. Then she went to the large, clear-fronted, commercial refrigerator and took out a tube of Vero clone E-6 cells, the culture medium her tests had shown worked the best for growing both fresh viral isolates and laboratory-passaged strains of the peruvia virus. Vero was made from the kidney cells of African green monkeys, and although peruvia was South American in origin, it seemed to prefer this medium. She took the panel and the Vero to her work area, then returned to the refrigerated storage unit and gently removed a sealed tube of cold pink liquid: peruvia. The spacesuit's double-glove system destroyed contact sensitivity, so slow, careful movements were vital. Inside her helmet, the sound of her breathing seemed to grow louder as she stood for a moment, grasping the tube of lethal pathogen and centering herself. She carried the peruvia isolate carefully across to her workstation and set it into the plastic test tube holder. Then she took up a pipette and began filling the wells with Vero.

Behind her, a tall spacesuited figure came through the Level Four airlock and stood watching her.

She finished filling the wells, then began the delicate task of infecting each well of culture medium with the peruvia isolate. She worked slowly, carefully. During this process, the virus was out in the open: in the syringe she was using to inject the pathogen into each well, and in the circles of cell culture she'd already infected with it.

Behind her, the figure moved closer, the shuffle of his boots against the tile floor blanketed by the roar of air in her helmet. He was behind her chair now, eyes wide, shouting into his helmet. But Lucy heard nothing. Suddenly his arms shot out, one hand grabbing for her air hose coupling, the other knocking against the arm that held the syringe of peruvia as he shoved her sideways in her chair.

Lucy screamed silently as she fell sideways, seeing the tip of the syringe, wet and deadly, flash across the surface of her glove. God, don't let it be torn, she prayed, but she could see the tiny tear line the needle had opened. What was happening? The syringe fell from her fingers as she pulled herself erect, scrabbling for the sealing tape that hung from her suit, looking around for her attacker, thinking, If it didn't get past the outer glove, I'm okay. As long as it didn't get past the outer glove.

Suddenly she couldn't breathe, and saw the air hose loose in his hands and thought, I've got to get out of here. She backed away from the silently shouting figure coming toward her again, his face clear beneath his faceplate as she gasped for breath: Carl Anders.

She ran through the lab toward the decon airlock and slammed through it with Anders close behind. The stale air of her helmet made her gag, but there was no time to plug her suit into one of the dangling hoses, not yet. She grabbed the metal emergency lock-bar and tugged it down into place. The movement used up the last of her oxygen reserves, and she felt herself starting to black out as she reached for a hose and fumbled with the coupling. She leaned against the airlock wall, greedily sucking in the cool, dry air that flooded into her helmet, then reached over and punched the button that activated the decontamination spray.

Standing under the chemical shower, she decon'd the ripped outer glove, praying the inner glove was still intact. When the seven minute decon cycle was over, she peeled off both gloves and inspected the thin inner one carefully. It looked okay, but that didn't mean much. She inflated it, holding it under the sidestream of water used for rinsing off their suits prior to deconing them.

Then she turned off the water and studied the glove carefully for leaks. Nothing. No holes. She sagged against the steel wall, weak with relief, then pulled back the emergency lock and went quickly out by the opposite door, slamming it shut behind her, hoping that Carl wouldn't dare to break decon by following her. In the locker room, she tore off her suit and threw on her clothes, then ran out into the main lab. In the hallway outside the entrance to the Level Four lab, she stopped and leaned against the wall as the enormity of what had happened hit her. He'd tried to inject her with peruvia. And he'd come damn close to succeeding.

Several lab workers looked up questioningly as Lucy hurried across the open-bench work area to her lab, but she just kept moving. She had her coat on and was reaching for her purse when her beeper went off. Shit. She checked the recall number: one of the intensive care units. She kicked the door shut and began dialing furiously, looking at her watch. Four and a half minutes until Anders was out of decon. After several tries, the page operator put her through to the attending. She barked medication changes and a promise to stop by on her way uptown.

Less than two minutes left . . . She banged down the phone and headed out to the elevator.

One minute to go . . . Come on, come on. Lucy jabbed at the elevator call button. Get me out of here.

The elevator arrived, its door sliding open. Anders would be out now, and looking for her. She hurried inside and punched the Close button, watching in relief as the door began to slide closed. Then a hand was thrust inside and the door sprang back, revealing a furious Carl Anders.

"You stupid, stupid woman," he shouted, his hand pressing against the door, holding it open. "How did you ever get Level Four clearance?"

"You tried to kill me. Get out of my way." Lucy forced her way past him into the reception area, but he grabbed her shoulders and spun her back around to face him.

"What the hell are you talking about?" he shouted. "I saved your fucking life."

"You came up behind me and knocked me over and stuck the peruvia syringe into my glove."

"I was reaching for your damn air coupling. The hose was ripping it out of your suit." Carl snorted derisively. "You stuck *yourself*, doctor."

"The suit coupling was separating?" Lucy stared at Carl in disbelief. "Why didn't you say something, let me know you were standing there instead of creeping up behind me?"

"I did, dammit. I shouted to you over and over, but you ignored me."

"I didn't hear you."

"Your helmet receiver must be faulty. Or my mike." They were both calmer now. "The syringe actually tore your glove?"

"Just the outer one. The inner one was good." She went to a nearby chair and collapsed into it.

Anders followed. "Didn't you check your suit before you put it on?" he demanded, standing over her.

"Of course I did," Lucy shot back. But there could have been a hidden tear on the underside, a weak spot, she thought. Attaching and unattaching the hoses on my way in could have weakened it further . . .

"If you don't believe what I'm telling you, check the damn suit yourself. Go on. See for yourself." Carl stomped off toward the hall, then turned back. "You actually thought I was trying to kill you?"

Lucy felt herself flushing; the idea seemed ridiculous, now. "I don't know . . . I didn't think anyone else was in there, and then suddenly you were behind me, knocking me sideways, grabbing my—"

"I was trying to get at the coupling."

"I didn't know," Lucy said quietly. "I thought you—after what you said to Bill about me, I guess I thought—"

"—that I would commit murder in order to get you out of my lab? Hardly." He glowered at her. "I don't like you, Dr. Nash. I don't think women belong in this kind of work, and to my mind, what happened in there just now is proof of it. Well, I've made my objections known, and I've been overruled." He paused. "But I'm a professional scientist, Lucy. I am not a murderer."

"I'm sorry I misunderstood what you were doing."

"Apology accepted." He stood there for a moment, then came over to her chair. He leaned down so that their faces were level. "On the other hand," he told her softly, his eyes boring into hers, "if I *were* trying to stab you with a syringe loaded with lethal pathogen, I wouldn't miss."

Bill thought he would explode as the girl with the seaglass eyes ran her tongue along the inside of his upper thigh. She'd been teasing him like this for hours, or so it seemed, bringing him nearly to the point of climax, then back down again with no release. His body was slick with sweat, his breathing labored. He lunged for her, ready to finish things, but she rolled away, laughing. Hell with this, he thought, and threw himself on top of her, parting her legs roughly and ramming himself inside. She cried out, but he barely heard her, thrusting deeper—what the hell was that? He stopped, heart racing, then slowly withdrew. The girl's eyes were laughing. He reached inside her and withdrew a small, folded paper.

The girl rolled him over on his back and mounted him, sucking him deep inside her body, holding him tight as a fist, her hips moving like pistons. "Read it," she breathed, riding him. He gasped, thrusting upward as he unfolded the soggy document with trembling fingers, his unfocused eyes straining. She bore down on him and he cried out and emptied himself into her, realizing at the moment of climax that he was holding a check, signed by Kiamos, for thirty million dollars.

Some twenty minutes later, the damp check safely locked inside his attaché case, Bill reboarded his waiting Lear. A faint smile hovered on his lips as he collapsed heavily into a plush leather seat. The small jet ran down the runway and leapt into the warm, moist air.

"A movie, sir? Some music? Refreshments?"

"I think I'll try and catch a few winks," he told the steward. "Wait; I'll have something to drink first. Perrier and lime, please. Make it a tall one."

"Right away, Dr. Miller. And shall I dim the lights, or do you want to read for a while? May I bring you a magazine?"

"No, I doubt I could concentrate at the moment." He smiled up at the steward. "Lower the lights, by all means."

The steward went aft to the small, well-equipped galley and Bill gazed idly out at the night sky through which they were climbing. As the plane banked to the right, a necklace of islands appeared in the window, their lights like diamonds against the black breast of the sea.

The steward appeared at his elbow, holding a tray. He set a filled, lime-rimmed glass on the low table, then added reinforcements in the form of a small ice bucket, a plate of lime slices, and a large green bottle. Bill gulped half of his drink immediately and topped it up.

"Fund-raising must be thirsty work," the steward observed, smiling.

Bill took another long pull at his drink, then settled back into the wide, soft seat. "You have no idea," he told the steward, glancing over at him through half-closed eyes. "You really have no idea."

Chapter Thirteen

"I won't let him scare me away from the lab," Lucy repeated. "I just won't."

"I don't know, Luce," Rick said doubtfully. "The man's unstable. Who knows what he's capable of?"

"I checked my suit," she said impatiently. "He was right. The coupling *was* loose. Another tug and it would have separated."

"Well, maybe he was the one who loosened it."

"Then why would he go into the lab after me? No, if he'd done it, he'd have stayed far away and let the damn thing come apart when I was alone. An accident. They happen."

"How about what he said to you afterward? You don't consider that a threat?"

"I did at the time, but now . . . I think he was simply trying to scare me. He's quite open about wanting me out, and considering the way he feels about women, intimidation would be his weapon of choice. Well, screw him." Lucy slammed her coffee mug down on the work surface. "I'm staying."

"Hey, I'm trying to save the world, here," Rick protested, mopping coffee from a pile of printouts. "You're not going back in there today, are you?"

"Not hardly." She picked up a coffee-stained paper. "Sorry about this."

"A duplicate printout. No harm done."

She scanned the page idly. "You still working on the bacteriophage project?"

"Yeah, but Anders asked me to do some protein analyses for him."

"This the chromatography study?"

"It *was*." He took the soggy paper from her hand. "Any chance of seeing you this evening?"

"I need to stop at the hospital on the way home, and I don't know how long it'll take. Can I call you later?"

"Sure."

Lucy started out, then stopped in the doorway. "Hey, we have a visitor. Bill's here."

"Miller?"

"Yes, he just went into Carl's office. I bet he's getting an earful."

"Hell with that." Rick went and put a supportive arm around her shoulders. "Everyone knows Carl broke protocol by coming up behind you the way he did. When he realized you couldn't hear him, he should have gone around in front of you, gotten your attention, pointed to the coupling. What he did was incredibly dangerous. We all know that what happened in there was his fault, not yours."

"Thanks." She kissed him lightly on the cheek. "Okay, I'm off."

". . . damn dangerous . . . told you women were too . . ." Lucy paused outside Carl's office, her coat over her shoulders. Carl was trashing her, of course. She looked around; the corridor was empty. She went up to the closed door and listened.

". . . been through all that," she heard Bill murmur. ". . . want to know about . . ." He spoke more quietly than Carl had done, and Anders's reply was equally moderated.

". . . simian hemorrhagic . . . fatal . . . not the same as . . . unless . . ."

Was Anders doing vivo studies on SHF in that locked animal lab? If only she could make out more than one word in ten. . . .

". . . new strain?" she heard Bill ask.

". . . completely effective," Anders replied, "but only *in vivo* testing will—"

"They say eavesdroppers never hear well of themselves." Lucy swung around. Rick stood behind her, papers in hand. "Carl wanted these molecular weights before five. A timely interruption might be in order." He gave her a conspiratorial wink.

"It doesn't matter—" Lucy began, but Rick was already knocking on the door. The murmuring within ceased. The door opened.

"Yes?" Anders scowled at Lucy, then at Rick. "What is it?"

"I have those molecular weights you wanted," Rick said. "Is this a bad time?"

Bill Miller appeared in the doorway. "We can finish this later," he told Carl. His eyes went to Lucy and he smiled. "Do you have a minute for me?"

"I'm on my way to the hospital, but—sure, Bill."

Rick went into Carl's office and Bill followed Lucy back to her lab, saying, "I won't keep you long."

Lucy seated herself in her work chair and Bill perched on a nearby stool. "I was horrified when Carl told me what happened today on Level Four," he said, his face serious. "I've told Carl he was completely wrong in the way he handled the situation. Dangerously wrong. We all owe you an enormous apology." He paused. "Apology hardly seems enough, considering what happened in there."

"I was partly at fault," Lucy said. "I should have checked the suit more carefully."

"That's very generous of you," Bill said, "since you could probably slap the IMA with a lawsuit. And win." He smiled, but his eyes were worried.

"I'm not going to sue you, Bill."

"Glad to hear it. The IMA's taken enough hits lately, what with Jean-Pierre . . ." He stood. "You're a real team player, Lucy. I appreciate that. And I hope this incident won't sour you on the job offer."

"It won't make a difference one way or the other," Lucy assured him truthfully.

The level of background noise had been rising during their conversation, and now Carl's voice rang out through the open work area. ". . . can't possibly be right, Hollander. Not anywhere near the estimates. How in hell—"

"What's going on out there?" Bill asked, following Lucy into the workbench area. Researchers were casting surreptitious looks toward Carl's office, embarrassed for Rick, yet curious.

"You must have set the field wrong," Anders was insisting loudly. He burst from his office, Rick in tow. "Show me how you set the damn chromatograph." They disappeared into Rick's lab, and for a moment there was silence. Then Carl's angry voice burst out again. "The current was too strong. I knew it. Let me review Chromatography 101 for you, Hollander. You put the protein gel suspension in the chromatograph, and you turn on the electronic field. It's polarized, right? So the proteins migrate from one pole to the other. They migrate at different rates, which is why we're able to separate one from another, and measure them. We okay so far?"

Lucy and Bill looked at each other in growing discomfiture.

"Now, if the electronic field is too strong," Anders boomed, "the proteins migrate too fast. So when you go to cut the gel, you end up cutting the proteins in the wrong damn place and the weights are all wrong."

They couldn't hear Rick's murmured response, but Carl's answer was loud and clear. "Simple mistake?

An undergraduate makes a simple mistake like this, not a Stanford scientist with a reputation like yours. Okay, okay, so you got the setting wrong. The point is, you should have seen that the molecular weights you got didn't fit the estimated criteria. You should have done it again. Do it again, *now*."

"You're going to find yourself with an empty lab if this keeps up," Lucy told Bill as they watched Carl storm back into his own office. "You can't keep people like Rick if you treat them like that."

"I know," Bill sighed. "I'll talk to Carl."

"You might have a word with Rick, too. And now I really have to get going."

He watched her disappear around the corner of the hallway, then went and knocked on Rick's open door. "I seem to be spending most of today apologizing for Carl Anders," he said.

Rick looked up, his face flushed and angry. "I came here because I believed in the work of the IMA," he said, "and because I was excited about the chance to do independent work in a state-of-the-art environment. But frankly, it's not worth it."

"Rick—"

"I didn't come here to do grunt work," he continued with some heat. "I'm not some little research assistant Carl can push around. I'm a damn good molecular biologist. And I don't need this shit."

"Carl's got a problem," Bill said softly. "He needs psychological help, and I'll see that he gets it." He paused. "Why don't you leave all that for now"— he gestured at the papers scattered across the work counter—"and let's go get some coffee, or a beer. I want to talk to you."

Rick hesitated. Had Miller found out about his fling with Renée?

"Come on, grab your coat," Bill said. "My car's outside."

*   *   *

"Carl was lucky you didn't sock him one," he told Rick as they settled themselves at the bar of the White Horse Tavern. "*I* would have." He waved the barman over, and they ordered beers. "You know this place?"

Rick shook his head. "I'm a Californian, remember?"

"It's an institution; at least, it was. A lot of us spent a fair part of our youth here in this bar, arguing about what was wrong with society and how to fix it." He sipped his beer, remembering. "We were going to change the world." He sighed. "Today, those kids are advertising executives, corporate attorneys. . . . Youthful ideals don't last, I'm afraid."

"Oh, I don't know," Rick said. "You seem to be doing your part."

Bill smiled sadly. "I suppose so. Although it doesn't seem like nearly enough." He reached down the bar for a bowl of pretzels. "You say you believe in the mission of the IMA," he said, passing the bowl to Rick. "Does that mean you've hung on to a little of your own youthful idealism?"

"I don't know that I'd put it quite like that," Rick answered. "The IMA fills an important need, and it makes me feel good to be a part of it. But if I hadn't been promised a chance to do my own research in a state-of-the-art lab, I wouldn't have come."

"Enlightened self-interest, eh?" Bill smiled. "I approve of that." He drank some beer. "I wanted to talk to you, away from the lab, because what I have to say is somewhat . . . delicate."

Shit, Rick thought, studying his glass. He *does* know about Renée.

"It's about Lucy." Rick turned to stare at Bill in surprise. "I understand you two have become . . . close. And I hope you won't misinterpret what I'm going to say." He paused. "You know about her affair with Jean-Pierre? All that?" Rick nodded. "Well, I'm very uncomfortable with her continuing to investigate his death."

"Why?" Rick asked. "I'd have thought it was in the interest of the IMA to clear his name."

"Sure, if it *is* cleared."

"You don't think it will be?"

"Frankly, no. And I've told Lucy so. I've also told her it could be dangerous for her. We're talking drug running."

"You seem pretty sure he's guilty."

"Who knows what he was involved in?" Bill said tiredly. "The point is, Didier's arrest and suicide has had a serious impact on contributions to the IMA. And without money, the IMA can't function. Fortunately the public has a short memory, and contributions are on the rise again. But if Lucy does manage to clear his name, she's going to want to announce it, make a big thing of it, which will bring the whole story back into the news again. And you know how people are. They won't really take in the fact that he was cleared, or else they won't believe it. They'll just think: 'IMA, dope smuggling.'" He shook his head, sighed deeply and reached for a pretzel. "And that's the *up* side. If, on the other hand, she finds evidence of his guilt, and *that* story gets out—hell, the man *was* carrying heroin. . . . You see what I'm driving at?"

"You want me to use whatever influence I have with Lucy to make her stop?" The idea seemed to amuse Rick. "Forget it." He broke a pretzel in half. "Besides, she's only ever mentioned it once. Are you sure she's still pursuing it?"

"She *did* tell me she was dropping it at one point, but it seems she hasn't." Bill drank some beer. "I just want you to keep your eyes and ears open. The drug arrest was bad for us, really bad. We'll need to do some serious damage control if any other unsavory information comes to light. All I'm asking is that you keep me in the picture; make sure I know whatever she knows. For the good of the IMA. Do you think you could do that?"

"No, I don't think I could."

"You said that working for the IMA made you feel good."

"Working, not spying."

"Oh, let's not get overly dramatic. I'm simply asking you to help me protect the IMA's reputation, and its fund-raising ability. All I want is a little advance notice about anything that could turn around and bite us in the ass." He clapped Rick on the shoulder. "Work with me on this, Rick. Carl can't stay in his present position much longer. And I know how to reward loyalty."

"I don't want to hurt Lucy."

"Hurt her? Just the opposite. I don't think she has any idea what she could be getting into. We can help protect her if the going gets rough."

"I suppose that makes sense," Rick said slowly. "She's got this female-macho thing; wants to brazen everything out on her own. I bet she didn't even tell you what Carl said to her. After he explained he'd been trying to save her life, that is."

"What did he say?" Bill frowned.

"Something like, 'If I'd wanted to kill you, I wouldn't have missed.'"

"Jesus." Bill's face registered his shock. "He really said that?"

"Afraid so. Uh, I'd rather you didn't mention it to Lucy. She'll know I told you."

"If you say so," Bill agreed reluctantly. "But I'm sure as hell going to talk to Carl about it." He hesitated. "What was Lucy's reaction?"

"She thinks Carl was just trying to scare her off. She refuses to let him, of course."

"Of course." Bill smiled. "Any woman who's comfortable in a Biosafety Level Four lab obviously doesn't scare easily. Which is precisely why you and I have to work together. To protect her from herself."

"Well, when you put it like that . . ."

"I knew I could count on you." Bill reached for his wallet and slapped some bills down on the bar. "Renée assures me you're dedicated to our work." Rick flushed, but Miller's expression was bland. "I'm rather fond of the countess myself," Bill said, "but there was never anything serious between us. Ah, Renée, such a free spirit. I hope you used a condom." He stood and retrieved his coat. "Stay and finish your beer. Soak up some atmosphere."

"Right."

"Oh, and you might consider ending whatever it is you're having with Renée, preferably by phone. You wouldn't want anything to come between you and Lucy. Especially now." He stood and retrieved his topcoat. "Keep me posted." At the door he turned back to give Rick a thumbs-up before disappearing into the gathering dusk.

Rick's face was grim as he drained his glass. "Get you anything else?" the barman asked.

Rick shook his head. "You have a phone I can use?"

"Back there. Next to the john."

The bar was starting to fill up. Rick made his way through the gathering crowd, reaching in his pocket for change. Situated between the men's room and the kitchen, the pay phone was a little public for his purpose. But the short hallway was empty at the moment, and the noise from the kitchen would cover his voice. In the next few minutes, he held two brief conversations. Neither of them was with Renée.

On the loading dock beneath the colorful King Banana sign, three men were loading a white truck bear-

ing the wholesaler's trademark illustration of a
dancing banana, a jeweled crown perched tipsily over
one anthropomorphic eye. Two others were carting
boxes of fruit out of the warehouse and stacking them
on the cement platform. No one looked up as Bill
Miller edged his way past the loading crew and over
to a battered door, where he rang the bell and was
promptly admitted. King Banana did good business,
and visits from jobbers were common, even at this
hour.

But having climbed the steep and dirty stairs, Bill
didn't stop at the frosted-glass door of the wholesaler's
office. Instead, he continued along the grimy corridor
to the men's room. Choosing the last of the three
empty stalls, he locked the door, then bent down and
counted five tiles in from the right-hand wall along
the bottom row. He pushed one side of the sixth tile
and it swiveled back to reveal an odd-shaped keyhole.
He inserted a key and twisted, and a section of tile
some four feet high and two feet across opened silently inward. He crouched and stepped through into
semidarkness, then reached back and flicked the lock
on the stall door. By the time the stall door had swung
open, the section of tile had locked seamlessly into
place again.

The hallway in which Bill found himself was narrow,
cold, and badly lit. He followed it around a right-angle
turn and up to a door set flush into the rough cin-
derblock wall. He inserted his key again and pushed.

Inside the small conference room, faces looked up
at the sound of the alarm. Slowly, a section of the far
wall swung outward and Bill entered, accompanied by
cold, stale air.

"Everybody here?" he asked. "Then let's get
started."

                    *   *   *.

Lucy poured herself a cup of old coffee and collapsed into a chair in the doctors' lounge. After half an hour with the attending and his AIDS re-admit, she'd left a message on Rick's answering machine saying it was going to be a long night. The coffee was disgusting, but she drank it anyway, needing its caffeine. God, she was tired.

I'm stretching myself too thin, she thought. If the IMA work were Level One, even Level Two . . . But the stress of Level Four was simply too great to add to her already full load. She gave up the coffee and deep-sixed the paper cup. No, it wasn't the stress of Level Four, she decided, as much as the stress of Carl Anders.

Why did he dislike her so much that he'd want to frighten her away? Okay, he didn't like women. But he was no youngster; surely he'd dealt with women scientists before. And Bill Miller was Carl's boss. Bill liked women, supported them. Was Bill aware of how pathological Carl's reactions were?

She thought back to her dinner with Bill and smiled. He was a real throwback to the sixties, she thought, a man who still fancied himself a sort of armchair revolutionary. A doctor who'd never lost his youthful commitment to healing the world, aiding the underdog. Concerned. Idealistic.

And perhaps just a little naive?

"Dr. Nash, to ICU Two North. Stat. Dr. Nash—"

Lucy rose quickly and headed out into the corridor.

How well did Bill Miller really know Carl Anders? she wondered as she ran for the stairs. To what degree did Carl actually share Bill's theories of social reform? And could there be some reason beyond the obvious that Carl Anders wanted her out of Level Four?

". . . six million dollars. And the Lewis Stanton Williams Foundation has approved a contribution of three million. But the big news is, Alexander Kiamos has given me a check for thirty million for our work." Bill smiled at the people assembled around the rough wooden table. "As you can see, the IMA has fully recovered from the, uh, problem of Dr. Didier's arrest."

"Not from where I sit." The speaker, a woman wearing a navy pea jacket, jeans, and Timberland boots, slid a financial printout across the table to him. "As you can see from the past three months' figures, my operation is still feeling the effects. My boss is concerned."

"Please reassure him. I'm sure the incident will soon be forgotten, and things will be as they were before."

"As long as that woman doctor of yours doesn't remind everybody."

"No risk of that, I assure you. She's being tightly monitored. And other steps are being taken, as well. Please inform your boss of that." The woman rose, and Bill stood, too. "Thank you for joining us today. Please give my respects to Mr. Tortoriello."

The woman nodded and went to the far wall, where she waited for Bill to work his magic with the hidden panel. When she was gone and the wall had swung back into place, Bill turned to the group around the table. "Now we can speak more freely," he said.

"You're sure *she* doesn't know?" inquired a portly, middle-aged man with thinning blond hair, his eyes flicking toward the hidden panel. "Or her, uh, boss?"

"Absolutely not," Bill answered. "Unless someone here has been careless." He eyed them sternly. "As you were, Carl." Carl began to protest angrily, but Bill cut him off with a wave of his hand.

"What's this?" the blond man asked, his eyes worried. "What happened?"

"Nothing that need concern you," Bill said quickly. "It's been dealt with. But it's an example of the need to maintain tight security in everything we do." He began collecting the various papers on the table in front of him, ignoring Carl, who was scowling across the table at him.

"Are you sure it was wise to involve Tortoriello?" asked a short, gray-haired man. "I mean, the results have been phenomenal . . . until Didier, of course. Still—"

Bill stopped, put his palms on the table, and leaned across toward the questioner. "The results are all that count, Oliver. Never forget that." He stood up, addressing his words to the meeting at large. "Working behind the scenes, my friends, we're performing a most important service: the creation of a new, a better world order. If we have to get our hands dirty doing it, so what?"

The blond man nodded enthusiastically. "It's the end that counts," he agreed. "The means are unimportant."

"Exactly. As every surgeon knows," Bill continued, stuffing papers into his leather attaché case, "sometimes you need to cut deep in order to save the patient. That is what I am prepared to do. That is what we must all be prepared to do." He snapped the case closed. "I believe we're finished here. You'll be called with the date of the next meeting."

He keyed the hidden wall panel open. "Carl? A word, please." He drew the scientist aside as the others filed from the room. "Ease up on Hollander. I don't want to lose him."

"He made a stupid mistake," Carl said impatiently.

"Dr. Nash, too," Bill continued, ignoring Carl's interjection. "I don't want to lose either of them. Understand?"

Carl shrugged. "You're the boss."

"That's right. Please don't forget it. You can go now." Carl departed, his face sullen.

When the wall was back in place and the room was empty, Bill went to a small closet. Donning the lab coat that hung ready, he transferred a small package from his attaché case to his pocket, then slung his topcoat around his shoulders.

Crossing the room again, he opened the wall panel and stepped into the catacomblike passageway, nervously fingering the vials in his pocket.

Chapter Fourteen

" ... So then the surgeon looks up. He says, 'There's a damn duck!' and he aims carefully and fires once, and the duck falls down dead. Then the internist looks up and says, 'Hmm, duck . . . rule out eagle, rule out sparrow . . .' "

Lucy smiled at Hank's retelling of the old "doctors on a duck hunt" joke. Although everyone around the banquet table must have heard it a thousand times, Hank's version, complete with gestures, was very entertaining.

"Suddenly the ER guy starts blasting away," Hank continued. " 'Boom! Boom! I got it, I got it! What the hell was it?' "

Lucy joined in the general laughter, enjoying herself. One of the nicest things about high-profile medical conferences like these, she thought, was the chance to socialize with others in the field of infectious diseases; to see people she'd lost contact with, and meet doctors whose names were more familiar to her than their faces.

Ten days had passed since her run-in with Carl. During that time, she'd made only one visit to the IMA Level Four lab, having had to cancel this week's session because of the conference. Although she'd approached Level Four with a certain amount of trepidation the previous Thursday, she'd soon lost herself in the work, proceeding without interference from a rather subdued Carl Anders. In fact, he seemed to go out of his way to avoid her, and treated her with formal respect when they were forced to converse. Rick had told her the lab chief had apologized to him for his outburst, and as she observed them together, chatting easily over some printouts, she thought Rick was too forgiving. But she managed to keep herself from saying so. She was only a volunteer, after all, with a medical career elsewhere. She could walk out any time she liked, but Rick had given up a good position in California to take this job with the IMA. It was different for him.

"I enjoyed your paper this afternoon," said the man on her right, a young doctor from Houston. "I don't do much AIDS work myself, but it helps to know what to look for."

"I'm glad it was useful," Lucy said, beaming. Her presentation that morning on manifestations of opportunistic infections in AIDS patients had been very well received, and the experience of speaking before such an august group had been exhilarating.

"So you're no longer at the CDC," said Barbara Coley, a virologist from Los Angeles. Though separated in age by some twelve years, the two women had hit it off at the previous year's conference and had exchanged several letters since. "How are you enjoying clinical work?"

"Very much," Lucy replied. The waiters began clearing away the remains of the baked chicken and asparagus.

"You don't miss the lab?"

"Actually, I'm doing some part-time work at the IMA's lab. International Medical Aid, the organization that sends volunteer medical people around the world," she added, seeing Barbara's baffled expression.

"I've heard of them," Barbara said, the light dawning. "Didn't they send a team to India for that cholera outbreak last year?"

"Before my time," Lucy replied. "But it sounds like them."

"So what kind of research are you doing?"

"I'm working with a new filovirus we found in Peru."

"But . . . I thought you'd left the CDC." Barbara looked at her questioningly.

"I did. The IMA has a small Biosafety Level Four containment lab."

"No kidding?" The older woman looked impressed. "They must do one helluva job of fund-raising."

Lucy smiled. "They do."

"So, they doing anything besides filovirus work?"

"Oh yes, they also have Level One and Two facilities. They're doing some bacteriophage work, and— actually, you may know one of our research associates. He's from California, too. Rick Hollander."

"The name sounds familiar. . . . Hey, you don't mean Richard Hollander. From Stanford?"

"Yes. You know him?"

"Mostly by reputation. I only met him once."

Lucy smiled. "Good or bad?"

"Oh, definitely good. Highly respected in his field, and rather a hunk, as I recall."

"That's him," Lucy said.

"They must have been nuts at Stanford, letting him go. He was there for years; ran his own show. Grad students would kill to work with him."

"Really?" Lucy frowned, recalling the botched chromatography study. "I didn't realize he was that senior."

"God, yes," Barbara said. "You're really lucky to have him. Have you met his wife?"

"What?" Lucy froze.

"His wife. Dotty. Not her name, her nature. Name's Eleanor. She's a trip."

"He, uh, never mentioned . . . I don't think she came east with him," Lucy managed to reply.

"Probably divorced by now," Barbara said. "Wouldn't surprise me. There were always stories."

So *that* was the family business Rick had to take care of in California at Christmas. Some great judge of character you are, Lucy berated herself; first a drug dealer, now a married philanderer.

"You working together?" Barbara asked.

"No . . . we're just, uh, friends."

"Well, you'll learn a lot from him. And if he *is* divorced, you should go for it. Although he may be kind of tall for you."

"He's only five or six inches taller than I am," Lucy said, frowning.

"Is that all? I got the impression he was taller." Barbara shrugged. "Well, I only met him once. Ah, peach melba, my favorite."

Somehow Lucy managed to get through the dessert and coffee, and even joined the group at the bar for a while afterward. But once in her room, she paced from chair to window to bed, veering between anger and despondency as she sorted out what Barbara had told her and compared it to what she knew, or thought she knew, about Rick. Any way she looked at it, she saw holes big enough to drive a truck through.

She slept badly and woke before her wake-up call, running over it all again while she showered and dressed. He didn't wear a wedding ring, but that didn't mean anything. And come to think of it, he rarely spoke about his past. On the other hand, while the California trip at Christmas could have been to see his wife, it could also have been to see an attorney, or to pack up his things. Barbara seemed to think the marriage was rocky; it was perfectly possible that he was now divorced. Innocent until proven guilty, she reminded herself. Ask him. Give him a chance to explain. This is a man you care for. You've shared his bed, for godsake. But don't do it from a hotel phone; talk to him in person.

Rick in person. That was another thing that was bothering her. How could so senior a scientist as Rick was supposed to be, screw up a chromatography setting and then not notice that his protein weights were off? And what was that business about him being too tall for her? It was true that she was short, but Rick wasn't particularly tall.

At least *this* Rick Hollander wasn't.

She picked up the phone and dialed Palo Alto directory assistance, then hesitated. This is crazy, she thought. Anyone can make a lab mistake. She herself had missed the loose air hose connector on her suit. And Barbara could be a lousy judge of height. She replaced the receiver, grabbed her conference folder, and headed for the eight a.m. breakfast meeting, smiling at her overactive imagination.

"I said this was the last time, and I meant it," he insisted. Renée smiled her lazy smile and began unbuttoning the shirt he had just buttoned. "Quit it," he said, annoyed. He grabbed her hands, but she pulled free and started on his fly. "Damn it, Renée."

"Be a good boy, Rick, or I'll tell your boss about us."

"He already knows," Rick said, freeing himself and retreating across the room. "Is that how you two get your kicks? Screwing other people and telling each other about it?"

"What a nasty little boy you are, *caro*. I have already told you: Bill Miller is nothing to me."

"Yes, and I'm nothing to you, and Count dePalma is nothing to you. We're all just toys."

"Do you want to be something more?" Renée looked surprised.

"God, no."

"Ah, that is all right then. So I will be away until Monday, but on Monday night—"

"No, Renée. No more. I can't."

"Of course you can," Renée told him, laughing. She went for his crotch again, but he fended her off, then took a firm hold on her arms, spun her around, frog-marched her over to the bed, and dumped her onto it.

"No means no," he told her with a sardonic smile. "Bill Miller's orders."

"Bill?" Renée sat up, indignant. "Bill gives *me* orders?"

"Not you. Me." Rick sat on the bed some distance away from her. "It's a business matter," he added. "Nothing personal."

"And what does Bill's business have to do with our fucking?" Renée demanded.

"He's asked me to keep an eye on Lucy Nash," he said, watching her reaction.

"Who?"

"The woman I was with at Bill's party."

"Yes, I remember her. . . ." Her expression turned contemplative. "But why should Bill want this?"

"Ask him yourself," Rick said. "The point is, we can't see each other anymore. It's too risky." He stood and went out into the hall, retrieving his jacket from the floor where Renée had tossed it after practically ripping it off him when he'd arrived.

"I think I would like to meet this Lucy again," Renée said, following him to the door. "Why don't you bring her to dinner here on Monday? Perhaps afterward, the three of us could—"

"Not a chance," Rick said tightly. "She's not like you."

"No? Too bad for you," Renée shot back. "Perhaps

I should take her to lunch and tell her what you like me to do to you in bed. That would be nice for you, no?"

"I wouldn't advise it," Rick said firmly, stepping out into the public corridor. "Unless you want to deal with a very angry Bill Miller."

"You think that scares me? Bill Miller?" Renée's eyes flashed. "He is nothing compared to—" She broke off, hesitated for a moment, and then flung herself at Rick, her open mouth against his, her hand cupping his groin. "You really want to leave me?" she whispered. She stroked him, feeling him grow hard under her fingers, then suddenly released him, and stepped back, a taunting smile on her face. "Go, then. Go."

"Compared to whom, Renée?" Rick asked softly. But the door was already closing.

The scheduled conference events concluded at four, but Lucy had signed up for an after-conference seminar. So it was eight-thirty in the evening when she collected her suitcase from the baggage carousel at LaGuardia and joined the taxi line outside the terminal. She was exhausted, but fortunately the taxi line moved fast, and soon she was headed into the city, the car's tires hissing on the wet road.

She paid off the cab and hurried into her apartment building, barely noticing the shadowy figure huddled in a nearby doorway.

Although she'd hoped to sleep late, she found herself reluctantly awake at seven-thirty the next morning, her mind buzzing. She got up, showered, and made some coffee. Then she sat sipping it and nibbling cinnamon toast while she jotted down a list of the day's to-do's. Clothes to cleaners. Buy milk & veggies. Cash check. Call Rick.

She set down her coffee and went to the window.

Her apartment looked out over the backyards of town houses, gloriously green in the summer, but rather bleak on this mid-winter day.

She carried the mug over to the chest on which stood the two roughly carved Peruvian statues. Stupid things, she thought; don't know why I keep them. But of course, she did. They were all she had left of Jean-Pierre—not her romance with him; that was history—but the puzzle she still hadn't managed to work out. Jean smuggled valuable art, but the experts agreed that these figures were valueless. Jean had hinted to Beno that he was bringing in a unique artifact. What he'd brought in was heroin. It made no sense at all. Maybe it never would. And did it really matter?

She wandered into the kitchen for a refill, feeling stale and edgy. Lack of sleep, she decided. And lack of closure.

She went back to the sofa, exchanging the coffee cup for her pad and pencil. Buy stamps, she wrote. Call Monica.

Her eyes drifted to the statues. She recalled how her father used to tease her, calling her Tenacity Nash, saying she reminded him of a bulldog he'd had as a child. But he'd said it with love. A career army officer, he'd encouraged her can-do spirit, her unwillingness to give up even when she was losing. She smiled at the memory of the old nickname. Her father had died five years earlier of congestive heart failure, and she missed him every day.

She got up and went over to the statues again. God, they were ugly. Still, she might have been wrong not to show them to Beno. Jean must have put them in his suitcase for a reason. Maybe Beno could help her figure out what it was. She glanced at her watch: after nine. By the time she got there, it would be around ten. Too early for a Saturday morning visit? Nah.

She dressed quickly, pulling boots over her jeans,

and a scarlet-and-white sweater over a white turtle-neck. Rick and Monica and the stamps and veggies could all wait.

She rummaged in the kitchen for a shopping bag and dumped the statues into it, covering them with clothes for the cleaners. Was she nuts to keep pursuing this thing? Maybe so, she thought, but hey, we bull-dogs are like that. Grabbing her green anorak from the hall closet, she headed out.

It was, as it had appeared from the window, a typi-cal February day, with the sun fighting a losing battle against the light overcast and streets slushy with the run-off from an early thaw.

She deposited her clothes at the cleaners, then grabbed a crosstown bus to the West Side and walked up Columbus Avenue. She noticed a bright yellow APARTMENT FOR RENT sign taped to the antique store's window as she passed. Another nearly covered the words STANISLAS ARTS beside the door to Beno's building. He's moved out, Lucy realized with a shock. He's gone. Why?

She went into the tiny vestibule and rang the bell repeatedly, but no answer came. Not that she expected one. Perhaps the antiques people would know some-thing since they were advertising the place for rent.

"You didn't hear?" asked the lanky young salesman she approached. "It was on the news."

"What was?"

"The old man was murdered," he replied, lowering his voice.

"Murdered? My God."

"Stabbed. The police think he was killed during a robbery attempt." He hesitated. "I'm sorry. Were you a friend of his?"

"Just an acquaintance," Lucy replied shakily. "When was he . . . when did it happen?"

"They found him Wednesday morning. News One

sent a TV crew. They interviewed Lorenzo—he's the store manager. You didn't see it?"

Lucy shook her head. "I was out of town. What happened?"

"Well, they found his body on Wednesday," the young man told her, warming to his subject, "but he'd been dead for two days. Can you imagine? Such bad luck."

"Bad luck?"

"He'd been gone since Christmas; on vacation, I guess. He only just came back last weekend. If he'd stayed away a little longer . . ." the young man sighed. "Well, as I said, the police think it was a robbery. His place was completely trashed. Isn't it terrible? And in this neighborhood, too."

"Yes, it's awful. Do they have any leads?"

"Not a one. He was killed with one of his own kitchen knives, poor man. There were no fingerprints on it except his. No one in the building remembers seeing anyone suspicious go in or out, but really, who can be certain what they saw two days before? Are you okay? You're shaking."

"I'm just cold. Uh, can I sit down?"

"Of course." He led her to a Victorian settee away from the window. "It's very upsetting, isn't it? And they say the city's getting safer," he added, with a snort of derision. "I'm Damien, by the way."

"And I'm Lucy. Who found him?"

"Well, Ida Friedkin—she lives on the floor above— was taking her dog for a walk, and the dog started whining at Mr. Stanislas's door and straining on his leash."

A middle-aged couple entered the store and began examining a wooden dining table. "Is this Georgian?" the woman called.

"I'm afraid you'll have to check with Lorenzo; he's

the manager," Damien told her. "At the desk back there."

The couple wandered away and Damien sat down beside Lucy, saying, "He thinks he's too good to work the floor, now that he's been on TV. Well, as I was saying, it turned out that Ida's dog had been sniffing at Mr. Stanislas's door for a couple of days, every time they went out, but she didn't think anything of it. And then on Wednesday, the dog pulled away from her and ran over and started pawing at the door, and it opened, and the dog went in and started barking, so Ida went in too, and there he was, lying on the floor, blood everywhere. . . . She came running into the store, screaming and babbling, and Lorenzo and I could hardly understand what she was saying, and when we finally did, we called the police."

"How terrible for her."

"Yes. And then after Lorenzo called the police, he called News One. Which is why *he* was the one who got interviewed on TV," Damien added waspishly. "You want a glass of water or something? You look awfully pale."

"I'm all right," Lucy said. She tried to remember whether she'd given Beno her phone number; she didn't think so. "Did he have any relatives?" she asked. "What will happen to his things?" It seemed callous, but she found herself hoping he'd taken his own advice about keeping notebooks well hidden.

"I really don't know. But if you're interested in antiques, we have some lovely things."

"Maybe another time." Lucy rose.

"Let me give you my card. We get new pieces in all the time."

Out on the street, Lucy stood for a moment, taking it in. Robberies happen; murders, too. It would be easy for someone who knew how, to break in through that vestibule door, get into Beno's apartment. . . .

She hurried back inside and found Damien. "You said the door swung open when the dog pushed on it," she said. "Did the police say whether it had been forced or broken?"

Damien looked surprised. "Didn't I tell you? That's the scariest part." The middle-aged couple approached the table again, a portly young man in tow: Lorenzo. Damien looked over and lowered his voice. "The police think Mr. Stanislas actually knew his murderer. They think he opened the door himself and let him in. Creepy, isn't it?"

"Very creepy," Lucy agreed.

"I mean, protecting yourself against strangers is bad enough," Damien said, walking her to the door. "But you'd never imagine you'd have to protect yourself from your friends."

"No," said Lucy slowly. "You wouldn't, would you?"

Outside again, she retraced her steps and stood staring at the door that led to Beno's apartment. Whatever he may have had that could connect her to him had undoubtedly been found by now. By the police. Or by the murderer.

"She hasn't told me a thing," Rick insisted into the phone. "Anyway, she's been in Washington for the past three days. At some medical conference."

"I'm depending on you," Bill Miller told him. "The IMA is depending on you. Lucy's own safety could depend on you."

"Now who's being melodramatic?"

"I'm worried about her," Bill insisted. "And it's been over a week since you and I talked. We still have a deal, right?"

Rick sighed. "Yes, we still have a deal."

"So when are you planning to see her again?"

"I'm not sure. I've called her a couple of times this morning, but I just get her answering machine."

"Keep trying."

"Bill, this isn't going to work if you pressure me. You'll just have to let me do it my way. I promise I'll call you if she tells me anything about the Jean-Pierre business."

A silence. "Okay, Rick. But don't let me down."

Still carrying the bag with the statues, and badly shaken by the news of Beno's murder, Lucy got off the crosstown bus and turned down Second Avenue. She was nearly past the greengrocer when she remembered her to-do list and pulled it from her anorak pocket. Buy veggies, she read. Buy milk.

"Hey, doc. Wait up." She stopped dead, the familiar voice ringing in her ears. "Help me get a cup of coffee, doc?"

She spun around and stared at the stocky figure in front of her, his paper cup extended. "I didn't recognize you, Ray," she said. "You look so good, I walked right by you." And he did look good: relatively clean, his graying hair cut short, new hightops on his feet. He must have gone to the rehabilitation center after all, she decided. But then, what was he doing back on the street? She dug in her jeans pocket for her wallet and peeled off two singles. "I was worried about you," she told him, dropping the money into his cup. "Where have you been?"

Ray stared at the money greedily. "Went to the stars," he murmured.

"The stars? Tell me about it." But he was already shuffling away, his collar turned up against the chilly air. Curious, she went after him. "I've got another dollar, Ray," she said. "If you tell me about the stars, I'll give it to you."

Ray stopped and swung around to look at her. "Went

to the stars," he repeated. "I got real sick, so they took me to the stars and I got better." He held out his hand for the dollar.

Someone must have taken him to a hospital, she thought. Perhaps the rehabilitation center had organized it. He must have been awfully sick; he'd been gone a long time. Funny, he hadn't seemed ill the last time she'd seen him. "What was it like in the stars?" she asked, reaching for her wallet again.

"It was warm," he said, idly scratching at his neck. "Real warm. And I slept in a bed. And there were angels, golden angels."

Lucy smiled. In her experience, nurses were indeed angels. "Do you know the name of the hospital?" she asked, holding the dollar above his cup. But she could see from his eyes that she'd gotten all she was going to get, today.

"Lived in a big star," he muttered. "A whole lot of us. We all lived in a big star and we flew around with the angels." He shook his cup impatiently, and Lucy let the bill flutter down into it.

"You take care of yourself, Ray," she said. "Get some food."

"Will do, doc." He turned away to wave his cup at another passerby, one hand scrabbling beneath the collar of his jacket again.

"Ray? What's that on your neck?" She moved in for a closer look, and felt a jolt go through her.

"Huh? Lemme alone," he protested immediately, turning up his collar and backing away from her.

"Wait . . ." But he was already moving down the street, cursing and muttering and waving his arms. She stood rooted, watching him go. I must be mistaken, she thought; it simply isn't possible. But in the moment before the collar had sprung back against his neck, she'd caught a glimpse of what appeared to be six deep-red, crescent-shaped scars.

Chapter Fifteen

The phone was ringing as Lucy came through the door, milk and veggies forgotten. Her mind was still grappling with the significance of Ray's scars as she lunged for the receiver.

"Welcome home," said Rick. "How'd it go?"

"Fine," she said distractedly. She tossed the shopping bag with the statues onto the sofa and wriggled out of her coat. Peruvia, she kept thinking. How could Ray have had peruvia?

"And your paper met with loud huzzahs from one and all?"

"It went fine," Lucy repeated, tossing the coat in the direction of the closet. Those golden angels . . .

A pause. "You sound funny. Anything wrong?"

Lucy sank into the desk chair. Everything, she thought; everything's wrong. Beno, and Crazy Ray, and this warm, sexy man with whom I'm more involved than I want to admit. . . . Her mind was buzzing with questions, and she couldn't wait until this evening, as she'd planned, to get at least one of them answered. "Rick, I have to ask you something."

"Shoot."

"Are you married?"

"Am I . . . ?" His voice became cautious. "Where did you hear that?"

"I mentioned your name to an old friend at the convention. Turns out she knew you slightly, some time back. She mentioned your wife, Dotty—I mean Eleanor."

"What old friend was that? What's her name?"

"Who cares? Is it true? Are you married?"

Rick sighed. "Technically, yes. But Lucy, I'm getting divorced. That's why I went back to California. To settle the last few details." Lucy was silent. "Look, I'll give you the phone number of the attorney who's acting for me. You can ask him yourself."

"Why didn't you tell me?" Lucy said quietly.

"I don't know. . . . I guess I thought it didn't matter. Or wouldn't, once the decree became final. Which will be soon, Luce, I swear." He hesitated. "I never meant to hurt you. You know, this is really awkward to talk about on the phone. Can we have dinner tonight? Discuss it face-to-face?"

"I . . . don't think I'm up for dinner tonight," she said. Beno Stanislas had known his murderer. Did Beno tell him about her before he died?

"That's not fair," he protested, misunderstanding her reluctance. "Okay, I admit I wasn't completely open with you. But Eleanor and I have been separated for months, even before I came here. Hell, that's one of the *reasons* I came here. Lucy?"

"A lot of . . . bad stuff has happened this morning," Lucy said slowly. "Your being married is just the cherry on the goddamn parfait."

"What bad stuff?"

"I found out that someone I knew was killed during a robbery last week. And—" She broke off, suddenly reluctant to talk about the scars on Ray's neck. I only had a brief glimpse of them, she told herself. I could be mistaken. I *must* be mistaken.

"Let me help, Luce. Have dinner with me." But Lucy was silent. "Don't do this," he said softly. "Don't let it end like this."

End? Suddenly Lucy was scared. Scared of Beno's

murderer, scared of the scars, and scared that she was
about to lose this man she'd truly come to care for.
She took several deep breaths and tried to center herself the way she did when she was about to enter
Level Four. Let's deal with one problem at a time,
she told herself. "If your marriage really is over . . ."
she began tentatively.

"My marriage was over years ago," Rick said bitterly. "If your friend, whoever she is, knows anything
about me, she'll know that."

Fair enough, Lucy reflected. Barbara had said there
had always been stories. She'd suggested Rick might
be divorced.

"Maybe I was wrong not to tell you," Rick continued. "But I didn't lie to you about it, either. And I
am getting divorced. I would never do anything to
hurt you. You have to trust that." He paused.
"This . . . relationship we have going is not just a roll
in the hay for me, you understand? I care about you,
Lucy. I care a lot. I won't ask if you feel the same
way. I know you have a need to take things slowly.
Hell, we've been seeing each other for over a month
now, and you've never invited me up to your apartment. You have your reasons, I guess, and I respect
that. I don't quite understand it, but I respect it. The
point is, I trust you even though I don't completely
understand you. And if we're going to keep on seeing
each other, you're going to have to trust me that
way, too."

How could I have doubted this man? Lucy thought.
He's like a rock: strong and safe and solid. A feeling
of relief flowed over her at the thought of something
safe and solid in the maelstrom of the morning's
events. "Let's not go out to dinner tonight," she said.
"Why don't I cook something here, instead? How
would that be?"

He was quiet for a moment. Then, "I'd like that very much."

"So what do you think he's up to?"

"You know as much as I do. You read my report."

"Come on, Rossetti. You're on ground zero. What's your take on it?"

"Don't have one yet."

"And you still don't know what it was she took from Didier's apartment, I suppose."

Rossetti shook his head. "No idea."

The older man studied the younger one across the scarred wooden table. "As my old Yiddish grandmother used to say, 'You can't dance at two weddings with one backside.' You understand what I'm saying?"

Rossetti sighed. "I'm not going into business for myself, if that's what you're suggesting." He reached for his beer, then changed his mind and pushed the glass away. "That was a helluva thing to suggest, Tom."

"Sorry, it's not what I meant." The older man reached for a potato chip, hesitated, turned it over in his fingers. "Doctor says I need to cut my cholesterol. No, what I meant was," he continued, looking back at Rossetti, "don't get emotionally involved." He popped the chip in his mouth and chewed. "Fuck him."

"Nice attitude," Rossetti told him. "Your doctor's not the one who's risking a coronary. And now," he said, rising, "if there's nothing else you'd like to accuse me of, I think I'll be going."

"Just remember what I said. And I want to talk again on Tuesday."

"That's only three days from now," Rossetti protested. "What could we have to talk about?"

His companion regarded him with a jaundiced eye. "Find something."

*   *   *

"Floating island," Lucy said, spooning the custard and meringue into blue bowls. "It's like eating clouds." She passed one to Rick. "I always think of it as comfort food."

"Comfort food?"

"You know, like mashed potatoes. And chicken pot pie."

"I don't know about the comfort part," Rick said, plying his spoon, "but it's certainly delicious. So, was that salmon *coubliac* comfort food, too?"

"No, that was just me showing off." She smiled and refilled their wineglasses, but her eyes were troubled.

He reached over and put a hand on hers. "Wonderful cook though you are," he said gently, "food can take you only so far. Won't you let me offer a little human comfort? Don't you think it might help to talk about your friend?"

"He wasn't exactly a friend, but . . . it's kind of complicated." She looked over at him. "Actually, I'd like to tell you about it." She hesitated—where to begin? "The man who was killed was named Beno Stanislas. I'd only met him once, about a month and a half ago. He was an art dealer."

"And how did you meet—?"

"Please, Rick. Let me tell it my way." She reached for her wineglass and took a small, meditative sip. "Beno's expertise was in primitive artifacts. He and Jean-Pierre did some . . . business together."

"Jean was a collector?"

Lucy smiled ruefully. "In a sense. He was a smuggler. He took valuable ancient artifacts out of whatever country the IMA sent him to, and smuggled them into the States. He'd made quite a few trips to South America for the IMA, and had an arrangement with a dealer in Lima. Stanislas was his New York fence. Well, one of them."

"Are you serious?" She nodded. "It's hard to imagine a doctor getting involved in something like that."

"That's why he was so successful at it, I guess."

"There must be big money in it," Rick suggested. "Look at Miller's collection. I suppose it could be tempting to the right guy."

"Jean liked to live well," Lucy said, remembering. "He said his family had money."

"Well, somebody did."

Lucy nodded. "Beno said many serious collectors don't care much about the source, only about the authenticity. I find that so strange."

"True collectors of anything are kind of maniacal," Rick said. "Fanatics."

"That's exactly how Bill described himself," Lucy said. "I've been wondering whether he was one of Beno's customers."

"The sainted Dr. Miller buying smuggled artifacts?" Rick scoffed. But he remembered how Bill had stressed the virtues of pragmatism.

"I asked Beno, actually, and he denied he even knew Bill. But I think it was Bill's name that got him to let me in." Rick's eyebrow went up. "He said not, that people had been hanging around, spying on him. He thought I was one of them, and he wanted a closer look."

"If Miller was in the market for smuggled art, why wouldn't he buy direct from Jean?" Rick asked.

"Maybe he would have," she replied, "if Jean had been able to keep the appointment he'd made with Bill. But Jean died two days before." She drank some wine. "On the other hand, even a fanatical collector like Bill would probably refuse to buy something he absolutely *knew* had been smuggled in. Stanislas, on the other hand, was a dealer; Bill could buy from him, or from any other dealer for that matter, and convince himself there was nothing illegal going on. As long as he doesn't ask too many questions."

"I never could understand the drive to own things like that," Rick said. "It's like the people who travel to exotic places and spend most of the time in souvenir shops."

"Yes, but these are some pretty fancy souvenirs we're talking about."

"The principle's the same. May I?" He helped himself to more dessert. "The beauty of nature is what appeals to me," he said. "Especially in such a fragile environment as the South American rain forests. They're the last unspoiled regions on earth—what's left of them, that is. The ecological balance is so delicate. Taking anything away with you is like . . . rape."

"You've been there?" Lucy asked, surprised.

"There's a lot of wisdom," he continued, ignoring her question, "in that old saying about taking only photographs and leaving only footprints."

"Bill wouldn't agree," Lucy said. "He feels his collection is helping to preserve ethnic heritages."

"Sure he does." Rick spooned up some custard. "Amazing, isn't it, how people can rationalize doing whatever it is they're determined to do. Even Jean-Pierre probably rationalized his smuggling: 'The legislation is unfair, promoting of free trade is good, I'm giving the world access to artifacts that would otherwise stay hidden and unappreciated. . . .' Although I don't see how anyone could rationalize drug running."

"Jean couldn't have been smuggling drugs," Lucy said decisively. "He didn't need to; he was making all that money smuggling art."

"A profitable sideline is always nice."

"Beno seemed to think so, too," Lucy admitted. "He'd read about the drug arrest and assumed Jean was guilty. But—"

"Maybe Beno fenced heroin, too?"

"No, he got furious when I accused him of it."

"And you believed him?"

"Yes, I did." Lucy shivered, remembering the old man serving her tea and biscuits. "It's . . . frightening to think that he's dead."

"Random violence is always frightening," Rick said. "But you live in a secure building, there's a doorman—"

"It's not random violence I'm afraid of," Lucy said quietly. "Beno Stanislas wasn't killed during a break-in, Rick. There *was* no break-in. He opened the door to his killer."

"But . . . why should that scare *you*?"

Lucy was silent for a moment. "If Beno told his killer about me before he died, I could be next."

"I don't understand."

"I found a notebook hidden in Jean's desk."

"What?" Rick leaned forward, frowning.

"It lists his suppliers, and various art galleries, and money he was paid, or maybe owed, I don't know. That's how I found out about Stanislas." She paused. "Beno warned me to keep it hidden."

"A notebook . . . Where is it?" Lucy looked at him in surprise. "I mean, you've hidden it somewhere safe, right?" She nodded. "Maybe you should—"

The shrill of the phone interrupted whatever he'd been going to say. "I can let the answering machine get it," she said uncertainly.

"No, go ahead and answer it," he told her. "I'll clean up." He rose and began stacking the dessert dishes. Lucy went into the living room and picked up the phone.

"You don't call, you don't write. . . ." Monica's voice was teasing. "So tell me about the conference. How did your presentation go?"

"It went very well," Lucy said. "I got your message, but things have just been . . . well, busy."

"You're forgiven. Hey, I was talking to Ted Wiley on Friday. He said to give you his best."

"Ted? How's he enjoying Texas? Quite a change from the CDC."

"He loves it. He was wondering how you guys are coming along."

"You mean, with peruvia?" Behind her, Rick appeared in the doorway between the dining area and kitchen. "We're working on protein analysis and gene sequencing."

"You ever find that second strain?"

"No. Carl Anders still insists there *is* no second strain," Lucy said. Rick moved closer. "It's all rather odd," she added.

"Talk about odd," Monica said, "that Anders guy sounds slightly over the edge himself. Hold on a sec." Lucy heard Howard's voice in the background. "Howard says to tell you Max thought your Christmas present was the best thing he'd ever eaten."

"That dog of yours is a menace." Lucy laughed. "Did you manage to take that photo you promised me? Or did he eat the film, too?"

Monica chuckled. "Film's still in the camera. One of these years, we'll finish the roll. So what are you up to this evening?"

"Actually, I have some, uh, company right now—" Rick disappeared into the kitchen. "But I swear I'll call you tomorrow."

"*Male* company?"

"Yes." Lucy turned toward the kitchen whence came the sound of running water.

"Well, let me not stand in the way of true love," Monica said. "Talk to you tomorrow, sweetie."

Still smiling, Lucy hung up and started for the kitchen, then changed direction and went along the hall to the bathroom. As she stood at the mirror, combing her hair and applying fresh lipstick, she was glad she'd told Rick about Stanislas. She felt calmer, having shared her fear. And as he'd pointed out, her building was secure; she did have a doorman. . . .

She opened the door and started down the hall, then froze. A cry rose in her chest. Rick stood in front of her, a large kitchen knife gripped tightly in his fist. "I wondered where you'd got to," he said as he walked toward her.

"Tweezers," Bill Miller said. Sister Margareta put them into his hand and he gently extracted the sliver of glass. "Got it. Some antibiotic salve," he told the thin, rumpled woman on the examining table, "and you'll be as good as new."

"No stitches?" the woman asked fearfully.

"No, just a bandage," he assured her.

"Don't get up," Margareta told the woman, putting a restraining hand on her arm. "Doctor's not finished yet."

"I can't compliment you and your staff enough," Bill told Margareta over his shoulder as he worked. "I took a real chance, getting permission to keep those patients here. If it had spread . . . Okay, my friend," he told the patient, "we're all done. Try and keep it clean," he added as the woman swung down from the table. "And the sisters will rebandage it tomorrow," he called after her as she hurried from the room. "Anyone else?" he asked Margareta.

"She was the last. Come and have some coffee." He followed her down the corridor toward her cubicle of an office. Beyond them, the large red quarantine sign had been removed from the double doors at the end of the hall. The doors were open, now; the overnight shelter program was back in business. "One hundred percent recovery," he murmured. "Very impressive."

"Thanks to your skill, doctor," Margareta said graciously. He settled himself on the small threadbare sofa as she filled paper cups with hot, dark liquid from her personal coffeemaker. "No milk, I'm afraid. But I do have sugar."

"Black is fine." He smiled and took the cup from her outstretched hand. "I can't tell you how pleased I am."

"You're a good man," she told him. "You take such joy in our successes. No, don't look so modest. So many people feel our . . . clientele is not worth troubling with. I'm very proud of our nursing staff, of course," she continued. "But without your antibiotics—"

"Not antibiotics," he reminded her gently. "The strain was antibiotic-resistant, remember?"

"Of course." Margareta grew flustered. "I meant . . . whatever drugs you gave them that helped them recover."

But Bill shook his head. "I really didn't do so much," he replied. "I just fended off any secondary infections. You're the ones who cured them. Your care, your dedication, your professionalism . . . You're angels of mercy, all of you." He smiled at her. "You're angels."

Covered from head to toe in spacesuits, their air supplies on their backs, they entered the deserted ward like astronauts arriving on the moon. They piled their equipment in the center of the room and unpacked the bleach and duct tape.

Carl looked around at the stained walls, the bare iron cots. Mattresses, pillows, sheets, all had been removed in biocontainment bags and burned. The room had no windows, and the air that blew through the ceiling vents was recirculated through a sealed, isolated air-flow system. One man set up a ladder and pulled down the venting grids. The grids and the ladder would remain here until the process was complete.

The men began to scrub the walls, ceiling, and floor
with bleach. They scrubbed the cots, the IV stands,
the cabinets, the desk. They opened the door that led
to the staff living quarters, empty now, and scrubbed
that, too.

Carl watched them carefully. When he was satisfied,
he asked for the tape. Together with his men, he
sealed up the joins between wall and floor, wall and
ceiling, anywhere that air could possibly seep through.

Now the men began unrolling a long, heavy electric
cable with outlets along its length, snaking it through
the two rooms in a thick black line. While the others
unpacked the electric frying pans, Carl went through
the rooms scattering pieces of paper containing spores
of *Bacillus subtilis niger.*

When the cable was in place, the men began plugging in the frying pans, setting each one to "high."
Carl followed after them, placing white crystals of
formaldehyde on each pan.

One last look around, and Carl signaled the men to
leave. When the last man was out in the corridor, he
plugged the business end of the cable into a heavy-
duty electrical outlet and closed the door. As the pans
heated up, changing the crystals to gas, two men
quickly tape-sealed the door from the outside.

For seventy-two hours, the room would remain airtight, filled with killing gas. Then Carl would come
back and take samples of the test papers and look at
them under a microscope. *Subtilis niger* was very hard
to kill, but he was reasonably certain that the formaldehyde would have done its work. And if the bacillus
was dead, then the other thing that lived here would
be dead, too. Or so he hoped.

Chapter Sixteen

Lucy screamed and ran for the bathroom, slamming the door closed behind her, fumbling with the lock, twisting it shut. Gasping for breath, she leaned against the sink and wondered what she could use as a weapon. There was alcohol in the medicine cabinet; if she aimed for his eyes . . .

"What the hell—?" Rick was at the door. "Lucy?"

There was a small window beside the toilet. She shoved it open and looked down at the seven-story drop to the tiny courtyard below. No way out, but she could scream. Maybe someone would hear her. Someone with his windows open in the middle of February. Right.

"Lucy? Are you all right?"

"So far," she shot back. "Disappointed?"

"What?" He rattled the doorknob. "Open the door."

"Why? So you can kill me the way you killed Stanislas?"

"The way I—?" A pause while the impact of what she'd said hit him. Then, "Oh God. You thought—?" Another pause, and then the sound of something being forced under the door. She watched in horror as the knife blade slid inside, its point toward her. "Here," Rick called through the door. "Take it." The blade continued its slow process along the floor, stopping for a moment at the handle. She heard Rick curse, and then the rest of the knife came flying under the door. Lucy bent and retrieved it. "You have it?" he asked through the door. "Then look at the blade. I was scraping the burned bits off your damn roasting pan. See?"

"You used my good knife to clean a roasting pan?" she exclaimed.

Rick laughed. "That's better." A silence. "So you can come out now."

"Not so fast. Why were you looking for me with a knife in your hand?"

"I was cleaning the goddamn pan, Luce, and your oven started smoking. Something's burning in there."

"Shit. The madeleines."

"*Ex*-madeleines. I called, but you didn't answer, so I came looking for you."

"Holding a knife?"

"Apparently so. An error of judgment, I grant you, but seeing smoke come pouring out of the oven sort of rattled me. So, you coming out?"

Lucy considered. "Did you turn off the oven?"

"No. Should I?"

"Unless you want the fire department up here. And dump the burnt offerings." She put her ear against the door and listened to the sound of him retreating up the hall. Then, very quietly, she turned the lock and cracked the door open. Peeking out, she watched his retreating back, then crept up the hallway well behind him. The reassuring scent of burning madeleines floated on the air. She watched him switch off the oven, remove the cookie sheet with an oven-gloved hand, and slide the blackened confections into the trash. "Let it cool before you wash it," she instructed from the doorway.

The metal sheet crashed to the tile floor as Rick whirled around. "Christ. You scared the shit out of me, Luce."

"Then I guess we're even."

They looked at each other for a long moment. Rick went and folded her in his arms and suddenly she was shaking. "It's all right," he told her. "Everything's all right."

He stroked her hair and whispered to her and held her, and somehow coffee seemed unnecessary and the dishes could wait until the morning, and then they were in her bed, their clothing strewn about the room, their bodies working together, his lips on hers, and she felt herself drowning in the feel and touch and taste of him. A long time later, damp and flushed and spent, they slept in each other's arms.

She half-woke around four, nudged from slumber by some sound, some movement. The room was in semidarkness. Beside her lay a dented pillow, a rumpled duvet. Where was Rick? Probably in the john, she decided; they'd drunk a lot of wine with dinner. She closed her eyes, but a tiny sound made them fly open again. Cautiously, without moving her body, she looked around the room, and came fully awake. Rick stood at her dresser, his hands busy. In disbelief she watched him go through each drawer, quickly and methodically. Then he tiptoed to the door and disappeared.

Moving slowly and silently, Lucy got out of bed and went after him. She heard him opening and closing kitchen cabinets. Going to put a stop to this right now, she thought, hurrying back to the bedroom door, heart pounding. She draped herself against the jamb, hoping she looked sufficiently like a woman who had just that very moment woken to find her lover missing. "Rick?" she called plaintively. "Where are you?"

He appeared in the hallway, holding a glass of water and looking flustered. "Lucy? Did I wake you? I was so dry." He took an ostentatious gulp and came toward her. "Want some? Have you been up long?"

She shook her head drowsily. "I had a nightmare," she said, "and then I woke up and you weren't there."

He put an arm around her and led her back to bed. "Poor Lucy," he said. "So jumpy. First she thinks I'm trying to murder her, now she has nightmares. . . ." He cuddled her in his arms, pulling the duvet around them. "I'm here, babe," he said. "I'm right here. Go back to sleep, love. I'll protect you."

So you'll protect me, will you? Lucy thought grimly, lying in his arms, willing herself to stay awake. And who will protect me from *you*?

"Did you sleep at all?"

"Not much."

The sat across the table from each other, sipping cups of strong Starbucks coffee. "You sure you're not hungry?" Rick asked. "This croissant is really good."

"It looks good," Lucy said, "but no."

Conversation had been faltering this morning, at least on Lucy's part. Rick had put it down to tiredness, which was partly true. He didn't know she'd seen him searching her apartment, didn't know she was wondering who this stranger was, sitting across from her. "So what are your plans?" he asked. "Shall we see a flick? Go to the Met? Or we could go downtown, wander around SoHo."

"Actually, I need to spend a few hours at the hospital today."

"Sunday?"

"Patients don't take the weekend off, I'm afraid."

"Well, can we meet later on?"

"I don't know how long I'll be, and I'm really tired. Can I have a rain check?"

Rick looked surprised. "Sure. Uh, are you all right?"

"Yes, just tired." She managed to smile. "What will you do?"

"Actually I have some work to catch up on, too. More coffee?"

"Half a cup, thanks. Then I'd better get going."

They parted outside the coffee bar, and Lucy, weary and confused, stood watching him until he turned the corner. Then, her heart heavy, she headed back home in search of Crazy Ray.

"Help me get something to eat?" he muttered as she came toward him. His hat was pulled low over his forehead, his jacket misbuttoned. He appeared agitated and confused.

She had a dollar ready, and dropped it into his cup. "How are you today, Ray?" she said brightly. "How's that neck?" He scowled at her, his eyes cloudy and unfocused. "You know who I am?" she probed. "I'm the doc, remember?"

"Don't need no doc," he said, eyes wandering.

"Don't you remember me?"

He regarded her with an expression of hostility, and a total lack of recognition. "Go away. Get away from me."

"I just want to see that rash on your—"

Ray's arms windmilled as he pulled away from her. "Thief!" he shouted. "This is *my* money!"

Lucy stepped back quickly. "I don't want your money, Ray."

"Can't have it. It's mine." He stumbled after her, yelling and flailing his fists. "Trying to steal my money. Get away from me."

Lucy retreated a safe distance, then turned back and watched as a mother and child crossed the street to avoid him. She sighed. He must have stopped taking his medication again. She'd seen these paranoid episodes before, and she knew it would be impossible to examine the scars until the mood swing had passed.

Ray ambled down the street, muttering and cursing, then stopped and banged his cup against the window

of a pizza store until a man in a stained white apron
came out and chased him away. The police would be
getting phone calls again, she thought despondently.
And if they acted this time, if they removed Ray from
the neighborhood before she had a chance to examine
those peruvia scars . . .

Then she thought: peruvia scars? Give me a break.

She turned and walked slowly back toward her
apartment building. It simply wasn't possible; it was
merely a figment of her overheated imagination. She'd
only had a tiny glimpse, after all. It could have been
anything.

She let herself into the apartment and locked the
door carefully behind her. As she hung up her coat,
she noticed the shopping bag. She'd shoved it into the
closet the day before while doing a fast cleanup in
anticipation of Rick's visit. Now she pulled it out and
removed the two carvings. Tossing the bag aside, she
went and set the statues in their usual spot on the low
chest. It's not over yet, kids, she told them. Tenacity
Nash is still on the case.

But which case? There suddenly seemed to be so
many: drugs, art, Beno's murder, Ray's peruvia
scars . . .

They weren't peruvia scars, she told herself sternly.
They couldn't have been. You're overwrought. You're
seeing things.

Sure I am, she thought. And Carl Anders didn't
threaten to kill me. And Beno Stanislas is alive and
well. And Rick wasn't going through my dresser drawers in the middle of the night.

The outer door was locked, as usual. He inserted
his cardkey, pulled it open, and walked quickly past
the deserted guard's desk to the elevator. He rode it
up to the second floor and got out. The steel doors
were locked shut, but they slid back when he turned

his key in the wall lock, and his cardkey opened the glass doors beyond. He passed through the dark reception area and the short, dogleg hallway, into the lab.

He paused for a moment, orienting himself in the pitch dark, then took a small flashlight from his pocket and played it around, spotlighting work counters, test tubes, beakers, microscopes.

He followed the beam through the lab, freezing at an imagined sound and dousing the light, waiting, proceeding. He entered a short hallway. Ahead, large red signs warned BIOHAZARD. NO ADMITTANCE. He continued down the corridor to the steel doors and pushed through them into the locker room.

Now he allowed himself the luxury of electric light. The flashlight went back into his jacket pocket. His clothes came off, his underwear, his watch. He bundled it all into a locker, then put on a sterile scrub suit, gloves, socks. With practiced ease, he sealed the join between socks and trousers, gloves and cuffs.

He went through to the staging area. Blue Chemturion spacesuits hung from a rack against one wall. He shuffled through them, found the one that had ANDERS stenciled across the chest, inspected it very carefully for tears, and then laid it out on the floor. He stepped into it and pulled it up around his body, put on the helmet, taped and Velcroed himself airtight, plugged in an air hose, cleared the faceplate.

LETHAL PATHOGENS. BIOHAZARD. He ignored the warnings, unhooked the hose, and entered the steel air lock. He barely paused, continuing through to the concrete boot room, connecting and disconnecting and reconnecting his air supply.

A few feet away, one final steel door, the entrance to Biosafety Level Four, separated him from his objective. Stepping up to it confidently, Rick Hollander went through the door and emerged in the Lethal Pathogens Lab.

Chapter Seventeen

Terrorist bomb cripples paris metro, Monday morning's headlines screamed. 33 dead, 116 hurt. algerian group claims credit.

"Terrible, just terrible," the doorman said, opening the plate-glass door for Lucy. "Poison gas in Tokyo, pipe bombs in Atlanta . . . now this. World's going nuts."

"Sure seems that way," Lucy agreed, hurrying out into the street. She'd seen the horrifying news report on television as she'd dressed.

Up early thanks to troubled dreams, she'd decided to clear her head with a visit to one of her favorite places: the gym. The events of the weekend had shaken her, and she hoped that mindless physical activity would have its usual calming effect.

Having ascertained that Rick hadn't found Jean's notebook the night before, she'd decided the safest thing would be to lock it in her safe-deposit box at the bank. With that in mind, she now retrieved it, shoving it among the clothes in her gym bag.

Ray was at his old spot in front of McDonald's. She greeted him as she went past, but got only muted curses and an angry, glassy-eyed stare in return. Well, at least he was still on the street where she could get hold of him when his mental state improved.

She made the rounds of the exercise machines, working herself hard, then finished up with twenty minutes on the treadmill. The news played soundlessly on the large television sets, shots of stretchers and twisted metal making an odd contrast to the rock music pumping through the gym's sound system.

The exercise was helping, she decided. Her fears, though still with her, somehow felt more manageable. Beno had seemed a pretty discreet guy; maybe he hadn't told his killer about her. As for Ray, it would be easy to check him and prove herself wrong, once his medication kicked in again. And Rick . . . Still running, she swigged from a small bottle of Evian. She had no idea what Rick was playing at, but surely she could keep him at arm's-length until she figured it out.

She finished her run, then showered, letting the warm water flow over her, relaxing her muscles and her psyche. She was just stepping out of the shower room when a dark figure sprang at her, sending her sprawling over a bench. She was up again in a moment, ready to fight off her attacker, but the threatening figure transformed itself into a blond, middle-aged woman in dark sweats.

"Are you all right?" the woman asked solicitously. "Sorry I ran you down. Moving too fast, I guess."

"I'm okay," Lucy replied, lowering her fists, her heart pounding. Good one, she told herself wryly; you almost took out the assistant manager.

It was barely eight-fifteen when Lucy, dressed in street clothes again, bought a newspaper and a cup of the club's cappuccino and carried them to a table by the window. As she read about the terrorist attack, her dark mood slowly returned. It was quite horrifying, she reflected, what fanatics were prepared to inflict on innocent bystanders in the name of a self-styled cause.

Man's cruelty to man brought back thoughts of Beno Stanislas. Not precisely an innocent bystander, but not guilty of any crime that carried the death penalty. Although, if he'd lied about his ignorance of the heroin Jean-Pierre had been carrying . . .

"Protecting yourself against strangers is bad enough," Damien had told her. "But you'd never imagine you'd have to protect yourself from your friends."

Maybe it's time to figure out who my friends really are, she reflected. Sipping the hot coffee thoughtfully, she decided it had been a mistake not to have told Bill about Jean's involvement in art smuggling. He knew the art world; maybe he could help her work out how art and heroin could be connected. Of course, knowing about Jean's art smuggling might add weight to Bill's conviction that Jean had been smuggling drugs. But she would risk it. She was tired of secrets: Jean's, Beno's, her own.

She finished the coffee and grabbed a taxi downtown to IMA headquarters.

"He's been in a meeting since eight," Alicia told her. "In the conference room. It shouldn't last much longer, if you want to wait."

"I do."

"Well, go on in. I'll tell him you're here. Can I get you some coffee?"

"No, thanks."

Lucy walked across the attractively appointed office toward the large windows. It appeared that Bill had been here for some time. The morning newspapers lay scattered across the coffee table, and an inch of congealing coffee lay in the bottom of the mug on his desk. The computer was on, its screen saver spiraling slowly.

Outside, Mother Nature had mistaken February for April, and produced a bright blue sky along with a crisp but pleasant air temperature of fifty-four. She looked down at the streets below: the rush-hour crowds scurrying about, cars and taxis jostling for position. What easy targets we all are, she thought.

"Lucy. How nice." She turned back from the window. Bill stood in the doorway, a paper cup in his hand. He smiled at her. "To what do I owe the pleasure?"

"I need to ask your advice about something," she said.

"Please. Sit down." He gestured toward the seating area in front of his desk, and she joined him there.

"Awful, isn't it?" She indicated the newspapers on the table in front of them.

"Terrible," Bill agreed solemnly, setting down the cup of fresh coffee. "We've just been talking about sending a team to help out. Not sure they'll need us, but I feel we should offer."

Lucy nodded. "I can't understand how people can do such things to each other," she said. "How do they sleep at night?"

"Quite soundly, I'm afraid," Bill answered. He sighed. "It's appalling, as you say. But the problem is that in today's world, how else can such downtrodden ethnic minorities make themselves heard?"

Lucy stared at him. "You're defending these killers?"

"No, of course not. I'm just explaining their rationale. . . ." He looked uncomfortable. "I condemn such action, of course." He frowned and looked at his watch. "I don't mean to seem rude, but I have a rather full morning. How can I help you, Lucy?" He sipped from the cup and set it down.

Lucy hesitated. Now that she was face-to-face with Bill, the idea of telling him about Jean's art smuggling didn't seem quite as red hot as it had in the gym. "It's about Jean-Pierre," she said slowly.

"Not that again," Bill interrupted impatiently.

"Yes, that again," Lucy replied politely but firmly.

"I learned something curious this weekend, and I wanted your opinion. But maybe I shouldn't bother you with it." She rose.

"Don't be so prickly," he said. "I just don't like to see you wasting your time. But if you've learned something important . . ." He smiled ingratiatingly. "I apologize. Sit down and tell me about it." He picked up his coffee again.

She studied him for a moment, reassured by the sincere interest she saw in his eyes. "Jean was an art smuggler," she said, resuming her seat. "He specialized in ancient artifacts. He relied on the good name of the IMA, and the fact that your personnel are treated with such respect, to bring things into the country whenever he came back from a mission." And that will teach you to patronize me, Lucy thought with satisfaction.

"So that was why he wanted that meeting with me," Bill exclaimed angrily. "He wanted to sell me stolen art."

"Very possibly. Jean usually sold his artifacts through a number of art galleries here in New York. But one dealer said he thought Jean was planning to cheat him by going directly to his clients."

"But . . . are you certain about all this?" Bill asked, frowning. Why hadn't Rick told him about this new development? Didn't they have a deal?

"Oh, yes. I found Jean's secret notebook—oh, you've spilled your coffee. Better put some water on—"

"Never mind my shirt," he said impatiently, dabbing at it with his hanky. "Tell me about the notebook."

"It lists all his contacts—the people he bought from, the galleries he sold to."

"Goddammit." Bill rose, still wiping at his shirt. "Drugs weren't enough for him; he had to smuggle art, too. When I think of the risk—"

"You don't understand," Lucy interrupted. "I agree that his art smuggling put the IMA at risk. But it actually proves what I've always maintained: that Jean wasn't dealing drugs."

"I don't see how," Bill said angrily, pacing. "To my mind, it proves the opposite."

"No, it doesn't," Lucy insisted. "Think about it. If Jean were caught bringing in heroin, not only would he be looking at a long jail sentence, but his medical career would be finished, his reputation destroyed. But if he were caught with illegal art, he could simply claim to be an amateur, say he had no idea he was doing anything wrong. The artwork would be confiscated, he might be fined . . . but it would be a slap on the wrist, that's all. No, it doesn't make sense that Jean would risk smuggling drugs when he could make all that money smuggling art."

"But he *was* smuggling heroin," Bill insisted, turning back from the window.

"Why do you want to believe the worst of him?" Lucy asked, puzzled. "He was a doctor, an IMA volunteer. Why aren't you on his side?"

"Because he put this organization at risk," Bill replied tightly.

Lucy sighed. Bill was right, of course. And yet . . . "The reason I'm here," she told him, "is to see if you can help me figure out how heroin and art could be connected, somehow."

"That's easy. He was smuggling both."

"No, Bill. I'm certain he wasn't."

"What then?"

"I believe the drugs were planted on him for some reason."

"What?" Bill stopped in midstride, contemplating her in horror.

"Someone put the heroin in his suitcase," Lucy insisted.

"But . . . why?"

"I don't know. But someone made damn sure he wouldn't have a chance to defend himself against the charge."

"How do you mean?"

"That death pill. Did you really buy that suicide story?"

"Of course." Bill looked surprised. "He was a doctor. He'd know how to prepare a death capsule of some sort."

"But why should he *want* to?"

"I'm sure he'd prefer death to a highly publicized trial—"

"And so we come full circle again," Lucy said tiredly. "You think he knew the drugs were there, and I don't."

"I guess we'll never know the truth," he said. "So as I've been saying all along, it's best to just forget the whole—"

"There's more, Bill."

"More?" He regarded her warily.

"You ever hear of an art dealer named Beno Stanislas?"

"Can't say I have," Bill replied, turning away from her to toss his coffee-stained handkerchief onto his desk.

"He was one of Jean's fences. I went to see him just before Christmas. He told me people had been spying on him. Last week he was killed in a botched robbery. At least, that's what the police say."

"And you believe differently?" He turned toward her with a disbelieving smile. "Really, Lucy."

"Don't laugh at me, Bill. Isn't it possible someone killed Beno because he knew too much?"

"Too much about *what*? Jean's art smuggling? Jean's dead. None of that matters anymore."

"Beno's dead, too, remember. So we won't ever

know what else Beno might have known too much about."

Bill came around to where Lucy sat and put a fatherly arm on her shoulder. "Don't you think you might be overdramatizing all this, just a little?" he asked. "You're overworked, overtired. You're letting your imagination run wild." He sat down next to her. She could smell the coffee drying on his shirt. "You came here for my advice. Well, here it is, the same as before: forget this whole nasty business."

"I can't."

"You must. For your own good." He shook his head regretfully. "You started this conversation by asking me to help you find a connection between drugs and art. Okay, I'll ask around. I know all the major players; maybe I'll come up with something. But understand this, Lucy. If I do uncover some sort of connection, you may not like what it is. I've warned you of this before. You start opening doors, you have to be prepared to deal with whatever lies behind them."

"But you'll give it a shot?"

He shrugged. "Sure. Although I still say you're reading too much into all of this. Just the way you did with Carl Anders's files."

"They were sangre negra files, Bill. What was I supposed to think?"

He shook his head, smiling. "That's what I mean. You act as if the most likely explanation is that Carl's Mexican sangre negra is your Peruvian one and that people are keeping things from you." He smiled sadly. "You need to step back, get some perspective." He reached over and squeezed her hand. "I have nothing but respect for you, Lucy. You're an excellent doctor, a helluva researcher . . . a fine, compassionate person. I promise I'll do what I can, as long as you promise me you'll concentrate on what you know: medicine. How's your peruvia research coming?"

"Very well," Lucy told him, feeling slightly whiplashed from the rapid change of subject matter. "The similarities with Ebola are quite striking."

"Are they?" he said vaguely. "Not my field, I'm afraid."

"No. Well, it raises some interesting questions, especially when you consider how isolated the area of the peruvia outbreak was. How did the IMA come to hear about it, by the way? I've forgotten."

"An anthropologist, working in the area, mentioned it to one of our South American representatives."

"Could you give me his name? I'd like to talk to him."

"The rep?" Bill frowned.

"No, the anthropologist."

"I don't see why you— Actually, I don't remember his name, offhand. It was all sort of word of mouth."

"I see," said Lucy. "And there's never been an outbreak of peruvia outside South America?"

"Not so far as I know. Why? Oh, those damn sangre negra files. I've already told you: it was a Mexican hantavirus." He began folding the scattered newspapers, some stained with coffee, and stacking them neatly in a pile.

"No, I wasn't thinking about that. I saw—" Lucy broke off. She wasn't really sure of what she'd seen on Ray's neck—not yet, anyway. And Bill had already accused her of imagining things, of overdramatizing. Without some sort of proof, he'd only laugh her off. "I know how committed you are to helping the homeless," she continued, changing her approach, "and I was wondering whether you're familiar with a mission or a mission-run hospital that has the word 'star' in its name."

Bill's head jerked around. "Star?" he said. "Not offhand. Why?"

"There's a street person in my neighborhood who fell ill at a mission." She smiled. "He said he got sick and lived in a star and flew around with gold angels. From the way he spoke, it sounded like they could be dealing with some sort of epidemic there. I thought there might be some way the IMA could help."

"Star . . ." he mused, returning to his paper folding. "Now I think about it, I believe Carl may have mentioned such a mission. I don't recall the actual name, but 'star' sounds familiar." He paused, thinking. "I seem to remember that Anders did some volunteer work there." He saw the look of surprise on her face. "He's a difficult man, Lucy, but his heart's in the right place. If it's the one I'm thinking of, Carl worked there only briefly. He said it was very poorly run. If you're thinking of offering your services, I suggest you steer clear of it." He placed the final newspaper on the stack. "If your friend's in need of medical attention, I can recommend several places you can send him to." He stood and went to his desk. "Shall I write them out for you?"

"That won't be necessary. He seems fine now." Lucy stood, too, gathering up her purse, jacket, gym bag.

"Good. Well, I hope I was some help to you, Lucy. And I *will* follow through on that art-heroin connection." He turned and smiled at her. "You were right to come and tell me," he said. "I'm sorry if I was a little negative, but you took me by surprise."

"Of course. Well, thanks for your time, Bill." She smiled at him. "And your advice." She started to leave.

"Uh, Lucy? What have you done with Jean's notebook?" Lucy froze, then turned to stare at him. "I just want to make sure it's safe," he said quickly.

CODE RED   227

"It's locked away in a bank vault," Lucy said carefully. The gym bag suddenly felt very heavy. "It's absolutely secure."

"Good." He watched her walk out into the corridor, then went back in and swung the office door closed. Returning to his desk, he reached for the telephone.

"I get them at a little French bakery around the corner from my apartment," Rick said. "You want another?" He pushed the paper plate of assorted sweet rolls across the desk.

Carl swallowed the last of his apple turnover. "Thanks." He inspected the contents of the plate.

"The cinnamon rolls are good."

Carl carefully cut one in half, took a bite, chewed. "Delicious," he agreed. "Well, this is certainly a nice change from the usual breakfast fare around here."

"You mean you're not a fan of stale donuts and weak coffee?" Rick laughed.

"It was nice of you to bring them," Carl said. "And the coffee."

"Vanilla-almond's a big favorite of mine, too." Rick sipped the fragrant brew, then leaned back in Carl's visitor's chair. "Very civilized."

"Yes." Carl started on the second half of his roll. "I can't tell you how sorry I am about that outburst of mine."

"Ancient history," Rick said kindly. "Don't even mention it. A job like yours produces a helluva lot of stress. It had to go somewhere, and I happened to be in the way."

"Nice of you to see it like that."

"Well, I can understand what it's like for you. I've been there."

"You ran your own show at Stanford," Carl acknowledged.

" 'Course, we didn't deal with stuff like this peruvia

thing. Level Four work." He gave a delicate shudder.
"I can't tell you how much I admire your courage,
going in there every day." He drank some coffee and
watched Carl preen. "Talk about stress."

"You get used to it," Carl said bravely.

"Still, not many places offer that kind of challenge.
Aside from the CDC, of course." He paused. "You
ever find that second strain?"

"Second strain?" Carl stopped chewing.

"Peruvia. The second strain that guy Wiley found,
down in Atlanta. You ever find it up here?"

"How did you hear about that?"

"Lucy mentioned it. More coffee?"

Carl shook his head. "There *is* no second strain. I
told her that."

"But the CDC was so sure."

"They must have compromised one of their samples."

"Funny kind of contaminant, though. Doesn't seem
likely. Not that it's any of my business," Rick added
hurriedly. "Uh, have you tried the crullers?"

"I've had enough." Carl scowled and pushed away
his plate. "We both have work to do."

"Of course. I'll just clean up here." He began gathering up the paper plates, the soiled napkins. "So
how're things between you and Lucy these days? You
getting along okay?"

Carl eyed him suspiciously. "Yes. Why?"

"Oh, no reason. It's just that working on Level Four
is tough enough without the stress of being in there
with someone you can't stand."

"Can't stand?" Carl looked surprised. "I wouldn't
put it as strongly as that."

Rick tossed the used paper goods in Carl's trash
can. "Come on, Carl. You can be honest with me. I
know you don't like her." Carl shrugged and sipped
his coffee. "And after that incident when you saved
her life and she turned around and accused you of

trying to kill her . . ." Rick looked over at Carl. "I'm amazed you can work in the same lab with her."

"It's not easy," Carl allowed.

"Practically impossible, I should think. If it were me, I'd want a good, thick wall between us." He waited hopefully. When Carl didn't respond, he added, "Is that what you did?"

"What are you talking about?"

"I bet you set yourself up another lab, a separate one, inside Level Four, didn't you? Someplace private."

Carl paled. "Of course not. Why should I do such a thing?"

"Why, to get away from Lucy, of course." Rick emptied the plate of sweets into the white bakery bag, folded the top, and placed it on a corner of the desk, saying, "Why don't you keep these for later?" He resumed his seat, insisting, "You did, didn't you? I tell you, it's what I would have done."

"What you suggest is quite impossible," Carl began, but the telephone interrupted his denial. He answered it, listened for a moment, then put his hand over the mouthpiece. "Thank you for breakfast, Rick. Now, if you'll excuse me, this is a private call."

"Of course. Uh, we still on for a drink this evening?"

"I'll let you know. Um, shut the door on your way out, will you?"

Rick paused outside the closed door, but could make out only a low, intermittent murmur, so he headed back toward his own lab. Carl was obviously lying, he reflected. If the CDC said there was a second strain, it definitely existed. Yet he'd searched Anders's workstation thoroughly on Sunday, with disappointing results. If Carl truly hadn't found it in his own samples, why hadn't he requested a sample from the

CDC? That would be normal procedure. And if Carl *had* found it, why was he denying its existence?

He slumped down into his desk chair, watching the flying toasters drift across his computer screen. Where could it be? he wondered. Where had Carl hidden it? And, more important, why?

Chapter Eighteen

" ... **W**hich in this case proved to be 0157:H7, the same strain of *E. coli* responsible for the outbreak of food poisoning in Sakai, near Osaka, in 1996," Lucy dictated into the hand-held recorder. "In that outbreak, more than 6,000 elementary school students were infected with the 0-157 colon bacillus bacteria through the consumption of contaminated school lunches. Don't hover, Jake, you're making me nervous." She beckoned to him and pointed to a chair. "This strain was also responsible for the 1993 outbreak in the United States, during which 700 people became ill after consuming undercooked hamburgers. Four fatalities resulted. Typical symptoms of 0-157 include bloody diarrhea, abdominal cramps, and, in severe cases, renal failure." She switched off the recorder and set it on top of the *E. coli* file. "What's up?"

"Just the usual chaos. I hear you had quite a success in our nation's capital last week."

Lucy grinned. "With all due modesty, I must admit I was terrific."

Jake smiled. "Congratulations. I'm not surprised."

"Thanks. Look," she continued, reaching for the recorder again, "I don't mean to be rude, but can whatever it was you wanted wait? I'm getting ready for the departmental conference tomorrow morning."

"And I've got rounds in ten minutes. I just stopped

231

by to invite you to dinner next Sunday. And Beth says to bring along that guy you've been seeing."

"Rick?" Lucy looked doubtful.

"That his name? Seems you've been telling my wife things you haven't told me," he added mock accusingly. "Who is he?"

"His name's Richard Hollander. He works at the IMA lab, but I don't think—"

"Richard Hollander?" Jake looked impressed. "Stanford, right?"

"Yes." Lucy put down the recorder and gave Jake her full attention. "You know him?"

"No, but I've heard the name. You say he's running the IMA lab?"

"Not running it; working in it. He's got his own lab setup, does some private research . . . What's the matter?"

"Nothing. Only it seems kind of funny, a guy like Hollander working for the IMA."

"Does it? Why?"

"First of all, he's a control freak, or so I was told. And second, he's not what you'd term an altruist."

"I thought you said you didn't know him."

"I don't. But one of my residents worked with him briefly. This goes back a while. Guy did a year of graduate work in biochemistry at Stanford before applying to medical school. He said Hollander was brilliant, but very controlling. And not very generous about sharing scientific credit. Not exactly selfless, if you take my meaning." He paused. "Doesn't sound like the kind of guy who'd give up tenure at Stanford to become a do-gooder at a small, unknown lab."

"People change," Lucy murmured.

"Of course they do," Jake said soothingly. "Bring him to dinner."

"I'm . . . not sure about Sunday, actually. Can I let you know?"

"Sure. Hey, don't take what I said too seriously. I'm just repeating seven-year-old gossip."

When Jake Weiss had gone, Lucy sat for a moment in thought, then reached for her Rolodex and sorted through it. People change, she thought, but not that much. She pulled the phone toward her and began dialing. It took several tries, but at last she managed to track down Barbara Coley.

"Barbara? Lucy Nash. Yes, it was great seeing you, too. Actually, I'm calling to ask sort of a weird favor. Do you think you could find a photo of Rick Hollander? In a professional journal or something, I mean. Well, we're making a . . . a party for him, celebrating his first six months with the IMA, and I thought it would be fun if we could find an article he wrote, something with his picture, and enlarge it and . . . Really? That would be great. No, why don't you fax it to me if you find it. Yes, the sooner, the better." She gave Barbara the number of the office fax. "Thanks a million, Barb. I owe you."

She hung up and turned back to her half-finished report. "Upon positive identification of 0-157 in the stool samples of our patients, New York General issued a statement warning consumers about the dangers of eating undercooked meat and urging infected persons to seek medical aid immediately . . ." Her voice trailed off. A photo of Hollander would be helpful, but not definitive. The photo could be old, and people did change. She reached for the telephone again, dialed directory assistance for Palo Alto, and requested the general phone number for Stanford.

She copied the number in her desk diary, then hesitated, receiver in hand, wondering whether she was chasing phantoms. But he *had* been searching her apartment, she reminded herself. Why would a molecular biologist do that? She quickly punched in the numbers.

After much transferring, she was finally connected with someone in molecular biology and asked to speak with Richard Hollander.

"He's on an extended sabbatical until September," the woman told her. "Is there anyone else who can help you?"

"Not really. I'm an old friend of Rick—uh, Richard's. Do you know where I can reach him?"

The woman hesitated. "I'm new here," she said. "But if you give me your name and where I can reach you, I'll try and find out."

"Thanks." Lucy supplied her name and the hospital phone number, and hung up. Extended sabbatical?

Don't jump to conclusions, she told herself. Perhaps Rick's keeping his options open until he sees how things go at the IMA.

Well, she'd done all she could for the moment. She finished dictating the *E. coli* report and brought it to the office for typing.

She had consults starting at three-thirty, and rounds at five. She checked her messages often during the afternoon, and the fax machine, too. But it wasn't until six that the page operator reached her with an incoming call.

"Dr. Nash?" said a woman's voice. "This is the Stanford personnel department returning your call. Richard Hollander is doing some personal research at the IMA lab in New York. Would you like the phone number there?"

Lucy dutifully took it down and thanked the woman for her trouble. Well, that seems conclusive, she thought: Rick really is Richard Hollander. Although his brief search of her apartment was still puzzling and upsetting, she felt relieved that his identify, at least, was clear. She was also rather embarrassed at having asked Barbara to fax her that photo.

She finished making rounds and went back to her

office to retrieve her coat. She'd been silly to think that chromatography mistake Rick had made had been significant, she decided. As a senior scientist, Rick probably hadn't done his own chromatography in years; he had all those grad students to do it for him. No doubt he was in the process of getting divorced, too, just as he'd told her. And Barbara was a lousy judge of height. Chasing phantoms. And yet, his behavior on Saturday night had been distinctly strange.

Carrying her coat, she went back to the office to sign out. "Half a day?" Jake teased, coming in behind her.

"Very funny. Actually, I'm going down to the IMA lab for a little while," she replied. "I have an experiment running, and I missed my regular Thursday session last week."

"You work too hard."

Lucy laughed. "You should talk. You don't even have your coat on."

"Guilty as charged."

"Dr. Nash?" Pam, the office secretary, interrupted. "That fax you were looking for all afternoon, the one from California? It never came in, and I've got to leave."

"I'll be here awhile," Jake said. "I'll have the page operator give you a jingle if it comes through. They have your number down there?"

"Yes. But it'll wait till tomorrow."

"Whatever you say." He peered at her through his black-rimmed glasses, his dark eyes soft with concern. "You look tired, kid. Don't drive yourself so hard."

"I'm okay, Jake."

"Sure you are." He gave her a bright smile, but his eyes were worried.

"Wait here until I'm inside, would you?"

"Sure, lady."

Lucy got out of the taxi, fishing for her cardkey. It was a little creepy down here even during the day; at night, it felt downright threatening. She unlocked the small steel door and went through it, then turned and waved to the driver before swinging it shut behind her.

Jake's right, she thought, I'm pushing myself too hard. I don't really need to be down here tonight. The cell cultures will wait. The elevator arrived and Lucy stepped in, then hesitated, her finger poised above the second-floor button. Never mind, she was here now. She pressed the button and the door slid closed.

The second floor was quiet, but the lights were blazing. As she neared Carl's office, she heard the faint click of computer keys. So he was still at work. The lab space beyond seemed deserted, and she felt a faint frisson of fear at the thought of being alone with Carl. She edged quietly past his open door, darting a look inside. His back was to her, his concentration on the screen. She continued past, glad he hadn't realized she'd arrived. She'd be inside Level Four before he even—

She stopped. That hadn't been Carl Anders. Slowly, quietly, she retraced her steps and peered in at the figure seated in front of Carl's computer monitor. Dark hair. Medium height. Broad shoulders. Rick Hollander.

Silently, she edged into the room, trying to make out the words on the screen. He shifted in his seat and she froze, but he didn't turn around. He hit some keys and the screen changed. Lucy moved closer.

Now she could just read the file names he was scanning through, and her eyes grew big. Rick had called up Carl's peruvia files, and was examining them, one by one. Off to one side sat the printer, powered up and ready, a stack of printed pages already lying in its "out" bale.

As she watched, Rick called up the Search program

and typed in a command: SECOND STRAIN. How did he know the CDC had found a second strain? she wondered. And why would he think Carl would have a file on it? Anders had always denied its existence. She watched as the Search program came up empty, heard Rick's frustrated curse, saw him close the file. It was only then that she realized they weren't Carl's files he was searching through, but her own.

She backed out of the office, wondering about what she had just witnessed. Industrial sabotage? Or something worse?

As she turned back toward the entrance hallway, Rick emerged from Carl's office, a sheaf of papers in his hand. He caught sight of her and stopped dead. "Lucy?" She turned around and they stared at each other for a moment. "Get your days mixed, doctor?" he asked, his tone light but his smile stiff.

"I missed last Thursday," she said quickly. "I just wanted to check on . . . some things."

"Kind of late to be going into the hot lab," he offered. "Not a good place to be when you're tired."

"You're working late yourself," she replied.

A pause. "Just doing some stuff for Carl." His eyes drifted to the papers he held. "I'm just about, uh, finished. Want to grab some dinner? I'll wait for you."

"I don't think so," she answered. "Thanks, anyway."

"Well, I guess I'll just finish up and, uh, get going." He started for his lab, then stopped. "Maybe I should wait around for you anyway, drive you home. It's not a good area to be wandering around in, looking for a taxi."

"That's okay. I'll call a car service when I'm finished." She made herself smile at him. "Go on home, Rick. I'll be fine."

"You're sure?" She nodded. "Well, okay."

Lucy watched him amble casually to his lab and

disappear inside. She was still standing there when he emerged moments later, wearing his brown leather jacket and carrying a briefcase. "See you on Thursday," she said, forcing her feet to start moving.

"I was hoping sooner," he replied. He touched her hair lightly with his fingertips.

Saved by the beeper, she thought as it sang out, startling them both. She stepped back from Rick and checked the number: the page operator. "Excuse me," she said, retreating toward her lab. "This could be important."

"I better wait," he said, "in case you need a ride to the hospital."

"Dr. Weiss said to tell you that fax you were waiting for came through," the page operator told her. "You want me to get him for you?"

"No," Lucy replied. "It'll wait until morning." With Rick's identity no longer in question, the fax had lost its urgency for her. It wouldn't explain his curiosity about her dresser or her files. She hung up and sank into a chair, suddenly exhausted. There was no way she was going into Level Four tonight.

"Last chance for a ride." Rick stuck his head around her open door.

"I think I'll stick around a while," she told him. "Thanks anyway."

"Any time." Rick came and kissed the top of her head. "Don't stay too late." He waited a moment and, getting no response, gave her a quizzical look and withdrew.

Lucy listened to his footsteps retreat toward the elevator, then propped her elbows on the desk and her chin on her hands, and thought about computer files. It was obvious that Carl's mysterious sangre negra data had been intentionally deleted from the hard drive, and she'd always assumed that Carl himself had been responsible. But now she wasn't so sure. She'd never realized Rick had an interest in peruvia; he'd never questioned her about it. Yet now she thought about it, Rick had already been at work that morning she'd arrived early and discovered the files gone. Anders's office had been dark. Was Rick, not Carl, responsible for the disappearance of those locked files? Was that another little job Rick had done for him?

Just what *was* Rick's sudden interest in the filovirus? she wondered. And was it really so sudden? How could he have learned about the second strain, since Anders refused to acknowledge its existence? And what did any of that have to do with his search for Jean's notebook on Saturday night?

Omigod, the notebook, she thought. She'd forgotten to take it to the bank today. She shuffled quickly through the exercise clothes in her gym bag, sagging with relief when she felt it among her things. Tomorrow, first thing, she told herself. How could she have forgotten? She zipped up the bag and flipped through her address book for the number of the car service.

Chapter Nineteen

Lucy was waiting outside the bank when the guard came to unlock the doors on Tuesday morning. The safe-deposit vault opened at eight-thirty, and the departmental conference started at nine. She knew she was cutting it close, but she didn't want Jean's notebook in her possession one minute longer than necessary.

She signed in, produced the key to her box, and followed the clerk through the thick steel doorway into the vault. Together they unlocked the numbered compartment door. Swinging it back, the clerk drew forth the long metal box and carried it into one of the tiny client rooms, closing the door behind him as he left.

She took the leather notebook from her pocket and set it on the counter, then flipped open the box. A few pieces of her grandmother's jewelry, too valuable to wear, too meaningful to sell. Some old family photos. The deed to her co-op apartment. Several bonds she'd bought when she'd started earning decent money. She tucked the notebook beneath the bond certificates and reached for the lid of the box, then paused.

There was something else in there, too; something she might need. Slowly she removed a bulky envelope. Opening it, she withdrew a heavy object wrapped in an oily cloth that gave off a pungent smell. She stood for a moment, inhaling the sharp, distinctive scent, then slowly unfolded the cloth.

It looked just as it had when she'd put it there almost three years before: sleek, dull black, deadly.

You're crazy, she told herself. Leave it where it is.

Her father had taught her how to use it when they were living in Texas. She was twenty, home from college, and flirting with the idea of joining the military. They'd gone out into the scrub and set up tin cans, and her father had given her a long lecture on gun safety before he'd let her so much as touch it. Her mother had never liked having a firearm in the house, and when he died, she was grateful to Lucy for offering to get rid of it. She'd assumed Lucy would turn it in, or destroy it. She'd assumed wrong.

The gun was unlicensed, and Lucy knew she'd be unlikely to get one. It was doubtful whether the Beretta 92F, with its fifteen-round magazine of 9mm shells and its muzzle velocity of 1,280 feet per second, would be viewed by the authorities as a sport pistol.

She stared at it for a moment more, considering, then wrapped it up again and put it back in its envelope. From deep within the box she extracted several full ammunition clips, slipping them in beside the weapon. Then she closed the safe-deposit box, tucked the envelope into her commodious handbag, and told the vault clerk she was ready to leave.

The meeting had already started as she entered the conference room. Jake Weiss had saved a seat for her, and waved her over.

"You got my message about the fax?" he whispered.

"Yes, but I haven't picked it up yet. I just grabbed my report and came straight here."

"That's what I figured." He pulled a sheet of paper from between the files in front of him. "Here you go."

"Is this it? Thanks, Jake."

"No problem. An article by the boyfriend, huh?"

But Lucy didn't answer. Her eyes were fixed on the unfamiliar face staring out at her from the page. Granted, the quality of the photo, a three-quarters shot of a man standing on the steps of the University library, was poor, made poorer still by the fax transmission. The hair color looked about right, and the general build was similar. But the face . . . People change, she reminded herself. The article was dated some eight years before, the accompanying note from Barbara apologizing for not having found anything more recent. People could change a lot in eight years; he certainly seemed younger in the picture. Younger and taller. Rick would have aged, she thought, but it was unlikely that he would have grown.

The lights went out and the projection screen lit up. A case was presented, and then another. . . . She tried to concentrate; it would be her turn soon. But all she could think about was Rick at the computer, reading her files. . . . Rick in her hallway, a knife in his hand . . .

But if Rick wasn't who he claimed to be, why would Stanford's personnel department tell her Rick Hollander was working at the IMA? Why *was* he working at the IMA, come to that?

She thought about how chummy he and Carl had become, how quick he'd been to forgive Carl's insulting outburst. It didn't seem in character for the sort of person Jake Weiss had described to her.

She felt Jake touch her arm. "Lucy? Your turn." The department chairman was looking at her; everyone was. Forcing her mind back to the business at hand, she opened her folder and took them through her *E. coli* report. It seemed to go well.

After the meeting, she walked slowly back to her office, turning things over in her mind. She thought of Carl wanting to scare her away from the lab, of Rick searching her files to see what she knew about a second peruvia strain. She thought about Crazy Ray's scars, and going to the stars, and that Carl Anders had been involved with a mission with "star" in its name.

Was it possible that Rick, or Carl, or maybe both of them together, were using the IMA lab for their own purposes? And might those purposes include infecting Ray and others like him with the filovirus she'd brought back from Peru? The idea was horrifying, but also puzzling: Why would they do such a thing? To what end?

She thought of Bill Miller, the armchair revolutionary—naive, good-natured, and too trusting to realize what was going on right under his nose.

Entering her office, she booted up her computer and began making notes. Writing things down often helped organize her thinking. And God knew, she needed to put some order into the multiplicity of questions that were milling around in her head.

She typed furiously for several minutes, then stopped and read over what she'd written. Okay, she thought: next steps.

TALK TO BILL, she typed. No, too soon. She deleted the words and substituted EXAMINE RAY. He'd seemed semicoherent this morning; perhaps tomorrow he'd recognize her. FIND STAR MISSION, she added. THEN TALK TO BILL. Yes, that was the order of march. Go to Bill with facts, not guesswork. TELL BILL ABOUT RICK. Good; she could do that right now. No need to wait on that one, right? Wrong, she told herself. Supposition again. Stanford's personnel department would back up Rick's claim, and that would carry more weight with Bill than a blurry, out-of-date photo. Besides, Bill might tell Carl about her suspicions of

Rick, and that could be dangerous for her, especially if Carl and Rick had gone in business together for themselves.

STOP SEEING RICK was equally wrong, and she deleted it. If she was careful, her relationship with him could be a vital conduit of information. A dangerous game, perhaps, but only if he knew that she knew that he—

Her head hurt. She pulled a tin of aspirin from her desk drawer and shook two tablets into her palm. She stood, contemplating the screen. Keep it simple, she told herself. Examine Ray. Find the mission. Keep your relationship with Rick going. Talk to Bill Miller when you're sure of your facts and can prove them. Good. Right. Okay.

She selected everything, hit the delete key, and went out into the hall to get some water for the aspirin.

Carl Anders ripped away the tape and entered the abandoned ward. He wore a full bodysuit: boots, gloves, helmet. The formaldehyde gas should have done its work by now, but until he checked the papers, he couldn't be positive. Even after he'd seen with his own eyes that the subtilis niger on every paper was dead, he wouldn't be positive, only reasonably sure.

He picked up the samples in his thick double gloves, and carried them to the makeshift workstation. He was keenly aware of the air around him, heavy with the thick scent of decontamination, but his air supply was self-contained and he couldn't smell or taste it.

He spent a long time at the portable microscope he'd brought. Finally, satisfied that the room was as clean as he could make it, he hit a switch and started the ventilation system that would pump the sickly, telltale-scented air out into the building's closed respiratory system where it would be sterilized yet again, stripped of its odor, and returned. Within twenty-four hours, the formaldehyde would be only a whisper in the air around him. He fervently hoped that the filovirus that had once lived here would not be that even.

Rosetti pulled out a chair and sat down. "I'm glad you chose some place new," he said with a lopsided grin. "People were beginning to talk." He reached for the lager the older man had ordered in anticipation of his arrival. "You want to go first, or shall I?"

"Be my guest."

"Jean-Pierre Didier—that doctor who was arrested with the heroin? Turns out, he was an art smuggler. Specialized in valuable ancient artifacts. Sold them through a few galleries that weren't too particular about their provenance. And I know what it was she took from his apartment: a notebook listing the galleries and sales."

"Good work. You have it?"

"No, but it doesn't matter anymore, at least not for our purposes. Didier's out of business, and so is one of his fences, guy named Beno Stanislas. Stabbed."

"And you said we wouldn't have anything to talk about." His companion sipped his drink. "I want that notebook, Mike."

"Look, the art smuggling's a red herring. It's not even connected to the IMA, except that Miller may have bought some stuff through Stanislas."

"And you don't think that's significant? What if Miller realized what Didier was doing? What if he figured out that the stuff he was buying from what's-his-name—"

"Stanislas."

"—had been smuggled in by one of his own doctors, putting the IMA at risk?"

Rosetti shrugged. "Miller would have been ap-

palled. And he would have fired Didier, or whatever
you do to get rid of a volunteer. End of story." His
companion eyed him noncommittally. "You think otherwise? Miller's a highly respected doctor, Tom. Besides, Didier committed suicide, remember? It's your
turn, now. Was I right about dePalma?"

"Bingo. That place she was born in, Villarosa? It's
in Sicily. And guess who else was born in Villarosa?
Joseph Tortoriello's grandfather Paolo."

"Mafia."

"Right. Oh, and Count dePalma's title wasn't inher-
ited. It was purchased. The present count was formerly
known as Luciano Salerno. Came here from Sicily as
a boy; deported twenty years ago for criminal activities."

"Renée's a big contributor to the IMA,'" Rossetti
said meditatively, "and a pal of Miller's. But the mob
doesn't usually use women. So what's the connection?"

"You tell me, Mike."

"Wish I could."

"Oh, there's one more thing I think will interest
you. Someone's been calling Stanford recently, asking
about Richard Hollander."

Rosetti frowned. "Who?"

"Dr. Lucy Nash."

"Oh, shit."

"Indeed. Of course, we handled it. Told her Hollander was on sabbatical, doing private research at the
IMA lab." He paused. "But I think we have trouble
there."

"She's the one who's in trouble," Rossetti said
slowly. "If she's starting to question Hollander, it's
going to be a lot harder to protect her."

"Oh, I think she's more dangerous to us than we
are to her. She's part of the IMA, she works in Level
Four. She's got to be one of the inner circle."

But Rosetti shook his head. "I don't think so, Tom.
I'm sure she has no idea what's really going on."

"Then that makes three of us."

"Yes, but she found the notebook. And she's already been threatened by Anders. . . . I think she's in real danger." He sighed deeply. "And now we can't protect her anymore."

Chapter Twenty

The oranges looked good. She selected three, adding them to the small roast chicken, French baguette, and assorted vegetables in her shopping basket, and took it all over to the cashier.

"Stocking up?" the clerk asked as Lucy dug in her handbag for her wallet. "They're forecasting five, six inches tomorrow."

"So I heard. But they've been wrong before," she added hopefully.

"Feels like snow, though."

"It does." Lucy pocketed her change and took her groceries out into the cold, dark, Wednesday evening. Ordinarily, the thought of a snowstorm would have evoked cozy images of hot chocolate and cuddling with Rick. But these were not ordinary times.

"Hi, doc. Help me get something to eat?"

Lucy spun around as Ray shuffled out of a recessed doorway, his cup held out. "Sure, Ray," she said quickly, reaching for the change in her pocket. "You know who I am?"

Ray frowned. "Course I do. You're the doc." He watched carefully as coins cascaded into his cup. "Where you been?"

"I've been working," Lucy replied, refraining from reminding him that he'd been the one who hadn't been all there lately. "Uh, do you remember what we talked about last time?" Ray shook his head and began to move off. "I have more money for you," she called after him. "Lots more."

That stopped him. Cautiously he extended the cup again, but Lucy shook her head. "First I want to buy you a meal. You like McDonald's, don't you?"

"Sure."

"Well, come on. Aren't you hungry? I am."

But Ray stood confused. "You want me to go with you? Inside?"

"Of course, inside. It's too cold out here. I want to talk to you." Gently she led him to the restaurant and through the glass doors, and settled him at a table. People glared pointedly at them, but she stared fiercely back and they looked away. "You stay here and I'll get the food. What would you like?"

When she returned with the loaded tray, Ray had shed his anorak and unwound a filthy scarf from around his neck. He attacked the food with vigor, and Lucy forced herself to eat some of her burger.

"Last time I saw you, you had a sort of rash on your neck," she said. "I have some salve in my office that will make it feel better. Could I look at it?"

Ray paused in mid-bite. "You want to look at my neck?"

"That's right. I'm the doc, remember?"

Ray shrugged. "Okay."

Lucy rose and went around to where he sat. Gently she pulled back the grimy shirt collar. The crescent scars were unmistakable. Trying desperately to control her facial expression, she went back to her seat. "I have the perfect medicine for that rash," she said. "In my office at the hospital."

"It doesn't bother me," he said.

"I don't want it to get worse," she answered, but he didn't seem to hear her. He pushed away the empty cardboard burger container and started on his pie. It wasn't a very large pie; she didn't have much time.

"If you come back to my office with me now," she said, "I'll pay you ten dollars."

He looked up at her, his lips smeared with cherry juice, his pale eyes large. "Ten dollars?"

"That's right."

Ray scowled. "That's a lot of money. What do I have to do for it?"

"Well, we're, um, doing a study on, uh, neck rashes," Lucy improvised. "A special study. We examine people's necks, and, er, then we give them a little checkup, and we pay them for their, uh, time. And then we write about it."

"No kidding?" He popped the last of the pie into his mouth and looked at her with interest. "You'll pay me ten dollars just for looking at my neck?"

"Yes, I will. But you have to come with me right now. In a taxi."

"Where we going?"

Stay with me, Ray, she prayed. "We're going to my office at the hospital. That's where we do the study. That's where we keep the money."

"Don't need no hospital," he said. "Already been there."

"This is a different hospital," she said patiently. "And it's just for a few minutes. I bet they didn't pay you ten dollars at that other hospital."

"They paid me *twenty,*" Ray said. He dabbed at some fallen pie crumbs with a forefinger and licked them off, glancing up to see if she was buying it.

"We usually only pay ten," she replied, "but I guess we could pay you twenty." She tried to remember how much cash she had with her. She supposed she could borrow some at the hospital. "Are you finished eating?"

"Could you make it twenty-five?" he asked hopefully.

Lucy sighed. "Okay, Ray. Twenty-five. But only if you come with me right now."

He got up and began winding the scarf around his neck. "Okay," he said. "I sure can use thirty dollars."

"Twenty-five."

"Right." He struggled into his jacket and followed her outside into the cold.

The first taxi she flagged down pulled away as soon as the driver saw she meant to take Crazy Ray with her. She got the door of the second cab open and Ray inside before the angry Middle Easterner at the wheel knew what was happening.

"You shouldn't take him in a regular taxi," he protested in broken English. "It is not fair. My car is clean. Is not for him."

Lucy was unsympathetic. "Drive," she ordered firmly.

It was after six, and the hospital was drawing a deep breath in preparation for the evening onslaught. An ambulance was pulling up outside the ER as Lucy guided Ray through the front entrance and around to the elevators. They passed through a hallway leading to one of the ORs, and Ray shied at the sight of several gowned and masked surgical technicians striding purposefully past. But once they were in the infectious diseases corridor, things quieted down, and so did Ray.

She led him past her office and into a small examining room. "Why don't you sit up here on the table?" she suggested, but Ray shook his head and plunked himself down into a chair to one side. She put her medical bag up on the small desk, suddenly realizing she'd left her groceries in the taxi. Never mind, she thought; even at twenty-five dollars for Ray and nine-fifty for groceries, it was cheap at the price. "It'll be a lot easier if you sit up here on the table," she told Ray.

He eyed her cannily. "Thirty bucks?"

"Twenty-five's all I've got." She paused. "Tell you

what: I'll pay you another five if you'll get up on the table. And if you let me draw some blood."

Ray got up. "I'm outta here," he said firmly.

"Okay, okay, no blood. How about a chest X ray?"

"What you need a X ray for?" he asked suspiciously.

"It's part of the little checkup I told you about."

He studied her. "Okay, but no blood."

"Deal." Still scowling, Ray climbed up on the table and Lucy called down to Radiology to say she'd need an emergency chest film taken in ten minutes.

"Emergency?" Ray asked.

"I just said that so you could go home sooner," she told him. "You don't want to hang around this hospital, do you?"

"Hey, how'm I gonna get home?" he asked, it having suddenly occurred to him that he had no idea where he was.

"I'll pay for a taxi to drive you. Unbutton your shirt for me, please."

Lucy checked the scars again, wishing fervently for a blood sample, not so much to convince herself of her supposition, but to be able to prove it to Bill. Then she listened to Ray's chest and lungs, and checked his blood pressure. A slight wheeze in the left lung. Strong, regular heartbeat. Pulse slightly elevated, but that would be nerves.

"You finished yet, doc?"

"Just about." Lucy made notes on the examination form, and looked at the scars one more time. "Okay, get dressed and we'll go down to X ray."

"When do I get my money?"

"After the X ray." *And after I borrow ten bucks from the X ray technician.* She packed up her medical bag and took him down to the subbasement via the back elevator. Radiology was in another wing of the hospital, and the basement corridor that ran beneath both buildings was the most direct route.

"Spooky down here," Ray said. "Where we at?"

"We're underneath the hospital," she explained.

"Where we going?"

"To X ray." They walked in silence for a few minutes. Several nurses, hurrying past, barely glanced at them. "That hospital you were in, before," Lucy said "It was called 'star' something?"

"Yeah, stars. It was inside a big star."

"Inside a star? I thought you said it was *called* 'star.' "

"Star, yeah."

"Do you remember what was the matter with you?" Lucy pressed. "Did they tell you what you had?"

"What I had?" Ray thought for a moment. "I was sick."

"I know you were sick," Lucy said impatiently. Then, more gently, she added, "Did they tell you the name of the sickness?"

"Yeah. But I don't remember. *P*-something."

Jesus, Lucy thought excitedly. "Peruvia?" she asked, trying to calm her voice. "Was it called peruvia?"

But Ray shook his head. "Nope, that wasn't it. *P*-something . . . a *P* and a *T* . . . Some kinda letters."

Lucy racked her brain; what could he mean? "TB?" she asked at last. "Is that it? Did you have TB?"

"Yeah, yeah, that was it." His face brightened with recognition. "It was TB."

She considered. Tuberculosis was certainly possible, at least in theory. Several types of TB were on the rise among the city's homeless. But peruvia scars sure as hell weren't.

She thought about the symptoms of peruvia and wondered how anyone could confuse the disease with tuberculosis. Sure, both infections presented with fever and a cough. Sure, some forms of TB produced a rash. But there the similarities stopped. The hemorrhaging, the bloody eyes, the gradual liquefaction of the internal organs, all these were symptoms no tubercular bacillus had ever dreamt of. The chest X ray was vital, she realized. The chest X ray would prove Ray hadn't had TB. Unfortunately, it couldn't prove conclusively that he'd had peruvia. Only a blood test could do that.

"How much more would I have to pay you to draw some blood?" she asked.

Ray stopped, then started walking backward, away from her. "You said no blood."

"I'll pay you extra."

"No blood. Going home now."

She went after him quickly. "Okay, okay. No blood. I promise. Just the X ray." Stupid, stupid, she berated herself. "No blood. Look"—she reached into her handbag—"here's the money. Don't you want the money?" Damn, I need that chest film. It took her a few minutes to quiet and reassure him, but at last she managed to coax him into a slow shamble in the direction of the radiology department.

"Be about twenty minutes," the technician told her. "He can sit over there." Despite the hour, some eight people were ranged in chairs around the waiting room.

"Can I see you a moment?" Lucy took the technician aside. "I'm Dr. Nash, from Infectious Diseases. I just called down?" The man nodded. "Look, there's no way I can keep that guy waiting around here for twenty minutes. He'll simply bolt. You've got to take him next. Please." The man looked around her at the raggedy man with the bleary eyes. "All I need is a couple of chest films," she continued. "It's important. I need them stat. Oh, and can I borrow ten dollars till tomorrow?"

*   *   *

Clutching the manila envelope containing the X rays, Lucy got Ray, now cloudy-eyed and growing confused, into a taxi, and shoved some money in the driver's hand. "Take him to Second and Seventy-fifth," she said. "Just let him out on the corner."

"What if he won't *get* out?" the driver asked reasonably. It was warm in the car, and the seats were soft.

She thought for a moment, then opened the back door. "Ray? I'm giving the driver an extra five dollars. He'll take you to McDonald's, and when you get out of the taxi, he'll give you the money. Okay?"

Ray mumbled an assent, and Lucy pushed a five through the driver's window. She stood for a moment, watching them pull away, then carried the envelope back up to her office.

She'd had a quick look at the films on the radiology lightbox before she and Ray had left. No tubercular nodules, no scarring; nothing that would indicate TB. Not that she'd expected any. No, what had shaken her was that, despite the crescent scars on his neck, Ray's lungs showed no evidence of the sort of damage peruvia always inflicted, to a greater or lesser degree, on soft tissue, even in survivors.

She sat in her darkened office, the room illuminated only by the spill from the light box on her wall, staring at the films. How could Ray have peruvia scars if he hadn't had peruvia?

Chapter Twenty-one

She woke the next morning with a renewed sense of purpose. The promised snow had not yet developed, but excited TV meteorologists were assuring everyone it was on its way. Lucy grabbed a pair of boots from the hall closet as she headed out the door. She'd planned to hit the gym for half an hour on the way to the hospital, but had overslept. Now she hurried down the street, checking her watch and praying for a taxi, and hoping she wouldn't be late for rounds.

It was Thursday, her day for the IMA lab, but a series of new admits forced her to call Carl and cancel her session there for the second time in a row. On the one hand, she felt a little guilty; she didn't approve of taking on a job and not following through. On the other, she felt relieved. Working in Level Four was exhausting, and she wanted to use whatever reserves her hospital day left her with, to do a little sleuthing.

By four in the afternoon, the pace had slowed somewhat. She grabbed a sandwich and some juice from the cafeteria—her first food since morning—and took them back to her desk, collecting a NYNEX Yellow Pages from the department office on the way.

Taking a bite of sandwich, she opened the book to "Hospitals" and ran her finger down the list. Only one, Morningstar Medical Center, a small facility in Yonkers, sounded promising. She wrote its address on a piece of note paper, and paged through to "Missions."

Here there were many suggestive names: Angel Memorial House, God's Lighthouse, Le Candela. But no stars; not even an *estrella*. She turned to "Shelters," wondering what had possessed the phone company to create a separate category for this while lumping together under the previous heading the Nepal Mission to the U.N. and Grace Faith Church.

"Shelters" boasted only three entries, two of which held no significance to her. The third was Star of Hope Mission, with a downtown address.

She copied it out, then leaned back in her chair, notepaper in hand, and tried to decide which one to start with. Morningstar Medical Center would be better equipped to treat TB. For that matter, a mission shouldn't be treating a bunch of TB patients at all. But Ray didn't have TB, she reminded herself. And Morningstar was way up in Yonkers. It was unlikely, though not impossible, that Ray had wandered up there on his own.

On his own . . . She seemed to recall that the homeless people in her neighborhood had all disappeared about the same time. Maybe they hadn't wandered anywhere. Maybe they'd been collected.

By Morningstar Medical Center? Or by Star of Hope Mission?

Beyond her window, tiny flakes had begun to fall, making her decision for her. It would be folly to try to get up to Yonkers and back in a snowstorm. She stood and went to the window, craning to get a look at the sidewalks below. The snow was still very light. She could grab a cab downtown and have a quick look around. It might be hard to get a taxi back, especially if the blizzard materialized, but the buses might still be running. Besides, she had her boots and heavy coat; she could walk back if she had to.

Taxies were still plentiful outside the hospital as she came out into the cold, wet evening. "Can't take the West Side Highway," the driver told her as they pulled away. "Accident. Roadway's getting slick."

"Well, go the best way you know," Lucy told him, settling back. Lost in her thoughts, she was barely conscious of where they were until the cab skidded around a corner. "Where are we?" she asked, looking up. The flakes were falling faster now, and the street was dark.

"Nearly there," the driver said, slowing down. "Just around the corner."

Lucy nodded, and began to fish in her wallet, then stopped and stared out the window, suddenly realizing where they were. She turned and saw, disappearing behind them, a small, dimly illuminated steel door. They had just passed the IMA lab.

The cab turned one corner, then another. "It's a real maze down here," the driver complained. "End up driving around in circles, with all these one-way streets. That where you're going?"

Ahead, a giant blue star shed an eerie light in a wide arc across the newfallen snow. It's like a mirage, Lucy thought, or a vision. No wonder Ray had told her he'd lived in a star.

STAR OF HOPE read the flaking gilt sign above the door. Lucy got out and stood looking up at the brick building. Because she'd always taken the West Side Highway downtown, she'd never approached the IMA lab from this direction. And the garage where Rick kept his car was over toward the river, too. The taxi had made two right turns after passing the IMA lab; she must be on the street behind it. She glanced left and right, trying to orient herself, realizing that the IMA lab and Star of Hope would be more or less back-to-back. She felt a chill that had nothing to do with the snow that was coating her hair and shoulders.

She hesitated for a moment, then pushed open the mission door and went inside.

A fug of heat and food and unwashed bodies rolled toward her as she started up the bleak hallway. A line of people shuffled slowly up to and through an archway to the right, where an overworked man in a soiled apron was ladling steaming stew onto white plastic plates.

"May I help you?" Lucy turned. A severe-looking woman with kind eyes stood beside her. Taking in the clean coat, the boots, the face, the handbag, she added, "I assume you're not here for the meal."

"No, I've come to help."

The woman surveyed her, frowning. "I don't understand. You're not one of our regulars." Her accent was soft but distinctive. German? Lucy wondered. Dutch?

"No, I . . . I live around here." A number of loft buildings had been turned into residential housing, some legal, some not. In any event, the lie was believable. "I've often passed this way," Lucy continued, "and thought about volunteering. And then tonight, with the snow, I figured maybe some of your regular people wouldn't show up, and . . ." She smiled and gave a little helpless shrug. "Anyway, I'm here."

The woman studied her for a moment, then smiled. "You were right," she said. "We can use some help tonight. One of our servers and an overnight volunteer have both canceled. I am Sister Margareta. What is your name?"

"Lucy," Lucy said. "Lucy Nash."

Lucy thought she saw a flash of recognition in the woman's eyes. But her tone, when she spoke, was impersonal. "Come with me, please," she said, leading her toward the serving table. "Jonathan will show you what to do."

*   *   *

He pushed open the door and flicked on the light. The ventilation system had been going full blast for two days now, and the air was smelling pretty good. He jerked up the master switch and the loud *whoosh* of the exhaust fans fell silent. He could still recognize the faint, sickly odor of the formaldehyde gas that had worked its way inside the desk drawers and cabinets and joins in the linoleum flooring. The last of the odor would take a while longer to dissipate completely, but that was to be expected.

He wandered around, checking for anything he might have missed. The bleach had removed the tell-tale smears of blood and feces from walls and floors. The long electrical cord had been taken up, stored away with the frying pans and boxes of crystals. The staff, those who'd survived, had been paid off hand-somely, and sent back to the far-flung locations from which they'd been carefully, and separately, recruited. The families of the less-fortunate nurses and orderlies had received letters, purportedly from their kin, telling of high-paying new positions in Europe and Asia.

The room was ready. But he doubted it would be needed again. His results were complete and conclusive. They could move to the next stage now. They were ready.

"You guys were pretty lucky with that TB thing," Lucy said casually, placing a slice of bread and a square of butter on the plate Jonathan passed her, and handing it to the next person in line.

"What TB thing?" Jonathan frowned, concentrating on the pot of stew in front of him.

"All those homeless people who got sick. I knew one of them, a guy who hangs around my neighbor-hood. He told me."

The server looked over at her. "Don't know what you're talking about," he said. "No TB here." He passed her another plateful. 'You must be thinking of some other place.''

"No, it was here. My friend told me about the star outside. Said he got sick and you took care of him. Other people, too." She hesitated. "The nursing staff must be pretty good here, huh?"

Jonathan looked away. "Don't know what you mean," he murmured. "No TB here."

"Well, maybe he was wrong about the TB. But he did get sick here. And you did make him better."

"Not me," the man said with finality. "I didn't have nothing to do with it."

"Dr. Anders? It's Margareta. That colleague of yours, the one you said might be stopping by? She's here. I didn't say anything to her, as you instructed." Margareta paused. It seemed funny that Dr. Nash's dear friend Carl Anders wanted to surprise her if she showed up. It also seemed funny that Dr. Nash wouldn't identify herself as a doctor, nor mention Carl. Well, the IMA had been very good to the mission. Her predecessor had told her how the IMA had arranged for the repair of the building's crumbling rear addition several years before, enlarging the small shelter from ten beds to twenty-two, creating a storage room, and renovating the antiquated bathrooms and showers. And Dr. Miller had been so helpful and supportive during the TB outbreak. No, the IMA's internal affairs were none of her business. "It's about six, now, and I'm not sure how long she's planning to stay. But you said to call you, so that's what I'm doing. I hope you get this message." She hung up the phone and went out to see how Lucy was getting on.

Carl entered the small laboratory and headed for the computer terminal. Yes, everything was on schedule, he thought with satisfaction. All that remained was to change the mode of transmission. He lowered his suited body carefully onto a metal stool and typed a command on the keyboard. The screen changed, and changed again, as his lightly gloved fingers flew across the keys, creating computer models of gene sequences. On the counter some six feet away from where he sat, the red message light on his telephone blinked rapidly. Specially built for use inside the hot lab, the sealed instrument could access messages left on his office answering machine, transmitting them via a microphone tie-in to the headset in his helmet. Ordinary phone conversations could be carried on the same way.

Carl worked for several more minutes before the red glow caught his eye. He punched the replay button and listened intently. Then, with a muffled curse, he rose quickly and ran for the decon shower. Behind him, the computer screen glowed in the dim blue light.

Jonathan carried the large serving pot into the kitchen while Lucy went around the dining room filling the large black trash bags with used plates and cups and plastic cutlery.

"How are you getting on?" Margareta asked, appearing at her side. "Have they had the fruit cocktail yet?"

"No, Jonathan's gone to get it. I'm just clearing up a little."

"Let me help you." Together they moved among the tables, the sister smiling and greeting her shabby guests with the graciousness of a hostess at a fancy dinner party.

"I understand you had an outbreak of TB here recently," Lucy remarked as they worked.

"TB?" Margareta shook her head. "Here? Who told you such a thing?"

"A . . . friend of mine was . . . involved," Lucy replied carefully.

The sister relaxed. Carl had explained that this Lucy Nash he was half expecting was his colleague. Since Carl had obviously seen fit to tell Dr. Nash about the TB outbreak, it seemed silly for Margareta to continue denying it. "It's true," she confided, lowering her voice. "We were given a special permit to keep them here, poor things. We set up a complete quarantine in the shelter area, and of course we took extreme precautions. And God blessed our efforts. We had a one hundred percent recovery."

"Really? Isn't that wonderful," Lucy exclaimed, wondering whether the sister was lying, or simply misinformed. A one hundred percent recovery from peruvia was impossible; even a fifty percent recovery was unlikely. "And how did you first identify—"

"Everybody stay seated, please, and we'll bring around the dessert," Jonathan announced, interrupting her. "Lucy, can you give me a hand here?"

"Go on," Margareta told her, tying the trash bag shut. "I must see to the shelter. We have only twenty-two beds," she added regretfully. "Such a terrible night to have to turn people away."

Lucy took the tray Jonathan thrust toward her and quickly distributed the small bowls of canned fruit, her mind on other things. Had Margareta really believed the patients she'd quarantined in her shelter had been ill with tuberculosis? On the other hand, it seemed impossible that she would knowingly harbor a lethal pathogen here in the mission, even under tight quarantine conditions. Besides, no ordinary quarantine would be tight enough to contain peruvia. Extreme precautions, Margareta had said. Did that mean orange RACAL suits? Was that what Ray had been referring to when he talked about golden angels?

Now that the sister had confirmed the outbreak of what they'd both referred to as TB, Lucy was anxious to probe further, but when she went out into the corridor in search of Margareta, the sister had disappeared. Lucy went back to the dining room. The guests were spooning in the fruit, joking with Jonathan as he went from table to table collecting the salt and pepper shakers.

"Would you put these away?" he asked Lucy.

"Sure." She took the box of shakers and went through the dining room to the tiny kitchen. The entrance was fairly well blocked by several large, black garbage bags. Inside, a young man stood at a stainless-steel sink, scrubbing an aluminum cooking pot. "Why don't I get this trash out of here?" she offered, reaching around to set the box of shakers on a counter.

"Good idea," the dishwasher replied. "Coupla bins out front. Just stick 'em in and put the top on tight. Better take your coat. It's snowing pretty hard out there."

Sorry she'd suggested it, Lucy put on her coat and boots and dragged the bags to the front door. Several inches of fresh, undisturbed snow, bright blue with the reflection of the giant neon star, covered the sidewalk in front of the mission. She trekked across it to the plastic bins and crammed the bags in, feeling the snow settle wetly on her hair and cheeks and eyelashes.

Behind her, the door opened and the erstwhile guests, all but a lucky twenty-two, streamed out into the frosty night. At the end of the procession came the dishwasher, waving good night to her as he buttoned his coat.

"Bad night out there." Jonathan stood just inside the door, her oversized bag in his hand. "Is this yours? You shouldn't leave it around."

"Thanks." Lucy took the proffered handbag. "And I had some shoes—"

"They're in there. You can put that in Margareta's office if you're staying the night."

"I don't know about all night," Lucy answered, "but I'll stay as long as I can."

"Fair enough. Leave your stuff with Margareta and come on back to the dining room. After we finish up in there, we'll get out the blankets and pillows."

"Okay." Still wearing her coat and boots, Lucy started down the long corridor. She hoped Margareta would be alone when she dropped off her things, so they could talk some more. But Margareta wasn't alone. From behind her closed office door came the murmur of voices. Lucy raised her fist to knock, then froze.

"I got your message," Carl Anders was saying. "Where is she?"

"Working in the dining room, I believe," Margareta answered. "And what a night she chose to turn up. Two inches already, and still—"

"Never mind the weather," Carl said. "What is she doing here?"

"She helped with the dinner, that's all." Margareta sounded surprised. "Such a charming young woman. But I was surprised that you'd told her about the TB outbreak. I realize she's a colleague of yours, but—"

"What? She knows about that?"

"Well, yes. She said a friend of hers had been involved and I naturally assumed . . ."

Where had Carl come from? Lucy wondered. The snow in front of the mission had been unmarked when she'd gone to the trash bins. Was there a back door? But why would Carl come in the back way? She looked down at the linoleum tiles in front of Margareta's partly closed door; they were perfectly dry. The only wet footprints were her own. Carl had come from somewhere inside the mission. Interesting . . .

"I'll go and get her," Carl was saying. "You wait out in the hall, in case she tries to leave."

Lucy bristled; how dare he? Did he really think he

could prevent her from leaving? What did he possibly imagine he could do to stop her? Then she thought of the deserted streets outside and recalled his whispered threat that if he wanted to kill her, he wouldn't miss. Who knew what he was prepared to do? Still, Margareta wouldn't allow him to harm her.

"But I don't understand," the sister was protesting. "I thought she was a colleague of yours."

Carl's reply was low and Lucy moved closer, concentrating on his voice. "She's an impostor," she heard him explain. "I didn't tell you the truth because I didn't want you to frighten her away. But she's . . . not really a doctor; she only thinks she is. She gets . . . confused. She's been institutionalized a number of times, but the psych units are so overcrowded . . ."

Good one, Carl, Lucy thought. Now there was no way Margareta would believe anything she might say. Unnoticed, Jonathan appeared from the dining room. He went straight to the front door, flipped the lock shut, and shot the large steel bolt mounted high up on the door frame before disappearing back into the dining room.

"Poor girl," Margareta was saying. "She seemed so nice."

"She isn't a bad person," Carl agreed. "She just needs help. These delusions of hers usually pass in a few days. I've brought a sedative. After we've calmed her, perhaps she could stay with you for a while."

"Of course. I'll help any way I can," Margareta assured Carl.

Time to go, Lucy decided, and ran to the front door. She pulled at it to no avail, then looked up and saw the shot bolt, just out of reach.

Behind her, she heard a chair scrape back and realized she'd left it too late. In a moment, he'd come out into the hallway. She was at his mercy.

Or was she? Carl had come into the mission with

dry feet. If he'd gotten in, she could get out. The mission and the IMA lab must be connected somehow. But where? The buildings were back-to-back, she reminded herself, so Carl must have come in from the rear of the mission.

As Margareta's door swung open, Lucy raced back down the corridor toward the sleeping area, praying they'd come out facing in the opposite direction, toward the front door and the dining room.

"I hope we will not have a problem," Margareta was saying.

Lucy stood in an agony of indecision. Behind her was the sleeping room. To the right were the bathrooms. To the left was a brown door marked EMPLOYEES ONLY. She'd only get one crack at this. She flipped a mental coin, turned left, and pushed through the brown door.

She was facing a wall. A short, narrow hallway on her right ran back toward the rear of the building, and she turned and followed it to its end, stepping down into a small, modern addition, low ceilinged, dimly lit, and filled with junk. Folding beds, a broken chair, and similar discards filled half the space, and cartons of old clothing, books, and miscellany were stacked haphazardly here and there. A wide wooden wardrobe, its green paint peeling, stood against one wall; a steamer trunk leaned drunkenly against it. Set into the opposite wall was a modern closet with sliding doors. She opened them and found the blankets and pillows Jonathan had spoken of. I guessed wrong, she thought despondently. This room's too well used to house a secret passageway. I should have chosen the bathrooms.

Now what? She could go back and face Carl, brazen it out, and try to get Jonathan to unbolt the front door. She had her hospital identification in her handbag. But Carl had more credence than she, and he'd say her badge was a fake. Margareta and Jonathan would do as he told them, restraining her while he injected the sedative. Or whatever it was he'd brought with him.

Good idea, getting that gun out of the vault, she told herself sarcastically. It's real useful, hidden under your damn mattress. Not that she could quite picture herself shooting her way out of the Star of Hope Mission.

She sat on a carton and looked around. Jonathan would be coming in for the blankets soon. She got up again and paced to the short hallway she'd come down, then turned back. For a storage room in constant use, it certainly was a mess. The area in front of the blanket closet was more or less clear, but the rest of the floor space was practically obscured. And how did they ever manage to get to that wardrobe over there, the one with the two large, heavy-looking cartons in front of it? She wandered over and inspected the cartons. They were filled to the brim, their unseen contents topped with crumpled newspaper, but when she pushed one, it moved easily. They're empty, she thought in some surprise.

And there was something about the way those cartons were positioned in front of the wardrobe that bothered her, too. She pulled them out of the way and opened the door. The few items of clothing that hung there had been shoved to one side.

She stepped inside and felt along the back wall. Solid. Right wall: solid. Left wall: missing. Missing? With growing excitement, Lucy felt around the opening in the left side of the closet and found the hinged panel. Carl must have left it open in his hurry to confront her.

She got out again and studied the exterior of the wardrobe. It was some three feet wider on the outside than it was on the inside. She retrieved her handbag, then pushed the cartons as close to the wardrobe as she could while still being able to open the door. Squeezing between them, she stepped back into the wardrobe and fumbled with the door, discovering it was double-hinged to swing in as well as out. She swung it in.

The large, heavy-looking cartons had been camouflage, easy to shove aside when getting in or out of the wardrobe. She reached out and pulled them right up against the wardrobe, then swung the door back into place. In total darkness, she bent and stepped through the open panel, stumbling as she encountered the first in a series of high, narrow stairs.

Chapter Twenty-two

"She took out the trash," Jonathan said, "and then I told her to put her handbag in your office, sister. That's the last I saw of her."

"She must have gone," Margareta said. "When you went back into the dining room."

But Jonathan shook his head. "I asked could she stay the night, and she said she'd stay as long as she could. Didn't sound like she was going right then."

"She heard us," Carl fumed. "She was outside your office"—he turned toward Margareta accusingly—"and she heard me warning you about her."

"Yeah? What's she done?" Jonathan asked.

"She's a confused woman who needs our help," the sister told him severely. "She must have slipped out," she said, turning back to Carl, "while we were talking."

But Carl appeared unconvinced. "She could be hiding somewhere," he said. "Jonathan, you search in there." He gestured toward the examination and infirmary rooms. "Margareta, the bathrooms and showers."

"Maybe we should just let her alone," the sister suggested. "She didn't seem particularly dangerous."

"Yeah," Jonathan agreed. "Hunting her down like this seems awfully—"

"Necessary," Carl interjected. "Remember, she

thinks she's a doctor. You have overnight guests. Suppose she takes it into her head to 'treat' one of them."

Margareta's eyes grew big. "I didn't think of that."

Carl watched them fan out, then followed the sister to the rear of the building and stuck his head inside the shelter. Empty. He withdrew it and turned toward the EMPLOYEES ONLY door. If she'd gone in there . . . Stupid, he rebuked himself. Stupid, stupid.

They'd disagreed about building the hidden stairway as part of the renovation, but he'd insisted. What if something went wrong with the treatment? he'd argued. What if the mission staff got wind of what they were doing? They couldn't simply drag the bodies out the front door. He'd prevailed. But at that moment, he wished he hadn't.

He shoved through the door and strode down the hallway toward the storage room. My own fault, he berated himself. I shouldn't have panicked. Shouldn't have been in such a hurry; should have gone the long way round. Fortunately, Margareta hadn't noticed the old coat he'd grabbed from one of the cartons to make it seem as if he'd come from outside. Stupid, stupid. God, how he hated that damn Lucy Nash.

The stairs led upward through the blackness. She stumbled, bruising a knee, as she blindly followed their convolutions, moving fast, expecting at any moment to hear Carl's footfall on the stairs below, to feel his hand on her shoulder. The air was dank and stale, the metal banister rail cold. The stairway ended abruptly and she banged into the door in the darkness, rebounding, stumbling backward, pulling herself erect. Frantically, she searched with her hands for a doorknob, a lever, something. . . . She shoved at it in frustration and it creaked open. Like the wardrobe door below, it was double-hinged. She stepped through it into a low corridor, dimly lit by widely spaced low-wattage bulbs strung along the ceiling.

Okay, she thought; this will be okay. It'll lead into the IMA lab, and I can get out that way. I just have to follow it and I'll be fine. As long as I can stay ahead of Carl.

He scanned the storage area, relieved to see that the two large cartons were still positioned in front of the wardrobe. Reassured, he attacked the rest of the room, sliding back the closet doors, pulling clothing out of suitably sized cartons, shoving the folding beds away from the wall to look behind them. Nothing.

He went back into the main corridor. Jonathan was ushering men into the shelter room, promising blankets and pillows. "Any luck?" he asked the volunteer.

"No, man. Hey, you finished in the storage room? I need to get the blankets."

"Go ahead."

Jonathan disappeared through the EMPLOYEES ONLY door as Margareta appeared from the shower room, shaking her head and continuing on to her office.

Maybe Lucy did leave, Carl thought. There's nowhere else she could be; we've checked everywhere.

Not in the wardrobe, he thought. I didn't actually look inside the wardrobe. But she couldn't have gotten in there without moving the cartons, and the cartons were still in place. Hell, even if she *had* squeezed past them, so what? He'd just go in and pull her out. He started toward the door.

Unless she wasn't in there anymore.

But that was impossible. He'd closed the panel securely when he'd come through. Hadn't he? Suddenly, he wasn't sure. He'd been in such a blind, panicked rush . . .

"Let me give you a hand with those things," he said quickly as Jonathan backed through the brown door, his arms full. Together they distributed the blankets, then retrieved the rest of the bedding from the storage room. 'I'm going to take one more look around," he told Jonathan when they were finished. "But Margareta's probably right about her having already left."

"Whatever," Jonathan said. "I'll stay in here with these guys for a while, anyway. In case she shows up."

"Good." Carl went back into the storage room, pulling the cartons away from the wardrobe and yanking back the door. Empty. He reached inside, fumbling around for the panel, feeling the draft. Had he left it open, or had she?

He reached into his pocket for the small but powerful flashlight, bent his head, and stepped through the opening.

The low passage swung left and dead-ended at a large steel panel, its lock-light gleaming redly. At right angles to it, left and right, were two doors: an anonymous black door, cold to the touch and secured by three heavy iron bars, and a steel door, gray like the panel but smaller, and bearing a yellow biohazard symbol. Its lock light was dark. Lucy was mulling over the significance of this when the sound of a door slamming back against the wall somewhere behind her made her jump. No time to try her luck with the locked steel panel. She pushed tentatively at the inactivated door and opened it. Dare she go inside? The lock had been disarmed, but what of the biohazard it had contained? Approaching footsteps echoed in the passage, and a flashlight beam bounced off the wall around the corner from where she stood. She'd have to risk it. Carl had obviously come along here to get to the hidden stairs, and the room itself was unsealed; chances were, it was clean. Of course, these were just the sort of chances she was trained never to take, the sort of chances that could kill. But Carl could kill, too.

That was clear from the peruvia scars on Ray's neck. One hundred percent recovery rate indeed. Her heart in her mouth, she stepped inside and pushed the door closed.

A faint smell rode on the cold, damp air: formaldehyde. She knew what that meant. But the room was pitch dark, and she could see nothing. She ventured a few steps, hitting her shin on a piece of metal. She couldn't go blundering around here with Carl just outside, yet she had to find a hiding place. But how could she, when she couldn't see anything?

She headed back in the direction of the door, feeling for its frame, positioning herself to one side of the hinges. The open door would hide her. It was the best she could do.

Had she come this way or not? Carl asked himself urgently. He might have left the panel open in his rush to confront Lucy. She might have heard them talking about her and left the mission. He could still be safe, the secret secure. Or . . .

The red lock-light was still glowing; that was some comfort. If she'd gone through, the light would be green: She wouldn't be aware of the need to reset it. Nor would she realize her lab cardkey would work here, too, he told himself. If she even had it with her. That was another argument they'd had, he recalled. He'd insisted that two differently coded cardkeys were unnecessary; no threat could come from the mission side of the building.

So if she wasn't in there, and she wasn't in the corridor, and she hadn't left the building . . . He kicked open the small steel door on his right and flicked on the light. Not many places to hide in here, he thought. Only the closets, now filled with decontamination equipment, were large enough to conceal her. Nevertheless, he strode through the empty ward and into what had been the staff quarters.

Lucy stood motionless behind the open door, trying to quiet her breathing, willing him to leave. Then what? she wondered. She'd have to make certain which way he went. If he went through the lock-lighted door, she'd go back down to the mission and take her chances with Margareta and Jonathan. If he went down there himself, she'd have to try and get through the locked door and into the lab.

Satisfied at last, Carl came back through the room toward where she stood concealed. He hesitated for a moment before the open door, and Lucy was sure he would hear her heart thumping. He turned for one last look around the room, then reached for the door, pulling it partly closed as he stood in the doorway, pausing again as though sensing her now-exposed presence. Lucy held her breath. If he glanced to his right . . . But he didn't. He cursed briefly, flicked off the light, and shut the door behind him.

She gave him a minute, then carefully cracked the door and peeked out. She could hear his footsteps heading back toward the stairs, see the reflection of his flashlight beam dancing away down the passageway. She turned on the light and looked around. Bare bed frames lined the walls of the square, windowless room. Who had inhabited those beds, and why?

Wrapping her hand in the edge of her coat, she opened a closet. The electric frying pans, thick cable, and formaldehyde crystals told her what she'd already guessed: she was standing in a former hot zone. From the lingering smell, she knew that not very long ago something had been loose in this room, something that had required the heaviest known sterilization protocol to kill it. She desperately hoped the protocol had worked.

She'd had enough adventure for one night, she decided as she came out into the passageway. On the other side of that heavy steel door must lie the IMA lab. If she could get through it, she could get out of here and go home. Hiking through a blizzard in a bad neighborhood would be a welcome relief to secret passageways and hot rooms and the threat of Carl's syringe. She'd confirmed what she'd come here suspecting: Ray had been kept in the Star of Hope Mission, he'd been infected with peruvia, and he'd somehow survived. And Carl Anders was responsible.

She studied the door lock. It looked just like the one that guarded the regular IMA lab entrance. Wishful thinking? Worth a try. Carl wouldn't be expecting visitors from this side, after all, and certainly not anyone who worked at the IMA lab. She dug out her IMA cardkey and inserted it. The red light went out and the green light below it blinked on. Thank you, Carl, for being such a careless sonofabitch, she thought. She opened the door and stepped through, then stopped, frowning, as the door clicked shut behind her. This wasn't the IMA lab. Where the hell was she?

One blue and five black spacesuits hung on the tiled wall in front of her. The black suits were nameless, interchangeable. The blue one read ANDERS across the chest. It was still wet.

Okay, she told herself. So Carl has a second decon shower. Well, he'd need to, in order to leave Level Four this way. All that means is that instead of leading into the regular lab, this must lead into Level Four. All I need to do is suit up and go through it. But why hadn't she ever noticed a second decon shower entrance in Level Four? Decon showers were always clearly and boldly marked.

She inspected the suits. Although fabricated with nonreturn-valve air hose couplings, they were also equipped with self-contained airpacks. That made sense for the decon suits; presumably, these were what were worn when the ward she'd just come from had been nuked. But why should Carl's suit need an air-pack? Level Four had hoses.

Working as quickly as she dared, she stripped off her boots and coat, and pulled a sterile scrub suit up over her clothes. Way wrong, she knew, but she couldn't leave her clothing here for Carl to find, nor could she go home naked. Fortunately, Carl's sterile suits were extra large. She taped gloves and socks to the suit, then took down one of the black spacesuits, checked it for tears, and put it on. She paused, then chose a second suit and bundled her outer clothes and handbag into it. Helmet on, she checked her air supply; the airpack was working well. She had no way of knowing how much air it contained, but there would be air hoses once she got into the hot lab, so that shouldn't be a problem. Sealing the second suit that contained her things, she carried it through the decon shower and the tiny cement boot room, and stepped out into the hot lab.

But it wasn't the hot lab, not *her* hot lab. It was very small, for one thing, and there was only one workstation. And no air hoses dangled from the low, tilted ceiling. Against the far wall, a computer monitor glowed. Placing her belongings on the floor, she went toward it.

Carl unbolted the door and looked out into the blizzard. Was she out there somewhere? The snow in front of the mission door had been trodden down by the recent exodus of diners, but in the twenty minutes since, fresh snow had nearly covered their tracks. No recent footstep marred its white perfection, and that meant . . . what? That she'd left early enough for the snow to cover her tracks, too? Or that she hadn't left at all?

The flying snow stung his face and settled on his

hair and eyebrows, but still he stood there, staring out into the wild night.

> . . . a far milder strain, present in the original samples, that I have named peruvia b . . .

Ted Wiley's second strain, Lucy thought; Carl had it all the time. She scanned the research report quickly, taking in the topline information. Carl had left the computer on; he'd be coming back.

> . . . flu-like symptoms in chimps, while recent testing of peruvia b on human subjects produced headaches, fever, minor scarring . . .

Human subjects, she thought; humans like Ray. A hypertext extension offered the option to view a scanned micrograph of peruvia b. Staring at this second strain, Lucy noticed immediately that unlike Ted's version, all the viral lengths were either longer or shorter than the optimum length for maximum virulence. Carl had been working with it, refining it in some way. And testing it.

Okay, she thought; it's outrageous that Carl's been injecting people with this stuff. But maybe his doctored version of the milder strain, this peruvia b, might have an inoculant effect. Maybe some good can be rescued from his horrendous experiments. And indeed, as she returned to the report, she found the phrase ". . . inoculant effect against both of the other two strains . . ."

Other *two*? There's a *third* one?

> . . . experiments have shown that peruvia moribundi is far more virulent than the original peruvia. Controlled human testing produced a fatality rate of over ninety percent versus sixty percent for the original strain. . . .

peruvia b gives complete protection against the moribundi strain . . .

Lucy read quickly through the next few pages, then
leaned back in her chair, her mind reeling. Carl had
tinkered with the genetic structure of the original peruvia to create a far more deadly version. Why would
he do such a thing? She thought of the hot room she'd
just come from and shivered. Ray had been lucky.
He'd been given peruvia b, the mild version, the one
that caused only coughs and fevers and scars. The people in the hot room had been infected with the lethal version.

Another hypertext connection provided a micrograph of moribundi, its viral lengths all within the
range for maximum infectibility and virulence.

But how could Carl be certain that peruvia b gave
complete protection against peruvia moribundi? Perhaps Ray had been luckier than she'd realized. Recovery from peruvia b followed by infection with peruvia
moribundi would be the only way Carl would know
for sure. I don't think you're gonna win the Nobel
Prize for this one, buddy, she told Carl silently, her
lips white with contained fury.

She scrolled back to the top of the report, wanting
to dig deeper but fearing Carl's imminent return. She
was fairly breathless with anger . . . yes, breathless.

She felt herself go cold with fear. She was breathless, all right, but not with anger. The airpack was
giving out.

She stood up, looking around wildly. She had two
choices, neither one good. Run straight back through
to the locker room, breaking decon procedures and
spreading lethal pathogen all the hell over the room
and beyond. Or find a way through to Level Four and
the air hoses. The first choice might not be as bad as it
sounded, she thought; peruvia was transmittable only

through blood and bodily fluids. Ah, but who knew what refinements Carl had added in his creation of moribundi? Removing her spacesuit without deconing was risking death.

So was not breathing.

She fumbled behind her. Some airpacks had a small hook called a j-valve that, when pulled, released three minutes of extra air. She hadn't checked this one, so sure had she been of the presence of air hoses. It took a long, panicky minute before she found the hook and yanked it down. But three minutes' reprieve wasn't much. Breathing as shallowly as she could in her frightened state, she began exploring the small room.

"If she did overhear us, I doubt she'll come back," Margareta said, taking the vial Carl held out to her. "And I'm not comfortable about sedating her." She turned the small sealed ampoule around in her fingers. "What is this?"

"Just a standard sedative," Carl assured her. "Actually, Bill Miller prescribed it when I told him the woman might show up here."

"I'd feel a lot better about it if he were here to give it."

"I understand your feelings. But Doctor Bill can't be everywhere at once. And he was concerned about the safety of the mission." He paused. "Of course, you must do as you think best."

Margareta studied Carl for a moment. "Please thank the doctor for me," she said firmly, "but I'd rather not keep this."

"Whatever you say." Carl shoved the vial back into his pants pocket. "I'll be going now."

"Don't forget your coat." She rose. "I'll walk you to the front door."

"There's no need." He retrieved the worn coat and strode out into the hall.

Margareta followed. "I'm afraid I must bolt it behind you," she said. "We have had problems in the past."

Carl cursed the sister under his breath. He'd assumed she'd stay in her office, and he'd be able to use the rear passageway again. He hadn't known about any damn bolt. Now he'd have to go out into the storm, circle the block, and go in through the IMA lab. And in his good shoes, too.

It has to be somewhere obvious, she told herself frantically. He'd have no reason to hide it, at least not on this side. She was gasping now in the last of the air as she felt along the tiled walls for a hint of a join. Nothing. Okay, find the control mechanism, then . . . he must have some way of opening the door or panel or whatever way he gets into Level Four.

She went to his small workstation, hands scrabbling underneath the overhang, along the sides, hearing the hiss of air fade in her helmet, the resulting silence telling her she'd run out of time.

Heart pounding, she tried to calculate how long she could go on breathing the recycled air in her helmet before the carbon dioxide buildup made her pass out. Not very long; already she was feeling a little dizzy. She gripped the workstation, trying to calm herself. A button, a switch, she thought. The workstation area would be the place for one, but she'd felt nothing. Felt nothing . . . felt . . . She was spacing out from lack of oxygen, but there was something important about not feeling. . . . The gloves, she realized. Of course. The heavy gloves greatly reduced tactile sensation. She was seriously dizzy now, as she leaned down and examined the bottom of the overhang, barely focusing on the small metallic button mounted flush with the bottom surface. A button, she thought. That's nice. Pretty button . . .

Come on, come on! Drawing on some deep reserve, she fought back the carbon dioxide narcosis that was overtaking her, and pushed the button. A small section of tile to one side of the workstation began folding inward. Her vision dimming, she dragged herself through the opening. An air hose dangled in front of her. With the last of her strength, she managed to grab it and fumble it into the coupling on her suit, then stood weaving as fresh air flooded into her helmet. She sucked it in gratefully.

It was some minutes before she recovered sufficiently to take stock of her surroundings. She was at Carl's workstation inside Level Four.

Disconnecting the air hose, she hurried back through the opening and retrieved the black suit with her clothes and purse, then plugged in the hose again. She pushed the section of tile and it slid smoothly back into place. She studied its location so she could find it again, then realized that wasn't necessary. All she needed was the location of the control button on this side. Knowing where to look now, she soon found it on the underside of the work counter.

If only she had some portable air, she thought. She could go back in and read the rest of the computer report, check out the vials of virus Carl had secreted somewhere inside, take samples. . . .

But she didn't have a working airpack. And Carl was coming back.

She'd done all she could tonight, she decided, as she headed for the decon shower. And at this point, it might be a good idea to recruit some help.

Standing in the chemical shower, her outrage at Carl's testing program was rekindled. The IMA had sent her to Peru to combat a deadly filovirus, and Carl had used the samples she'd brought back to concoct an even more lethal one.

And an inoculant, she reminded herself. But no,

he hadn't created peruvia b. It had been present in her samples.

Now that was strange. How could a mild, inoculant version of peruvia have arisen simultaneously with the disease itself?

She thought about the old man in the Peruvian rain forest, and his wife. She'd collected two blood samples, one from each of them. By chance, one had gone to the CDC, the other to the IMA lab. These two samples were obviously the source of the second strain; she'd thought so months ago, when Ted Wiley had first mentioned its presence to her. But neither she nor Ted had understood then the difference between this second strain and the original peruvia.

When the old man had repeatedly referred to the disease as sangre negra, insisting it was an evil spirit that had returned, Lucy had assumed he'd experienced a similar sickness before. Filoviruses had only recently been discovered, and so far, they all seemed to have very similar symptoms.

But peruvia b wasn't a similar filovirus; it was the *same* filovirus. And if it had returned . . . No, that didn't make sense; peruvia b didn't produce the same deadly symptoms as peruvia. The old man must have experienced a different filoviral illness. But if that were so, what was the peruvia b virion doing in his blood?

The shower shut off and Lucy hurried out. In the locker room, she quickly divested herself of the black spacesuit and scrubs, and donned her outer clothing and boots. Shoving the scrubs and bodysuits into three different lockers, she grabbed her handbag and went out into the main lab space.

Carl trudged through the snowy street, his feet wet and frigid, his hands shoved deep into the pockets of the old, too-small, mission coat. The snow had lessened somewhat, but the wind was high, swirling the freezing crystals into his eyes and around his throat. You're a dead woman, Lucy Nash, he promised her silently. A dead woman.

She stepped from the elevator into the dark and silent lobby, ran across it, and yanked open the door. The marauding wind nearly plucked it from her hand as she braced it open and hurried outside. It banged shut behind her, the sound lost in the wind. God, it was cold. She moved quickly, heading east, away from the river, her destination clear in her mind.

Carl rounded the corner, digging with frozen fingers for his cardkey. He shoved it into the lock, then looked down. Footprints led away from the door, their outlines blurred by the blowing snow. That meant she'd gotten through; she knew everything now. He had to go after her. But how long had she been gone? What route had she taken? Her footprints were already growing faint; he'd lose her trail within a block. It was hopeless. He shivered in the thin coat. His shoes were soaked through. He could no longer feel his toes.

The airpacks had been nearly empty, he reminded himself. She wouldn't have had time to do more than read the research file he'd left open. So she knew about the three strains; so what? It was private research, that was all. And the TB outbreak? Hell, they'd rounded up the homeless people and brought them in for treatment in the first place. They could round them up again, get them off the streets. Then let her try and prove it wasn't TB.

No, she didn't know everything.

Lucy stumbled through the drifts, fingers and toes icy, her body shaking with cold. But despite her discomfort, her mind kept turning over the puzzle of the second strain.

The old man in the jungle; he was the key.

She dredged her memory for details of their confrontation all those months ago, replaying it in her head. He'd raved that sangre negra had been brought by white men, hadn't he? And she'd assumed he'd meant non-Peruvians, foreigners. There was certainly a tradition of that sort of thing; European explorers and colonists had brought syphilis and influenza to the New World. But during the three weeks she'd spent with them, she'd found the Peruvian Indians in that remote region to be very literal. Could it be that, by *hombres blancos,* he'd meant people dressed in white? Doctors? Nurses? Medical technicians? Could that be why he'd cursed the medical personnel who'd tried to treat him, and run off into the jungle?

She thought of Carl's sangre negra files, dated two years before. A hantavirus in Mexico? Or peruvia in Peru?

And hadn't Rick spoken of having visited Peru? Take only photos, leave only footprints, my ass, Lucy thought. She was beginning to suspect Rick and Carl had left something very different. But to what end? Another of Carl's human experiments?

She tripped over a rise in the snow and fell to her knees, too cold to feel any pain. What was Bill Miller's role in all this? she asked herself, struggling to rise. Was he a partner or a pawn? Carl must have learned about her interest in the Star of Hope from Bill, but that didn't make him guilty of collusion. He might simply have mentioned her query to Carl in passing. Doctor Bill was an eminent, highly respected physician, after all. Naive in his political thinking perhaps, with a tendency to romanticize primitive cultures. But a man with a good heart, committed to serving the less fortunate.

She staggered on, her whole body shivering. Five more blocks, she told herself. Just five more . . . Four, now . . . She was too cold to think clearly. She was too cold to think at all. Three more blocks . . . two . . .

She was nearly incoherent with cold when she finally climbed the steps, leaning against the railing for support as she rang the bell.

"Lucy, for the love of God," he exclaimed. He put his arm around her and she clung to him as he drew her inside, pulling off the frozen hat, the snow-covered coat, the soaked gloves.

"Carl's research . . ." she murmured through frozen lips. "I saw . . ."

"Don't try to talk," he said gently. "Let me defrost you first." He held her close, stroking her back, her wet hair.

Her arms came around him. She could feel the animal warmth of his body against hers. It would be all right now; everything would be all right.

He kissed her gently, his lips caressing her cheek, her neck. "Oh, Lucy," Doctor Bill whispered, "I'm so glad you're here."

Chapter Twenty-three

"Glad I caught you at home."

"Where else would I be?" Rossetti asked reasonably, glancing at the snow-caked trees that swayed like crazed ghosts beyond the kitchen window. Tucking the portable phone under his chin, he took a beer from the fridge.

"Are you alone?" Tom asked.

"Unfortunately."

"Good."

"Easy for you to say."

"Can the repartee, Mike. I'm calling to warn you. We've been hearing things recently that suggest something big is in the wind."

"You mean, with the drug connection?" Rossetti carried the beer through to the living room and settled himself on the sofa. "It's Renée, isn't it?"

"Not exactly. Renée's important, but not in the way you think. The Tortoriello family set her up, of course; the old man's no fool."

"I thought the mob didn't use women."

"They don't," Tom replied. "This is different, a new wrinkle. We did some checking, thanks to you, and here's the way we see it. When Luciano Salerno was deported, he lost everything. So when the Tortoriellos up and offered him an elegant title and a bunch of money in exchange for his marrying Renée and staying out of the way, he agreed. Now Tortoriello owns a beautiful Italian countess who's lavish with her sexual favors, and who's also some sort of poor relation—old man Tortoriello grew up with Renée's family in Sicily—so he feels he can trust her."

"But if she's not running a drug operation—"

"Oh, she's more valuable than that. We think Renée serves as a discreet liaison between the Family and any wealthy, unscrupulous miscreant with whom Tortoriello wants to do business."

"Like drug running?"

"And money laundering, yes."

"Which one is Miller doing?"

"Some of both, I would guess," Tom answered. "But that's just fund-raising. No, something much larger is being planned. Something global."

'Planned by whom? Tortoriello?"

Tom hesitated. "We're not sure, but I don't think so. Over the years, we've found traces of various shadowy financial networks that back worldwide terrorism. Certain Middle Eastern governments, of course. And arms dealers with no political agendas. But lately, the mix has become more complex. Remember the group that took out a piece of Colombia's major oil pipeline some months ago? Along with thirty vehicles and some fifty assorted soldiers and police?"

"Yeah. Leftist rebels, weren't they?"

"Yes, but consider the ramifications. These rebels were involved in drug trafficking. They were retaliating against a government program aimed at destroying the coca fields. They were backed by thousands of small farmers who insisted that growing coca was the only way they could earn a living."

"Sounds like something Bill Miller might approve of, in his naive, 'sixties' way."

"It's exactly the sort of thing he'd approve of. And possibly provide financial backing for. But not because of any leftist leanings—even sixties throwbacks aren't naive enough to finance a drug-growers' revolution in the name of truth and love."

Rossetti frowned. "You mean, if he's involved in drug trafficking, it's in his own best interests to keep the coca fields producing."

"Yes. Except that I don't think he's that big into drugs," Tom answered slowly. "*If* he's dabbling in drugs, *if* he's using his doctors as unwitting mules, it's just a sideline, a means of fund-raising. What disturbs me is what he's raising funds *for.*"

"For the IMA, of course," Rossetti answered, surprised.

"And what exactly is the IMA?"

"A charitable organization that—"

"I've read their literature, Mike. No, what the IMA is, is Miller's baby."

"And Carl Anders's."

"Anders, yes . . ."

"So what you're suggesting," Rossetti recapped, frowning, "is that Miller's using drugs to raise money for purposes unknown. And that Didier didn't know he was carrying heroin when he was arrested. He was caught on a random check?"

"Maybe. Or maybe Didier found out what Miller was really doing and Miller decided to get him out of the way before he could talk. A little heroin in his luggage to discredit him, an anonymous call to the DEA. And then a death pill in his cell. The mob could help with that part."

"I thought Didier committed suicide."

"You also thought the IMA was a charitable organization."

"So Miller's using the IMA to raise money to support left-wing terrorism? That's your theory?" Tom was silent. "And how, exactly, does this 'second strain' virus thing fit in?"

"You tell me."

"I can't, Tom." Rossetti thought for a moment. "Maybe Anders is playing a lone hand. Maybe Miller doesn't know what Carl's doing. God knows, *I* don't."

"Now who's being naive?' Tom sighed. "Whatever's going on at the IMA, you can bet on one thing. Nothing happens without Miller's approval."

"I'm not sure I agree. Carl Anders—"

"Forget Carl Anders," Tom said harshly. "Anders works for Miller. You ever wonder how Miller got approval to build that Level Four lab? Well, wonder no more. It appears the CIA may have been involved."

"Miller's a spook?"

"Not Miller; some friends of his. The trail's muddy but suggestive."

"But if the lab is CIA-based, then Miller's on our side."

Tom gave a cynical little laugh. "And which side is that, precisely?" Mike was silent. "Anyhow, we're not talking officially sanctioned covert stuff, more like a rogue offshoot. But never mind all that. The important thing for you is, we're getting the feeling that whatever is going to happen, is going to happen soon. We need to know what, and we need to know when."

"I don't see how I can do more than I'm already doing."

"I know, I know. Just keep your eyes and ears wide open. Let me know about anything that seems the least bit . . . irregular. Even if it doesn't *seem* important."

"Will do."

"And Mike? One more thing."

"Yeah?"

"Watch your ass."

Gently, his arm around her shivering form, Bill led Lucy into the living room and settled her on a sofa facing the fireplace. "Let me get you something hot to drink," he said solicitously.

But she shook her head and, taking his hand, drew him down beside her. "I have so much to tell you," she said, her eyes serious. "And none of it can wait."

She began to speak, her cheeks pink in the sudden warmth of the room. As her words tumbled out, Bill stared at her with an expression of horror as she described the recently decontaminated ward, the secret labyrinth between the mission and the IMA lab, the scars on Crazy Ray's neck, Carl's secret Level Four lab, and the peruvia research report she'd read on his computer screen.

When she finished, they both were silent. Then, "God, Lucy," Bill exclaimed softly. "What a fool I've been. What a trusting fool."

"You'll have to close down, of course," she said. "We'd better call the CDC right away. And the Environment Protection Agency isn't going to be very happy, either."

But Bill shook his head. "I can't do that."

"You have to. You're putting the entire city at risk."

"I don't think so. Whatever went on there is over, and the lab itself is completely contained. I'll close Anders down, of course. But I won't risk what I've built, all the good things the IMA is doing in the field and at the lab, your own work included." He paused. "As you can imagine, it wasn't easy, getting permission to build a Level Four lab. It took support, influence from people at the highest levels. The same . . . friends who supported that effort will support me now in cleaning up this mess quietly, in a way that will avoid publicity and allow us to continue our good work." He took tender hold of her shoulders and looked deeply into her eyes. "You must let me do this my way, Lucy. I know you have friends at the CDC, but you mustn't call them. There's too much at stake here, more than you know. You must leave me to deal with this." His face tightened. "And believe me, I will." Lucy frowned but nodded her agreement, and Bill visibly relaxed. "You're still cold, aren't you? I can feel you shaking. How about that hot drink? A cup of cocoa?"

"It does sound good."

A plaid woolen throw was folded over the back of a nearby chair. He draped it around her, then went and added a fresh log to the fire in the grate. For a moment he stood watching the leaping flames. Then, "Be right back," he promised, and headed for the kitchen.

Lucy snuggled under the soft wool. The horrors of the night seemed more manageable, now that Bill knew about them, too. Together, they'd put a stop to Carl Anders's mad experiments.

He soon returned with two steaming mugs, and Lucy gulped hers eagerly. It had been a long time since she'd had anything to eat or drink. He smiled down at her. "You're looking better already," he told her, sipping his cocoa.

"I feel better. But I ought to go home soon. It's late."

"No way," he said. "It's still snowing like crazy, and nothing's moving out there. Stay here tonight. I'll make up a bed in one of the guest rooms."

"But I—"

"Please. Let's not even discuss it. I have a few phone calls to make," he continued, "and then I'll fix us some sandwiches and we'll talk about how we're going to deal with all this." He beamed at her. "You are one courageous young woman, Lucy Nash." He patted her arm. "Rest and get warm. Doctor's orders."

The hot drink was coursing through her. She turned, smiling, to watch his retreating back, then relaxed against the sofa cushions and stared at the fire. The dancing flames were almost hypnotic. It had been a long night; her eyelids felt heavy. When he returned some ten minutes later, she was asleep.

Bill stared down at her, then bent and lifted her in his arms. She murmured and cradled against him, but didn't wake up as he carried her upstairs to his bedroom. He set her gently on the bed and unwound the wool coverlet from around her, dropping it onto a chair. He pulled off her boots and thick socks, hesitated, then started to remove her skirt. She stirred and opened her eyes, and he immediately stopped, drawing the bedspread over her legs.

"Rick . . ." she murmured.

He frowned. "What?"

"How well do you know Rick?" she asked thickly.

"Hollander?" Bill's eyes narrowed. "Why?"

"Saw him in the lab . . . trying to read Carl's files. . . ." Her eyelids flickered. ". . . Sure you can trust him?"

Bill frowned. Hollander was on *his* side, wasn't he? Was this accusation of Lucy's the result of a lover's tiff? Was that why Hollander hadn't been able to warn him of Lucy's recent activities? Or was there something more here? "Lucy? Wake up." He shook her by the shoulders, but her eyes remained closed. The strong soporific he'd given her, to allow him time to set certain plans in motion, had certainly worked quickly. Well, it didn't matter; he knew perfectly well who constituted the greatest threat to the operation, and it sure as hell wasn't Hollander.

He pulled back the bedspread and unzipped and removed her skirt, admiring her strong, slim legs. His eyes wandered to the dark patch beneath the white lace panties. He caressed it, feeling the warmth against his palm. He glanced at her face. She was well under; no need for caution. Roughly he pulled off the panties and parted her legs, his fingers moving inside her. She moaned and shifted on the bed, but he ignored her. He was in control of her body now. She had no say in the matter.

With damp fingers, he unbuttoned her sweater and peeled it off, then reached around and unclipped her bra, tossing both items onto the floor. He took her nipples in his mouth one at a time, sucking, nibbling, biting, as he fumbled with his zipper. This feeling of power over her, of complete possession of her, was almost uncontrollably exciting. Shucking his trousers and briefs, he straddled her, taking his member in his hand and parting her lips with it. Still sleeping, she brought a hand up to push him away, but he held her off, working himself into her mouth. Teach you a lesson, you interfering bitch, he thought.

His pleasure built steeply, too steeply, and he stopped abruptly, determined to make it last. He hesitated, then slid down her body, his tongue working. At last he entered her, lifting her buttocks to ram himself deep inside. Still unconscious, she moaned again and tried to roll away, but he held her impaled, thrusting ever deeper, rough and fast and hard, pummeling, punishing. You'll feel this tomorrow, he thought furiously, exultantly. You'll feel my power.

The monkeys howled and shook their cages as Carl Anders appeared. They hadn't been fed since morning, but the man in the sealed yellow suit carried nothing save a hypodermic needle and several filled vials.

He surveyed the animals briskly, showing no regret for what he was about to do. He'd never liked monkeys much, and these twelve animals had been mere research tools, to be studied and discarded.

The monkey in the far left cage bared his teeth as Carl approached, anticipating dinner, angry at the delay. The man struck swiftly, plunging the long needle through the hairy skin and emptying its contents into the bloodstream. The animal jerked back, but the needle was already out, ready for refilling. During the experiments, Carl had been scrupulous about using a fresh needle for each injection, but now it didn't matter. The experiments were over, the monkeys no longer of any use. Miller's phone call had been very specific.

By the time the syringe was full again, the first monkey lay slumped in its cage, its breathing slow and stuttery. Quickly Anders worked his way down the row of cages, injecting each monkey in turn. The animals grew quiet, fear overwhelming hunger.

The animal experiments had not been a success, Carl reflected. He'd been unable to transmit peruvia to the monkeys in any recognizable form, although their blood samples had shown the presence of viral antibodies. Nor had he been able to transmit the simian version of peruvia to human subjects. Not that he'd been surprised; all the research agreed that simian hemorrhagic fever wasn't transmittable to humans, either. Still, he'd hoped. . . .

The last monkey shuddered and lay still. Anders shoved a long stick through the bars and poked at it. Getting no response, he cautiously unlocked the cages and began pulling out the dead animals, dropping them one by one into large, heavy, black decontamination bags.

"Lucy? I didn't know whether to wake you or not. It's nearly eleven."

Lucy swam up from treacly sleep to see Bill Miller, dressed in business clothes, standing at the partly open door. God, she felt tired. "What time did you say?"

"Ten of eleven." Bill smiled warmly. "When I came back with the sandwiches, you were passed out on the sofa. You must have been exhausted."

She sat up and looked around. "Where am I?"

"In one of the guest rooms. I'm afraid your clothes will be a little wrinkled. I didn't feel right about undressing you, so I let you sleep in them. Aside from your boots, of course. Would you like some breakfast?"

Suddenly the time registered, and Lucy threw back the cover. "I'm due at the hospital," she said, swinging her feet off the bed.

"Better check your answering machine first. Things are kind of haywire, thanks to the storm."

"Is it still snowing?"

"No, it stopped around dawn. The sky's clearing. Wish I could say the same for the streets." She stood up, swaying slightly. "You okay?"

"A little dizzy." She found her boots beside the bed and began to pull them on. "Some coffee might help."

"I'll bring you a cup."

"That's okay. I'll come down."

"Whatever you like. There's a phone by the bed, if you want to call in."

Lucy reached for the instrument, then grimaced at the dull ache in her abdomen. Must have pulled something when I fell in that drift last night, she thought. Although it didn't feel like muscle pain, exactly. Her skirt seemed to have worked its way around during the night. She adjusted her clothing, smoothing the wrinkles as best she could, then picked up the phone and began dialing.

Bill was eating toast in the breakfast nook. "Honey or marmalade?" he asked as she hurried through the archway.

"Neither, thanks." Lucy slid carefully into a chair across from him. The dull ache in her gut was troubling, and when she'd used the bathroom, she'd found a blush of blood on her panties. What the hell had she done to herself? "Look, I've got to get going.

They're shorthanded at the hospital; people are having trouble getting into town. Which brings up another problem."

"Oh?" Bill carefully poured coffee into the cup in front of her.

"Ken Walsh left about a million messages on my machine. He wants me to fly to the Ivory Coast today." Walsh was in charge of sending IMA doctors on overseas missions. "I don't see how I can possibly go, but if it's really peruvia—"

Bill's face took on an expression of astonishment. "Peruvia? In Africa?"

"That's what he said. At least, that's what the reports suggest it might be."

"God, Lucy, you *have* to go."

"Bill, I can't."

"Two days, three at the most." He paused, thinking. "This is Friday. . . . We'll fly you back on Monday for sure, okay? Please, Lucy. There's no one else we can send, no one else who's actually worked with peruvia, who has the clearance to deal with it."

Lucy shook her head. "It's impossible. Don't you think I *want* to go? If it really is peruvia, it's an amazing discovery. But I don't see how—"

"Call the hospital. See what you can do." Bill paused. "Besides, it might be a good idea for you to get away for a bit."

"How do you mean?"

"After what you discovered last night, I don't think Carl Anders is going to be very happy to see you."

"I wasn't planning to pay him a visit."

"The man's already threatened to kill you, Lucy. You said so yourself. He'll be a lot more dangerous to you, now."

"He's dangerous to us all."

"Yes, but I know how to deal with him. For your

own safety, if not for the peruvia project, get out of town for a while."

"I don't know. . . . Even if I did agree to go, I can't believe any flights are taking off today."

"They have one runway open at Kennedy. I heard it on the news. I can arrange for a helicopter to fly you over there from the East River terminal. That's just a few blocks from here."

"I'll need to pack. . . ."

"I'll get a car to take you to your apartment, wait while you throw some things into a bag, and then take you to the helicopter pad. What time's the flight?"

"I don't know. I haven't called Ken back yet."

Bill got up. "You have some breakfast," he said, all energy and bustle. "I'll call Ken and make the arrangements."

"I'm not big on running away from things." Lucy frowned.

"You're not running away from anything," Bill insisted. "I'm afraid it'll all be right here waiting for you when you get back on Monday evening."

"I guess you're right. And if it really *is* peruvia . . ."

"Then we need you there."

"Well, I'd better get busy," Lucy said, deciding. "I'll have to call the hospital, and . . ." And Rick, she thought. They'd arranged to meet for dinner tonight; part of her attempt to learn what he was really up to. "I have to cancel some things," she finished lamely.

"I'll use the phone in the study," Bill said, "so you can use this one." He paused at her chair and touched her cheek. "It's the best way, Lucy. For everybody."

It was quite amazing what money could do, Lucy reflected a short time later, as the Lincoln Town Car skidded through the partly plowed streets toward her apartment building. A helicopter was standing by, her ticket was waiting for her at the airport, and even the hospital administration had been supportive of her sudden trip which, considering how shorthanded they were at the moment, was a small miracle in itself. The pain in her gut had subsided somewhat, and the strong coffee Bill had brewed had cleared her head. The car drew up in front of her building and she leaped out, excitement about her forthcoming trip building fast.

She waved a hand at the doorman and hurried through the lobby, mentally sorting through her clothing. She wouldn't take much, she decided; a large overnight bag should do it. She'd only be gone a few days, and most of that time she'd be wearing scrubs and a sealed field suit.

Inside the apartment, she quickly stripped off her clothing and threw it onto the bed, then took the world's fastest shower. Still damp, she pulled on jeans and a shirt, then dug out her passport and driver's license and began to pack.

There was a holiday feeling in the air. Schools were closed, and children were body surfing off the roofs of buried cars and bombarding each other with snowballs. Many businesses seemed to have declared a snow day too, and people trudged, slightly bemused, through the drifts in search of a store that hadn't yet run out of milk.

Rick checked his watch as he entered the lobby of the building that housed the IMA offices just before noon. It had taken him nearly an hour to make the trip uptown from the lab. The receptionist was among the missing, so he wandered down the hall, asking directions of the sparse staff.

"He'll just be a minute," Alicia said, rising. "Can I get you some coffee?"

"That would be great." The secretary disappeared and Rick settled into the chair beside her workstation. He was glancing idly at the papers on her desk when she reappeared, cup in hand.

"I think you'll be more comfortable in the reception room," she said coldly, handing him the cup.

"Uh, right. Thanks." Embarrassed, Rick took the coffee and was turning away when Alicia's intercom buzzed.

"You can send Hollander in now," Bill's voice instructed.

Rick reversed direction and hurried past a tight-lipped Alicia, into Bill's private office.

"Close the door," Bill ordered from behind his desk computer. Out of the corner of his eye, Rick saw Bill eject a disk with a bright green label and slide it furtively under some papers before waving the younger man to a seat.

"I thought we had a deal," Miller said without preamble, coming from behind his desk.

"We do," Rick agreed.

"Then why didn't I know Lucy was still pursuing the Jean-Pierre thing? Why didn't you tell me about Didier's notebook?"

Rick did his best to look surprised. "What notebook?"

"Don't bullshit me, Hollander."

"I swear, Bill, she didn't tell me." Bill looked unconvinced. "Look, I have no reason to hold out on you. We both want the same thing: to protect Lucy from herself, right?" Rick hesitated. "The thing is, we had a little . . ."

"Lovers' quarrel?"

"Yeah, sort of."

"What about?"

"Come on, Bill. I can't tell you that."

Bill rose and paced toward the window, then turned. "Lucy tells me you've been trying to get into Carl's computer."

"What?"

"She said she saw you. She asked me whether you could be trusted."

"Jesus." Rick shook his head sadly, but his thoughts were churning. How to handle this? he wondered. "Jealousy is a terrible thing," he said at last.

Bill watched Rick carefully. "Go on," he said.

Rick sighed. "She found out I'd been seeing Renée."

"I thought I told you to break it off."

"I did . . . I tried. Renée kept calling my apartment, leaving messages on my machine," he continued, inventing freely. "Lucy heard one of them. Hell, you know what Renée's like."

"So Lucy's trashing your reputation because she's jealous of a woman you used to date."

" 'Date' isn't quite—"

"That doesn't sound like Lucy."

"A woman in love—" Rick began, but Bill waved an impatient hand at him.

"Maybe, maybe not." He studied Rick closely. "Frankly, it doesn't really matter."

"What do you mean? Look, I'm having dinner with her tonight. I'm sure I can smooth things over. I'm still your man."

Bill lowered himself into a chair across from Rick. "I don't need you to be my 'man,' as you put it. I'm through trying to protect Lucy Nash."

"How come?"

Bill gave a helpless little shrug. "I've done all I can. Lucy's a big girl; she'll do what she wants to do. One of the things she wants to do, by the way, is to give up her work at the IMA lab, effective immediately. She's not coming back."

"Not coming back? But her experiments—"

"Someone else can take them over. I'm considering closing down all the peruvia research, anyway."

"I can't believe she just up and quit," Rick said. "What reason did she give?"

"You can ask her tonight," Bill said neutrally. "At that dinner you mentioned. I believe she'll say that she's been spreading herself too thin. She wants to devote more time to fieldwork." He paused. "She told me fieldwork has always had great appeal for her, and that it's even more appealing, now that Jean-Pierre's dead."

"What does Jean-Pierre's death have to do with her wanting to do more fieldwork?"

"I wondered that myself," Bill said slowly. "Well, I'm sure you'll want to be getting back to the lab." Rick rose, and Bill walked him to the door. "So glad we had this little talk. I must say I'm reassured to know that Lucy's accusations of treachery were motivated by jealousy. I've always had the deepest regard for your work."

"And I for yours," Rick said as the door closed behind him. He hesitated, then turned and silently cracked the door open a tiny fraction. Putting his eye to the narrow slit, he watched Bill slide into his desk chair, then fumble around in the mess of papers and retrieve the bright green disk. For a moment Bill looked up as though feeling Rick's eyes on him. Then, with a furtive gesture, he inserted the disk into the computer drive.

She's not coming back. All the way downtown, Bill's words echoed in his ears. When had she made that decision? Why hadn't she told him? Perhaps she was planning to, this evening. He hurried through the small reception area and into his lab. The message light on his phone was blinking.

Pressing the replay button, he heard Lucy's voice canceling their dinner plans. As he listened, he became more and more concerned. She was flying to the Ivory Coast immediately, she told him, to deal with a medical emergency that might be related to peruvia. She'd be back on Monday evening, and they'd get together next week.

He sank into a chair, brow furrowed. This trip was awfully sudden, he thought. "Fieldwork has always had great appeal for her," Bill had said. "It's even more appealing, now." Why now? Rick had the feeling he was being set up for something, but what?

"She's not coming back," he repeated silently to himself. Not coming back to the lab. She's off to Africa and she's not coming back. Oh, shit, he thought, she's not coming back at all. He grabbed for the phone and began dialing furiously.

Lucy had set the large overnight bag down in the corridor and was locking her apartment door when the phone began to ring. Should she answer it? She glanced at her watch. No time, she thought. Let the machine get it. She picked up the bag and ran for the elevator.

Chapter Twenty-four

"**Y**ou told me there were no survivors."

"I was wrong. But—"

"Shut up, Carl." Bill Miller's face was dark with anger. It was Anders's fault he'd had to call this emergency meeting above Banana King this Friday evening. Anders's fault that Lucy had learned what she had, and that he needed Tortoriello's help again. "If two people survived the sangre negra trials two years ago," he continued, "there could be others."

"So what? No one knows—"

"No one *knew*," Bill snarled, leaning over him. "Someone sure as hell knows now."

"No, she doesn't," Carl insisted. "The report she saw in my computer didn't mention the earlier trials."

"And you don't think she'll figure it out? It's bad enough two of the blood samples she brought back from Peru contained the peruvia b virion. But denying it existed while accidentally sending one to the CDC—Jesus." Bill slumped into a chair. "If I hadn't been able to arrange for Ted Wiley's funding to be cut . . ." He shook his head in disgust. " 'No survivors,' you said. 'Everybody dead. Saw the bodies myself.' " He glared at Carl. "I'm surrounded by fools."

"Listen, Bill, it's damn lucky there *were* survivors. If those two *indios* hadn't come to the research station to be treated for fever, we'd never have discovered peruvia b. We'd never have realized the sangre negra had spontaneously mutated in their bodies, the way Ebola did in those monkeys in Reston, Virginia, back in 1989."

"I know all that," Bill said impatiently. "The point is that you—"

But Carl was on a roll. "The point," he insisted, "is that without those two survivors, we'd never have known peruvia b even existed, let alone that it was an inoculant. Hell, I tried to duplicate the mutation in the animal lab and I couldn't. I'm damn grateful for those two survivors, and you should be, too."

"Don't lecture me," Bill told him angrily. "Thanks to you, everything we've worked for all these years could have gone right down the toilet. If Lucy hadn't come to me last night—" He rose and stalked the length of the room, turned, paced back again, his body stiff with tension. "What the hell were you thinking?" he demanded. "Chasing her through that damn mission, letting her discover the lab, the moribundi ward— Never mind," he broke off angrily. "I'll deal with her now."

A buzzer sounded. Bill brought himself under control, then hit the control switch that worked the secret panel. It swung open to admit Renée, followed by several men. Bill waved them all to seats around the table. He himself remained standing.

"We have trouble?" Renée asked.

"Nothing we can't handle," Bill said tightly. "But we'll need the help of your people. For which we'll pay well, as usual."

"I told Mr. Tortoriello it was not a good idea," she said, stripping off her navy peacoat, "to deal with amateurs."

"Nonsense," Bill replied tautly. "Everything was going beautifully until Didier was arrested. *You* were supposed to make sure that sort of thing never happened." He glared at her.

Renée shrugged. "It seems the Customs people got a tip from an art gallery owner," she said. "Something about smuggled artifacts. That's what they were looking for when they found the heroin. There was no way we could have known. You have anything to drink around here?"

"You know I don't."

"Pity. Anyway, we took care of Didier in jail. He never got a chance to defend himself against the charges, at least not convincingly. And Beno Stanislas has been taken care of, too. A little gift from my boss."

"Beno . . ." Bill's face filled with sudden understanding. "Didier's art dealer."

"Yes. Beno thought Didier was cheating him, or so he told our people. He and that stupid Didier put the whole operation in jeopardy." She looked around the table. "I think we should close it down."

"You may be right," Bill agreed, taking a seat across the table from her. "We'll discuss it after you take care of Lucy Nash."

Renée smiled a catlike smile. "What would you like me to do to her?" she purred. "And do you want to watch?"

"I want her murdered, Renée. And no, I don't want to watch."

Renée stiffened. "I do not do murder."

"Of course you don't. But your people do." Renée frowned. "Lucy was Jean-Pierre's lover, so we'll tarnish her with the same brush."

"Heroin."

"Yes. The IMA has already sent her to the Ivory Coast."

"The Ivory Coast?" Carl repeated. "What's happened there?"

"Malaria, as usual," Bill said shortly. "But I had Ken Walsh tell her it might be peruvia."

"She'll see right away that it's not," Carl objected. "She'll suspect—"

Bill shrugged. "Reports from the field are not always accurate. Besides, it no longer matters what she suspects. You see, when she comes through Kennedy Airport, someone will have tipped off the Customs people, citing her former relationship with Didier. Her bags will be thoroughly searched. Heroin will be discovered. When approached by the authorities, I will reluctantly inform them that she had recently asked to be given more field trips, presumably in order to continue Didier's smuggling of drugs and artifacts. His notebook will be found among her possessions."

"She'll deny it all," Carl broke in. "She'll tell them about my research—"

"What?" Renée turned to frown at Carl.

"She won't say a coherent word, I assure you," Bill quickly assured her, shooting a furious glance at Anders. "And once she's in custody, your people"—he turned back to Renée—"will do to her what they did to Didier."

"That might be a little difficult," Renée said slowly. "Our resources in the women's detention facilities are not as good as in the men's."

"Well, work something out," Bill said impatiently. "It's important to both our organizations. I'll provide you with Lucy's flight number and arrival time."

"It will be expensive," she warned him.

"Of course it will," Bill agreed dryly.

Renée frowned. "I still don't understand what Carl was saying before—something about his research?"

"It's nothing you need to worry about," Bill said smoothly. "Just a little internal friction. Lucy's been working at the IMA lab, and Carl's made it fairly obvious that he doesn't care for her."

"I see. And Rick Hollander? Is he still keeping an eye on Lucy for you, or can I have him back now?"

Her smile was lazy and arrogant, telling Bill clearly that she didn't really need his permission.

"Once Lucy's dead, you can do whatever you like with him," Bill told her, smiling grimly as he recalled his recent meeting with Rick. Lovers' quarrel indeed. Another job for Mr. Tortoriello's boys when the time is right, he thought. He rose. "Thank you for joining us, Contessa," he said, coming around the table to kiss her hand. The others stood, too, as Renée shrugged on her coat. Bill went and opened the wall panel, letting in a gust of cold, stale air. "Gentlemen, would you stay behind for a moment?" he added as Renée stepped out into the dark corridor. "Just some financial housekeeping," he explained as she turned back questioningly. She nodded and disappeared down the hallway. Bill closed the panel behind her, waving the men back to their seats, the smile fading from his face.

"Stupid mistakes have been made," he told them sternly. "Arming the rebels in Colombia was one thing, but allowing them to blow up the pipeline in the name of drug running? That was stupid. I never authorized that." He glared at them. "There will be no more stupid mistakes. We cannot afford them, not when we're so close." His eyes glittered with fanatic zeal. "The dream is about to become reality, gentlemen. The creation of a new world order is at hand. All that remains is to perfect human airborne transmission." He scowled at Carl.

"I thought . . ." Anders began, then stopped, swallowed, and started again. "I was successful in mutating the simian strain," he explained earnestly. "The simian strain did become airborne, but it turned out to be harmless to humans. That happens sometimes, and—"

"We don't want to hear about your failures," Bill interrupted. "How soon can you report success?"

"I'm not sure. But soon," he added quickly, seeing Bill's face darken.

"This is troubling," said the man to Carl's right. "How long are we expected to wait? My people have contributed much money," he added in accented English. "They want action. What if airborne transmission is impossible?"

"Then we go with what we have," Bill said confidently. "It'll be nearly as effective. Airborne transmission is ideal, but not strictly necessary. Believe me, with what we have right now, the world will listen to us." He stared fiercely around the table. "I promise you, the world will listen. And obey."

"Jesus, Tom, I've been trying to reach you all afternoon."

"Been up to my ass in meetings," the older man replied. "Something wrong?"

"The IMA just sent Lucy Nash to Africa."

"So? She's gone on medical missions before."

"Yeah, but I have a bad feeling about this one," Rossetti said. "It's too sudden. I think she may have learned something, and they're planning to neutralize her."

"In *Africa*?" Tom sounded doubtful.

"Why not? Or maybe on the way there. Or on the way back. You've got to pull her out."

"Pull her out?" Tom protested. "She's not *in*."

"The hell she isn't. She's in it up to her—"

"You know what I mean. I didn't *put* her in. She's a civilian."

"And she's in danger. Can't you take her into protective custody or something?"

"And blow the whole operation? Good plan." Tom sighed. "Look, Mike, all we have are suspicions. The hot lab's license is legit. There's no proof that any laws are being broken, or that Miller and the IMA aren't what they seem."

"But you know better," Rossetti insisted.

"I *suspect* better," Tom corrected him. "Without actual proof—" He broke off. "We're getting close," he began again. "Like I told you, something's in the wind. I can't afford to let Miller get suspicious now. And if Nash was sent to Africa because of something she knows, our interfering would be the worst thing we could do."

"Not for her. Can't you track her through our embassy in the Ivory Coast?"

"*Track* her?" Tom replied incredulously. "You can't actually be suggesting that someone follow her into the bush, stand next to her while she doctors people. Even if it were practicable, which it isn't, don't you think it's a tad obvious?" He thought for a moment. "Tell you what: give me her flight numbers and we'll check to see if she got there, and whether she leaves on schedule."

"I don't have them. But she's flying back sometime Monday."

Tom sighed. "I'll see what I can do. Although I'm still not convinced she isn't part of whatever's going down. I know, I know," he added quickly, as Rossetti began to interrupt. "You don't agree. Well, even assuming you're right and I'm wrong, I am not, repeat not, prepared to do anything that might jeopardize this operation. So unless you can come up with concrete evidence that her life is in danger, Lucy Nash is on her own."

Chapter Twenty-five

Lucy jounced uncomfortably on the sprung seat of the old Ford taxi, breathing in the warm smell of wet vegetation and wondering for the thousandth time why the hell she'd been sent here. How could an experienced field technician have confused the symptoms of malaria with those of an unknown filovirus? Why had Ken Walsh been so anxious to whisk her off to Africa that he hadn't waited for lab confirmation of the blood work? And why, if peruvia had been a serious possibility, had she been sent in alone, without experienced biohazard backup people? The past three days had been a complete waste of her time, and she was feeling tired and ill used. She paid off the driver, grabbed her bag, and strode into the airport, anxious to be on her way.

"Dr. Nash?" Lucy stopped, turned. An unremarkable man of about thirty-five, a pale toothbrush mustache decorating his upper lip, stood beside her. "We meet again," he said, smiling and offering a beefy hand. "Jack McNulty, remember?" Lucy frowned; he looked familiar, but she couldn't quite place him. "Mayaruna Airport? Back in November?"

Her face cleared. "Yes, of course," she said. "You're the South American rep."

"Was," he said. "Africa, now." He hesitated. "So sorry to hear about Dr. Didier. Helluva thing." Lucy nodded but said nothing; what was there to say? He

311

glanced at the case she carried. "Where's the rest of your luggage?"

"This is it. I wasn't here very long."

"Well, let me check it for you," he offered. "Just give me your ticket, and—"

"That's not necessary," Lucy said.

"Oh, the IMA is a full-service organization," he said with a friendly wink. "Besides, the check-in line's awfully long." He gestured toward the crowd milling around the departures counter. "Find a seat somewhere and I'll see to everything."

"Thanks." Lucy fished in her bag for her air ticket and handed it over.

"And I'll need your bag," he said, reaching for it.

"It doesn't need to be checked," she explained. "I'm carrying it onto the plane with me."

He hesitated. "They're inspecting all hand luggage these days," he told her. "It's frightening what some people try to take on board. Don't worry, I'll have it back to you in a jiffy."

Lucy relinquished her hold on the case and he picked it up. "Have a seat over there," he suggested, "so I'll know where to find you. Oh, and can I bring you something to drink? Soda? Coffee?"

"A soda would be nice."

"Something canned and sealed." He nodded approvingly. "Wise choice in this part of the world."

Lucy watched him disappear into the crowd, then wandered over to the bank of seats he'd indicated and slumped into one of the orange plastic chairs. Mayaruna Airport, she thought. So much had happened since that rainy morning, none of it good. Her mind drifted back to the weeks with Jean-Pierre in Peru, to their farewell at the airport. "There's something for you in my luggage," he'd said. Two ugly statues and six kilos of heroin. Thanks a lot, Jean.

"Sorry to take so long," McNulty dropped down

into the seat beside her. "Here's your bag, safe and sound. Ticket's right on top. And I got you a cola. Hope that's okay."

"Cola's fine." She took it from him, a little surprised to see that he'd snapped the top and inserted a straw.

"I told you we were full service," he said, noticing her expression. "You've got twenty minutes or so before they start boarding." He leaned back in his chair and stretched. "Looking forward to going home?"

"Yes," Lucy said. "Frankly, I don't know why I'm here at all. Surely you have people on site who can handle malaria."

"Malaria? Is that what it was? Afraid I don't know much about the medical side of things. I just meet and greet." He looked over at her. "Drink up."

Lucy took a small sip. It was warm and very fizzy. "How do you like the Ivory Coast?" she asked. "Rather a change from South America."

"It is and it isn't," he told her. "All airports are pretty much alike."

"But surely you get out of the airport now and then," she teased.

"Oh, sure. Actually, I like traveling around, seeing different places," Jack said. "I grew up in Virginia. Beautiful, but a little too quiet for me. So my dad suggested I join the IMA. He's an old pal of Bill Miller's."

Lucy suddenly remembered the conversation she'd had with Bill soon after Jean-Pierre's death, when she'd wondered aloud whether Jack could have put the heroin in Jean-Pierre's bag and Bill had assured her such a thing was impossible. Bill had mentioned that Jack's father had worked at Langley. No one said "Langley" like that unless he meant CIA. Why hadn't it seemed significant to her before? Had McNulty Junior been a spook, too, at one time? She frowned. "Where else have you been stationed?" she asked, attempting a casual tone despite the disquieting thoughts that had begun chasing each other around in her head.

McNulty thought a little. "South America, mostly," he said. "And now here. Oh, and I spent a year in Turkey, but that was quite a while ago. Uh, why don't you finish your drink and we'll go through to the gate?"

"You're coming with me?"

"Sure. I have a gate pass. As I said, we're a—"

"—full service organization." Lucy managed a laugh. "Okay, let's go."

"Uh, better drink up first. I don't think they'll let you take that through security."

"Really?" She lifted the soda. *"Salud."* She took the straw between her lips, then raised her eyes to look at him. His eyes were fixed on the can, his expression tense.

"Bottoms up," he said.

She stopped in mid-sip and sat perfectly still. Stupid, she berated herself; stupid, stupid. A cold, white fear flooded through her. She released the straw and thrust the can toward him. "Hold this for me, will you?" she said, striving to keep her tone calm and easy. "I need to use the john." She picked up her bag and turned away quickly so he wouldn't see her face.

"You can leave your case with me," he called after her, but she ignored him and kept moving.

Inside the ladies' room, she locked herself into a cubicle and rummaged frantically through her bag. Nothing. She leaned against the metal wall, stiff with dread. I actually went to him for help, she thought fearfully; I told him everything. I fell asleep in his goddamn house. I made it so easy for him. Her hands were shaking as she looked at her watch; time was running out. She bent down and removed the contents of the case, piling everything on the damp and dirty

floor. She ran her hand around the sides of the empty
bag, then along the bottom, and felt the lining shift.
An edge of the fabric was loose in one corner, its
underside tacky. She pulled at it and it began to lift.
The fabric had been glued to a piece of stiff cardboard
cut to mimic the bottom of the bag. It had been done
recently; the glue was still sticky. This false bottom
had then been glued into place over—what? A quick
tug and up it came, revealing a space some two inches
deep between the false and true bottoms. Nestled in
this space were five flat plastic bags of white powder.

Quickly Lucy removed the first bag and held it over
the toilet, ripping the plastic with her fingernail. The
powder cascaded into the bowl and she flushed it
away. She emptied the next bag, flushed; then the
next. When all the bags were empty, she flushed them,
too. She went to the sink and washed her hands, then
soaked some paper towels and washed out the bottom
of the case. When it was thoroughly clean and dry,
she repacked the bag and left the ladies' room, shoving the false bottom into a large trash can beside the
door as she went.

McNulty was pacing just outside, the can of soda
still in his hand. "You okay?" he asked, studying her
face. "You look sort of funny."

"Stomach bug," Lucy said shortly. "Which way's
the gate?"

"Over there." He thrust the soda toward her.
"Cola's good for settling the stomach."

"True." Lucy took the can and went through the
motions of drinking, sucking the liquid up into the
clear straw but holding her tongue over the top of it.
Seeing the cola rise in the straw, seeing her appear to
swallow, McNulty nodded and smiled. "That'll fix you
right up," he said approvingly. "You'll see."

"I feel better already," she told him as she ditched
the can. She worried about what symptoms to fake

and how soon he'd expect them to start, but the flight
was boarding as they reached the gate, and it turned
out not to be a problem.

He'd come so close, she thought as the plane lifted
off. So damn close. If McNulty hadn't pushed quite
so hard . . .

They banked and began to climb through the
clouds, heading west. She pictured McNulty hurrying
back to the departure lounge, dialing a phone number.
Yes, she drank the soda. Yes, she took the goods with
her. Everything went according to plan.

That's what you think, Doctor Bill, she thought with
cold fury. You haven't won yet.

Their arrival at Kennedy Airport in New York was
late but uneventful. She cleared Immigration without
any difficulty and was heading for the Customs area
when several grim-faced federal agents intercepted
her. They escorted her to a small room where they
emptied her travel bag and searched it and its meager
contents thoroughly. Obviously surprised at not finding the contraband Lucy had dumped into a toilet
hours before, they questioned her extensively, then
called in a policewoman and subjected her to a strip
search. During the ordeal, Lucy said as little as possible, her plan already well-formed. When, eventually,
they were forced to release her and her possessions,
she hurried through the empty terminal to the taxi
stand.

"He's a dupe?" Rossetti stared at Tom across the
scratched Formica table. He shook his head in frustration. "Just three days ago, you suggested Miller was
using the IMA to run drugs to raise money for left-
wing terrorism. Now you're saying he's being used,
that he's an innocent—"

"That's not what I'm saying," Tom replied heatedly.

"It isn't that simple." He cast a furtive look around the nearly empty diner.

"You bet it's not simple. You want to tell me what's going on?"

The older man turned the cracked coffee mug around in his hands. "We've been tracking two different . . . situations over the past few years," he continued at last. "I asked for this meeting because it's suddenly occurred to . . . somebody that the two might be connected."

Rossetti nodded sagely. "Clear as mud."

"I know. Just listen." Tom waved away the waitress in her tired pink uniform, then turned back to Mike. "Situation One: Is a well-known, respected doctor financing left-wing terrorism? This is something you and I have discussed before. Here's Bill Miller, an eminent medical man, a selfless healer, a sophisticated art collector, a wealthy supporter of charitable causes—"

"And a left-wing drug runner."

"Don't jump the gun." Tom drank some coffee. "Yvette was a Parisian living in Brittany when—"

"Yvette?"

"Bill's mother. French. She met his father toward the end of the Second World War. Dad was a decorated naval officer. They married, Miller *père* was reassigned to a mid-level job at the Pentagon, and they settled in Virginia. Bill was born there. His father was well placed, his mother played her European Culture card for all it was worth, and the family enjoyed a reasonably affluent lifestyle. Nice house, good schools, hobnobbing with middle-level diplomats, military and cultural attachés, that sort of thing."

"CIA people part of their social circle?"

"I should think so; it comes with the territory. Anyway, Yvette convinced Bill to attend the Sorbonne in Paris after prep school. He lurked on the fringes of various university political action groups, left-wingers to neo-Nazis, but apparently never became a card-carrying anything. His mother died during his third year, and he immediately transferred to Harvard, then went on to Harvard Medical School. His old man died about ten years ago."

"And Bill went on to found the IMA. Cue the music, roll the credits."

"Come on, Mike. The point is, Miller's lived an exemplary life—"

"Aside from the drug running."

"We can't prove that," Tom cautioned. "What I've been trying to tell you is that some of his international fund-raising contacts are rather . . . interesting." Tom sipped his coffee. "Which leads us to Situation Number Two."

Mike held up a hand to silence Tom, then signaled to the waitress for a refill of coffee. When the woman had departed, he said, "Go on."

"Number Two is this: In recent years, rumors have surfaced about a shadowy figure, a powerful man who clothes his extreme right-wing beliefs in left-wing polemic. A man who favors ethnic cleansing and elitist world domination. A man with sufficient financial and political backing to attempt to bring it about."

"Featuring himself in the starring role?" Tom nodded. "And you're suggesting Bill Miller could be . . . ?"

"No, of course not. The politics are wrong. But Miller could be being used."

"By this shadowy figure?" Mike shook his head. "I thought we agreed that Miller supports left-wing terrorism, not right-wing."

"Yes, but so does The Shadow, at least outwardly."

"So you think this guy could be using Miller to promote left-wing terrorism? Why?"

"Several reasons." He took a gulp of tepid coffee,

then pushed it away. "One, Miller's great at fund-raising. I'm talking multimillions. Two, despite his urbane up-bringing, Miller seems a bit naive, politically." Mike frowned. "What?"

"Nothing," Rossetti said, looking troubled. "Go on."

"Okay, three: Miller's got excellent international contacts—family friends, his years at the Sorbonne, his medical eminence. . . . That could be very useful to the right person. Four, there's the IMA, a perfect setup for collecting and laundering money. And five, Miller has the support of some well-placed spooks. Remember what I told you about the approval of the IMA Level Four lab?"

Mike nodded. "Okay, I see what you're driving at. But why would this shadow of yours want to promote left-wing terrorism if he's a right-wing fanatic?"

"Think about it," Tom urged, his voice low. "What's one possible result of widespread left-wing terrorism? Besides murder and mayhem, that is." Rossetti shrugged. "A widespread right-wing backlash," Tom told him triumphantly. "Hell, it's already happening; read the newspapers. This guy could be promoting left-wing terrorism in order to promote a right-wing backlash, one that could ultimately lift him to power. Manipulated correctly, Miller could be very, very useful to such a man."

Rossetti shook his head. "I'm not convinced. It's all just . . . supposition."

"You're right; it is. But if these two scenarios *are* connected, if Miller *is* being run by The Shadow, he may have something else up his sleeve."

"What?"

"That's for you to find out, Mike." He smiled grimly. "That's why we pay you the big bucks."

Chapter Twenty-six

"I can't come to the phone right now, but if you leave your name and number . . ."

Rick slammed down the receiver of the pay phone. Her flight had landed two hours ago, and he'd confirmed she'd been on board; where the hell was she? His face tight, he pulled up the collar of his anorak and flagged down a cab.

The lobby was dark and quiet. The night guard lounged behind the polished reception desk, drinking coffee and reading the *Daily News*. Over toward the elevators, a young man in a brown coverall mopped listlessly at the green marble floor. "Help you?" the guard inquired languidly as Rick approached.

"Going up to my office," Rick told him briskly, brandishing his attaché case. "Getting ready for a big meeting tomorrow."

"Sign in," the man told him, jerking a thumb at a lined notebook.

Rick scrawled "Louis Pasteur, IMA," and started for the bank of elevators. "Uh, is the nineteenth floor unlocked?" he asked, turning back.

The guard glanced at the notebook. "You're with the IMA?"

"That's right. Uh, we've got an emergency situation."

"You don't have keys?"

"Not with me. They beeped me, told me to get right

over here." He waited tensely for the guard to ask
the obvious question: How come he had his attaché
case with him but not his keys? The question never
came.

"If the outer door's locked, José can open it for
you," the guard told him, waving a hand toward the
floor mopper. "He's the one lets in the cleaners."

"I better take him with me," Rick suggested.
"Speed things up."

"Whatever," said the guard, returning to his paper.

"There you go." José unlocked the small door set
at right angles to the thick plate-glass double doors
reading IMA in discreet gold letters, and swung it open.

"Thanks," Rick told him. "Uh, I'll need you to unlock my office, too."

The man looked doubtful. "You don't have your
office key?" he asked, eyeing the attaché case in
Rick's hand.

"Left 'em at home, I'm afraid," Rick replied, and
smiled engagingly. "This meeting tomorrow kind of
caught me on the run."

José thought for a moment, then shrugged. "Okay,"
he said. "Which one's yours?"

Rick thought back to his recent meeting with Miller,
trying furiously to remember where his office was.
Coming in through this side entrance had disoriented
him. "Along here," he said. Bill's was a corner office,
he recalled, at the end of a hallway to the left of the
main reception area. He strode purposefully down the
corridor in what he thought was the right direction,
flicking on a few lights so he could read the name-
plates beside the closed office doors. "Over there," he
said, spying Miller's nameplate with some relief.

The porter fiddled with the lock and the door swung
open. With his thumb, he depressed a button on the

side of the door above the lock. "Just pull the door closed when you leave," he explained. "It'll lock automatically."

"Thanks." Rick waited until he heard the distant sound of the side door closing, then entered Miller's office and shut the door firmly behind him. Flicking on the light, he crossed to the desk and searched through the few papers stacked there. The disk wasn't there, but he hadn't really expected it would be. The center drawer was unlocked and filled with the usual pens, pencils, breath mints, and paper clips. The side drawers were locked.

The desk was a beauty, all polished rosewood and brass. Rick admired it for a moment, shrugged, removed a hammer and screwdriver from the attaché case and smashed the drawer locks open. He went quickly through the contents, pawing through files, shaking the contents of envelopes out onto the desk, and hitting pay dirt at last as he ruffled through the pages of an unused legal pad.

Turning on the desk computer, he inserted the bright green disk, slid into Miller's leather chair, and began to read.

The shabby figure shuffled slowly along the street, shoulders hunched against the cold, a dirty paper cup extended, without much hope, to the few passersby. It was late, time to bed down in the doorway he'd staked claim to. His stomach growled. He hadn't thought to eat before, and now he was hungry.

Two women approached, made a wide detour around him, and hurried away. He pulled his gray balaclava down over his ears and looked after them, muttering loudly.

For several minutes the snow-encrusted street remained empty. Then a man in a smartly cut overcoat came strolling down the block, a paper bag in his gloved hand. As he drew alongside, a smell of hot grease wafted toward the shivering figure, drawing him like a magnet.

Listlessly, he extended his cup. To his surprise, the man stopped, fished in his pocket, and came up with some small change. Not enough for a meal, the beggar thought, cursing and turning away.

"Ray?" the man called softly after him. "Aren't you Ray?"

Ray turned back, scowling. "So what?"

"I brought you something to eat." Ray's eyes went to the brown bag. There were grease stains on it. "A burger," the man continued, "and fries. And hot chocolate." He extended the bag. "Take it."

"Why you bringing me food?" Ray demanded suspiciously, but his hand was already reaching for the bag.

"It's a present," the man told him.

"Present?" Ray puzzled over this foreign concept briefly, then shrugged; food was food. He drew out the burger, unwrapped it, and took a large bite. It was good. "Why you giving me presents?" he inquired, his mouth full.

"It's not from me. It's from the doc."

"Doc who?" Ray took another bite.

"You know. The doc. That nice woman doctor you talk to, sometimes. She thought you might be hungry."

"Oh, yeah, the doc," Ray mumbled, chewing. Gripping the bag tightly, he headed for his doorway. It would be nice to drink the hot chocolate in his doorway.

The man hesitated, then went after him, watching as the shabby figure seated himself on the low step out of the wind and pried up the lid of the steaming drink. "Enjoy your meal, Ray," he said. "Stay warm."

Ray waved him away and began attacking the fries

while he waited for the cocoa to cool a little. The man crossed the street and moved off a few yards, then stopped and turned back, watching as Ray began gulping down the hot liquid. Nestled in his doorway, Ray finished the food and drink, then leaned back and closed his eyes, suddenly tired. The man stepped back into the shadows and waited ten minutes by his gold wristwatch. Then he recrossed the street and knelt down beside the dormant figure.

"Ray?" he said softly. "Want some money, Ray?" There was no reply, but he'd expected none. Stripping off his leather glove, he felt among the rags that covered Ray's chest, paused, then moved his fingers up to the neck, feeling for the carotid artery. Nodding with satisfaction, he retrieved the empty cup that had held the cocoa. Casting his eyes left and right, he rose and walked quickly down the street. At the end of the block, he dropped the cup into a trash bin, turned the corner, and disappeared.

How long will it take them to find out I was released? Lucy worried as she hurried through the darkened reception area. How long before they realize I didn't go home? It was clear they hadn't yet learned the true state of things; the lab was unguarded. You were so sure of me, Bill, she thought. Too sure.

Quickly she stripped off her clothing, donned scrubs and a spacesuit, and ran through the decon shower into Level Four, grabbing a small biocontainment hatbox from a storage closet on her way. The suit was designed to be plugged into ceiling air hoses; Anders's secret lab had none. She'd have to work fast, going back and forth between the two Level Four labs to plug into the air supply. First stop was her own workstation, where she gathered up all her samples and dumped them into the hatbox. Moving on to the lab

refrigerator, she did the same with the peruvia samples
stored there. Then, going quickly to Carl's work station, she hit the button that opened the hidden wall
panel. She took several deep breaths to pump up the
oxygen level in her lungs, then disconnected the air
hose, picked up the hatbox, and went through.

A small commercial refrigerator stood beside Carl's
secret workstation. She set down the biocontainment
box and wrenched open the fridge door. Vials of pale
pink liquid glowed faintly in the interior light. There
were two open, molded-plastic test-tube holders containing three vials each, and two similar ones, one behind the other, each holding six vials. She was stunned
to see that although the holders themselves were labeled, the individual tubes were not. More than careless, this was a highly dangerous practice. She scanned
the labels on the vial holders. The two six-packs contained peruvia b; the others, peruvia and p. moribundi respectively.

Her original plan had been simply to remove all the
virions from the lab. But seeing that the vials themselves weren't labeled, she now decided to substitute
tubes of the harmless inoculant, peruvia b, for the lethal strains she would remove from the fridge, and to
put water-filled tubes in place of the vials of peruvia
b she would be moving, in the hope of delaying the
discovery of her theft.

She fumbled the peruvia vials out of their open test-
tube holder, cursing her clumsiness in the thick gloves,
and placed them gently into the small biocontainment
box. Opening one of the packs of peruvia b, she
quickly transferred three vials into the peruvia holder.
Her lungs straining, she opened the pack of p. moribundi, and lifted out the three vials, setting them on
the work surface before fitting vials of peruvia b in
the three empty places. In a storage cabinet, she found

a carton of empty test tubes with rubber stoppers, and additional molded vial packs.

She was growing lightheaded, and hurried back through the panel for a fill-up of air. As she sucked in the deep, cool breaths, she wondered again whether Miller knew she'd escaped the trap he'd so carefully arranged, and felt her stomach contract with tension. Once he realized she hadn't gone back to her apartment, he'd know immediately where she must be. How long did she have before they came after her?

Back in Carl's lab, she took a vial holder from the cabinet and labeled it in red with one of Carl's markers, then knelt down and took the peruvia vials out of the hatbox. She set them carefully into the labeled vial holder and replaced them in the hatbox. She went back to the cabinets and took down three test tubes. She filled them with water, then dipped the tip of the red marker into each. She stoppered the tubes, shook them lightly, and set them into three of the six empty spaces in the peruvia b holder. The faint pink tinge wasn't an exact match with the peruvia b tubes in the second six-pack, but it was pretty close. She pushed the second pack well back in the fridge, just in case.

She was reaching for three more empty tubes when an alarm bell began ringing faintly inside her head. Oxygen starvation? she wondered, then noticed a light flashing above the opening between the two Level Four labs and realized the alarm bell was real. Someone must be entering Level Four from the IMA side. Her lungs were screaming for air as she dropped the tubes back into their box and slammed the cabinet and fridge doors shut, then grabbed the biocontainment box and ran through the opening in the tile wall. She shoved the hatbox inside a storage cabinet on the IMA side and jammed an air hose into her suit. She'd taken several quick breaths and was casting around for a hiding place when she remembered the three moribundi vials she'd left on the work surface. Pulling free of the air hose, she rushed back through the wall and grabbed the three vials, then hesitated. Which way should she go? She spun around, her mind racing. Could she get out of the lab via the Star of Hope side? No, she'd need portable air to use Carl's airless decontamination shower. Could she hide somewhere on the IMA side, then slip into the decon shower once the unwelcome visitors had come through it? Did she have time to close the secret panel? She turned back to find her questions meaningless. Three figures in black spacesuits equipped with portable air packs stood between her and her escape route.

"I told Bill you'd come here," Carl said through his helmet microphone as the two men took hold of her. The distortion of the headset built into her suit did nothing to mitigate the menace in his voice.

He came toward her, his eyes narrowing as he spotted the vials in her hand. Carefully he pried them from her fingers. "Indulging in a little industrial sabotage, my dear?" He opened the fridge and peered in. "Stealing the inoculant, I see," he said, removing and examining the half-empty peruvia b six-pack. "And the rest of the virions, too, no doubt, if we hadn't stopped you." Lucy struggled against the hands that held her but only succeeded in using up the remainder of her air.

"Filovirus research is dangerous work," Carl continued, slipping the three tubes he'd taken from her into a bio-pouch suspended at his waist. "Very dangerous, indeed. As you're about to find out." He returned the half-empty six-pack to the fridge and removed the moribundi three-vial holder. "Take her through to her workstation," he instructed the goons. He lifted out one of the test tubes and replaced the holder in the fridge before following them into the IMA section.

Then he pressed the button beneath the counter and returned the tile wall to its original solid state.

"Put her down on the floor near her workbench," he ordered. "And plug in her air hose. We can't have her suffocating. That wouldn't give the correct impression." He smiled, watching as they manhandled Lucy into position. "Tape her up." One of the men unrolled a length of strong tape and despite her struggling, managed to bind her wrists together, then her ankles.

Still holding the tube he'd taken from the moribundi holder, Carl wiped its rubber stopper with an alcohol swab and took a fresh syringe from Lucy's work cabinet. "No, the impression we want to create," he explained to Lucy, as he inserted the syringe into the vial in his hand and carefully drew off two cc's of liquid, "is that of an unfortunate laboratory accident."

He held up the syringe, admiring the faint pink glow of its contents. "Hold her steady," he directed. He turned the syringe around, gripping it like a dagger. "The mortality rate of peruvia moribundi," he told Lucy conversationally as he walked toward her, "is about ninety percent. You already know that, of course, since you read my report."

Lucy cried out and shrank away, but the black-suited men held her securely.

Carl kept coming. "I'm afraid this will hurt," he told her. He leaned down and wiped at the leg of her suit with an alcohol swab.

"You're insane. You can't—"

He lunged, stabbing the syringe through the protective suit and into her thigh, sending the virus coursing through her bloodstream. Her screams sounded loud in her helmet. This can't be happening, she thought wildly. Then she realized what he'd actually done.

Carl withdrew the syringe and applied a strip of tape to the nearly invisible hole. "Wouldn't want anything else to kill you," he explained, patting her shoulder. "Not that there's much risk. Despite my best efforts, nothing in here is airborne. You can release her now," he told the men. "Wait for me in decon."

As the men retreated, Lucy tried to rise, but Carl kicked her lightly in the stomach, sending her sprawling. "Moribundi kills within thirty-six hours or so, so you just sit tight," he told her mildly. "Of course, we'll lock the decon shower from the far side. The mission side's already secure." He leaned back against the work counter, staring down at her. "I did warn you, Dr. Nash, that if I went after you with a syringe of lethal pathogen, I wouldn't miss." He shook his head sadly. "Women don't belong on Level Four. I've always said so."

"Where are you taking the vials?" Lucy whispered, eyeing the bio-pouch.

"Ah, so glad you asked." Carl withdrew one of the tubes. "When we introduce peruvia moribundi to the world, my friends and I plan to be immune." He swabbed the vial's rubber seal with alcohol, selected a fresh syringe from the cabinet, and inserted the needle tip into the vial.

"No, Carl. Don't!"

"Oh, it's not for you," he said, ripping open the join between his suit and glove and swabbing the skin beneath his scrubs. "The inoculant is for me." He slipped in the needle and Lucy watched in horror as the level in the syringe went down. When it was empty, he tossed it onto the counter. "Good-bye, Dr. Nash," he said. He walked quickly to the decon shower door and pulled it open. "So nice to have known you." He stepped inside and shut the door behind him.

With difficulty, Lucy rolled to her knees, then levered herself erect. She stood there, swaying slightly, her eyes fixed on the door through which Carl had exited. In a day or so, someone would come to "discover" her accident. But there would *be* no accident. Because of her vial switching, Carl had unwittingly injected her with peruvia b.

And he'd injected himself with peruvia moribundi.

Chapter Twenty-seven

"I need your help."

Renée looked askance at the flushed and breathless man before her. "It is very late. You should have called first."

She swung the apartment door closed, but he shoved it open again before it could latch. "It's important," he told her.

"Perhaps to you." Renée scowled at him, drawing the semitransparent negligee around her body in a gesture that emphasized what she was purportedly attempting to hide.

"To both of us. Please."

She frowned slightly but stepped back, allowing him to enter the dimly lit living room. "You have ignored me for too long," she said sternly. "Suddenly you arrive here in the middle of the night and expect me to fall into your arms? I think not."

Rick shook his head. "That's not why I'm here," he said quickly, trying to keep from his face the relief he felt at her words. "I have far too much respect for you to—"

"Well, perhaps I will forgive you," she told him, taking his hand and leading him to the sofa. "Do you want a drink?"

"No, thanks. Renée, I—"

"I think I will have one." She went to the small bar against one wall and poured herself a scotch, neat.

"I'm sorry I woke you."

"I wasn't sleeping." She turned back toward him. "You said you needed my help?"

"Yes. I've lost Lucy."

Renée's eyes blazed, "Your little romance goes sour and I am supposed to care? How dare you—"

"Not like that, for godsake," Rick exclaimed quickly. "I mean, I've lost track of her. You know Miller told me to stay close to her. I went to the airport this evening," he continued, telling the tale he'd rehearsed on the way over from Bill's office, "but Lucy wasn't there. At least, she didn't come through baggage claim." Renée's expression had softened a bit, though she still eyed him warily. "Surely you don't think I care about her personally," he declared. "After a woman like you? No, Lucy is just business; Bill's business."

"I see. And Bill sent you after her?"

"You know he did. I told you so, weeks ago."

"I mean tonight."

Careful, Rick thought. She knows something. "Not specifically tonight," he answered slowly. "It's sort of an on-going thing. Why? What happened tonight?"

"If Bill hasn't told you . . ."

"Actually, I got a message to meet him. He said he had some news." Renée raised an eyebrow. "But I was afraid he'd ask me about Lucy and—God, you look beautiful."

"You think so?"

"Blue is a wonderful color for you."

"Better than no color?" The negligee dropped from her shoulders and pooled on the ground around her feet. She lifted her breasts in her hands and offered them to him, smiling her sleepy smile.

"You know I can't do this," he said, filling his voice with regret. "Not as long as Lucy—"

"Forget Lucy," Renée told him harshly. "Lucy's dead."

Rick went white. "Dead?"

"As good as."

So she's not dead yet, he thought frantically. There still might be time— "What happened?"

"Bill and Carl took care of her," Renée explained. She kneeled in front of him and began stroking his crotch. "We don't have to worry about her anymore."

"The drug scam?" Rick asked, his mind working furiously. "Heroin in her luggage, like Jean-Pierre?"

Renée's hand stopped moving. "You knew about that?"

"Bill told me." He took her nipple between his fingers. "Is that how they dealt with Lucy?"

"Ah, *caro*," she sighed, her eyes closing. "Don't stop."

Rick stopped. "First, tell me."

Renée's eyes flicked open again. "The heroin, yes. But it didn't work. No one knows why. It doesn't matter. Fortunately that stupid woman went straight to the lab. Carl Anders is arranging something."

"Arranging what?"

"An accident, Bill said."

"What kind of accident?" Rick asked, his voice tense.

Renée shrugged. 'What does it matter? Mmm . . . I have missed you."

"You'll have to miss me a little longer," he told her, brushing away her searching hands. "I have to meet Bill."

"Not now?"

"Right now. But when I come back—" He bent and bit her nipple and she gasped with pleasure. "Wait for me?"

"Perhaps." She smiled archly.

He ran for the door, wrenched it open, and went through it, banging it closed behind him.

The streets were deserted and the taxi made good time. Good enough? he wondered tensely, urging the driver on. They pulled up outside the IMA lab and Rick threw money at the man and leaped out, unlocking the outer door with his cardkey and hurrying through the small unguarded lobby.

He'd feared the steel doors, left open during business hours, would be locked in place across the plate-glass entrance, and was surprised to find them swung back against the wall. Of course, he realized; to make a lab accident believable, the doors would have to be left open.

He hurried through the darkened reception area, quickly searching every lab, every storage closet. Nothing. That meant only one thing.

He sprinted down the hall to the Bio Level Four staging area. Quickly he stripped off his clothing and donned scrubs and spacesuit, then hurried into the decon shower.

The shower's exit door was locked, and he had a quick moment of panic before realizing it was bolted from his side. He slid the bolt open and stepped out into the Level Four lab, calling, "Lucy? Can you hear me?"

Exhausted from hours of traveling, her time sense confused, Lucy had fallen in a troubled sleep on the floor beneath her workbench. Now she woke and looked around, startled. Was that Rick's voice, calling her? But he wasn't cleared for Level Four access; in fact, he'd declared the entire concept frighteningly claustrophobic. But of course Rick isn't who he says he is, she reminded herself grimly.

"Lucy? Where are you?"

She debated answering. Had Rick come to release

her, or had Carl realized he'd injected her with the wrong virus and sent him to correct the mistake? The decision was taken from her.

"Lucy?" Strong arms pulled her from her hiding place and began carefully slicing the tape away from her ankles and wrists with a second scalpel. "Are you okay?"

Lucy waited until her hands and feet were free, then scrambled up and grabbed a scalpel from the workbench. "Get away from me," she warned, brandishing it at him.

Rick stepped back, stunned. "What are you doing?"

"I know you're not Richard Hollander," she declared. "You're in league with Miller and Anders."

"That's not true. I—"

"You told me yourself that you weren't cleared for Level Four, that the whole idea made you queasy. Now all of a sudden you ride in here like the goddamn cavalry—"

"I *am* the goddamn cavalry," Rick said fiercely. He reached for her arm, then remembered the scalpel. "Come on, Lucy. If I were on Miller's side, would I have cut you free? Would I even *be* here?"

Lucy hesitated. That was true enough. Still . . . "Don't think I'm not grateful you came charging in here," she told him more calmly, "but who *are* you? And don't tell me you're Richard Hollander from Stanford."

"Can't we talk in decon?"

"I'm not deconning yet."

"But we've got to move," Rick urged. "You don't understand—"

"No, *you* don't understand." She hesitated. "There's something I have to do first."

"What?"

"I can't tell you until I know who you are and what you're doing here."

Rick nodded. "I guess it's time," he agreed. "As you say, I'm not Richard Hollander. Professor Hollander's enjoying a sabbatical in Japan."

"How nice for him. Go on."

"I'm here because it's highly unusual for a private lab to be licensed for Level Four work."

"To put it mildly."

"Especially when the license approval was backed by a couple of lads at the CIA, apparently acting on their own. But the license itself was obtained legitimately and all the design and inspection procedures were adhered to. There was nothing illegal about the IMA operation, at least nothing anybody could find. So they put me in place to nose around, see what I could come up with."

"They? The CIA?"

"You think I'm a spook?" Rick seemed to find the idea amusing. "No, I'm a scientist, just like you. Well, not exactly like you. I'm with the military; USAMRIID. They lent me to the FBI anti-terrorist unit."

"You're with the Army Medical Research Institute? My father had friends there. I can check you out."

"Please do. But can we get out of here first?"

"You still haven't told me your name."

"Major Michael Rossetti." He gave her a small salute. "My friends call me Mike."

"Of which you have many, I'm sure," Lucy said, setting the scalpel back on the workbench, "what with the scrupulous honesty you bring to your interpersonal relationships."

"Surely you don't think that what we had, uh, have, together is anything to do with—"

"I'll allow you to attempt to convince me of that, sometime," Lucy told him with a tiny smile. She hesitated. "Actually, I've heard of you. My friend Monica was involved in a joint study—"

"Monica Geyer? Anthrax?"

"That's right." Lucy sagged with relief. He had to be telling the truth. Or was there some other way he could have learned about Monica and the anthrax study? Her smile died.

"I guess I can't blame you for still being suspicious," Mike said. "Maybe it'll help if I tell you about the computer disk that's taped to my shin."

"You have a computer disk taped to your shin? That's against all safely protocols—"

"It was too important to leave in the dressing room. It's a copy of a disk I found in Bill's office." He paused. "I'm not sure how much you know about what's really going on here, but that second viral strain really does exist. And there's a third one called moribundi—"

"I know. Carl injected me with it. It's all right," she added quickly, hearing his sharp intake of breath. "He only thought he did. I'd been packing up the viruses, planning to take them out of here, and I switched the vials. He actually injected me with the inoculant."

"Thank God for that."

"He gave himself the moribundi."

"Jesus. Does he know?"

"No, he wouldn't listen to me. He needs to be found and quarantined before he accidentally infects anyone else."

"I called Tom—my FBI contact—when I read the disk. They'll be looking for him as soon as they can get a bench warrant. Miller, too."

"Can you reach him? Warn him about the virus Carl's carrying?"

"I'll try."

"There's something else you should warn him about. Carl said something about a plan to introduce moribundi to the world."

"Blackmail with a lethal pathogen," Mike said. "It's all on the disk." He looked around. "There's supposed to be a secret lab somewhere—" He turned back to study Lucy. "You found it, didn't you?" She nodded. "And Bill knew you found it and sent you to Africa. Why did you go?"

"I thought Bill was innocent. I thought he didn't know, that he was being used by Carl."

"I thought that, too, for a while. When did you realize?"

"When I found the drugs in my suitcase." She studied Mike through the faceplate of her helmet for some moments. "Okay, I believe you. At least, I believe you're not on Miller's side." She went to Carl's workstation and pressed the hidden button. "All the virions are in there," she explained as the section of wall folded inward. "It'll go faster if you help me. Oh, there's no air inside, so take a deep breath."

Lucy retrieved the biocontainment box she'd hidden and together they went into Carl's secret lab. Working quickly, they packed up all the vials and sealed the box shut. Lucy closed the wall between the two labs, and they carried the box with them into the decon shower.

Seven minutes can seem like a long time when you're standing in the mist of a chemical shower, waiting for the timer to release you. But it was barely long enough for Mike to tell Lucy what he'd found on the computer disk, and for Lucy to square it with what she herself had come to suspect.

"Three years ago," Mike explained, "Carl, funded by Miller, secretly created a new filovirus called sangre negra."

"But the IMA Level Four lab didn't exist back then."

"It didn't need to. Carl did the work secretly at a Mexican lab where he was already working in Level Four on a hantavirus of the same name. Used the name to camouflage his work with Ebola."

"Ebola? What's Ebola got to do with this?"

"Ebola was the starting point," Mike explained. "See, Carl had had some experience with Ebola—not many people have—and he'd hoped that by changing the genetic coding for two of the viral proteins, he could create a strain that would give immunity against Ebola." Lucy nodded; this explained the uncanny resemblance to the Ebola virion that she'd seen in her research. "He seeded this strain in a rural, isolated area of the Peruvian rain forest," Mike continued, "but it proved highly lethal, wiping out a large proportion of the indigenous population."

"But not everybody," Lucy said. "At least two people survived."

"Yes, but Carl didn't know that, then. He went back to the lab and tried again, this time creating peruvia. By now he was working in the new IMA lab. He chose a spot some twenty miles from the original test site, and, under the guise of IMA medical air, managed to inject it into the small, local *indio* population. It proved to be a milder version of sangre negra, but still too potent to use as an inoculant."

"You mean, IMA doctors actually participated in the experiment?"

"Not knowingly."

"Jesus."

"His next try," Mike continued, "produced moribundi, a real killer. By now he must have been getting pretty worried about being able to come up with the inoculant he'd promised Miller. But then you were sent to Peru, and he got lucky."

"The second strain I collected from the two *indios* who ran away. The strain that turned up in the CDC sample."

"And in one of the samples that went to the IMA lab. The *indios* had survived sangre negra three years before and trekked through the jungle, ending up near

the settlement Carl later chose for testing peruvia.
There may have been other survivors, too; we'll never
know. Anyway, it turned out that, inside the *indios'*
bodies, the original sangre negra virion had mutated
into peruvia b, a new strain that gave full immunity
against both peruvia and moribundi. Doesn't say how
Carl knew that, though; there doesn't seem to have
been another trip to Peru."

"There didn't need to be," Lucy said, remembering
the deserted ward with its sickly smell of formaldehyde. "He gave moribundi to a group of homeless
people. Kept them locked in a hidden room above the
mission—"

"What mission?"

"Star of Hope. It backs up to the lab building. Another group was kept in the mission itself. They were
the lucky ones."

"Lucky?"

"They were given the inoculant first."

"Christ," Mike said.

"And Miller's planning to inoculate himself and his
supporters, and use moribundi as blackmail? What
for?"

"Power. Wealth. He's got the backing of several
major international financiers, the ruling political
wackos of two small but fantastically wealthy
nations. . . . Miller has a vision of the way the world
should be run, and the clout to try and make it run
that way."

"You mean, his left-wing politics aren't just talk?"

"*Left*-wing? You didn't actually buy that bleeding-
heart act of his, did you? No, Miller's so far right, he's
practically falling off the edge. Tom says they've been
hearing about some shadowy right-wing fanatical Mr.
Big who's into world domination. He thinks Miller's
being used by this guy. But he's wrong."

"How so?"

"Miller *is* this guy."

For a moment, Lucy was silent. Then, "Where do the drugs fit in?"

"Fund-raising. A little side deal between Miller and the Mafia, courtesy of the Contessa dePalma."

"Renée? I never did like her."

"Neither did I," Mike replied truthfully.

"Did Jean . . . ?" Lucy began tentatively. "Was he . . . part of it?"

"I don't think so," Rick replied gently. "He had his little art scam, but he wasn't a drug runner. The FBI suspects Miller's been using IMA medical personnel as mules for years, without their knowledge. And they weren't the only people he used. Most IMA contributors have no idea of its true purpose." He glanced at the hatbox on the floor between them. "What are you planning to do with that?"

"I hadn't gotten that far," Lucy said. "I just wanted to get it all out of there, out of their reach, and then call the CDC."

"My car's in a garage nearby. We can lock it in the trunk until the CDC can send someone to pick it up."

"Okay. But I want you to give me the car keys first."

"I saved your life and you still don't trust me?"

"I'll check you out with USAMRIID from a pay phone at the parking garage. *Then* I'll trust you."

"You're going to have to wake up some pretty important people to get me identified at this time of night."

"I am and I will."

Mike looked at her with new respect. "Well, after we've established my identity, maybe I can buy you an early breakfast while Tom and the boys track down Miller and Company."

But Lucy shook her head. "Since Bill and Carl think I'm trapped here, dying of peruvia moribundi, I want to go back to my apartment. You can fix us something to eat, and I can take a much-needed shower." And there's something there we just might need, she thought to herself.

Mike frowned but said nothing.

The decon shower shut off and they left, carrying the hatbox out with them.

Chapter Twenty-eight

The black Range Rover glided quietly to the curb, flashing its headlights impatiently. A tall figure, muffled in fur, came out of a small, elegant building and approached the vehicle. The driver rolled down the window.

"Why didn't you call me sooner?" he asked curtly.

The fur-clad figure came around and slid into the front passenger seat. "It didn't seem all that strange at first," she said. "It was only later, when I thought about it . . ."

"Didn't seem strange?" Bill put the car into gear and pulled out into the empty street. "The man turns up without warning, in the middle of the night, asking where Lucy is—"

"Begging me to make love with him," Renée corrected angrily. "He said he only wanted to know about Lucy because he was afraid you would ask him about her when he met with you."

"Met with me? At three o'clock in the morning?"

Renée shrugged. "I thought he was working for you."

"So did I," Bill said grimly.

"You are too careless." Renée opened her coat, revealing black leather pants and a striped sweater. "You should never have told him about using your doctors as mules."

The car swerved, almost sideswiping a parked delivery truck. "He knew about that?" Bill demanded.

"Yes, and about planting the drugs on Lucy, too."

"Shit," Bill banged the wheel in frustration.

"Mr. Tortoriello will not be happy about this."

"He won't be overjoyed with you, either," Bill shot back. "If you hadn't told Hollander—" The sound of the car phone interrupted him. "Yes?"

"It's Carl. You were right; she's gone. The virions, too. But I have a vial of each of the important ones."

"You idiot," Miller exploded. "You should have secured the building when you left."

"*You* were the one who wanted everything to look normal," Carl protested. "Locking her inside Level Four was a good plan, until that cow started talking about it. Even then, we should have been all right. Hollander isn't cleared for Level Four."

"Apparently that didn't stop him," Bill said bitterly.

"Well, how was I supposed to know? He always said—"

"Shut up, Carl." Miller paused, thinking. "Get back inside the lab and stay there. I've got men combing the city for Hollander and Nash. We'll bring them back there and do the job right."

"Uh, I don't think that's a very good idea," Carl said diffidently. "Not anymore."

"And why is that?"

"There seems to be some sort of, well, surveillance."

"What?"

"What's wrong?" Renée asked. "What's happened?" Bill waved at her to be quiet.

"They arrived after I'd left the lab," Carl was saying. "I was just at the corner when I heard the car, but it never came past me. I turned around and saw it park across from the lab entrance, but nobody got out. Look, I have the vials with me. I could meet you at the office—"

"And you don't think they'll have the offices covered, too, whoever they are?" He thought for a moment. "Go to Banana King," he said. "Wait for me on the loading dock. Stay out of sight." He disconnected before Carl could reply, then dialed a number. "It's Miller," he said to someone on the other end. "Anything?"

"You won't like it. The guard's book shows that a guy named Louis Pasteur signed in about an hour ago. The porter opened up the IMA offices for him."

"Louis Pasteur?" Bill asked incredulously.

"Cute, huh? The porter says he unlocked a large corner office for the guy." My office, Bill thought. "After Pasteur left, the porter went back to make sure everything was locked up. Your desk was damaged and your computer monitor was on."

Bill went cold. "Can he describe this Mr. Pasteur?" He listened tensely, telling himself that lots of people had brown hair and eyes. But he knew who it had to be. He'd always found it a little odd that someone of Richard Hollander's stature would choose to work at the IMA lab, but Carl had wanted the man; Carl had been flattered. Carl had been had. And so had he.

Hollander had mentioned the drug trafficking to Renée. Hollander had suddenly been able to enter Level Four unassisted and unafraid. And now Hollander, or whoever he was, undoubtedly knew the rest.

"There were a couple of unmarked cars out front," the man continued, "so I went out through the subbasement. Want me to stick around?"

"Definitely not." He slammed down the phone. He had to get his hands on Hollander. Lucy was less of a problem; she'd be dead in hours. But Hollander . . .

"I am not going to Banana King," Renée announced loudly. "I wish to be taken home. This is nothing to do with me."

"The hell it isn't. If you hadn't told Hollander where his girlfriend—"

"Girlfriend?" Renee exclaimed. "He said Lucy was just business, that I was the woman he wanted. He was so passionate, so—"

"He was lying, dammit. It's Lucy he's in love with. Don't you understand? He's not really—" He broke off; no need to tell her all of it.

"He lied to me? You are sure of this?" Renée's face contorted with fury. "Bastard," she spat. "Bastard. We will go and find him."

"Just what I had in mind."

"And when we do . . ." She snapped open the leather handbag that lay in her lap and drew out a small pistol.

"Christ," Bill said. "Not that. I'll handle it my way."

"*Your* way is not good enough. This we know."

"Damn it, Renée—"

The car phone shrilled, and Bill grabbed the receiver and listened, then banged it down again. "A car with California plates just entered the all-night garage underneath Lucy's building," he reported, stepping hard on the gas. "For godsake, put that thing away."

"I do not take orders from you," Renée shot back, but she put the pistol back in her handbag.

"That's better. We need to work together on this."

Renée shot him a sour look. "We'll see."

"I have a feeling it's against the rules of the co-op board," Lucy said dryly, "bringing a box of lethal pathogens into the building."

"Wait'll they see the CDC pickup team." Mike went to the phone. "Go take your shower. I'm going to try Tom again."

"And make a pot of strong coffee, will you? I don't even know what day it is, anymore."

When Lucy returned some ten minutes later, wearing blue jeans and a sweatshirt and toweling off her hair, Mike was sitting on the living room sofa, turning Jean-Pierre's ugly wooden statues around in his hands.

"You reach Tom?" she asked pouring herself a cup of the dark brew he'd prepared.

"No, but I left a message for him with the duty officer." He waggled one of the carvings at her. "I didn't know you went in for this kind of thing. New acquisitions?"

"Not really," Lucy replied, coming to sit beside him. "Jean had them in his suitcase the night he was arrested. They were here in the apartment when you came to dinner."

Mike shook his head. "I didn't see them. And believe me, I'd remember." He traced the joins in the wood where Lucy had glued the statues back together. "What happened to them?"

"Customs sawed them apart looking for drugs, but they didn't find any. I put them back together for old times' sake. Ugly, aren't they?"

"Awful. But valuable, I guess. Didier knew his business."

"That's what I assumed, too. But when I showed them to some experts, they said they weren't worth a dime."

Mike looked up sharply. "They're valueless? Then why'd he bring them back?"

"That puzzled me, too. He told me at the Mayaruna Airport there was something for me in his suitcase. But these?"

"What else did he say?"

Lucy thought back. "He was jumpy, nervous. I thought it was the weather; it was raining like hell. He said there was something for me in the suitcase and then he warned me to be careful. Hey, what are you doing?"

"Trying to break this sucker apart again." He

smashed the statue against the edge of the marble coffee table again, chipping the wood. "You wouldn't have a chisel and a hammer, would you?"

"I'll get the toolbox. But I don't understand why—"

"Just a hunch." He set the statue back on the table next to its partner. "Jean-Pierre was an expert in valuable artifacts, yet he brought back these horrors. Customs believed they were empty or they'd never have returned them to you."

"They *were* empty."

"Look, Customs got a tip Jean was smuggling artifacts; that's why they stopped him. But when they saw the drugs, they figured they'd found whatever there was to find."

"And you think they missed something? But the statues are hollow."

"Jean-Pierre was an art smuggler, not a drug runner. Go get the tools."

Working quickly, Mike separated the two halves of the male statue and studied the thin cross-section of wood. "Hold it steady," he instructed, handing her the bottom half. Positioning the thin chisel carefully, he tapped gently, grunting with satisfaction as the edge of the chisel slowly sank into the wooden skin, separating what appeared to be a one-layer shell into two thin layers. He flaked off a section of the inner layer and continued gently separating and flaking until, near the bottom of the statue, the inner shell splintered away, revealing a tiny compartment. Inside lay something concealed in surgical cotton. He took it out and unwrapped it. An intricately carved tube of amethyst, an inch-and-a-half long and just under an inch in diameter, gleamed in his palm.

Lucy gasped. "What is it?"

"I'm not sure," Mike said. "But I bet it's worth a fortune." He examined the cylinder carefully. "Looks

Middle Eastern. Is your computer connected to the Internet?"

"Yes." She booted up her PC, logged on through her provider network, and handed over to Mike, who surfed rapidly through various art indices.

"It's a carved cylinder seal," he said triumphantly. "From Mesopotamia—that's Iraq to you. Dates from somewhere between 2500 and 3500 B.C."

"Jesus."

"Indeed. Most were made from semiprecious stones or precious metals." He hit some keys. "According to the *New York Times,* sanctions against the Iraqi government are causing wealthy Iraqis to sell off items from their private collections in order to stay solvent." He scanned down the article. "It seems there are highly specialized markets for these things, primarily in New York, London, and Tokyo."

"Jean hinted to Stanislas he was bringing in something special."

"This is special, all right." Mike logged off and shut down the PC. "Let's open the other one."

Together they pried apart the wooden lining of the female carving. Two cylinders had been secreted in this statue, one of intricately worked gold and silver, the other of exquisitely carved topaz.

"So that's why he was meeting Jorge Melendez." She frowned. "What was Melendez doing with Mesopotamian cylinder seals?"

"Art smuggling is an international business," Mike reminded her. "Who knows how many times they've changed hands?"

"They're so beautiful," Lucy said, examining the seals. "But I still don't understand something. If the only reason for the statues was to hide these cylinders, why did Jean keep telling me there was something for me in his suitcase?"

"Because there was: the statues." Lucy looked over

at Mike questioningly. "Smuggling artifacts meant there was always a chance of being arrested," he explained. "He also must have known that if Stanislas found out what he was doing, he might take revenge. Which he did."

"You mean *Stanislas* tipped off Customs?"

"Yes. You said yourself he suspected Jean-Pierre was selling directly to his customers. Stanislas decided to teach Jean a lesson. He never expected him to be carrying drugs, too."

"Neither did Jean."

"True. Anyway, whether it was Stanislas or McNulty or Customs that was worrying him, Jean must have hoped that if he ran into trouble, you'd come forward to claim his things. The cylinder seals were so well hidden, the chances of their being found accidentally were practically nil. You knew nothing about art; you'd assume the statues were his gift to you and you'd keep them. Later, he'd find an excuse to take them back and remove the artifacts." Mike paused. "He didn't count on being killed." Lucy winced. "Sorry." He took her hand and held it gently between his.

"I wonder what it was about our mission that suddenly started bothering him?" Lucy said thoughtfully.

"What do you mean?"

"Just before he boarded his flight, Jean told me to be careful. That warning had nothing to do with the statues. Something else was worrying him. Jack McNulty, perhaps. Or . . ." She thought back to their conversation on the way to the airport—the old *indio* who ran from the compound, the local name for peruvia, returning spirits. "He'd been to South America before."

The phone rang loudly, startling them both. "Don't answer it," Mike said quickly. Lucy looked surprised, but obeyed.

Her answering machine clicked on. A beat, and Renée's voice oozed from the speaker. "Rick, *caro,* are you there? I know you are." A pause. "You don't answer me? But it is I who should be angry at you. You promised to come back to me tonight, to make love to me the way we used to. I waited and I waited but you never came. Why, *caro?*"

"You *what?*" Lucy jerked her hand free. "You and Renée?"

"It's not what you think," Mike said, flushing.

"What I think is—" Lucy began furiously, but Mike shook his head.

"Later," he said. "Please."

"Rick?" Renée's voice cooed. "You are in a terrible danger. You must leave quickly or you will die." A pause. "Still you do not answer? But I know you can hear me, so listen. Lucy Nash has a deadly sickness. You will catch it if you stay there. Rick?"

Motioning Lucy to silence, Mike picked up the phone, punching the speaker button so that Lucy could hear the conversation. "Renée, it's me. What's that about Lucy being sick?"

"That accident I told you about," Renée said. "They injected her. She's dying."

Lucy shook her head violently and Mike nodded; she'd already told him about the switched vials. To Renée, he said, "Where can I go? Anders knows I rescued Lucy. He'll be after me. Miller, too. We're safer here."

"You're not," Renée said flatly. "Bill knows you're there; his men saw you drive in." Rick looked over at Lucy, who'd gone pale.

"We're still safer if we stay here," Mike insisted, frowning.

Renée laughed. "You think Miller's men can't find a way around a doorman? You think they can't get through a locked apartment door? Come to my place. He wouldn't dare attack me."

"I won't leave Lucy."

A pause. "Then bring Lucy, too," Renée said. "But hurry. I am waiting outside with a car."

"Why would you want to help me?" Mike asked. "You know I lied to you."

Renée sighed. "Yes, I know. But Bill Miller lied to both of us. He has used us. He is evil."

"And you're suddenly on the side of the angels? A force for good?"

"You know me better than that. My motive is pure self-interest. Our arrangement with Miller was limited to drugs. It didn't involve killing Lucy. Or you."

"You telling me the Mafia's above all that?"

"Don't be stupid. But something has gone very wrong, and my boss wants me to limit our exposure. I'm offering you protection in return for your silence about our involvement in the drug scheme. How about it?"

The intercom buzzed and Lucy went to answer it. "Gas man coming up to fix that leak," the night man said.

"What? No, stop them."

"They're already on the way," he said, sounding puzzled. "With all their equipment. Said it was an emergency."

"There's no leak here."

Mike looked over at her, his expression tense.

"Gee . . . well, I don't know what to tell you," the night man was saying. "You better talk to them."

"Okay, Renée," Mike said, deciding. "We're on our way. Wait for us out front." He banged down the phone and turned to Lucy. "Grab a jacket."

"You trust her?"

"Of course not. But we can't stay here. I'll leave word for Tom."

Lucy nodded. "Be right back." She disappeared in the direction of her bedroom and Mike gathered up the cylinder seals. He was dropping them into his pants pocket when she came running out again, a long, heavily padded leather jacket around her shoulders and a handbag under her arm.

"She'll be expecting us to come through the lobby," Mike said. "Is there a service entrance?"

Lucy nodded. "It comes out on the side street."

The outer hallway was still empty as they ran to the fire stairs, but they heard the whoosh of the approaching elevator as the metal door closed behind them.

Renée folded the cellular phone and handed it back to Miller. "That went well."

"You were perfect," he told her admiringly.

"I am excellent at my work," she said, preening. "But this is your last chance, you understand?" She fingered her purse. "Then we do it my way."

Mike went first, cracking open the exterior door and looking around at the small dark courtyard. "Stay in the shadow of the building," he whispered, slipping out into the cold night. Lucy followed, exhausted despite the coffee and shivering in the sudden cold. They paused beside the brick wall and surveyed the side street beyond. "We could wait a long time for a taxi to come past at this time of night," Lucy said, frowning.

"It's that or walk," Mike replied. "Walking, they'll see us for sure. They'll have people everywhere."

They remained hidden in the shadows for several minutes. "There's one," Lucy said suddenly, as a yellow taxi sped by.

Mike ran into the street, but the cab was well away, and he was afraid to call out after it. He was turning back when another taxi appeared, cruising slowly. He flagged it down and motioned to Lucy. "Come on!"

The taxi slid to a stop just beyond them, and he and Lucy piled in.

"The Nineteenth Precinct police station," Lucy ordered. "East Sixty-seventh Street." The driver didn't reply as he stepped on the gas.

A kneeling figure rose up from the front seat where he'd been concealed. "Dr. Nash, I presume," he said. The evil-looking pistol he trained on them gleamed dully in the glow from the streetlight. "And you must be Richard Hollander. So glad you could join us." The solid chunk of the central door-locking mechanism engaging made Lucy jump. "No sudden moves, please, doctor. You, too, Hollander. Hands where I can see them."

"She's been injected with a lethal virus," Mike said. "If you don't let her out of here, we'll all die."

"Dr. Miller thought you might try that one," the man replied calmly. "Which reminds me . . ." Keeping the gun trained on them, he reached across the seat-back toward Lucy. "I'll take that handbag, doctor."

The driver spoke softly into a portable phone. "We're on our way." He glanced over at the man with the gun. "He wants to know if she's got them."

Without taking his eyes off the two passengers, the gunman rifled through Lucy's commodious purse with his free hand. "Yeah, she's got 'em," he confirmed.

Around the corner, the black Range Rover sped away, heading west.

Chapter Twenty-nine

The taxi headed south along the Hudson River, just another late-night cabby trying to make a buck. Past Canal Street the driver turned east, and for a terrible moment Lucy was sure they were being taken back to the IMA lab. But the cab made a quick right and left and pulled up in front of a shabby two-story warehouse attached, either side, to more of the same. Two armed men, half hidden in the shadow of the overhanging metal roof, came cautiously forward.

One of them approached the vehicle and looked in through the front passenger window. "Vince?" he asked softly.

"Who else? Give me a hand with these two."

The guards helped Vince extricate Lucy and Mike from the backseat, and escorted them up six cement steps onto a narrow loading dock. A steel door was set into the solid metal barrier that closed off the interior of the warehouse from the loading dock. One guard unlocked the door and stepped aside, and Vince prodded his prisoners through the opening, following closely, his gun drawn. The taxi had disappeared into the night by the time the guards, having locked the door again, resumed their positions in the deep shadow of the overhang.

The interior of the old warehouse was dim and cold. Bluish light pooled beneath hooded, low-wattage fixtures suspended from the low dropped ceiling. Crates of produce were stacked here and there in the gloom, and the over-sweet smell of rotting bananas was palpable and unpleasant.

Bill Miller stood in a puddle of light, speaking on a cellular phone. His jacket was off and one sleeve was rolled up.

"Head out to sea," he was saying, his words echoing between the old metal ceiling and the filthy cement floor. "Tell the launch to power up and stand by. We—ouch! Jesus, Carl."

"Sorry." Carl, surgical gloves on his hands and a transparent splash hood set on his head like a sunshade, withdrew the needle and placed it carefully back on a draped tray set on a nearby carton.

Bill ended the conversation and set the phone beside the tray. "I see our guests have arrived." He rolled down his sleeve and reached for his jacket. Beside him, Renée peered into the shadows.

"Lucy is here?" she said nervously. "But I have not had *my* injection." She turned angrily to Carl. "Hurry up. I don't want to catch it."

"It doesn't work that way," Carl said. "Anyway, you don't need—" He caught Miller's eye. "Okay," he relented, filling a fresh syringe.

"No!" Lucy ran toward the group as Carl plunged the needle into Renée's upper arm. "Stop." A bullet whizzed by her, cutting a swathe through her jacket and grazing her upper arm at the shoulder. She stumbled, grabbing at her arm, but continued toward Renée as Carl hurriedly withdrew the needle and stepped back.

"Lucy!" Mike started forward, but Vince jerked him back, pressing a strong forearm hard against his windpipe. He leveled the gun at Lucy, ready for another shot.

"Don't shoot," Bill called out. "Damn fool," he murmured. "He'll hit one of *us*."

Vince frowned but lowered his gun as Renée came forward and grabbed hold of Lucy, pinioning her arms behind her.

"Or spatter us," said Carl from the darkness into which he'd retreated.

Renée looked toward Carl's voice, puzzled. "Spatter?"

"With her blood," Carl explained. "The virus is passed on in the blood and fluids."

Renée stared at Lucy's torn jacket. "But we have all had the injection," she said. "What is there to fear?"

"It doesn't work that fast," Carl told her tiredly.

With a cry, Renée released Lucy, shoving her away. Lucy staggered forward, the wound in her upper arm throbbing.

"Stay where you are," Bill warned Lucy, "or the gentleman with the gun over there will shoot your lover." Vince grunted in agreement. "Carl?" Bill looked around for the missing scientist. "Jesus, Carl, where the fuck are you?"

Anders stepped out from behind a stack of cartons. "We're dealing with moribundi, for chrissake. I'm not suited up. I have no intention of risking—"

"You'll do what I tell you," Miller replied angrily. He looked at the scientist in disgust. "No one would guess you spend your days in a Level Four lab."

"That's different," Carl protested. "I wear a body-suit, I—"

"Shut up and prepare the injections," Bill told him testily. He turned to Lucy. "We've brought some sedatives for you and your boyfriend. His will be laced with moribundi. The sedatives will make it easier to have your bodies taken up to the lab."

"Up?" Lucy looked around curiously. "You mean, this building connects, too?"

"Connects to what?" Renée asked.

"To the lab," Lucy explained. "See, the mission—"

"Shut up," Bill ordered. He stepped forward and slapped her hard across the face. "You're too smart for your own damn good."

Lucy backed away, her cheek burning. Behind them, Lucy could hear Mike struggling unsuccessfully to pull free of Vince's iron grip. As long as Vince held a gun to Mike's head, she was helpless.

"Not that it matters anymore," Bill was saying. "I'm closing the lab. Finding your bodies, yours and Rick's, will make me realize how dangerous the Level Four operation is. I'll be distraught over losing two of my best scientists, and I'll close the whole place down." He smiled. "Carl can finish his work anywhere. Even at sea."

Lucy continued backing away. "His work?" she asked. "You mean blackmailing the world with peruvia moribundi?" She saw Renée's eyes widen, saw her turn toward Bill questioningly. Good; if she could co-opt Renee . . . "That's why you were immunizing yourself with peruvia b just now: so you can infect the rest of the world with moribundi and raise yourself and your friends to power."

"What's she talking about?" Renée demanded. "You are infecting the world with a virus?"

"She's lying," Bill said.

"It's true," Lucy insisted. "Think about it, Renée. What kind of charitable organization uses drug running to finance its mission?"

"Don't listen to her."

"Drug running's one thing," Lucy continued, riding over him. "Direct involvement in international terrorism's quite another. Did you and your boss really sign on for that?"

"That's enough," Bill said angrily, stepping toward Lucy, but the contessa interposed herself between them.

"Let her finish," she demanded. "Go on, Lucy."

"Get out of my way, Renée; you don't understand. Carl, get the sedative. Let's finish this now."

"Wait." Mike's voice rang out in the musty room. "I want to make a deal."

Bill looked across the warehouse floor to where Mike stood, a pistol against his temple, one hand in his pocket. "A deal?" He smiled grimly. "You have nothing to deal with."

"You're wrong. We found the artifacts Didier smuggled in, his last trip."

"Didier smuggled drugs."

"That's because you put them there. When Customs found them, they called in the DEA and stopped looking."

"And you didn't? You found something? And you conveniently happen to have whatever it is with you?"

"I do."

"How very nice. I'll take them from you once you're sedated. Why should I bargain with you for them?"

"Because I'll destroy them. I can, easily. They're very small and very fragile."

"I'd rather inject you," he told Mike, "because it fits the cover story better. But shooting you is always an option." He took a small pistol from his jacket pocket. "Toss them over."

"Go ahead and shoot," Mike said. "They're in my hand right now. All I have to do is squeeze. Conscious action or dying spasm, the result will be the same. Which would be a real shame. They're very rare."

"For godsake," Renée said angrily. "Shoot him and let's get out of here."

"What are they?" Bill asked Mike.

"Don't be a fool," the contessa said. "Can't you see what he's—"

"Walk him over here, Vince," Bill ordered, ignoring her. "Slowly. Lucy? Please don't move." His gun moved from one to the other, settling on Mike as he added, "Cover her, Vince. Okay, Rick, let's see if what you have is worth your life."

"Not my life. Lucy's."

"Lucy's dying of moribundi, remember? There's nothing I can do for her. But you still stand a chance. If what you have is as valuable as you say."

Slowly Mike took his hand from his pocket, fingers curled, and extended his fist toward Bill.

"Stop this nonsense," Renée fumed. "You cannot let him go and he knows this. He's stalling, playing with you—"

"Ancient Mesopotamian cylinder seals," Mike said, uncurling his fingers. "Museum quality."

"Jesus." Letting his pistol hand drop, Bill stretched his other hand toward the tiny treasures. "I've never seen—" A shot rang out, and Bill spun away, a small, neat crease in the shoulder padding of his jacket.

"I warned you," Renée said. "Now we do it my way."

But Vince was being paid by Bill, not Renée, and he fired across Lucy at the contessa. As Lucy dove sideways, Renée fired back. The impact of the two heavy bullets drove Vince's body backward across the floor where it crashed, lifeless, against a stack of banana crates.

Bill had recovered from the shock of being shot at and was firing at Renée. One of the slugs took her in the neck, and her blood spurted out in a high arc.

Carl ran for cover, knocking the medical tray to the floor and scattering equipment, as Lucy instinctively ran toward the dying woman.

"Get away!" Mike shouted urgently. "Get back."

Lucy hesitated, then stepped back quickly, horrified at what she'd nearly done. Renée had been injected with moribundi. Her spurting blood was deadly.

Misunderstanding Mike's warning to Lucy, Bill sprang forward and wrapped an arm around her throat. "Don't move," he warned her. "Carl, get the seals."

"The what?" Carl crouched fearfully beside the crate that held the tray of vials.

"He means these," Mike said. "Here. Catch." He tossed them into the darkness, well beyond Carl's rising figure, and dove at Miller, driving him backward into a stack of crates, splitting them open. But Bill's arm clamped more tightly around Lucy, dragging her with him, her body shielding him from Mike's flailing fists as the over-ripe fruit cascaded around them. The three figures grappled briefly before Bill managed to raise his gun and smash it into the side of Mike's head.

Mike slid away unconscious, and Bill levered himself erect, his forearm still around Lucy's throat, his gun hand firmly around her body. Her arm throbbed with pain, and a thin stream of blood coursed down beneath her jacket.

"Your boyfriend's out for the count," he said into her ear. A sickly sweet smell of mashed banana clung to his clothing. On the floor at their feet, Mike moaned but remained unconscious. "So glad I didn't have to shoot him. We'll inject him now, before he comes to. Then it'll be your turn. Go ahead, Carl."

"Don't do it," Lucy told the frightened scientist as he pulled his eyes from the bloody scene and began gathering up the fallen vials and syringes with trembling hands. "He shot Renée. He'll kill you, too. He doesn't want any witnesses."

"Shut up," Miller told her. To Carl he said, "Don't listen to this bullshit. The plan can't work without you."

"The hell it can't," said Lucy. "You've already made the virsues, Carl. What else does he need from you?"

Miller tightened his arm against her throat, nearly choking her. "You're a real pain in the butt, Lucy

Nash. You're a snoop. You're a liar." He paused. "And you're not even very good in bed."

"What?" Lucy managed to gasp.

"Of course you weren't awake at the time, so perhaps it isn't a fair assessment."

"What . . . are you talking about?" She forced out the words.

"The other night, when you came to tell me about the mission and the secret lab. So trusting of you. So stupid. The sedative in the cocoa worked very well. It's the same one we're using tonight." He reached his gun hand under her jacket. "We had a wonderful time together," he told her, caressing her breast with the pistol barrel. "Couldn't you tell? Didn't you have some memory of it the next day?"

"You bastard," Lucy spat, remembering her unexplained pain. "You raped me."

"And I enjoyed every minute of it."

She began struggling again, but he jabbed the gun hard into her ribs causing her to grunt with pain. "If you weren't infected with moribundi," he continued, "I'd suggest we do it again tonight. Although, as I say, you didn't contribute very much to the festivities." He glanced over at Carl. "Jesus, man, how long does it take to fill a damn syringe?"

Carl's coloring, normally pallid, had paled to a ghostly white. "Nearly ready . . . it's just—" He broke off as he carefully added several cc's of pale pink liquid to the colorless fluid already in the syringe, then offered the needle to Bill with shaking fingers, his eyes sliding off to watch the blood pool beside Renée's body.

"Don't give it to me, you idiot," Bill exclaimed impatiently. "Use it on *him*. What's wrong with you?"

"I, uh, didn't expect all . . . this." Carl waved the long needle at the bloody carnage. His breathing was fast and shallow, his eyes hot and red-rimmed. "I don't feel very well." He leaned heavily against the banana crates, the syringe drooping in his trembling fingers.

"You can faint later. Inject the bastard." But Carl didn't move. "Okay, I'll do it." Gratefully, Carl extended the syringe again. "No, put it down on the floor over there, next to him. Good." Bill hesitated. "You'll have to take Lucy from me." He peered at Carl. "Can you do that? Maybe we should sedate her first. Give it to me."

Carl went to the tray. "It's not here. Uh, when the tray went over . . ." He scanned the floor. "I don't know where it—" Bill eyed him dangerously. "I'll fill another," he said quickly.

Behind them, Mike groaned and looked around blearily, then fell back. "There's no time," Bill snapped. "We have to take Rick out now, while he's still groggy." His eyes went to the outer door. Should he send Carl to bring in one of the guards?

Mike moaned again, and his eyes flickered open. Lucy, feeling Bill's attention wander, began twisting her body from side to side in an effort to pull free, but he tightened his hold against her neck, pulling her head back.

As he did so, he was abruptly aware of the risk he was taking by holding her so close. Unlike Carl, he was unprotected by gloves or face shield. Suddenly he wanted to be rid of her. "Pull yourself together," he snapped at Carl, "and come help me."

Carl took several deep breaths. "I'm feeling better." He reached a gloved hand up under his face shield and swiped at his damp forehead. "I'm okay now. Oh, shit."

"What now?" Bill asked impatiently.

"My glove's torn. I have to change it. I have extra gloves. . . ." He fumbled on the tray, tipping it over and sending its contents cascading onto the cement.

"Dammit, Carl," Bill exploded, wishing for Vince's help, cursing Renée in his mind. "Just come and take Lucy from me. And for godsake, don't let her get loose." Carefully he transferred the struggling woman into Carl's strong arms, his gun at the ready.

Lucy was exhausted, nearly overwhelmed by fear, pain, and lack of sleep. She tried desperately to maneuver her hand behind her, to reach the rear waistband of her jeans beneath her jacket. No go. That's it, then, she thought. It's all over.

But as she glanced up at Carl's scared but determined face, an idea came to her. As she felt Miller's grip slacken and Carl's tighten around her, she managed to wiggle a hand up under the front of her open jacket and press it against the bullet wound, keeping her eye on Bill. As soon as he turned his attention to Mike, she pulled her hand free and shoved it under Carl's hood.

"Moribundi blood," she whispered smearing it on his cheek, feeling his hold loosen as he pulled away from her in terror, hearing Carl shout as she twisted free, feeling Carl's breath as she elbowed him hard in the chest, then sprinted toward Mike and beyond, kicking the syringe away into the darkness as she ran for cover.

"You stupid bastard!" Bill shouted.

"She's infected me. I'll die." Carl's voice was high and panicky.

"The skin's not broken," Miller told him firmly. "You'll be okay."

"I have to decon. I have to wash my face."

From somewhere outside came a gunshot.

Both men started. "What the fuck was that?"

"I don't know. But I have to decon."

Bill's hand tightened on his pistol as he peered into the gloomy depths of the warehouse. "Use the chemical sink on the way through, but do it fast, understand? The launch is waiting. Tell them to take you to the ship."

"What about . . . all this? What about you?" Carl was shaking.

"Renée's traceable to the Mafia. Unless Tortoriello wants to go public about his role in the drug running, she'll be chalked up to a gangland dispute. Lucy'll be dead in hours; Rick, too, once I inject him." Pocketing his gun, he bent over the fallen tray. "This the vial?"

"Yes."

"Okay, get going." Pulling on a pair of surgical gloves, he grabbed a fresh syringe, inserted the needle tip, and drew up a small amount of fluid. "Wait. Take the pathogens Lucy stole."

"Where are they?"

Syringe in hand, Bill looked around, spotting the handbag Vince had brought from the taxi. He jerked his chin at it. "In there."

Carl retrieved the bag and began pawing through it.

"Just take it," Bill urged. "Go. Go!"

"But they're unwrapped," Carl breathed, drawing out a handful of vials. "She didn't even— Hey, these are antibiotics. Bill, they're *antibiotics*!"

His face purpling with fury, Bill grabbed the vials from Carl, examined them briefly, and hurled them at the ceiling. "Take the vials from the tray," he ordered. "They're enough to get us started. You can make more in the ship's lab. Move."

He watched as Carl grabbed the vials and disappeared through a small interior door. When he turned back, Mike was sitting up, swaying slightly. The side of his head was caked with blood, and his eyes struggled to focus. Drawing his gun again, Bill contemplated the younger man. "It seems you still have something to deal with," he said.

"But *you* haven't," Mike said, his expression clearing as he looked around. "Lucy's gone."

"Not far." He hesitated. "And now that I think about it, I *have* got something. Lucy?" he called out into the darkness. "I haven't infected Rick yet. Want to trade?"

"Don't answer," Mike shouted.

"Moribundi's a terrible way to die," Bill called. "You'll find out for yourself, of course, but Rick doesn't have to. Give me the vials you took from the lab, and he goes free."

"Don't believe him, Lucy. There's no way he can let me go."

"Not true. Neither of you matters to me anymore. Carl's gone, and he's got enough virus to kill rather a lot of people. The plan goes ahead a little earlier than scheduled, that's all. You'll talk about what you know? Terrific. It'll help convince people I'm serious about doing what I threaten to do." A pause. "Okay, Lucy. You leave me no choice. Injection or bullet, Rick's going down."

"Wait." Lucy stepped out into the circle of light. "You can have the viruses."

"No," Mike exclaimed.

"They're in the garage in my apartment building." Mike groaned, but she ignored him. "They're hidden in the trunk of Mi—Rick's car. The key ring's in my rear pocket. I'm going to reach for it. Okay?"

"Go ahead," Bill said.

Mike had gone very quiet.

"And you promise you'll release him?" Bill nodded. "All right." Lucy reached her right hand back toward her rear pocket and tugged. "They're stuck," she said. "I'm going to reach back with my other hand and free them."

"Let me do it."

He took a step toward her, but Lucy retreated into the shadows. "Don't come near me," she warned. "If you want the keys, you'll do this my way."

Bill stopped. "All right."

Lucy walked slowly forward, reaching her other hand back. The rear hem of her jacket lifted. Suddenly her left hand came forward, key ring jingling. "Here!" she shouted, flinging the keys hard at Bill's head, her right hand coming forward in the instant he flinched and ducked, firing her father's gun once, twice, calling to Mike to roll clear as the blood spattered and she fired again.

The pounding of a battering ram against the outer door was loud in the silence that followed.

Chapter Thirty

Lucy stood weaving, the smoking weapon dangling from her hand, as she stared down at Bill Miller's mangled body. Mike rose to his feet and went to her, putting an arm around her shoulders and drawing her away from the virus-laden blood. Lucy's legs began to buckle as he led her to a crate near the wall. She collapsed onto it, leaning against him.

"Where'd the gun come from?" he asked softly.

"It was my dad's." She looked down at the pistol as if seeing it for the first time. "I wasn't sure I'd be able to do it," she said softly. "You think you know what you're capable of, but until you have to . . ." She trailed off.

"You've never fired it before? You're a helluva shot."

"I've shot at tin cans and bottles and stuff, sure. That's not what I meant. I meant shooting at *people,* killing them. . . . Even in self-defense. I wasn't sure I could do it." She shivered. "I'm a doctor."

"And you removed a cancer and saved the patient."

"The patient's not out of danger yet," Lucy replied. "Not while Carl's still out there."

"How's your shoulder?"

"It hurts, but I don't think it's serious."

"You don't look well," Mike said, studying her. "Your eyes are all red."

"I feel rotten. I've got a fever, I think." She suddenly drew away from him, alarm in her face. "Better keep your distance."

"That's okay. It's the good virus, remember."

"I hope that's all it is," she replied, remembering her hand brushing Carl's sweating cheek. Behind them, the hammering at the outer door continued, but in her exhausted state, Lucy seemed almost unaware of it. "No form of peruvia is 'good,'" she murmured. "It's an inoculant now, but it could mutate again. We both need to decon. Quarantine, too. And the warehouse has to be sealed immediately." She cast a look back toward the bodies. "Can you get to Bill's phone? Call Tom?"

"I suspect that won't be necessary," Mike replied as the steel door crashed inward. He ran toward the figures in black coveralls, shouting, "Stay away from the bodies!"

"Mike? That you?"

"For godsake, Tom, stop them. The blood's infected."

Tom barked an order, then turned back to Mike. "Is Lucy with you?"

"Over there."

"I thought you guys were safe at the Nineteenth Precinct."

"We didn't make it that far. How'd you find us?"

"Truth to tell, we weren't looking for you. The lab surveillance team thought they heard some shots, and sent a man around the corner to check it out. They found Miller's car parked down the block, but no shooter. No one put Miller's car together with this place; they just figured he must have made the lab surveillance guys and abandoned the car. When I heard about it, I sent a team to bring the car in, and one of the cowboys outside"—he jerked his chin toward the loading dock—"took a potshot at them. That's when things came together." He paused.

"Smells like shit in here." He turned to stare at the bloody scene laid out beneath the circle of cool light. "What the hell happened?"

"Miller's dead, Renée dePalma, too. That's Vince, over there; he's just hired heat."

Tom shook his head. "How?"

"Renée did Vince, Miller did Renée, Lucy did Miller . . . I missed some of the bits in the middle."

Tom turned to stare at Lucy. "She shot him?" He went and gently took the pistol from her hand. When she didn't respond, he bent down and studied her face for a moment. "You did the right thing," he told her softly. "You did what you had to do." His eyes widened as they went to her bullet-ripped sleeve. "Were you hit?'

"Yes, but not badly," she replied. "Better not touch it. Did you get Carl Anders?"

"No, he hasn't shown up at the lab yet. Our men are still—"

"He's here," she said. "He's upstairs."

"What? Up where?"

"Not sure," Lucy murmured. "The lab connects with the Star of Hope Mission . . . a hidden staircase in a wardrobe in the storage room. Miller said something about taking us up to the lab, so I guess it connects through here too, somehow. Carl went through there." She pointed toward the interior door, now ajar.

Tom shouted instructions to one of the men, who led three others through the door at a run.

"We need a decontamination team here, fast," Mike told Tom. "In RACAL suits. We'll need a transport team, too, and hospital standby. And portable decon."

"You've got it," Tom said, waving his men back against the wall. He reached for his walkie-talkie. "Unit One to HQ. Over."

The instrument crackled a reply, but Lucy leaned

over and put a hand over it. "I don't think you should report this over an open line," she said quietly. "I can give you some numbers to call." Tom knelt down beside her and pulled a pad and pencil from his coverall pocket.

"Hey, you hear something?" Mike turned toward the bodies, listening. Tom gestured for quiet, and in the ensuing silence, the beeping of a cellular phone sounded faintly.

"Miller's phone," Mike said. He started toward it.

"No." Lucy reached out to him. "Don't touch it."

Tom took a pair of plastic crime-scene gloves from his pocket. "These help?"

"Yes." Mike pulled them on. Keeping well away from the gore, he retrieved the phone, along with several alcohol swabs from Carl's tray. He swabbed the instrument and said a silent prayer. "Yes?" he said softly into the phone.

"Miller? Is that you? I can barely hear you."

"It's Carl," Mike whispered, cupping a hand over the phone. "Go ahead," he told Carl, hoping the heavy static he heard would disguise his voice.

"I'm on the launch. We're nearly at the ship. You want me to send it back for you?"

"Tell him yes," Tom said softly.

"Yes, send the launch back here."

A brief silence. Then, "You're not Miller," Carl said accusingly. "Who the hell is this?"

"This is the FBI," Tom said, taking the instrument from Mike's hand. "Miller's dead. The lab's been sealed off. We know about the Star of Hope Mission, too. It's all over, Anders. Give yourself up."

"You're lying." A pause. "Put Miller on."

"He's dead."

"Bullshit." Another pause. "Where are you?"

"Where are *you*, Carl?"

"Never mind. There's a warehouse around the corner from the lab. You'll find a woman in there, Lucy Nash. She's dying of something called peruvia moribundi."

"It's not true," Mike whispered to Tom, who waved at him to be quiet.

"There's no cure for moribundi," Carl continued. "I should know; I created it. I have a vial of it with me, enough to kill thousands of people. Put Miller on the phone or I'll release it."

Tom put a hand over the phone and looked questioningly at Lucy.

"He can't just release it into the air," she said. "It's only transmittable through blood and fluids. Anyway, I switched the vials. What he thinks is moribundi is really the inoculant. But for godsake, don't tell him that."

"Miller's dead, and that's the truth," Tom said into the phone. "We know what he was planning, and it won't work without him. Give yourself up. You can't—"

"I can and I will," Carl said. "With or without Miller. We've come too far. There's no going back." A click and Carl was gone.

"We'll get him," Tom said, pulling out his own phone and dialing furiously. "The Coast Guard, the Navy—"

"Tell them not to board," Lucy said quickly. "Not without RACAL suits. It's not just the vials of virus. Carl's dying." Tom looked up. "He injected himself with the deadly strain. He thought it was the inoculant. He gave it to Bill and Renée, too. Carl's dying of moribundi."

Tom tossed Miller's phone to Mike. "You two get on the horn, order up whatever you need. I'll get after Carl." He wrinkled his nose. "What the hell *is* that stink?"

"Rotting bananas," Mike said. "The place is filled with them." He looked over at the blood-spattered fruit. "I'll never eat another banana as long as I live."

Chapter Thirty-one

Sunshine bounced off the plastic sheeting surrounding the hospital bed. Beneath the thin coverlet, Lucy ate a last spoonful of Jell-O, sneezed twice, and lay back against the pillows.

The door opened and Mike looked in. "Feel like visitors?" His words came dimly through the heavy plastic. "Tom's with me."

"Sure," she said, beckoning them into the room.

Mike drew his chair up close to the bed. "How do you feel?"

"Rotten. But flu-rotten, not dying-of-some-strange-incurable-disease rotten. So even though you're free to wander the streets of the city that never sleeps while I'm stuck in this damn tent for the next three weeks, I guess I can't complain." She smiled at him. No trace of virus had been found in his blood, and after careful decontamination, during which all of his clothes had been removed and burned, he'd been released to the outside world. Lucy, on the other hand, having lost her clothing, too, had, not unexpectedly, been placed in quarantine at New York General, where tests had confirmed that the only peruvia in her blood was the mild b strain. Although she'd slept through the first ten hours of her incarceration, she was already heartily sick of the idea.

"How's the shoulder?"

"Not as bad as it felt. The bullet just nicked it. Did the hatbox pickup go okay?"

"Yeah, the CDC was prompt and discreet," Mike replied. "I had a tough time convincing them we'd actually taken the box through a seven-minute decon shower, but when they realized I was serious, they seemed very grateful."

"I'll bet." Lucy smiled.

"The ambulance threw them at first," Tom interjected. "They thought there'd been an accident with the virus. Once they realized—"

"What ambulance?"

Mike shot a look at Tom. "I was hoping to put off telling you until you were feeling better," he told Lucy.

"Too late now. Spill it."

Mike sighed. "When we got to your building, an EMS crew was working on a homeless man down the street. Someone reported him to the police this morning, said he was lying drunk in a doorway. But the EMS guys said he died sometime during the night. They think he probably froze to death."

"Ray." It was a statement, not a question, and Mike nodded. "Do *you* think he froze to death?" she asked.

"It's possible, Lucy. It was bitterly cold last night." He squeezed her hand through the plastic sheeting. "The decon team found the cylinder seals, by the way," he announced, eager to change the subject. "I told Tom you might want to donate them to a museum."

"Are they mine?"

"Technically, I think they are. You want to sell them?"

"I might," Lucy mused. "All that money could help a lot of people."

"You don't have to decide right away. Get well first."

Lucy nodded. "I notice you've both been avoiding the big issue. No word from Carl yet?"

Tom shook his head. "How fast does the virus kill? Could he be dead already?"

"Not dead, but certainly dying. You locate the ship?"

"We think so. A small Liberian-registered cargo vessel, owned by a corporation of convenience. We traced it back to a guy named Kiamos." He checked his watch. "There's a cordon of Coast Guard cutters in a wide circle around it, and a Navy decon vessel with USAMRIID personnel aboard. If they try and make a run for the mainland or the open sea, we'll get 'em. But I'll feel a lot more comfortable once this thing is over."

"Your media blackout's been surprisingly successful," Mike said. "I haven't heard a thing on the news."

"We've been lucky so far. It won't last."

A nurse entered, carrying a bag of saline solution which she hung on the IV stand. "Are either of you Mr. Wrightson?" she asked.

"I am," Tom said, rising.

"They're transferring a call in here for you from the nurse's station. Please don't talk too long," she added as she left. "Dr. Nash needs her rest."

"What am I, twelve? Talk as long as you like, Tom."

The phone rang and Tom snatched up the receiver. "This is Wrightson. What's happened?" He listened for a moment, his eyes growing solemn. "I see. All of them? Good God. Yes, I'm heading back to the office now." He replaced the receiver.

"Well, we've got him," he said. "They tried to run. They were stopped and boarded." He reached for his coat. "Anders had injected everyone on board with what he thought was the inoculant. They're finished." He sighed. "Most of them are ordinary crewmen.

They haven't the faintest idea of what's happening or why."

"And your men have the vials of virus?" Lucy asked, her eyes sad.

Tom nodded. "They found a Level Four lab aboard, small but functional. Carl had already begun to replicate the virus there."

"Miller was planning to move his operation offshore," Mike said, "once they'd announced their intentions to the world. It's all on that disk I gave you."

"What will you do now?" Lucy asked Tom.

"We'll hold the ship at sea until all the men have died. Several USAMRIID personnel have offered to give them what comfort they can—" He broke off.

"Go on. It's worse not knowing."

"The bodies will be removed, the entire ship sealed and decontaminated, the lab dismantled, the viruses destroyed."

"And the media?"

"Told as little as possible."

"This Kiamos," Mike said. "You'll get him, of course. And the others."

"You think so?" Tom raised a cynical eyebrow. "That disk of yours contained no names, remember. Kiamos will claim he lent his boat to Miller for use as a hospital ship, or a research station; how was he to know what Miller really intended? Of course, any financial support he gave Miller would have been paid to the IMA. For charitable causes."

"But we know better."

"Yes. And by looking through the IMA's financial records, we'll know whom to keep an eye on." He shrugged. "But that's about all we *can* do."

"What will happen to the IMA?" Lucy wondered aloud. "Miller and Anders aside, it performed a valuable service."

"I suppose if new financial backing can be found . . ." Mike began.

"And suppose others *should* come along, offering to support the noble work of the IMA?" Tom said grimly, pulling on his coat. "Can you afford to trust such an offer, after this? How can you be sure their intentions are pure?" He strode to the door and opened it. "You're thinking what a cynical old bastard I am. And, of course, you're right. But . . . do you truly believe we can ever really know what's in another's heart?"

"Rather a bleak view of the world," Mike said as the door closed behind Tom.

"Comes with the territory, I expect. Still, he has a point."

Mike shrugged. "About the IMA, perhaps. But I know what's in your heart. And you know what's in mine."

Lucy smiled at him. "Oh, I know what's in your heart, all right. It's your identity I'm still not sure of. Are you really this Mike Rossetti character? I mean, you're not about to step into a phone booth and emerge as Clark Kent, are you? You won't suddenly decide you'd rather be Dan Quayle or Harry Reasoner or Mel Gibson? Although Mel Gibson *would* be rather— Hey, you're not allowed under here. What if the nurse comes back? She'll quarantine you in here with me. Which would certainly be nicer than being in here on my own. Okay, whoever you are, you talked me into it. Just watch that shoulder, fella."